A MIDDLE CLASS EDUCATION

IT was a wind of change that blew John Chote into Sturdley College at Oxford—just why, neither the college nor Chote ever seem really to have discovered. It was probably the same condition of bewildered unbelief which caused the college authorities to grant him a scholarship to a New York university, although their relief at his departure for America may well have been tinged with some apprehension of the result.

Chote in fact made a mess of his time in America —indeed, he hadn't distinguished himself much at Oxford. But the native, caustic wit that pulled him through three years of drinking, gambolling and frivolity there, was sharply alien to that other world across the Atlantic, and in disgrace he retreated whence he came—the lower strata of English small business, for which he was neither made nor marred by a middle class education.

In this novel about Oxford in the mid-fifties, we believe we are offering the first work of a writer destined to become of major importance. An Oxford graduate at present living in America, Wilfrid Sheed has written a book which is extremely funny and extremely serious. Behind the witty, caustic, and Rabelaisian inconsequence of an undergraduate's life lie problems which gnaw at the roots of university education today. Changes of environment, of direction and of emphasis, make for heavy burdens to place upon the shoulders of young men who, twenty years ago, would never have aspired to a university degree. Can they bear them? And is the attempt, successful or unsuccessful, worth while?

It is a problem which Wilfrid Sheed does not take lightly. But in the course of his description of undergraduate life at Oxford and in the New World, he has written one of the funniest and most caustic first novels it has been our privilege to read.

A Middle Class Education

a novel by

WILFRID SHEED

CASSELL · LONDON

CASSELL & COMPANY LTD
35 Red Lion Square · London WC1
and at
MELBOURNE · SYDNEY · TORONTO
CAPE TOWN · AUCKLAND

———

Copyright © 1960 by Wilfrid J. Sheed

First edition in Great Britain March 1961
Second edition April 1961
Third edition April 1961

Set in 11 pt. Baskerville type, leaded, and
printed in Great Britain by Cox and Wyman Ltd.,
London, Reading and Fakenham

AUTHOR'S NOTE

AT the height of the post-war confusion, Sturdley College absent-mindedly decided not to take me—pretty rich when you consider what they *were* taking in those days. It worked out all right, though. In the same confusion—which for all I know is still raging—I stumbled into a college altogether different: to wit, comelier buildings, more rational inmates, and absolutely antithetical dons. I owe the last two plenty, and as they have no place in a book of this kind, you won't find a trace of them. On the other hand, I hope to have settled some scores with Sturdley.

W.S.

CONTENTS

OXFORD

Be taught by this to speak with moderation,
Of places where, with decent application,
One gets a good, sound, middle-class education.

HILAIRE BELLOC

Begin with an individual, and before you know it you find
that you have created a type; begin with a type, and you find
that you have created nothing.

F. SCOTT FITZGERALD

THE *summer term at Oxford was only four wet and wintry weeks old, but already the tourists had begun to appear like crocuses. A large body of Americans was moving cautiously along High Street, ready to fire their cameras at the first sight of anything suspicious. A group from Australia was closing in from the opposite direction, surging up purposefully from the railway station; and a third party from Manchester was already standing outside one of the smaller colleges, planning its next move. 'Let's start with this one and work our way up,' they decided. It had a squat, friendly façade, propped between two larger ones like a drunk between friends.*

A pair of knowledgeable scouts went on ahead to sniff out the situation: to learn whether and how much tourists were suffered in these academic tumbledowns. Most of them knew too well what it was to be escorted from innocent-looking rooms and tranquil, unexpected gardens by red-faced canons, curators, baronets, and they didn't want it to happen here, not on this lovely day.

'Founded by Sir Thomas Sturdley in 1357,' said one of the diviners, thumbing at his yellow book. 'Completely rebuilt in the nineteenth century in a rather unfortunate neo-Gothic style.'

'I didn't want to mention it outside,' whispered the other, 'but I have a nephew in this college.'

'It seems that the Reverend George Fosberry, eighteenth century divine, was a fellow of Sturdley for thirty-five years. Now that's worth knowing, isn't it?'

'I hope we don't run into him, that's all I can say.' He peeped round at the unfortunate architectural trimmings.

'If you ask me, I never could see what all fuss was about

I

this place. Just a lot of rich boys wasting their own good time and other people's good money. Isn't that so, Oswald?'

Oswald didn't answer; they had had the same argument in Salisbury Cathedral, and Blenheim Palace, and God knows where else. His friend had no respect for tradition; he came only to sneer.

The first quad was empty: blank windows and flies browsing in the ivy. Oswald mopped his brow with a puff of green handkerchief. It was hot inside his swaddle of mackintosh and grey serge. 'I don't think we should go any farther, James,' he said. 'I feel uncomfortable.'

'Come along now.' They probed a quad to the right, which was equally empty, and another beyond that, which was hardly a quad at all, but somebody's garden. A large man in shorts gazed at them speculatively: his torso was bare and white as the moon. They withdrew in some confusion.

'That's quite enough,' said Oswald.

'One more to go,' said James; but Oswald had his way for once, and they left the last quad unexplored.

'By and large,' James summed up, 'Oxford probably hasn't changed much since the war. The same familiary influences, father to son and such, are still in evidence, a sort of vertical clubmanship, you might say. . . .' Oswald winced. These American sociology books might be all right for some, but they hadn't done his friend a bit of good: he knew less, felt less, than ever he had.

'You wouldn't say that if you knew my nephew,' he said, *but he did not pursue the point.* His nephew came from a decent family: his grandfather was a dean, and his father was a good man too. But the boy himself was evil, at least by Oswald's standards. Not evil in any spectacular way that James would understand. It was just that things went wrong when he was around; drought, pestilence—girls he didn't even know got into trouble, respectable boys turned up in haystacks, prayer-books vanished from pew racks in mysterious circumstances. There were more things on heaven and earth than were dreamed of in his friend's sociology.

According to James's oft-repeated theory, the proportions

2

always came out roughly the same in every generation. Parsons usually begat parsons (or anti-parsons), rugger players begat rugger players (or anti-rugger players), dons ditto dons; behind one of those blank windows even now, a young man would be sitting in cobwebs discussing the shortage of staff, and sundry inconveniences—Yanks and black fellows and so on—as vehemently as his grandfather before him. Even eccentricity (wearing a bathing suit to chapel) was handed down indefinitely, like granny's wedding dress: England renewed herself on all levels.

But people like his nephew must be changing all that. Twenty years ago they would never have gone to places like Oxford. They dispersed in those days, lived off their wits, became isolated boils on the social body. Now they clustered and seethed in places like Sturdley, and—well, something curious might come of it someday. One never knew.

The others were waiting impatiently. 'What's it like?' 'Is it one of the ones we were supposed to visit?' 'Is it one of the famous ones?'

James assured them in turn. 'It's moth-eaten through and through. . . . Undistinguished sort of place. . . . We caught one of the governesses gardening in the nude.' Oswald smiled secretly and toyed with his umbrella. They set off in a high good humour: it was nice to know that there were places like Sturdley, even in Oxford. It did wonders for one's confidence. It made Christ Church seem almost possible.

Section

I

*A Sturdley
Chronicle*

1. Resting

SOMEWHERE in the distance a bell rang faintly, then another one closer, then one to the left, down by the river, and finally the college clock itself, booming a few feet away. Oxford was celebrating the hour of 7 P.M., with its usual grave over-emphasis.

The tower of Sturdley College dropped its squat ungainly shadow inward over a mixed assortment of average libertines and pedants who trampled casually across the precious grass with their hands in their pockets, on their way to and from the college bar and the college library. There was still one little patch of bright yellow grass in a corner of the lawn, like a blanket spread for a picnic, on which six undergraduates were uncomfortably crouched. In a few minutes the shadow would be driving their blanket remorselessly into the neat flower bed, and thence up the bright green creeper on the far wall.

The six sunbathers were dressed to the chin in angular grey suits, which gave them a waxy stiffness, clothing dummies stuffed into the corner of a shop window. Immediately after lunch, they had been interviewed in turn for the annual Sturdley scholarship to America, and they had been sitting on the lawn ever since, first waiting for the result, then brooding over the injustice of it. It had been a terrible shock to all six of them. Their faces were glistening red by now, from too much brooding in the unaccustomed sunlight; and they were digging up aimless conversation, like tired children, and burying it again.

'That's an extraordinary suit you're wearing, John,' yawned one of them. John waved a stubby leg in response. It was a Sunday-best suit, eight years old, senile and unresponsive.

7

'Capital for interviews,' said John, squinting around cautiously. He didn't know these fellows too well. 'It makes the wearer look solid, dependable, and terrifyingly mature. I would never have snagged the bloody scholarship if I'd been wearing one of your flashy American suits.'

'Ah, so *that's* how you did it,' murmured a disappointed rival, still wincing from the slap in the face—passed over for a scholarship honour by John Chote. Of all the quite incredible people.

'The Americans won't like it,' said a whimsical scholar, his mouth working pleasurably. 'I mean the suit. It doesn't look very efficient.'

'It doesn't look friendly; it hasn't got "warmth". One can see the description now. "Portly austere-trousered Britisher John Chote. His trousers lack warmth." '

'The Americans expect us to look unusual,' said Chote. 'Who am I to disappoint them?' Pitter-patter—was this how these studious chaps always talked?

'I thought they liked everybody to look the same. Convict haircuts, padded shoulders and lashings of toothpaste.'

'That's just propaganda put about by the Communists in Hollywood,' said John Chote. 'Real Americans are madly interesting and individualistic. Like Brad here.'

Bradshaw Soames had come, according to his habit, to sit with them and listen to their exotic talk for a while. Since coming to England, Bradshaw had sprouted long hair and thick glasses and a tweed sports jacket with a mighty flap in the back, preparatory to setting up his shingle as Anti-American number one at Sturdley.

'Are you kidding?' snorted Soames. 'You can't tell Americans without a scorecard.'

'Sometimes I don't think you love your country as you should, Bradshaw. What will Colonel McCormick say when you get back? Not to mention the junior senator?'

'It has its points, I guess—you know the jazz, young and eager and all that crap,' answered Soames distastefully, 'but I wouldn't try to deny that it's boring as hell, even for the sake of the gentleman you mention.'

8

'You're just a snob, Bradshaw,' said Chote. 'You think decadence is everything.'

The sunlight was beginning to edge up the wall, and the lobster-faced candidates stood up one by one to shake themselves.

'Are you coming down for a pint, John?'

'No, thanks. A little spadework in the Senior Library . . . must start earning the damned scholarship sometime.'

'Ah-ha. The Americans would call that "character building", wouldn't they, Brad?' asked a cadaverous scholar, still frisking gently.

'It's football that builds character in America,' said the gloomy Soames, 'not reading.'

'Quite right, too,' said somebody. 'Excellent plan.'

Chote wandered away with his hands in his pockets, and the others fell at once to talking about him in low, exasperated voices.

'Honestly, I don't know. One doesn't want to be uncharitable—but really, one asks oneself—Chote!'

'Well, why not? He's not such a bad chap when he's sober, and when he isn't trying too hard to be funny.'

'Yes, but a scholarship. I mean to say, the laziest specimen that ever crawled out of the mud. The dons must be losing their collective grip. There's *no* other explanation.'

'I suppose it's a matter of good will, more than anything else. You know what the warden is like: as long as Chote makes a few friends for Britain, everything is rosy,' one of them summed up gloomily. 'God, what friends they'll be!'

A plastic golf ball with holes in it sailed past Chote's ear and into the hallway which led to the Senior Library.

'Watch out you clot.' A tubby undergraduate with a niblick under his arm bustled up to retrieve the flimsy ball. 'Don't examinations frighten you at all, Gadsby?' Chote asked him. 'Golf is the best relaxation in the world,' said Gadsby. 'Eisenhower, Churchill and the Duke have all played golf at various times of stress, I believe. Have you seen my bloody tee?' Ralph Gadsby scampered around in a circle.

Behind an unfortunate neo-Gothic façade and between real Gothic walls, the next layer of Sturdley fauna lurked in thin concealment. Under the stone archway it had become suddenly cool and dark. The sun never reached the old, damp stones; and in the winter they made a kind of natural icehouse. But in hot summers they had offered pleasant relief for generations of students who had worked too hard, or drunk too much, or indulged too passionately in theological controversy—or possibly all three, for the walls went back far beyond the age of specialization.

Up the stairs, and under dim brown panelling, Chote trotted his way into the Senior Library. It was organized in alcoves, each designed to contain one table, four chairs and, perhaps in some Utopian brochure, four keen, silent scholars. Between the alcoves stood the bookcases, spindly and bulging with ancient and disconnected volumes on college history, rock gardening and Roman Law, reflecting the discursive tastes of centuries of eccentric wardens. At the moment the chairs in the first two alcoves seemed to be missing. In the second, a small, shy-looking fellow was trying to study standing up, bent awkwardly athwart the table. He gazed reproachfully at Chote, licked his lips, and then decided not to say it after all. It was, by and large, unspeakable.

'Where are all the chairs?' Chote asked breezily.

'They're at it again,' answered the shy one in a toneless voice, and he shifted self-pitying to the other foot.

The poker game had floated to rest in the fourth alcove. Indistinguishable words with the leisurely oompa-pa of English profanity came rolling out of the prim alcove on a wave of thick blue smoke, the rhythm punctuated and chopped up by shrill cries of pain and loss. Chote swung into the alcove to find a gaggle of twenty or so desperate men huddled around the table clutching cards, swearing and smoking and chattering like monkeys. 'By God, don't you even *shuffle* in this country?' boomed an American voice.

'Why it's Chote. Have a hand, Chote.'

'It's like the bloody Klondike,' said Chote. 'Don't you chaps realize that Schools starts in two weeks?'

'This is a perfectly normal form of hysteria, old man. Examination nerves.'

'By God, how're you dealing?' howled the American voice. The cards were going out in twos and threes, little batches of unshuffled cards.

'Do you realize that Thomson hasn't got a chair to work on?' Chote asked them.

'Who's Thomson?'

'Thomson is a second-year man,' said Chote. 'They say he's going to get a First, and put Sturdley on the map at last, after six hundred years or more of dismal obscurity. Doesn't anybody *care*?'

'What the devil is he doing in the Senior Library if he's only in his second year? This is a serious place, by God.'

'I didn't even know where the Senior Library *was* in my second year.'

'All right, deal me a hand, you miserable baskets. It seems to be the only chance of getting a seat in this mockery of a library.'

He divided his posterior impartially between two chair halves and somebody handed him the bloated deck. 'Sixpence in the middle, you bloody man, Chote.' As the hands went out, the swearing started up again, like an old-fashioned gramophone being wound up, first gently and then swelling to a sour roar. With so many people playing, it was hopeless to bet on anything less than three face cards of a kind—if that. The hands showered back into the centre like autumn leaves. 'Bugger all, as usual.'

Thomson's spectacles appeared around the edge of the bookcase pursued grimly by Thomson. He had come to Oxford to get an education, and he couldn't help feeling bitterly disappointed. He glared at them, licked his lips remorsefully and walked away.

'Poor bastard. I was like that when I came up.'

'Of course you were,' said Chote. 'And so was I. And so was Browning.'

'Until you discovered that the college had a bar and that girls had et cetera, et cetera.'

'Look at us,' said Chote. 'Everyone here is in his last year. Schools starts in two weeks. Which of us ever thought it would end like this? What *happens* to your character when you come to this bloody place?'

'Who dealt this crap?'

The smoke was getting so thick that the players could scarcely see each other. Most of them were sulky because they were losing money with Schools so close, and the profanity was turning shrill and cacophonous, like cats crying. The American, Gene Fosdick, of Plainsville, Connecticut, was getting more and more irritated by the way they were dealing. 'Christ, what a way to play poker.' The light through the thick window was beginning to fade and the players crouched and squinted over their cards. Every few minutes somebody would moan, 'I came up here to work. And I had to run into you buggers.' The ancient volumes frowned down on them; Chote for one knew what they must be thinking. In all their years at Oxford, they had never witnessed such a crowd of idle. . . . The players seemed to bow their heads in silent acknowledgment.

'I can't afford to lose any more,' Chote said at last and he got up from his uncomfortable pseudo-seat. There were innumerable mounds of books lined up forlornly in front of the bookcase, like piles on a lawn, and he bent over to find his. He had put them down that morning and there they had sat all day.

'Don't tell me you're going to work, John?'

'It's too late for that,' said Chote sadly. 'I'm going to the F.A. to get some beer while I can still afford to.'

'That's a bloody marvellous idea.' Two other players pulled away from the crowded table, like petals ripped from a jagged flower, and bent down to look for their books; then quietly back past the empty alcoves, past the staunch Thomson, who knew the value of time. When they got to the door, Chote wheeled and trotted back to the gaming table.

'The Dean's coming up the stairs,' he panted. There was a harsh scraping of chairs as the players struggled to get away from the table, flies writhing helplessly on their sticky paper.

There was no rule against playing cards in the Senior Library, because the question had never officially arisen. But one's instincts sent up dour warnings; especially two weeks before Schools.

The din of retreat and the sudden eruption of fifteen frantic undergraduates streaming as one out of the tiny alcove should certainly have given the Dean something to think about. Hastily, chairs were pushed from alcove to alcove, chipping and clashing like bumper cars, until they were distributed with rough justice. Books were torn from the shelves and flung onto tables. Meanwhile the Dean, with bony legs pumping innocently, was urging his bicycle farther and farther into the salubrious countryside north of Oxford.

'You *ba*stard, Chote.' But Chote had already gone. 'After three years of Chote, one ought to know better.'

'He makes one absolutely ill.'

'Eternal youth is all very well. But Chote carries it too far.'

'He gets on my tits, really he does,' somebody summed up.

'Only Ralph Gadsby comes close to him in point of childishness—and possibly Alan Browning.'

Gene Fosdick still sat at the table holding his cards, waiting patiently for play to continue.

'What's all the excitement about?' he asked.

'Chote said the Dean was coming.'

'So what? The Dean's a sport.' Fosdick was several years older than the English undergraduates, and he took his discipline lightly. 'I know what the Dean would have said; he would have said what deans always say: "Play the ace, you fool." What's the matter? Doesn't anybody want to play a little cards?'

The others were beginning to leave in twos and threes. Chote's little caper had taken the heart out of them. Fosdick shrugged, and began to deal himself hands in an imaginary game. Soon the library was empty except for Fosdick and the wraithlike Thomson, who had returned to take up once again his quest of the phantom 'First'—first-class honours, the legendary Oxford stamp of approval on the first-class brain. And

13

Thomson knew by some instinct that if he didn't have a first-class brain, he didn't have anything.

Chote and his muckers walked moodily to the college lodge. They stared for several minutes at the college bulletin board; nothing new had appeared on it for days now: the same scholarships to Kenya; the musty, second-rate appointments; the chapel readings. They glanced into the pigeonholes where the college mail was placed. 'I haven't had a letter in three years,' said Chote. But he went carefully through all the 'C' mail, turning it over and over. 'There's less than there was this morning,' he said to himself thoughtfully.

Bradshaw Soames tiptoed up behind them and reached a long arm into the 'S' pigeonhole. Magically, out they came: letter after letter, all to Soames, together with a wedge of circulars, club notices and folded bits of paper saying '8 P.M. Be there' and such, all very much to Soames. He belonged to just about every club in the university, and consequently *got* something out of Oxford which Chote and his friends, who belonged to nothing, could only goggle at. 'What *sort* of mail do you get at this time of night?' somebody asked curiously.

'Come and have a drink, Brad,' said Chote. 'When Chote wastes time, *everybody* wastes time.'

'Not me. No drinking until after Schools.'

'Well, yes. I agree with you in principle. I made the same promise myself. But it's too late to do any work now. The brain is tired.'

'I'm going to try to get in a couple of hours before I hit the sack.'

'God,' moaned Chote, 'you make me feel like an absolute swine.' He staggered forlornly out of the lodge, with his friends just behind him. 'Do you know, they're sending me to America in exchange for Soames?' he said over his shoulder. 'It's a bloody sobering thought, isn't it? I only hope they know what they're doing.'

The other two might at first glance have been taken for close relatives: the same medium height and sandy hair, and the kind of mild expressions that can only come from centuries of mowing and rolling. Their clothes were also similar, down to the black patches on the elbows of their brown sports jackets, and the shabby, anonymous grey flannels. They lived in the same digs down the Cowley Road, and shared the same pleasures, getting fuzzy on beer roughly five nights a week and trying their luck with the local nurses on the other two.

However, there were differences too. For one thing, Godfrey Hook's coat seemed a little too short for him and his trousers rather too large, especially around the knees where they ballooned out forlornly. He frowned a lot, as if worrying about these technical problems, and this in turn gave him often a reproachful and somewhat pained expression, like a certain kind of stage parson's. Despite his anguished protests, many of the local nurses were convinced that he really disapproved of them and consequently wouldn't have anything to do with him; and at Sturdley, his colleagues were inclined to regard his ferocious attempts at debauchery as rather a joke, however seriously he took them himself. They didn't go with the face, somehow.

His background was the trouble; generations of scrupulous moderation had done their work. The son of a clergyman in Devon, his mildness ran very deep. Depravity, even modified depravity, had obviously not come easily to him, and when he left Oxford he would, students of form supposed, become respectable again with all decent haste. A wholesome girl, a bishop's daughter in fact, was waiting for him in Devon, waiting inexorably, to repair whatever damage had accrued to his façade. In a few months, so it was conjectured, his old friends would find it difficult to get in touch with him : letters would be answered slowly and grudgingly, and pretty soon, the long silence. Oxford would come back to him like a fever, making him toss and turn about three times a year while his wife watched understandingly, and pulled his covers up.

The other friend, Alan Browning, had long ago been classified by one of the more astringent dons as 'Sturdley College smooth' : a reference mostly to a remarkably persistent smile that expanded his smallish features in all seasons, a slight, quasimarcelled wave to his hair and a rather smart way with his grey flannels. He was the son of a schoolmaster in the soggy North Midlands, and according to official history had gone bucketing too far along the road to ruin to turn back. Brought up to despise strong drink and the baser passions (dancing and playing cricket on Sundays) he was, in his parents' eyes as well as his own, damned beyond hope with the first swallow— which had certainly saved a lot of time and anxiety all round. From the age of fourteen or so he had begun going discreetly and conventionally to seed, behind barns and in darkened school corridors. In the Army and at Oxford, his decline had accelerated and spread itself. His father came to inspect him at Oxford in the middle of his second year, and quickly sensed that something was wrong. Alan took him on an erratic sight-seeing tour in the afternoon which aroused the first hazy suspicions; by nightfall Mr. Browning knew the worst: as Alan said good night, he backed into a lampstand in the lounge of the Mitre, and fell to the floor, laughing with hysterical relief. The next day his father sent him a stiff note, saying that he wouldn't be needed at home when his university days were over. Mr. Browning knew better than to compromise with that kind of thing.

All the same, and to everybody's vague wonderment, Hook and Browning were inseparable companions—one of the many groups of two (sometimes stretched to three by way of Chote) of which Sturdley was mostly composed. They apparently papered over their differences with yards and yards of small talk. In three years, no one had ever heard mention of religion or politics, even in jest. In matters of applied morality, they must, one assumed, both have made some concessions, which 'Parson Hook'—as he was sometimes called—might or might not live to regret; in everything else they were well hidden behind masks (a grin and a frown) of comedy. But people who knew them well found them a curious pair.

It was nine-thirty when they got to the Forester's Arms. A clutch of second-year men were already singing loudly enough to aggravate the tic in the landlord's flabby pink jaw, forgetting now and then to slide over the dirty word, wailing at their mistake with discordant pleasure.

'Ho, it's Chote. Have a drink, John. It's your round.'

Chote and his friends settled themselves in a corner as far away as possible from the singers, who were on the nightly verge of being asked, wistfully and ineffectually, to leave.

'What's the matter with Chote?' piped a tiny inebriate. 'You too proud to sit with us, Chote?'

'You're a pack of drunken sods,' answered Chote, which seemed to satisfy the little man well enough. They returned to their song. 'The Lord's my Shepherd' this time, with many a sacrilegious growl and squeak.

The Forester's Arms was an average, humdrum, commercial pub run by a worried man called Wilson. He was worried chiefly because of the Sturdley undergraduates, who insisted on coming to his pub year after year and annoying whatever town trade his unctuous bonhomie had managed to accumulate during the vacations. Local businessmen in decent suits would come in, especially during the summer, to drink small, expensive glasses of gin, in well-behaved silence. Then came term again and for no reason at all, the undergraduates from Sturdley would pour in and stumble over his clients and spill beer on them, and generally rough them up. By the middle of each term, the local businessmen would have stopped coming to the Forester's Arms ('It's not your fault, Mr. Wilson'), and the poor man would be obliged to live from the sale of draught beer for a few weeks. The worst part of it was that he didn't even *like* undergraduates—his sympathies were all with the peaceful burghers, and he did his best to attract them with pretty barmaids and slick furnishings, which were in turn menaced brainlessly by the undergraduate hordes. He couldn't understand why they had to pick on *him* all the time. He didn't like them and he didn't encourage them, except in so far as his professional charm tended to encourage everybody. It was a *businessman's* pub. Why did *they* have to come here?

Chote and his friends were among the worst; Godfrey Hook in particular knocked things over practically every time he moved, and Browning got into obscure trouble with the local people and their wives; and all three of them paid next to nothing at the bar. 'How are you this evening, Mr. Chote?' asked Mr. Wilson with nervous politeness. Damn it all, he just couldn't help being polite: it was his nature, that was all, and it was a bad day when a man had to be sorry for being polite!

'Very well, Mr. Wilson. I say, those chaps are making an awful bloody row. Why don't you throw them out?' Mr. Wilson smiled weakly and moved away.

'I hear you've got the Yank scholarship, John,' said Godfrey Hook. 'I can't understand how an idle beggar like you gets away with it.'

'Neither do I,' said Browning, looking at him closely. 'It's blooming uncanny. I mean, you did say you were lazy, didn't you?'

'Certainly I'm lazy,' said Chote stoutly. 'Nobody has ever questioned my laziness.'

Browning was still staring at him. 'Absolutely uncanny,' he said.

'Do you think you'll like it over there?' interrupted Hook. 'Americans are so dashed serious about everything. Look at Soames.' He frowned at the thought.

'I think American humorists are much better than ours. That's one of the chief reasons I want to go.'

'I don't know. The chaps they send over here are serious enough,' said Browning, leaning back luxuriantly on the shiny red leather couch which had been originally designed to buoy up some tired businessman and friend.

'Well, that'll make a nice change after this place. Everybody tries to be funny around here; every time anyone speaks, it has to be a joke. Or else, of course, it has to be in dialect. God, but it gets dreary. In America, I believe they specialize. The funny people make the jokes, and the others keep strong and quiet.'

'The men keep quiet,' said Browning, 'but I believe the women never stop talking at all. I couldn't stand that. I like quiet women.'

'I can understand that,' said Hook, 'in your case. I prefer a meeting of the minds myself. By the way, did I tell you about

18

the smashing nurse I met last night? Doris Flounce. Absolutely smashing.'

'Oh, no!' said Browning. 'Not a meeting of the minds with Doris Flounce. I simply don't believe it.' He bounced satirically on the stiff leather.

'Do you, by any chance, know Doris?'

'Do I know Doris? Who am I not to know Doris? Three years ago, Charles Wagstaff was inviting her to his room for his "token-tea parties"—a potful of cold water and a stale crust, never too closely examined. And that was three years ago, before Doris had really found her form.'

'You mean I have a chance with Doris?' Hook asked eagerly.

'Yes, Godfrey, even you have a chance with Doris.'

'How absolutely smashing. By the Rood,' said the Parson, 'I'll invite her to the Summer Ball and try my luck.'

The singers were attempting to harmonize another hymn, with various results. The tiny leader of the revels, who had never been able to carry a tune when sober, was bravely crossing swords with the tenor part; the others were scattered up and down the scale, the fast singers versus the slow singers, whipped to frenzy by a timpani on trays and tabletops. The local people were getting up ostentatiously and heading for the door. Mr. Wilson was a decent chap, but this was really the last straw.

'I really must ask you to stop singing,' said the unhappy Mr. Wilson as he watched his dapper little clients vanishing silently one by one.

'Have a drink, Mr. Wilson.'

'Three cheers for Mr. Wilson. Hip-hip,' and they began cheering in slow rhythm. 'Hip, and again hip for Mr. Wilson.'

Chote was at Wilson's elbow. 'You're quite right, Mr. Wilson. They're absolute rowdies. I wouldn't stand for it if I were you.'

Wilson looked up startled. He felt his grip slipping away. With someone like Chote on his side, he could depend on nothing.

'Three more cheers for good old Mr. Wilson. Let's make it a rouser this time.'

'Come on, Mr. Wilson. We'll throw them out together.'

It was already nine fifty-five and the pub was due to close in five minutes. 'Time gentlemen please,' wailed Mr. Wilson. 'Gentlemen, *please*.' And then, as with so many incipient Oxford riots, everything faded away. It was bad taste to reach a climax, cloddish to pursue a joke one second too long.

'Good night, Mr. Wilson.' They melted away in a moment. There was no point in bullying the man. 'Thank you, Mr. Chote,' said Wilson, feeling that he ought to conciliate his old enemy. 'That's all right,' said Chote. 'Let me know if this sort of thing occurs again,' and he too was gone.

They stood around outside with their hands in their pockets deciding whether to give up and go home, or to carry the party over to a nearby Burmese restaurant for another hour or two. The one or two who had decided definitely one way or the other were trying to persuade the amorphous remainder; the men of action stood sulkily to one side, mumbling their slogans, 'Well, come on if you're coming.' They were sick to death of people who couldn't make up their minds. Hook and Browning were trying to frame a group policy.

'What about you, John?' asked Hook, scuffing his feet against the cobblestones.

'I haven't enough money,' said Chote. 'That bloody poker.'

'I'll lend you enough for a cup of coffee. I expect I owe it to you, anyway.'

'No. My landlady awaits with the warming pan.' Chote's landlady, the home-made legend : recklessly, foolishly in love with him, giving him no peace; drifting (so it was said) in and out of his room in a gossamer kimono at all hours of the day and night.

'You poor bloke,' said Hook, frowning with envy.

'You know, I've half a mind to put up a fight tonight,' said Chote as he drifted off towards his digs in St. John's Street.

In Cornmarket Street he passed some surly Americans in leather jackets, tottering aimlessly around and around and around, asking each other what the hell you could do in this town after ten o'clock. They seemed to come from a different

20

world from the active, rewarding one of Bradshaw Soames; but perhaps there was some connection that one didn't perceive.

St. John's Street was unearthly quiet; it seemed to have been preserved just so for a long time and the next sound one expected to hear was the clatter of hoofs and wooden wheels. Halfway along on the right, Chote began to go through all his pockets, only to find that he had come out without his key: then through them again, very slowly, pulling out bus tickets and bits of fluff; the third damned time this term. Talk about examination hysteria.

He rang the bell. He was the only lodger Mrs. Worsley had. He heard her rustling down the stairs. The door opened slowly, and a stout, middle-aged woman, tastefully dressed in faded chair covers—or so it seemed to Chote—peered suspiciously down at him.

'I'm sorry, Mrs. Worsley. I, er, seem to have, er. . . .'

'You young gentlemen are a proper nuisance,' she said.

'I'm sorry, Mrs. Worsley. I hope I didn't get you out of bed.' It was impossible to tell from her clothing whether he had or not.

He pushed past her and climbed the stairs. 'Good night Mrs. Worsley. No tea tonight thank you, Mrs. Worsley.'

He went into his room and turned on the light. He took off his shoes and his coat. Methodically he emptied out the coffee-pot and filled it again. Then he turned on the table light and opened one of his lawbooks. Five hours later, he got up with a yawn and took off his socks—the only clothes he hadn't removed already—and climbed into bed.

Browning and Hook had gone to the Rangoon for coffee, and with luck and some management they had soon found themselves at a table with two girls, somewhere between fourteen and thirty-five, thinly pretty, and starchy with make-up. The girls looked at them resentfully—they had perhaps been preserving the space for stray Americans—but Browning set out at once to revive fallen spirits and make them feel wanted.

'I say old man, we *are* in luck tonight,' he whispered hoarsely. 'Two smashing girls.'

One of the girls, who looked as if a bag of flour had been emptied over her head, frowned stiffly; but the other one, more flexible in the face, started to giggle right away. Browning pressed forward.

'Friendly too. You can tell right away. Sweet natures. Adorable creatures.'

Hook appeared to be embarrassed and a little distressed by the tawdiness of the line. 'You ought to have a striped coat and a little bag of brushes,' he muttered; but Browning was in full swing, and the giggling girl was beginning to show pink through the plaster, an encouraging sign. 'Easy to talk to, full of smart sayings, a thousand laughs a minute,' Browning pattered on artlessly. It seemed to be just the right approach in this atmosphere of peeling brown walls and chipped crockery and little curry-stained waiters.

'Oh, for God's sake,' said Hook.

'What was that?' Browning asked the girls. 'I didn't catch your last remark. So sorry, but you'll simply have to talk a little louder.' The girl with the giggle was moving steadily into paroxysms, swaying giddily against her grim companion and looking up at her plaintively : 'I can't help it, honest I can't,' her swimming eyes pleaded.

Hook looked at Browning disdainfully. 'Just like ruddy tap water.'

'I know what you're thinking,' said Browning. 'You probably think my friend here is a touch forward, a bit of a wolf, eh? Well I assure you he's perfectly safe. He only got out of the seminary last week.' His eyes were getting big and syrupy, his voice was a low, fatuous croon. 'I think you have a lovely smile,' he said to the prim one, and her vast red lip began to tremble. 'That's it. It won't hurt a bit. Go on, try it,' and in a moment she was grinning away, a gold tooth shining brightly in the front of her splashy mouth.

'Let me buy you some coffee,' said Browning, magnanimous in triumph.

From there on it was all downhill. Browning chattered away like a magpie, while both girls giggled, and wiggled about pleasurably. He asked for their names. 'I'm Marge and this is

—now come on, you might as well tell them, Loreen.' 'I'm Loreen,' mumbled the girl with the gold tooth, abandoning her last stronghold.

'I'm Horace, and this is Jeremiah. Honestly. Marge, you have lovely eyes. Loreen, you have gorgeous hair. I'll bet it's your own, too.'

Hook tried to rally his forces. He still had no idea what someone of his particular sort ought to say to girls of this kind, even though Browning had introduced him to dozens of them over the last two years or so. He had experienced some bad reverses lately, just as he thought he was getting the knack. He tried now to look amused—tolerant but commanding, although he didn't suppose for a moment it would work. 'Don't pay any attention to him,' he said loftily, 'he's quite mad. But he gives me very little trouble, considering. It's really a pleasure to look after him on the days that they let him out.'

Browning moved to his next goal like a mechanical robot. First he tried a few borderline jokes: there was a brief drawing of breath, and then the giggling started up again, more enthusiastic than ever. Browning pushed confidently over the borderline. 'Isn't he awful?' screamed Marge. 'Yes, awful,' agreed Hook, with stiff sadness.

The girls must have exchanged some signal: Loreen was beginning to look hard and unmistakably at Hook. 'I like your quiet friend,' she said to Browning.

'Most people love Jeremiah,' said Browning. 'Especially women under seventy.'

'The quiet ones are often the most dangerous,' said Loreen thoughtfully.

'That certainly applies in spades to Jeremiah,' said Browning. 'They don't make them more dangerous, anywhere.'

Godfrey flexed his jaw and squinted through his cigarette smoke. Perhaps this thing wouldn't develop any further. Not tonight, anyway. But soon Browning was staring into Marge's eyes and offering to take her home, and Loreen was simpering at Hook, and tapping his knee briskly with hers, as if to test his reflexes. Blast the girl: he could hardly even bring himself to look at her. 'Where do you live?' he asked reluctantly. 'Headington,' she answered eagerly, and they all got up to go, before Hook had even a chance to make a formal offer.

Browning had his arm around Marge as they went down the stairs, and Hook reached out blindly for Loreen. He could feel her compliant ribs twitching under his clumsy grip, as if his hand was too cold.

'Watch out for that man,' said Browning. 'Don't let him get you into any corners.' Loreen laughed and wriggled closer. 'Good luck, old man,' Alan whispered. Godfrey smiled as well as he could.

Outside, the couples separated. Browning, waving and leering encouragement, moved off smoothly and purposefully. Hook felt in his pocket, and confirmed what he knew already: he couldn't begin to afford a taxi. 'I'm sorry. It'll have to be the bus.'

They walked arm in arm to the bus stop. He asked her what she did for a living, and she said she was a waitress, and what did he do. He said he sold bicycles. Browning would be doing it better with glib talk about the Daimler in London; or else the glamour of the right kind of poverty, his attic and his paintings, or some other damned seductive nonsense. Selling bicycles, oh no! thought Hook bitterly. It was not only dull: it was also unbelievable. I'm just no bloody good at this kind of thing.

They sat holding hands on the last bus to Headington. Hook asked her about her family, and she asked him about his. 'My father is in the circus,' he said. 'He's an acrobat.' 'Oh,' said Loreen.

He didn't even know what *kind* of thing he ought to say next. Something about books? cricket? politics? Patently not. That kind of talk led one nowhere.

'Your friend is quite a character, isn't he?' said Loreen.

'Yes, isn't he?' said Hook warmly. He paused. 'He certainly is.' Loreen turned her head and looked out of the window.

They walked quickly to her house, their hands still clamped together, clammy as dead fish. He tried putting an arm around her, but he was aware that this made his short jacket

24

shoot up at the back and he knew what that made him look like. Just no good at this kind of thing. . . . And after all, did he want to be? He didn't particularly like the girl. Inarticulate tramps might be all very well for Browning who knew how to get the best out of them. Nothing wrong with that, of course. Also, one was rather tired tonight. . . .

The best thing was to get it over with quickly. He pushed roughly at the garden gate and steered her quickly to the front door. A gruff kiss catching a good percentage of the mouth and leaving a taste of chemicals: 'Good night Loreen. I hope I'll see you again,' and it was all over, as painless as that. She stood there a moment, mouth open, eyes wide open. She looked now perversely young and appealing. The chunky make-up slapped on with a heavy, inexpert hand might be concealing youth, after all, and not age. Extreme youth, perhaps too young even for the American military, and ergo, much too young for Godfrey Hook. He kissed her again more gently and accurately, and walked away. At the gate he turned: she was still staring at him open-mouthed—perhaps not so young after all. Oh, to hell with it—too late now.

He was a long way from home, and the last bus had gone. It was a nice night, though, clear and soft, with even a few stars, rare enough in those skies. Hook started back in a steady trudge, along the silent dowdy streets. Chote and his landlady, Browning and everyone: his blood steamed and hissed. To-morrow they would talk about it at great length. Some day, he might be able to do that, too: heaven knows, he had tried hard enough. But at twenty-three, time was surely beginning to run out.

The only thing would be to tell Browning that he just hadn't been in the mood for robbing the cradle tonight—the usual dribble, in fact. He was glad he didn't have to explain to Chote as well.

His head was a-hum with the whispering sense of another failure. He had failed Browning and behind that he had also failed the bishop's daughter in Devonshire, who was frowning dimly in her stained glass window. Well, never mind about that now. Schools in two weeks, chaps: the hope of a good job, the affluent future, all the latest daydreams. His tight work schedule had been forcefully dishevelled because he had been obliged to take a thirteen-year-old (yes, she couldn't have been more than that) home to the neighbouring town of Headington —there to kiss her dutifully smack on the chemicals and leave her forever.

Perhaps she was wondering how it was that she had failed to please the dashing bicycle salesman : but perhaps happy to be alone, all the same, free for the night from pressing friends like Marge who made her go to those terrible restaurants, and free from bicycle salesmen, and from the whole alien heave and push. If she were only a little older, it might be nice to see her again, and show her that he really wasn't that sort of chap. . . .

Take her down to the old Family Parsonage, in fact, and sit her in the front parlour with the Reverend Hook, where they could all have a good talk about the hydrangeas and the short-age of domestics—in no time at all she would see the emptiness and, yes, the dullness of her former existence : night clubs and love-making, indeed, when one could be sitting around the parsonage, talking up a storm about hollihocks. . . . That was his world, but he didn't believe in it. He just had to live in it. While his blood boiled and bubbled and his friends boasted.

Maybe after Schools. Maybe at the Summer Ball. Maybe Browning would help him.

2. Studies in Still Life

SUNRISE over Oxford is reputed to be a pleasant sight. The spires and towers take gradual outline against a pale sky; the dark quadrangles brighten slowly; grass, flowers and ivy resume their normal felicitious colours. College servants mount their bicycles and begin to wheel silently and discreetly into town for the long day's work. The rain clouds often hang back for an hour or two, to complete the salubrity.

It was a sight that John Chote had never actually seen. In his first year he had once come within a whisker of it. On the last day of April that year he had sat up all night in a punt on the river, waiting for the choirboys to welcome May with fruity purity from the top of Magdalen tower. But by the time the sun rose he was sound asleep as usual, under a dewy blanket, with purple lips and baby's pout. The vigil had been, while it lasted, a cold and bitter one (rendered immensely more uncomfortable by cheap, flat claret and bad cigars), and he had never attempted to repeat it.

Today (a balmy Thursday in May), he missed the sunrise by a particularly wide margin. The lusty mid-morning sun streamed into his room and swarmed across his bed. At ten o'clock Mrs. Worsley came in with breakfast. She shook him with a massive, life-giving paw.

'Yes, Mrs. Worsley.' His words failed to filter through the rumple of blankets.

'It's ten o'clock, Mr. Chote. And a lovely morning.'

'Yes, Mrs. Worsley.'

'Can you hear me, Mr. Chote? Are you awake yet?'

'Getting up right away.' He lay rigidly still. Perhaps she would go away in a minute.

If Mrs. Worsley was tight-lipped and accusing at night, she was—the only word for it—loose-lipped and forgiving (up to a point) by morning. The morning, as she often pointed out, was her 'good time'.

'*Such* a lovely day, although I think it's beginning to cloud over a little. Very hard to tell at this stage.'

Very hard, and very unnecessary, was Chote's first real thought of the day. Her voice sounded like a gong, booming, BOOMING, BOOMING. He looked up at her slowly; his face was white, puffy and suspicious; black hair, which hadn't been cut for two months, thatched across his eyes like a guardsman's bearskin. The smell of marmalade and cold toast began to work its dreary persuasions on his cloudy nostrils. How utterly second-rate one's whole life was.

27

'All right, Mrs. Worsley, you win.' He sat up and looked at his plate : a limpid yellow eye gazed back. 'Pretty thing,' he said.

'It's none of my business,' said Mrs. Worsley, 'but I think you'd enjoy your breakfast more if you didn't go out drinking every evening. I don't know if I ever told you this, but my late husband died of drink.'

'Yes, Mrs. Worsley. You've told me about that.' Why did one go on eating cold fried eggs, year after year?

'I was so stricken with grief, and everything, that I didn't take any more boarders for five years. You're the first I've attempted since my breakdown, you know. Such a good man when he wasn't drinking.' She moved closer, hovering warmly overhead. 'You remind me of him a little bit sometimes. You're almost like a son to me, Mr. Chote.' He shuddered and edged away. His red flannel shoulder blade came to rest against the wall behind his bed. Mrs. Worsley went out shaking her head.

By eleven o'clock, Chote had tumbled out into the tranquil street. His hair was loosely organized by now, and his face was beginning to mend. His stocky torso was wrapped in a tweed sports jacket, reinforced at the elbows and cuffs with the inevitable black leather. At the college lodge he met Browning and Hook, quarrelling over whose turn it was to buy *The Times*. Chote took his accustomed place in the argument; slowly and painfully they retraced the whole term. It was demonstrated at once that Hook had bought it least often. 'But I'm no good at crossword puzzles, so I don't care if we *don't* get the beastly *Times*!' said Hook. 'You have no social conscience,' said Browning testily. 'Chote, you look awful. Up working all night, I suppose.' Chote grimaced. 'Good Lord,' he said.

They headed for the paper shop at last, it being decided that Chote should pay threepence and Browning a penny, with Chote having the right to keep the paper after the crossword was done. When they got to the shop they found, as they usually did, that *The Times* was sold out. 'Blasted bad start to a day,' said Chote, as he usually did.

The café was swarming with undergraduates, the doorway

clogged with people trying to spot familiar faces through the smoke. One delicate-looking fellow with a tightly rolled umbrella and a floral waistcoat peered at the heaving mob for a moment or two and said in a high voice to a like-minded companion, 'My dear, there's *nobody* here.'

All the men from Sturdley who were taking Schools in two weeks' time were clustered together, sipping coffee and doing crossword puzzles as the shadow lengthened over them : it was still too early in the day to play cards, and one had to do *something*. 'God, this insouciance is a strain,' said one of them sadly.

Three more chairs were dragged over to a small table which already bulged bulbous with chairs. The waitresses cursed and muttered as they tried to squeeze behind the groaning backs.

'God, John, you look awful today. Drinking again I suppose.'

'It's that incredible landlady of mine,' said Chote. 'She's at her worst just before Schools. It's a form of midsummer madness. I believe her husband died from it.'

The others half believed him; because it was such an appealing story; and because Chote seemed to be that sort of fellow : marvellous touch he had.

'I wish you'd invite me to your digs sometime, John.'

'Not a chance,' said Chote, rolling his eyes mechanically.

'I believe you're really a secret worker, Chote, a solitary bookso.'

'Never say that, about anybody.' Chote turned his head to get another look at the mob. A tall, dapper man called Bill Gosworth was swaggering, mincing towards them through the fog, his immaculate trousers already warm from the morning's lounging.

'Good morning, chaps,' he said languidly. 'Schools in two weeks. Don't forget to be there, will you?'

'How do you feel, Bill?' asked Chote. 'After last year, you must feel delightfully calm.'

'Truth is,' said Gosworth with a neat little yawn, 'I've got so much rowing on in the next few weeks, I don't know if I can fit in Schools at all.'

There was a respectful silence. Gosworth had died a year ago, in mysterious circumstances. Apparently brim-full of the old dash and confidence, he had sauntered into the Schools building and collapsed in an unaccountable heap. After solemnly handing in several completely blank papers, he had given up completely, and taken to his bed for a fortnight. That made him an unhappy symbol: for three years no one had put on a better show of suave, stylish, invulnerable what-have-you —the kind of thing that had made Oxford a byword in the good old days: of the dozen or so conceited poses (austerity Oscar Wilde) in contemporary Sturdley, his was undoubtedly the best, a poem in self-satisfaction; and then Schools had broken him in a moment, snapped him like a dry and humble twig. He still wore the best clothes and belonged to the best clubs and said some of the very best things: but his pose depended squarely upon impeccability; and this year he wandered the streets and cafés everlastingly, like a broken-down actor toiling away manfully in darkened theatres and chilling casting agencies.

'I hear you've got the Yank scholarship, Chote, you lazy blighter.' Chote nodded. 'You know, I was given the dashed thing myself last year,' continued Gosworth, flicking at last year's specks on his lapel. 'For various reasons I decided not to take it.'

'Couldn't fit it in with your rowing, I suppose,' said Chote. Gosworth smiled thinly, and after the correct interval—there was no special rule about this, it was just correct—he was sauntering off to his fifth table of the day. 'After four years, I suppose one knows everybody in Oxford,' somebody said. A year ago, Gosworth had done this business supremely well, flitting about with his little load of pollen; now he looked more like an old man trying to cadge drinks as he moved methodically from table to table: a Lord Jim of the coffee-houses, always scurrying away before someone remembered who he was.

'Do you think he'll make it this time?' asked Chote.

'I don't know,' said Hook. 'I've done tutorials with him, and he's pretty good, verging on the brilliant, in fact. I can't understand how he failed last time.'

'Schoolers nerves,' said Chote ominously. 'They get everybody in the end. It really starts in earnest, so I'm told, the moment you tie on your white tie and wriggle into your squalid cap and sordid, verminous gown. You know something's up when you spot that unfamiliar green face in the bathroom mirror—arr, yes, that's you all right. Then there's the wait outside in the hall, with hundreds of other sweaty men, all shuffling their ghastly feet in unison. A great moan goes up and they start moving at once in a bloody great surge into the examination room. And there it is at last: the little piece of paper, grinning up at you, twelve questions or so that the Spanish inquisitors would have blushed to ask. Everybody begins writing except you. You're still reading the paper and shaking uncontrollably like a ruddy leaf.' He remembered a film he had once seen in which a fellow had tried to talk a friend into getting seasick, only to become seasick himself. As he listened to the impersonal clatter of china and the slurping roar of the undergraduates (the intellectual elite grubbing for nourishment) he felt the cool, frivolous finger slipping in again between the third and fourth ribs, feathering his heart. It seemed like a damned silly thing to be afraid of; the only consolation being that everybody else in the whole café (big, husky chaps some of them) was or would one day be hagridden by this same childish fear.

Several of the dons were having a mild lunch of cold beef and cucumber in the sunny Senior Common Room. The Chaplain, roundish and overwrought today, was talking to the Warden, large and bland and oval, and the law tutor, thin and rumpled: three stock characters from the great English repertory company. The Warden who more or less ran Sturdley was called by his charges the 'Scoutmaster'—a tribute to his long, scraggy, frequently beshorted legs, and his guileless mien. He was, in fact, a misplaced businessman who had been called in during the difficult days after the war to raise money and to handle the new paperwork. Thus, although he had been a good enough scholar in his day, and was now as eccentric as any two other dons, there were those who felt that he was a bad portent. Sturdley had enjoyed a motley collection of wardens over the centuries, to be sure, including every imaginable kind of

31

scoundrel, but never before had it tried an out-and-out businessman. Mr. McLavish was an ominous sign of the times:
the first of the bureaucratic dons. And the rumour that he
had possibly saved Sturdley from bankruptcy by selling great
chunks of time-honoured property had done little enough to
soothe the critics.

The worst thing about the Warden was his apparently cava-
lier attitude to scholarship. The selection of Chote for the
American scholarship was the latest alarming example, and it
had given rise to much anguished debate among his colleagues.

'I think we may be making a big mistake in sending Chote,'
said the Chaplain. 'You remember how the Americans complained about Wiggs.'

'Chote's a damned hard worker,' said the law tutor.

'So was Wiggs,' said the anxious Chaplain, 'and they talked
about cutting off the scholarships after Wiggs.'

'I don't pretend to understand the Americans,' said the
Warden. 'They send over such dull heavy fellows. I'm sure
they only do it to impress us. Wiggs may have been a bit wild,
but I'm sure he never indulged in a pantie raid. Extraordinary
extremists, the Americans.'

'I think Chote will be very popular over there,' said the law
tutor. 'He's a friendly chap, quite good manners if he tries.
Well,' he corrected himself after a glance at the other two,
'perhaps not. But he isn't affected like most of the English
people one meets in America. I'll never forget some of the prigs
I came across last year. . . .'

'I wish he wouldn't play cards in the Senior Library,' sniffed
the Chaplain. 'I went in there yesterday to get a book and
there he was swearing like a sailor. The whole scene reminded
one of those dreadful American war novels.'

'That one hears about. Quite,' said the Warden.

'Well,' said the law tutor, 'I think he'll create a lot of good
will in America. Look at the way Wiggs married that American
girl. Frightfully fraternal. I wouldn't be surprised if Chote
did the same.'

The three of them puffed thoughtfully. The Warden coughed,
the only way he knew of breaking silence.

'I suppose I shall have to do something about that card-playing in the Senior Library. Thomson has been complaining again. And besides, I can see them from my window, and it's damned distracting.'

'The point about men like Chote,' said the law tutor doggedly, 'is that they are the best examples of what Oxford produces : reasonably good scholars, and yet not unbalanced by it. You know, no twitches, no shakes. Chote has a lively intelligence and he can apply it to whatever comes up.'

'Especially if it's beer or cards,' said the Chaplain somewhat primly. 'Frankly, I disagree with you completely. I think that Chote has a fair native intelligence which he has not quite succeeded in stifling during his three years at Oxford. He hasn't learned anything here, except a certain additional glibness. That type never amounts to anything. And after all,' he went on plaintively, 'it isn't as if we didn't have plenty of good solid material : George Fibley, Norbert Jones, even Alan Browning would do. . . .'

'Two clods and a draper's assistant,' the law tutor summed up briefly.

'There you have the eternal debate,' said the Warden, settling himself into it comfortably. 'We do teach glibness, I suppose. It can take years for an employer to see through a good Oxford man. And by then it's often too late, of course.'

'Well, I put my money on Chote,' said the law tutor. The Chaplain snorted. The Reverend Mr. Smythe didn't even find Chote particularly plausible, if it came to that.

'And,' continued the Warden, pointing his pipestem at the Chaplain, who ducked his head, 'at this stage, the undergraduates themselves have little enough idea of their own worth. Judging from my own recollections, I think many of them see themselves as complete charlatans, who have bluffed their way through Oxford, and will have to continue to bluff their way through life. Of course, if that really is their intention, we equip them supremely well for it.'

He caught the Chaplain's eye and smiled benignly : perhaps one was still a charlatan ?

'It isn't Chote's background that you object to ?' said the

lawyer (who was still comparatively hot from the steaming womb of Manchester) to the Chaplain. 'He isn't exactly county, is he?'

'Nonsense,' said the Chaplain haughtily. 'Curiously enough, Mr. George, it might interest you to know that I was born in the very same part of London myself, of very much the same sort of family.'

'It does you great credit,' said the law tutor, never at a loss, 'but perhaps that very fact makes you oversensitive to the difficulties which attend such a climb when undertaken by others.'

'Nonsense,' said the Warden to the two junior executives. 'Mr. Smythe has exhibited no more prejudice in this discussion than you have. His arguments have been perfectly reasonable. Fallacious, I happen to think, but perfectly reasonable.'

A young English tutor came wandering over to the puffing group.

'I say,' he said, 'sorry to butt in, but I see there's a Marx Brothers picture on in town—*Horsefeathers* I think it is. Does anybody know if it's any good?'

'Not quite vintage,' said the Warden thoughtfully. 'Very good, but not quite vintage.'

To get through the college lodge, the Warden had to wade through a vast throng of undergraduates; he smiled faint, absent-minded greetings all around. The Warden was on his way to *Horsefeathers*; the undergraduates were debating whether to undertake a little work, or to play cricket, or to go to the cinema, too.

Gradually the cricketers and the workers detached themselves, leaving the soft underbelly of Sturdley: the 'chaps' who had been playing cards the day before and drinking coffee that morning.

'It's Schools hysteria. There's no point in fighting it.'

'It's just a question of which flick we haven't already seen this week'—always a problem by Thursday. Next week, they would all go down to the river to watch the boats come in: it would be Eights Week. But now they were still haunting the cinemas.

'I see there's a Marx Brothers starting today at the Scala.'

In twos and threes, they passed out of the lodge to follow the Warden to *Horsefeathers*. 'After all,' said Chote, 'one must relax sometimes. Let's face it : one isn't a machine.'

The procession wound its way toward the Scala, each explaining to each that it was just a question of revising a few notes, and presto! Schools was in the bag. The crowd got bigger and bigger as it went along, swelling snowball-like; the Warden striding along in front, like the Pied Piper, followed by hundreds of scuffling young men in patched sports jackets.

'Which one is *Horsefeathers*?' asked Godfrey Hook. 'Is it the one where they're stowaways on a ship?'

'Somebody always asks that bloody question,' said Chote gruffly—angry because he ought to have been working. 'It's the only one where they aren't stowaways on a ship.'

'What I want to know is this : what happens to your will power when you come to this place?' muttered Ralph Gadsby.

The cinema was full and humming with anticipation. There was always at least one Marx Brothers film a term, and a huge crowd always turned up, to try to memorize the lines. For the next few days, the Oxford air would be thick with half-baked Grouchoisms. The nightmare plot lived up to expectations : not quite vintage, perhaps, but well worth a twelfth visit for Chote and a seventh for the Warden.

On the way out, Chote asked Browning, 'Didn't I see the Warden chuckling obscenely in the back seats?'

'I give up. Did you?'

'The funny thing is that yesterday, during the scholarship interview, when he asked me why I wanted to go to America, and after I had given him the usual "widening horizons, exchange-of-ideas" crap, I said it was also because they had such smashing humorists over there.'

'What did he say?'

'He said, "That's hardly a conclusive reason one way or the other, Mr. Chote hm, hm." But I can't help thinking it helped, all the same.'

They wandered back to college, bent and hushed by little quasi-hangovers, temporarily dried up and empty like wax fruit. 'The college bar doesn't open for two hours,' said Alan Browning. 'It looks as if we'll have to work after all.'

'One hour for tea, one hour for work,' corrected Chote. 'Just a question of reorganizing the jolly old notes.'

'That's right,' said Hook. 'I have all the stuff written down. It's just a question of moulding it into shape. M-o-u-l-d-i-n-g.'

'There's such a thing as knowing too much,' pointed out Chote. 'One doesn't know what to say first. The big thing in an exam is to utilize all one's puny supplies of information, while giving an impression of vast reserves which one just hasn't time to call upon.' (It was a year when Stephen Potter had a lot to answer for.)

After a leisurely tea, and then minutes in the lodge, looking hopelessly through the pigeonholes ('Look at the mail accumulated by this bloody man Soames. Yanks are so ruddy communicative') and swiping gracefully with cricket bats which had been left lying about, the three of them made their sluggish, halting way toward the Senior Library.

The cards had vanished. But down the centre aisle of the library a game of cricket was in full swing, based (with British ingenuity) on a ball of paper and a ruler. Thomson was watching it, on the verge of tears. Every few minutes the shaggy ball drifted over to him, and an angry cry would go up for him to return it post haste. Work in such circumstances was out of the question.

'A neurotic manifestation,' said Chote. 'You chaps aren't really enjoying this, you know. It's just a clumsy retreat into childhood.'

'Don't we know it?' said the bowler, Ralph Gadsby, yesterday's golfer. 'You'll join us of course?'

Chote was taking his turn at the ruler when the Chaplain pattered in with an 'Ah, Mr. Chote.'

'Good afternoon, sir,' said Chote, stabbing at his pocket with the ruler.

'Enjoying a little much needed relaxation, Mr. Chote?'

'Yes, sir. I suppose so, sir.'

'Do you often relax in this way, Mr. Chote?'

'No, sir. Very seldom.'

36

'Not an ideal choice of venue, do you think?'

'No, sir. A very unfortunate choice.'

The Chaplain was a mild man and a good scholar: and like many such at Oxford, he had no idea what to do with people like Chote. Ideally, one felt, there should be no need for discipline at a university. Besides, one wasn't quite sure how great one's own authority was supposed to be. If only one had time to go back and consult with the other dons. He rather wished that Gadsby hadn't spotted him in the first place: he didn't feel up to the encounter at this particular moment.

'I hope you will be more careful in your choice in future.'

'Yes, sir,' said Chote to the Chaplain's hasty back.

'Thank God I've already got the scholarship,' said Chote. 'I suppose they can't strip it off me in some bloody great ceremony, can they?'

They left the library quietly. 'Apply yourself, lad,' they said to the inevitable Thomson, who was bowed over his books once again. The bar was now open and there was no point in wasting any more time in the library. Just outside the mouth of the bar, they ran into the Chaplain again.

'A little much needed refreshment, Mr. Chote? After the day's work?'

'I left my gown down there, sir,' said Chote, and the Chaplain passed on. 'Last week,' he added.

'Why does he always have to pick on me?' moaned Chote softly.

'Because he likes you and wants to help you,' said Browning.

The college bar was a tiny cave, with its own special assortment of smells and echoes, some of them dating back for centuries. There was a dartboard in one corner and a shove-ha'penny board in another, both of them doing a brisk trade. The non-participants clustered around to criticize and spread confusion; still others were swarming round the bar, heckling the bartender.

There was one spasmodically peaceful corner, with a table, where thoughtful people like Thomson could sometimes sit and sip sherry with their quiet friends. This evening Chote and his companions grabbed it, for they were in a comparatively serious mood. The elegant Gosworth, all dressed up for the evening, came over. 'Are you coming drinking tonight, John?'

'Not me,' said Chote. 'Thursday night is my night for womanizing.'

'Anyone special?' asked Gosworth.

'No. The usual. Daffers.'

'That's not very enterprising of you, John.'

'I'm too old to change my ways,' said Chote. 'My uncle who was up before the war recommended Daphne, although he said that she was showing signs of wear even in his time. She's been such a comfort, teaching me how to tie my shoelaces and so on—I can't very well desert her now, can I?'

'Did you really have an uncle up here, old boy?'

It didn't really matter: one could say that one had such an uncle if one didn't, and deny that one had him if one did. Like many others at Sturdley College, Chote had managed to bury, in a shallow grave, an undistinguished past; and he was comfortably aware that even his closest friends could not have given much account of him.

At Sturdley there was only a handful of men who had gone to the top public schools, and acquired the fine, luminous unconsciousness; and about the same number had gone to nameless grammar schools and still spoke, defiantly, reluctantly, with the meatier accents of their provinces; in between, there was a great pink featureless mass, Britannia's flesh. Chote had gone to an obscure public school, Brinkley College in the Chilterns, reputation so-so, where he had acquired a passable variant of the BBC voice: that was more than enough for Oxford to know. The admirable rules about personal questions and personal revelations covered the rest of him like a Victorian morning coat and trousers. He didn't have to lie about his origins; he had only to keep quiet.

On the whole, he was most often seen in the company of other indefinite men like Hook and Browning (Hook, an old Brinkleyan, Browning a good grammar school): perhaps that was a slight clue. Well, more than a clue. He was pretty sure that they knew, and they assumed that he knew that they knew . . . but nothing was ever said. He was an agile liaison man between the oppressors and the oppressed and many of his best friends were et cetera, et cetera. At Sturdley there was no apparent bitterness between the extremes but some awkwardness; and any man who could make himself at ease was generally welcome—especially if he was a licensed buffoon. Problems might arise when parents and girl friends with the red, raw, class characteristics came to visit; at these times, there was apt to be a certain amount of cutting, dodging and downright hiding on the part of the touchier elements.

To John Chote class was a faint impediment, like a limp, keeping him out of a few clubs, and perhaps later a few jobs, and away from a few other goodies that perhaps he didn't even know about. It didn't bother him much (except on rainy days) because if these things were decided on merit, he would very likely wind up in just about the same place. All the same, it would be nice to go to America and see how he got on without his limp for a while. One assumed that America had its own silly-as-buggery class system, but they would hardly expect him to play at it. He had seen the American Rhodes scholars at Oxford moving without embarrassment among all manner of men, accepted everywhere—at the Bullingdon, the Clarendon, the Oddfellows, or whatever the bloody places were called. There was one particular fellow from Brooklyn, who used to swear at tipsy intervals that he would never go home again : he had had a slight limp, too, very slight but nagging. Perhaps Chote would stay permanently in America for the same sort of reason. An educated alien could make himself at home all right : the class struggle was strictly a family affair. And talking of family—but enough. It was time to be thinking about Daphne now, setting the glands to work, getting warmed up, preparing oneself for the feast.

The established way at Sturdley was just to listen to Browning for a while—if one could stand it. He was holding forth at the moment about last night's Marge—No, really, he couldn't have done that . . . no, it was too much to believe. Browning's little face crinkled with pleasure as if knowing that he had his audience hooked now, and that disgusted, disapproving, enervated as may be, they would listen to the end.

Daphne Collins sat billowing in a moss-green dress on the sofa. She was almost as chunky as he was, placid and well to the left of plain. She had worked unobtrusively as a nurse for several years at one of the countless Oxford hospitals. She was one of those girls you could ring up at any moment and send for, and within half an hour, there she was. Or, if one preferred, one could go to her room and sit there all evening. It didn't seem to make any difference to her. At any rate, she never admitted a preference.

In his franker moments, Chote would admit that there wasn't a wealth of passion in the affair. 'I'm going over to sublimate with Daffers,' he used to say. There was a convention of delicacy about these affairs of the heart and he was never asked (even by Alan Browning) to describe his relations with Daphne any further than that—and he never did. If one's friends assumed the worst, that was perhaps all that one could reasonably hope for.

He was sitting with an arm round her and a lawbook in his lap. She sat very still, staring straight ahead with the large, saucer eyes. He read his book with a judicial grimace. 'Bloody, bloody law,' he said.

She got up to put the kettle on. 'I bought some chocolate biscuits,' she said. 'Is that all right?'

'Good show.' He shut his book, stretched and yawned, and swung his crepe-swathed feet onto the shabby sofa. Why on earth, he wondered idly, had he allowed Browning to talk him into buying these repulsive shoes? They must be almost two years old by now and still no signs of wearing out.

'I'm going to America for a year,' he said.

'Oh. That's nice. . . . We shan't be seeing you for a while, I suppose.'

'No, I suppose not.' Obviously not, he thought. Naturally.

'Will you write to me?'

'Certainly. We'll keep in touch.'

'It should be a wonderful year for you.'

Her face remained expressionless as usual, but he received a message of discomfort. This business of leading a sane, breezy sex life had its drawbacks: a series of poignant little partings, each leaving its own tiny scar. There had never been any question of marriage or love with Daphne, he had made no false promises, and yet surely he was committing a palpable act of desertion.

He kissed her, and she made her usual puddingy response. If leaving Daphne made one feel so agitated, how would one feel as one withdrew from the series of richer, more romantic entanglements which, let's face it, one had always planned for oneself?

He watched her making the tea, her plump back arched over the pot, and he felt for a second as if it were she who was leaving him, disappearing into the sink. For three years she had ministered to him with biscuits and jam and such, and now she was off with the teapot under her arm.

It was too bad of her to leave like this, while he had so much on his mind. He felt like calling peevishly after her. But then, look at the number of undergraduates who wound up engaged to nurses and shopgirls, probably after just such sessions as this. Not that one had anything against nurses and shopgirls of course; but one remembered the stark little ceremonies and, in particular, the horrible clash of relatives—the girl's family pouring down from Lancashire in chartered buses. . . .

They drank their tea in silence, and she washed out the cups. It was heartbreaking to watch her in such typical activity: filling teacups, washing them, drying them, carefully rounding up the crumbs from the chocolate biscuits. He started to speak, and then adapted his words while they were still rattling around in his mouth. It wasn't fair to offer her any encouragement.

'Are you coming to the Summer Ball?'

'If you like.'

'Good show.' It was time to go and she opened the door for him. He kissed the lifeless mouth and pressed the sturdy pink hand. God, I'm a swine, he thought to himself as he galumphed down the steps. 'You forgot your book, John': and she brought it down to him and handed it over gravely, with ritual courtesy. 'What would you do without me?' she said. 'Forget your head I suppose.'

Cruelty, cruelty—he had practised an awful lot of it one way and another, for a chap who didn't believe in it. But what could you do, what did other people do? Cover it up with jokes, ribaldries, and Gosworth-casualness, atone for it by proposing an insane marriage, toughen up with cold baths? Perhaps he would think of something after Schools.

He looked blankly at the clear sky. Hmm, pleasant weather we're having for a change, he suddenly realized. 'I must have a talk about that with Mrs. Worsley.'

It wasn't exactly Venice, but it was pleasant enough. The punt drifted a few yards, and then shot forward, drifted and shot, over the dark waters of the Cherwell; round corners and under branches, a light splash and a sweet silence, repeated over and over again in leisurely rhythm. Occasionally other boatloads swooped mysteriously past in the dark.

Browning stood at the back, wielding the pole lightly, a graceful confident figure in dim outline, supple, sure of himself, swaying lithely under the branches, and manœuvring the corners with a touch. Godfrey Hook, lying back on the cushions, knew that if he was handling the pole himself, he would be whacking the punt heavily against both banks in turn, and getting his pole caught in the weeping willows.

Hook's clumsiness went back a long way, several generations at least. As long as he could remember, his father had been tumbling off ladders and running out of petrol. The Reverend Mr. Hook never seemed to be quite safe anywhere. On Sundays, young Godfrey used to watch with trepidation as his father cautiously mounted the pulpit: surely he would trip this time and come sprawling? Godfrey's little palms would sweat uncontrollably and his mouth would gradually dry out as he waited for his father to stumble down over his words, lose his drift, sail away into an ocean of incoherence. The Reverend Hook never did lose control to that extent. He would get a grip on his sliding spectacles, clear his throat with manly determination, and start again : but Godfrey was sure that his father would slip over the edge one day and never come back.

Gloomily, he watched himself growing inch by inch into the same mould. A childish tendency to fall down all the time led the grim procession of ineptitudes: he couldn't make a bed without lumps in it, or keep his trousers up properly, or throw a ball straight. He knew it was coming, and he waited with resignation for each new challenge to appear and defeat him. He came to think of himself and his father as characters in an old two-reel comedy, tottering, staggering and stumbling together through life. His schooldays at Brinkley College were still a suppressed nightmare of embarrassments.

By reason of tenacity, he did at last manage to master a few physical arts, at least adequately. He learned to ride a horse pretty well, and to shoot a gun. His two years in the Army were nothing like as bad as he had expected : if he concentrated twice as hard as anybody else, he found he could do most of the routine things quite unobtrusively: much better than the Reverend Hook could have, anyway.

But the old apprehensions still dogged him. He never knew when he might take a left turn instead of a right on the parade ground, or slip on a cake of soap in the bathtub and break his angular bones. The fact that such things never actually happened did not prevent him from expecting them to, almost with certainty. The statistical awareness that in fact he underwent no more accidents than the next man came just too late in life to make any real difference.

His generalized clumsiness followed him indoors, or so he feared. At any moment, he felt, a situation might arise, in a pub or a drawing room (or worse) with which he wouldn't be able to cope. In the circumstances, the wisest move seemed to be to sit still and play things safe. He had few friends in the Army, and they were rather quiet, uneventful chaps, and he didn't honestly like them very much. On the other hand, even after hearing thousands of them, he didn't know how to react when he heard a dirty story. So he didn't have much choice. During most of his leisure moments he used to sit in the barracks by himself, writing long letters to the bishop's daughter, carefully cementing their relationship: that, after all, was his world—undemanding, quietly productive, dead right in its values.

He was reluctant to go to Oxford at all, but his father had been at Sturdley in the old days (when it boasted no more than eighty mediocre undergraduates, studying for the lower rungs of the ministry and the civil service) so Godfrey hunched his shoulders and prepared himself to weather another three years of loneliness, exile and anxiety over his balance. To soften the harsh aspect, he proposed marriage to the bishop's daughter, who accepted him with dignified enthusiasm; and during the last summer before he went up to Oxford, the two of them spent many blissful hours together, planting primroses and such in the rectory garden, and planning a quietly fruitful future.

During his first week at Oxford he wandered about by himself watching the trees change colour, counting the days until he could go back to Devon for good, only three years hence. The only people he met (besides Mr. Smythe the Chaplain, with whom he had a most satisfactory talk) were the inevitable club representatives: Conservative, Labour, Communist, Anglican, rugby and all the others. He paid out his half-crowns to them, and dandruffed his mantelpiece with small white cards, which entitled him to assuage his loneliness at upwards of twenty-five meetings a week, all starting at 7.45 P.M. precisely.

In his second week, he ran into John Chote, who was also making a round of the clubs. Chote was heckling a Communist speaker over his grammar, accusing him in a roundabout way of not being a good Englishman. 'You might at least do us the small courtesy of learning our language.' Hook recognized the voice with a thrill of fear. Chote had been his chief tormenter at Brinkley College, graceful and brutal. He had also been a schoolboy success, as these things go, captaining cricket and rugby and debating among the slim student body: Hook had been a resounding failure, by any standards. Nevertheless, Hook went diffidently up to him, and introduced himself bravely, as a Brinkley man must.

44

'I don't suppose you remember me: A godforsaken chap with pimples.'

'Shnook, Crook, Hook.' Chote would have the advantage as long as they lived. He sounded bored, as if Hook had been talking to him all night. 'The thoroughly repulsive, pockmarked man on my right is one Alan Browning. Alan and I were in the same ghastly regiment for two years, pacifying Austria, raping South Wales, and so on. Alan, I want you to meet my old school chum, Basil Shnook.' Alan Browning smiled hello, quite the most charming smile Godfrey had ever seen.

He took it for granted that they would both drop him again in a matter of minutes. He had never had any friends half so slick and knowledgeable. On the way home that evening they chewed the details of at least a dozen different nurses; and when they got to Sturdley, they went up to Browning's room to drink ill-gotten gin. This manifestly *wasn't* Godfrey's world, and these wouldn't be his friends. In a while, Browning began to walk round the room on his hands and Chote climbed out of the window and started to caper up and down on the withered tiles. Hook goggled: after a tumblerful of gin, it was all he could do to keep from sliding out of his chair. He left in a state of sentimental fluff, glad to have spent an evening with these smooth fellows before leaving Oxford three years hence. A moment later, Chote and Browning heard him clattering heavily down the rickety steps. He was on his feet in a flash, blood streaming from his ear. 'Are you all right, old boy?' Browning's friendly voice dripped concern from the top of the banister. 'Quite all right. Only a scratch,' answered Hook cheerfully. 'Carry on, men.'

For several weeks Hook remained in suspended animation, waiting to be dropped. Chote could hardly contain his boredom. And yet every evening they picked him up and took him on their accustomed rounds: pubs, mostly, and out-of-bounds dance halls. They seemed to take it for granted that he would come; and it never really occurred to him not to. An isolated stab of remorse came in the form of a letter from his fiancée telling him to keep his chin up. 'Only three more years, my dearest Godfrey. Courage.' He wrote back to tell her that he was settling in well and making some friends. Felicity was glad about this, of course, but apprehensive, especially as his letters grew shorter and less frequent: 'I feel that we're growing apart, Godfrey,' she wrote back sternly. He would have a lot to answer for at Christmas.

What on earth did these flashy chaps see in him? Like an ugly man doing well with a beautiful woman, he was sure that he would inevitably be found out—and, of course, dropped immediately. He just couldn't think of enough funny things to say or do, and if he did think of something it was always several seconds too late. These skilful chaps must surely have noticed: if not, it was only a matter of time. Whenever he was alone with either of them, his tongue locked automatically, and if it was Chote, he would shrivel in the ensuing boredom. Browning made him feel much better: and what was more, offered relief to the new sizzle in his blood. But he had to take them both together. And so, the three-cornered friendship continued somehow; and when that first Christmas came, Felicity berated him stoutly and icily for his growing aloofness. 'You seem almost like a stranger these days,' she told him severely. 'Something has happened to you, Godfrey.' There was iron behind Felicity's tenderness.

Ever since, Felicity had been hanging on grimly, sworn to be true to him come what may. Godfrey began to drift for a bit. One simply couldn't keep up the effort of trying to impress one's friends indefinitely. After all, perhaps they actually liked him for his amazing inappropriateness: possibly it amused them to keep a tame parson of their own, faintly corrupted, to display in their various dens and holes.

It wasn't too stiff a price to pay for admission to Babylon (Bishop Wagstaff's preaching had always made Babylon seem wonderful but unattainable). For a while, he even took to exaggerating his parsonish characteristics, hoping to amuse his friends even more hugely. He succeeded, too. Browning likened him to the disturbed clergymen who sell the Sunday papers, and together they persuaded him to masquerade as a deranged prelate in a college revue. He had a famous time staggering about the stage with his collar turned round and flapping loose, like a slack mouth. Some of his old clumsiness slipped away that night; and he found himself being accepted as a tolerably amusing fellow, all over Sturdley. In fact, he was asked to repeat his sacrilegious performance several times over, which he did with prodigious success, mouthing deliciously absurd pieties. At last he had found a form of wit he could master.

He felt a little guilty about it, but after all, it was all in fun. He had never felt anything but pity for his woebegone father, with his stiff little principles and his two left feet. He had seen through the Reverend Hook's fragile theology years ago, and he had only remained virtuous because there seemed to be no alternative.

Nevertheless, there was still Felicity, waiting, waiting, waiting. Every vacation started with the same scene of mute reproach. She watched in grim silence as he bicycled doggedly off to the village pub. With grim determination, he would down his beer, his watery symbol of emancipation, and wobble slowly back on his bicycle into the orbit of the large sorrowful gaze. It wasn't much fun, he had to admit : but once he had taught her to take him as he was, everything would be all right. Browning had assured him warmly that it was only a matter of training. And fortunately the Reverend Hook showed not the faintest sign of knowing what was going on : a blessing that could almost always be counted upon in his case, but still extremely welcome. Meanwhile, Felicity seemed to be biding her time patiently, until the season would come at last for her to get her hands on him full time. Then she would see. . . . Perhaps even the Reverend Hook had gone through a period of mild folly at that age. It was really nothing to get alarmed about, a mere seasonal complaint . . . and after all, Godfrey always came back to her during the vacations. . . .

'That sod Chote is a lucky sod,' said Browning absently, toying with the punt pole.

'You mean getting the scholarship ?'

'Yes, pretending to be a lazy bugger while all the time he was planning and plotting and scheming'—he gave a strenuous heave with the pole—'and, worst of all, being a bloody politician with the dons.' Hook peered at him through the gloom,

47

trying to make out the present set of his features. It was still hard, continuous work for him, sorting out the jokes that were meant to be serious.

'I daresay we all work a little harder than we pretend,' he said. 'As a matter of fact, I put in for a scholarship myself. You know, that unpretentious one to Columbia.'

'I daresay there is a good deal of deceit going about the place—though for myself I can honestly say, with the hand on the booz, that my laziness is at least comparatively genuine. I'm not at all sure that Chote could say the same.' There was a fairly clear note of irritability in his voice. But could one be sure?

'It's quite accepted practice,'' said Hook. 'Everybody at Oxford is a bloody great impostor, of one sort or another.'

'I suppose so,' muttered Browning. 'Still, I sometimes think that Chote carries the arts of fraudulence a little too far.'

'Do you?' asked Hook with interest. After three years he still felt like the outsider in the group. But this sounded like the real thing, all right. 'I've always thought that he had about as much integrity as the next Oxford man, which is to say damn all. It simply isn't what one looks for up here,' he said.

'You chaps who are bred to the cloth sometimes reveal depths of cynicism that we of the laity can only marvel at,' said Browning. The punt glided round in an indolent crescent, and began to nose gently back towards home. 'I agree that most of us up here have our little poses,' he continued, 'all of which bring a richness and variety to the family circle. Yerss. Quite so. Ding-dong. But one would hesitate to call it really deceitful in most cases. Willoughby-Pyke isn't deceitful. Anyone has a right not to be plain unadulterated George Pyke of Sheffield. And Gosworth isn't deceitful. Everybody knows he's a fraud. A public, chartered fraud.'

'But this doesn't apply to John, eh?'

'No, not precisely, no.'

'What do you suppose he's hiding?' asked Hook.

'God knows,' said Browning. 'Nothing I suppose. It's a delicate distinction. One mustn't rule out the possibility that one may be talking unmitigated crap. I mean . . .' This surely couldn't be embarrassment, thought Hook. Not Browning, embarrassed. '. . . with a chap like you, one knows where one stands, if you know what I mean. With John, one doesn't.'

'Ah,' said Hook, not disagreeing. This seemed to be a curious development indeed. Chote and Browning always appeared to be absolute equals in charming insincerity. It must be a question of O.K.-insincerity versus the other kind. Thank God he had blundered into the right camp himself.

'I don't know,' said Browning, who seemed to be straining uncharacteristically to put the thing just right. 'I don't mean to say that I've gone over to the big chin. Heavens, you know me. It's just that, well, Chote seems to be *all* act, a sort of india-rubber chap, with no shape of his own at all.'

It was so quiet on the river that Browning's words sounded unnaturally significant and final. He seemed to sense this reverberance, unnaturally harsh and clear, and he added quickly, 'No, that's much too strong. I really am talking tripe after all.' He pushed peevishly at some unoffending weeds which were straggling past.

Hook stretched against the cushions, languorously angular. Should one say, 'Yes, but I see what you mean about Chote'? This could mean a new level of friendship with Browning, a higher understanding. But after all, he didn't *really* know what Browning meant, what was eating the blighter. He had his own scruples about Chote, but they might not be the *right* scruples. He stood to lose two friends if he criticized Chote for the wrong reasons. And then, where would blessed relief be found? And the secret of gracefulness?

' 'I don't know why I said all that,' said Browning echoing the uncertainty. 'Schoolers nerves, I daresay. I don't really believe a word of it. John's a splendid chap.'

Hook dangled his fingers luxuriously in the cool, dark water, and didn't say anything.

'It's just that confounded way he has of sneaking off by himself all the time, and turning up suddenly with scholarships clutched between his teeth,' pursued Browning.

'He always was like that, even at school,' said Hook. 'An uncommonly successful chap. But then, after all, isn't that part of his charm?' Browning didn't answer.

'Oh, by the way,' he said. 'Did you have a rewarding life experience last night with that rather enticing bit of frippet?'

'What do you take me for?' said Hook, glad to get it off his chest at last. 'A cradle snatcher?'

'Hmm,' said Browning.

3. Taking It Easy

THE news of Chote's scholarship lapped gently against the two Rhodes scholars, Gene Fosdick and Bradshaw Soames.

They hadn't much else in common: each thought the other represented all that was worst about Americans abroad. Soames (according to Fosdick) stood for naïveté, keenness, the embarrassing question. Fosdick (Soames's version) was stuffy, cautious, unconsciously quaint.

There was indeed a fine antique finish to Gene which rendered him almost venerable to the touch. An admiring Englishman once said of him that the first moment one laid eyes on him, one thought: By George, this bloke is mature! Nobody minded about this except Soames. If maturity was the pose that suited the fellow's aptitudes, good luck to him. Fosdick was considered, in fact, something of a connoisseur's delight.

It was the sporting situation that threw them together. During the past winter, Soames had been captain and Fosdick secretary of the university basketball team—a dogged body of five Americans and one very tall Englishman which whiled away the clammy evenings in drafty auditoriums and aircraft hangars, and other bleak improvisations, jousting with assorted segments of the U.S. Air Force. (The winter before that, Fosdick had been captain and Soames secretary.)

During the summer, with the basketballs stowed safely

away, they played tennis together on the Sturdley sports grounds. Twice a week they merged with the bicycled mob on High Street: white trousers, cricket bats, handkerchiefs at the throat—the healthy-minded youth of England in full cry.

Today they were swinging off course. It was the last day of Eights Week, and the Sturdley boats would be puffing in at intervals during the afternoon. Girls in print dresses would be urging them sweetly on from the Sturdley barge, together with the Warden in his shorts and ghostly oarsmen from the past, who came up every year. It was a feast of folklore not to be missed by Soames. And Fosdick, who found human nature very much the same everywhere he went, but with subtle differences, saw at least mild pleasure in the prospect.

'How do you think Chote will go down in America?' asked Bradshaw as he plied his pedals vigorously.

'All right, I guess. He ought to be popular anyway.'

'It seems like a funny kind of choice. I mean, he's not exactly what you'd call academic material.'

'Americans,' said Fosdick, gazing around with his mild eyes, 'always make the mistake of equating scholarship with solemnity.'

All right, you know-it-all bastard, thought Soames. If Fosdick ever found anybody as mature as himself, he might be able to have a decent conversation with him: as it was, one had to put up with this omniscient crap.

'I didn't mean that,' he said peevishly. 'You know the way we expect graduate students to work their tails off. Chote seems pretty much of a time-server to me.'

'It takes a while to understand the English character,' said Fosdick, swerving his bicycle around a bulbous lorry.

Oh, for Godsake. 'I know that.' Soames had to pant to keep up. It made it all the harder to strike the right note with this superior sonofabitch. 'I just don't see a facetious guy like Chote. . . .'

Fosdick got off his bicycle. They had reached Christ Church meadows, a stretch of soft shade between commerce and the river. Fosdick seemed to be gazing off into the middle distance.

. . . 'Other Englishmen aren't like that' . . . Jeez, I'm boring him again, thought Soames. 'I mean so kind of, I don't know, phony.' Fosdick was definitely losing interest. Ah, to hell with him. Soames didn't know why he bothered with him. But when there was a silence, he blamed himself for it.

He began looking around for English company, in which he wouldn't feel quite so young and flighty. There would be plenty of it down by the river anyway: a roar of mixed English vowels came wafting up from the barges. The girls and the old oarsmen were giving it all they had: and what a *comfortable* noise they made, thought Soames.

Americans, he decided, were too. . . . No, he left that one to Fosdick. He wheeled his bicycle faster over the stony path leading to the barges.

Six o'clock. The Chaplain opened the door a crack and peered cautiously in. Two men in white trousers were bearing Thomson swiftly toward the far end of the library on their shoulders: Chote, by the look of it, and one of his deplorable friends. Thomson sat erect and stiff in his good grey suit, obviously determined to rise above his trying circumstances. He had been accustomed since early youth to these periodic bedevilments by the cloddish, ruffianly elements (though one did think that at Oxford—well, after all, dash it) and he knew the imperative importance of keeping one's dignity at such times. In the long run, they would learn to respect one, and perhaps even leave one alone.

The Chaplain shut the door softly and shuffled away. The strains of 'Lloyd George knows my father, father knows Lloyd George' followed him foolishly down the stairs. What was a man to do in these dreadful situations?

He found the Warden sitting by the open window of his study, looking across at the Senior Library and puffing thoughtfully on his pipe. 'Ah, Mr. Smythe,' he said absently. 'Do have a chair won't you?'

'Look at what they're doing,' said Mr. Smythe at once. 'Can you see what they're doing? Are they still doing it?' He darted towards the window to get another look.

'What on earth are you talking about?' asked the Warden amiably. 'Who doing what?'

'They, you know, Chote and his friends, have been carrying poor Thomson about the library like a sack of potatoes. Just a minute ago. I saw it myself.'

'Oh, that's all right. They've put him down now, and they seem to be talking to him. It all looks quite friendly and civilized.'

Mr. Smythe paused. After all, he had done his duty in reporting the incident: if the Warden chose to take a thoroughly irresponsible line after that, well that was surely his own affair. One doubt alone still plagued him: 'I really don't see how we can send Chote to America after this,' he ventured. 'This seems to me to be the absolute last straw.'

'Oh, do you think so? I should have thought he would be capital value at their football matches and—what's the word one wants?—"pep" rallies. He has such uncommon supplies of enthusiasm. . . .'

Mr. Smythe paused again: one had to tread carefully when the Warden was in one of his skittish moods. 'I have no objection to schoolboy spirits,' he said slowly, 'within reason.' Painful memories stabbed playfully at him. The year before, Chote had occupied the room above his own; and he had been forced to listen, night after night, to the crashing of furniture, and the unspeakable songs, and sometimes the derisive snicker of an empty bottle careening down the drainpipe outside his window. Only the year before that, he had been junior housemaster at a small country school. The muffled noises of the dormitory had certainly imposed a mild strain; and when the appointment to Oxford finally came, one welcomed it with joy: an alluring prospect of semi-retirement among the peaceful spires, a chance to follow one's quiet pursuits (with even less hubbub) in the most civilized surroundings imaginable. And instead he had found himself sitting up in bed every night wondering how soon Chote's vulgar cockney body would come hurtling through the ceiling in a shower of plaster and broken glass. 'No objection, within reason,' he said. 'After all, I have spent most of my life among schoolboys and I flatter myself that I

53

know something about them. But this is a totally different proposition. Chote is, to put it bluntly, a pure hooligan, a thoroughly bad hat, little better than a spiv in fact.'

The Warden smiled. 'Perhaps you're right, although I don't happen to think so myself. Time, of course, will tell.'

This was really too exasperating. 'I should have thought that time had told us enough already,' said Mr. Smythe waspishly. 'Look at what happened with Wiggs: the Americans were simply livid about him. And Chote is exactly the same type.'

'Well,' the Warden threw up his hands gently, 'I'm afraid I don't agree, that's all. Actually Wiggs reminded me rather more of Alan Browning. And I'll grant you that Alan Browning would be a decidedly risky proposition.'

'Really? I should have thought him infinitely preferable to Chote. I'll grant you that he has his rough edges. And he still has a certain amount of growing up to do. But all the same, there's a world of difference between him and Chote.'

'I won't argue with you about that,' said the Warden. 'Look —they seem to be leaving the library and taking Thomson with them. You don't suppose Chote is planning to lead the lad astray, do you?'

'I wouldn't be surprised,' said Mr. Smythe earnestly. 'Only look at what he's done to Godfrey Hook: Godfrey hasn't been to chapel in two terms, and I believe that his father is really most concerned. And Alan Browning—I'll wager we'd see a world of improvement in that lad if Chote left him alone for a while.'

'Leading Alan Browning astray?' said the Warden with surprise. 'Oh no, I can't accept that at all. No, really, that's too much.'

'Well, I believe it,' said Mr. Smythe stoutly. 'I think Alan has very good instincts, and I know that he has a good background—pious people, in the very best sense. He may be a little weak, a little tractable—you can see that in his face, in the eyes and mouth. He's the sort of boy who can be drawn into trouble by bad acquaintances. But fundamentally he's sound.'

'Well,' said the Warden, 'appearances can indeed be misleading and I may be wrong about both of them. I've always thought there was something rather sinister about Browning —but then, I haven't had your experience among boys.'

'Oh, I'm sure you have,' said the Chaplain modestly. 'I didn't mean that as a boast, I assure you.'

'Anyway,' said the Warden, in tones of one firmly summing up, 'there's really nothing more to be said. I hope that my judgment proves correct in this instance.' Mr. Smythe knew that there was no chance of this judgment being changed : the Warden might be a bit fatuous, but these captains of industry made a fetish of will power. 'We shall see in God's good time. In the meantime, I don't suppose you'd care to have a friendly wager on which of the two does better in Schools?'

The Chaplain couldn't help looking just a little horrified. His colleagues at school had warned him not to expect too much from a place like Sturdley, a very cellar of Oxford life. But a Warden who wagered money on his own students. . . .

'I had in mind about sixpence,' said the Warden. 'But of course, if it's against your principles—'

'I suppose sixpence would be all right,' said Mr. Smythe dubiously. 'There wouldn't be any harm in that. Very well. Sixpence.' The words tumbled out uncontrollably. He hadn't meant to agree to the wager at all. Still, it was only sixpence.

'I'm afraid I'm what you would call "bad company", eh?' said the Warden jovially. He began rummaging for the sherry decanter.

'No, no, thank you very much.' Mr. Smythe was on his feet and doing his ritual shuffle to the door. It was a way of taking one's leave of important people, learned years ago and never abandoned : bowing and smiling and rubbing the hands and all the time backing away as fast as the feet would carry one. He made the door without tripping or stumbling over any of the Warden's sparse furniture. But when he got outside, he found that his palms were unaccountably sweating, and trembling a little, so that he had to put them in his pockets.

On the last night of Eights Week, the men who row break

training and go native. The transition is too abrupt, of course, and by seven o'clock there is a gurgling at the washbasins, and sometimes at the windows as well. After that, the burden of celebration and the advantage of the extension have to be taken over by those who are used to it, the chaps who celebrate every night.

Chote and his friends had brought Thomson along as a kind of talisman. Sturdley's first boat had finished in the first division, an almost unprecedented performance, and they felt that Thomson should acknowledge it in the customary way. 'You're a bad Sturdley man, Thomson.' 'You're a historian aren't you? Well, history was made today.' Thomson saw of course the futility of their arguments; but something else in the frenetic atmosphere seemed to nag at him. He looked at them dubiously. Although he was a far cry from Bradshaw Soames, somewhere in his vast brain a voice told him that it might not be wise, or even possible, to avoid *all* personal experience. 'We'll buy you a drink, Thomson, for the sake of Her Majesty.'

And now here he was sipping tentatively at a pint pot of beer, peeping over it from time to time at the scenes of alien riot and disorder. Was this really the stuff of history? It was a thoroughly unnerving and repulsive thought. 'I think Thomson has begun to go like the rest of us,' somebody whispered.

By eight o'clock, the pub was filling up like a tube train in the rush hour. Customers were pressed like butterflies against the bar, while glasses of beer were passed slip-slop over their heads. Others were jammed against the walls, hardly able to get their glasses to their lips. At eight-thirty the undergraduates began to swarm onto the sturdy antique tables, which were soon covered with swaying, swearing flesh. Occasionally one of them clambered down to get another drink and there would be more swearing underneath. Mr. Wilson working frantically behind the bar didn't know whether to laugh or cry. Perhaps, after all, the sales of beer would finally exceed the anonymous damages.

At nine o'clock, for some incomprehensible reason, Queen Elizabeth decided to speak to her sodden subjects over the

BBC. Hasty attempts were made to make the pub sound respectable, but it was too late. Some Welsh oarsmen who had never even bothered to train began mimicking Her Majesty and laughing in falsetto. Red, bibulous faces turned up towards them; fishlike mouths groped for words which would express enough disapproval without giving way to pompous patriotism. 'Sodding well wrap up, can't you?' It was a delicate matter. Furtive Englishmen pulled vainly at Welsh trouser legs and tried to bring them off their table.

It was that kind of evening, two days before Schools. The radio went off and there was a sharp roar, as if somebody had turned the pub's volume up too quickly. A policeman poked his head into the steam for a minute to see what was going on. 'It's all right, officer,' he was assured. 'We're just initiating some new Mau Maus.'

'Drink up, Thomson,' said Chote. 'Schools is still a year and two days away. Cheers.'

Thomson wasn't listening. He had an appointment with destiny.

'I'm going over to have a word with those filthy swine.'

'Capital idea,' said Chote.

'To tell you the truth,' said Thomson, 'I don't care for their attitude one little bit.'

'That's right,' said Chote, woozily provocative. 'They can't get away with that sort of thing in an English pub.'

'Just show me where they are. I think somebody ought to have a word with them.'

'They're over there I think.' Thomson followed his vague directions, pushing courteously through the crowd—'Excuse me . . . *ex*cuse me . . . sorry.' In a few minutes he was back, still frowning. 'I couldn't find the swine,' he said.

'Still,' said Chote, 'pity to let them get away with that sort of thing.'

'I know,' said Thomson. 'Perhaps I'd better look again. Where did you say they were?'

'Look over there. That chap in the green scarf was the one who started it.' 'I think I see the chap,' Thomson said dubiously. His small, intense shape, huddled in an enormous

57

raincoat, disappeared again into the crowd—'Frightfully sorry . . . *ex*cuse me.' Chote chuckled to himself : that was the only thing to do with the intellectual elite. Put it to work for you. Tracking down subversives.

He wasn't as drunk as that, and he knew it. He began to feel the unmistakable tightening of intestines : the pain that came from trying not to think about something. A vague acquaintance was standing at the bar, a fellow who was also reading law, and he shuffled over to him, past a dripping claque of merry peasants who had taken to beer-throwing.

'Schools in two days,' he said.

'I know,' said the vague acquaintance.

'Do you mind if I pick your brains?' said Chote.

'No, go ahead. *Pick* my brains. *I* don't care,' said the fellow heartily. And together they went through possible questions until eleven forty-five came and Mr. Wilson plunged into his hopeful croon : 'Time, please, gentlemen, *please* gentlemen, time.' It wasn't just Schools that was bothering Chote, but a feeling that something had gone badly wrong somewhere. A scholarship to America—what a bloody farce. He ought to be staying home with Daphne. But it helped to talk about Schools. The mob was staggering out now in a weaving line, leaving Mr. Wilson to clean up the slop and wipe away the smells.

Men in all imaginable stages of drunkenness were standing or tottering about in the rain, singing and giggling and turning green in the cold air. Chote wanted to get home quickly before he sobered up. But somebody was coming up on him from behind and tugging at his arm. It was little Thomson, looking owlishly affectionate.

'I say. I hope you don't mind my saying so, Chote, but you're a frightfully nice chap.'

'Why, thank you, Thomson.'

He continued to walk away, but Thomson trotted along beside him.

'Quite frankly I don't think I've ever met a nicer chap.'

'Thank you a thousand times, old boy.'

'I don't know what it is about you. I just feel that you're a tremendous chap, that's all. In fact I feel quite privileged to know you.' He looked up with earnest bleary eyes. His brown hair was pasted down severely with rain water. 'Never realized before what a nice chap you are.'

Chote turned into Cornmarket Street. 'Better bugger off now, there's a good chap.'

'Yes, I suppose so,' said Thomson. 'Don't feel a bit like it though.'

'Probably the wisest thing to do.'

Thomson continued to trot along with him, his gigantic brain all but asleep; plunging down like a great fish through dark layers of prehistory. 'I say, you *are* a nice chap. Hope you don't mind my saying so? I mean, you're not offended or anything? I felt I ought to tell you. . . .'

Chote turned when they got to St. John's Street. 'Good night, old boy.' Thomson stared, still more owlishly. 'Er, good night, Chote.' He paused. 'I say, where are we?' Chote silently pointed the way back along Beaumont Street. 'Of course. Well, good night, Chote.' 'Good night, old boy.'

Thomson disappeared to sleep off the only debauch he was ever to experience and his only brush with history. It was the last time he ever spoke to Chote. In fact, from then on, he could hardly bring himself even to look at Chote.

Chote walked the last few yards with a heavy lurch, and he talked to himself in a drunken whisper. But it was no good. The vice was slipped back on his stomach. He had fooled them, that was the truth, and now they were calling his bluff. He couldn't go through with it. He'd confess everything and marry Daphne. Only fooling of course, but God, he felt depressed.

It was pointless to study any more : he already knew all he was going to know. Every additional piece of knowledge could only enter by displacing another piece, like three comedians trying to share a bed big enough for two. But it was the only way to keep from thinking. He opened a book on tort which he already knew by heart, and went through it once again. 'Roll on next week,' he said to himself in a voice heavy with self-pity. But in a few minutes he felt better, and in less than half an hour he had fallen asleep over his book. And from his coat there came an overpowering smell of stale beer.

The next day Felicity Wagstaff came up to Oxford to 'buck up' Godfrey Hook at the last minute, and generally assist him in girding his loins for the stern trials that lay ahead. It was a bloody inconvenience for Godfrey, who had planned to work all day. 'Surprise, surprise,' panted Felicity from the foot of the stairs; and Mrs. Fosse, the landlady, stood beside her, beaming and flushing as if she had engineered single-handed one of history's great rendezvous. 'There's a young person to see you, Mr. Hook,' she crowed coyly.

Felicity had never been to Oxford before, and Godfrey, feeling a bit swollen and slow from the evening before, was obliged all the same to take her on a stately round of sight-seeing. 'My father says that one ought to relax *thoroughly* on the day before an important examination. So here I am.' He thought at first that she must be joking; but her face was cathedral-solemn. 'What's this? Is it something one has heard of?' she asked, pointing earnestly at Magdalen College, the first landmark on their route.

Grimly, they made their way up from Magdalen Bridge, with Felicity chattering in a prodigious effort to relax him, and Godfrey incorrigibly tense, trying to show a little of his impatience, but not too much. Felicity, out of the corner of an anxious eye, could see that the forthcoming exam was rattling her fiancé badly, and she really began to put her back into making him feel at ease. '*When* did you say this funny little tower was built?' 'I don't know. It wasn't here yesterday.' Poor Godfrey : she had never seen him so nervous before.

'Who's that funny-looking man? He seems to know you.' John Chote was shuffling forlornly towards them. Godfrey propped him up and introduced him.

Felicity began to haul off a white glove.

'Don't bother to shake hands,' said Chote. 'My hands are already shaking nicely, thank you. I wouldn't encourage them.'

The two worlds of Godfrey Hook stood still for a moment staring blankly at each other, and then moved off again into their own orbits.

'Is he a friend of yours?' asked Felicity.

'Yes, as a matter of fact, he is.'

'He looks quite nice,' she said doubtfully.

Browning then came across in the Sturdley quad. Alan looked Felicity up and down and Godfrey was seized with a brief fear that he would start spieling the line, soupily praising her eyes and her hair, and moving on swiftly to *double-entendres* about her torso and et ceteras. He had never seen his friend with a 'nice' girl, but he had often heard him say that all women were alike if you just pushed the right button. Supposing Browning had been right all along—supposing Felicity were suddenly to melt away under the pressure of his vulgar compliments, and start carrying on then and there like all the other women Browning knew? Absurd, of course. Alan was talking to her quite pleasantly, about the salubrities of the weather, and the whatnot of Oxford, and she was nodding without any trace of abandon.

'Alan's a very good friend of mine,' he said as they walked away. 'A thoroughly nice chap.'

'He seemed all right,' said Felicity, without much enthusiasm. 'I didn't much care for the way he looked at me, though.' Hook felt a mixture of alarm and consolation. Here, at least, was a woman magnificently immune from Browning's techniques, and that was good : he had never imagined himself holding a girl, any girl, that Browning might chance to want. He had pictured his friend cutting a swath through faithful wives and frosty virgins almost at will—people like Browning were like that. But it was encouragingly clear that, even had he wanted to, he would never have managed to cut a swath through Felicity.

On the other hand, Felicity had bridled ominously at a minimum display of lasciviousness, and that was discomforting in its own way. He knew what Browning thought about that kind of female virtue and although one might still have lingering reservations about Browning's moral conclusions, the chap undoubtedly knew his *facts*. Alan was a man of vast experience, and he was remorselessly clear about the motives of virtuous women. Hook knew, of course, that there was some cynicism as well as science in all this : but three years of bawdy anecdotes and aphorisms had

61

left their mark, and it wasn't easy to respect Felicity's high-mindedness. One could already see her fuzzily outlined in grey flannel, snuffing out the candle and resolutely closing her eyes. . . . They went to Worcester College, and brooded among the swans. Felicity was tired of trying to cheer him up with her questions : she didn't really care *when* the beastly buildings had gone up, or who had lived there. The whole thing was a terrible mistake, she should never have come. It had been all right, she thought, before they had met that lecherous friend of his in the Sturdley quad : Godfrey had been admittedly a bit on the dismal side before that but talking a little, and brightening gradually. But ever since running into that dreadful man, he hadn't said a word, and he had been frowning quite horribly into the bargain. Perhaps he had been reminded of his examinations again by seeing his dreary little friend on his way to work. Oily, undistinguished chap, what her father would have called 'Thoroughly middle class.' It was depressing to realize that Godfrey had such, well, dog-eared friends as the two she had met today. Hook shied a pebble into the pleasant waters. A swan swung gracefully out of its path. Poor Godfrey, she thought. Detestable, detestable examination.

Chote and Browning sat leadenly in the college library going through their notes over and over again, relaxing by thinking about the worst.

'By the way,' said Chote, 'did you happen to sight Godfrey's formidable fiancée steaming up the High?'

'Yes, I did as a matter of fact,' said Browning. 'Rather like a battleship and her escort, I grant you. It's a curious effect. Actually, he is an inch or so taller than she is, I believe, but he looks like nothing at all beside her, practically transparent.'

'I fear she'll gobble up poor Godfrey, boots and all,' said Chote. 'He looks like such a tender thing. Funny, one never noticed it before.'

'Was she what you expected?'

Chote shrugged. 'How little one knows one's friends sometimes. I really hadn't the faintest idea of what sort of girl Godfrey would be concealing. Something with mouse-coloured hair, I suppose, and spectacles.'

'Well, you were right about that anyway. But then, you knew that she was English.'

They looked at their notes blankly for a minute or two.

'Do you think they'll be very, very happy?' asked Chote.

'You must be the man from *Woman's Weekly*. I don't know. She looks a little too hot for him to handle.'

'That's funny. She seemed a bit on the chilly side to me.'

'Good Lord, no,' said Browning. 'Chilly? Don't you believe it. I happen to know something about the daughters of non-conformist clergymen. . . .'

'You're a bloody liar, and a braggart to boot,' interrupted Chote amiably. Browning didn't bother to argue. His reputation was beyond question and therefore all jokes about it were compliments, one way or another. 'She looks pretty passionate to me. I think Godfrey will find himself out of his class pretty quickly. I only wish I was living in the house next door when the great awakening comes.'

'You absurd little man,' said Chote. 'You don't think she'd send for you in an emergency do you? Not while there's a dependable fire brigade and a trusty police force. . . .'

'Well, I rather fancy she liked me at first sight. It might ripen into something beautiful. You never know.'

'Oh, come now. Conceit has blinded you to the facts. Just because she didn't strike you with her enormous fist, or kick you with her vast boot, doesn't mean that she actually liked you, old boy. As a matter of fact, I think I was the one she fancied.'

Browning raised his eyebrows and looked at Chote with silent curiosity. At last he said, 'Well, there's enough of her for both of us, I suppose, *and* some left over for the fire brigade. Talking of which, are you coming down for tea?'

'Well, yes, I suppose so. Not that I want to, mind you.'

'We might run into the star-crossed lovers. Where do you think they would be having tea?'

'Where would *you* take a bishop's daughter? The Mitre, I suppose.'

They actually found Godfrey and his lady at the Randolph, and greeted them with many hollow exclamations of delight.

63

Hook knew that they had never had tea at the Randolph before, but he was too far sunk in gloom to care. Felicity lowered her head and addressed her food. She heard them scraping their chairs up and plumping down on them heartily: this was the worst thing that could have happened. Godfrey's nerves hung in loose shreds. He obviously didn't know whether to talk their language or her language : whether to concentrate on impressing them as a master of women, or her as a man among men. He compromised on a grim, uncertain silence, looking paler than ever beside his mighty escort.

Chote and Browning talked merrily away, burning up cakes and tea as amorous fuel, and ludicrously competing for tiny signs of Felicity's favour. Chote didn't want to take her away from Godfrey, and he didn't know whether Browning really did either. It was just one point in an endless game.

Felicity obviously didn't realize that there was a game in progress. She imagined that it was usual for these smart young men to talk too much and try to be funny, and generally ooze rudeness from every pore. She couldn't help feeling annoyed at the effect that they had on Godfrey—much of his new character was explained by them. Thank God he would soon be leaving this empty atmosphere for good. Meanwhile, she wished they would just go away. She tapped her foot and kept her eyes on her plate.

They stayed for an hour, flirting obliquely and watching for minute signs of progress. She smiled a couple of times, more out of nervousness than anything else, and they took as much encouragement as they could from that. Eventually she was driven to asking the morose Godfrey about trains to London; and then, since even that didn't budge them, getting up firmly and saying goodbye. She had meant to stay longer, but perhaps it was just as well to go. There didn't seem to be anything else she could do here.

'Terribly shy, of course,' said Browning on the way back to Sturdley. 'Therefore hard to tell.' It was hopeless for either of them to pretend that he had got very far with her.

'Not much sense of humour, I thought,' said Chote. 'But as you say, terribly shy.'

64

'She seems to have a sobering influence on Godfrey,' said Browning. 'I've never seen him looking so spiritual. Altogether a bit discouraging.'

Browning was smiling: the seductive manner still lingered in his face, like a local anæsthetic, freezing his features. For a moment, Chote felt a vague feeling of disgust. Browning, he suddenly realized, had been trying. Nobody had been playing but Chote. The Playboy of the Upper Fourth.

4. Working

SCHOOLS, in a tiny parody of death itself, has a miniature valley and a shadow. Around suppertime that day Chote began to laugh mysteriously. He went down to the college bar to find all his friends laughing. They played darts oafishly and sang Christmas carols. They had passed safely through the shadow.

The second-year men looked on uneasily at this Dance of Death. They had no exam this year. Schools this night donned for them its red whiskers and fright-wig.

The feeling was still there the next morning, by gad. Chote looked at the dark-blue suit hanging prim over the chair at the end of his bed, at the white bow tie on the table by the window, at the black socks and black shoes on the floor, looked at them and began to laugh again. Bring on the pain, bring on the misery! He hummed 'Silent Night' to himself as he climbed into his uniform: head clear, pulse admirable, stomach empty; voice quite superb (well, it *might* come in handy). Schools could even be a pleasure for such a well-endowed chap.

'Morning, Mrs. Worsley, good morning, good morning.'

'A little nervous, sir?' she asked dolefully.

'Not a bit not a bit not a bit.'

'It's only an exam, sir.'

'Quite right. Absolutely right. That *is* the whole point isn't it?'

He wondered whether he would, like the mythical undergraduate who had doed himself on Benzedrine, wind up scribbling his signature *ad nauseam* on the desk. His conversation this morning seemed a little repetitious, but this would doubtless right itself, doubtless right itself. This was the time, if ever it was going to be, to pinch one of Mrs. Worsley's pendulous jowls. She must have sensed his mood, because for once she kept her distance.

He strolled over to the college, sniffing up the June weather, hands in pockets, and whistling fitfully. When one felt as confident as this in the face of Schools, it seemed a pity to keep it a secret, after all. If one wanted to set the seal on oneself as an incorrigible personality, an unrepentant scoundrel who died as he had lived, this was obviously the day to do it.

In the lodge, Bill Gosworth was pacing up and down, taking quick dramatic pulls on a cigarette. Chote had never seen anyone so low on pigment: Gosworth must have been scrubbing himself all over with one of those splendid detergents that washed whiter than white. Chote clapped him on the back, and he shivered alarmingly, like a condemned building.

'Cheer up, old boy. It's only an examination. A test for schoolboys.'

'Oh my God,' said Gosworth, looking at him with yellow eyes. He was twisting the tassel on his mortarboard viciously, jerking it loose. 'Only an examination!'

'You've got nothing to worry about,' said Chote. 'You've got a job whatever happens, haven't you?'

'I don't know whether I have or not. I don't suppose any firm wants a man who has failed Schools twice.' A man mightn't even want himself in those circumstances, thought Chote. Pity, pity, pity.

'Who's talking about failing?' said Chote. 'Everybody tells me you're a brilliant chap.' Gosworth without his suavity was an obscene sight; Chote reached into his bag of phrases to find a loincloth. Gosworth lit another cigarette and stood, head bowed, silent, not even pretending any more, not caring who

66

saw him in this state: no pride left, hardly any Gosworth left. Chote turned away. Gosworth's soul did not look particularly well in the nude.

Browning and Hook came into the lodge, reasonably composed.

'You look cheerful enough, John. How do you do it?' asked Hook. 'Alan tells me it's all a front.'

'Look at that chap,' he whispered, pointing at Gosworth. 'Just look at him.'

The sight of Gosworth had added to Chote's confidence, as if he had just supped well off Gosworth's dwindling supply. He felt himself becoming offensively breezy. 'Alan, you look like a bank clerk in that rig.' 'Godfrey, you look like a farmer dressed for church.'

They started down High Street together. Masses of black gowns, mortarboards and washed-out faces were descending slowly on the Schools building. A visitor seeing Oxford for the first time might have thought for a moment that the town was populated by learned albinos. Tourists, who assumed that the boys were going to their daily classes, marvelled at the order and decorum of the procession, the air of medieval solemnity. These young men took education seriously (doubtless a key to England's enduring success).

Inside the huge building, there was a low hum of agitated small talk.

'How do you feel, Chote?'

'Wunnerful, just wunnerful,' he said, in what was meant to be an American drawl. Any facetiousness at all would add now to the impression of unspeakable coolness under pressure.

'I must confess that I feel a trifle unenthusiastic myself.'

Most unenthusiastic of all were the girls, most of them looking so forlorn in their severe black suits and black stockings that it seemed heartless to make them go on any further. In comparison the men looked almost healthy—relatively pink or swarthy as the case might be. The examination was a minute late, and the feet began to shuffle noisily on the stone floor in a kind of dirge. Then the inner doors opened, and the black mob surged through, bats into hell, flapping and groaning. Chote still had his hands in his pockets and observed, as from his own pockets, the anxiety around him with intense, almost feverish now, amusement. 'I wouldn't give sixpence for your chances in a saliva test,' whispered Browning. Inside the exam room they were rushing about, now rapidly and harum-scarum with insect cunning. He sauntered very slowly to his desk, pulled out the chair very, very slowly and sensuously, picked up the exam paper casually—still deliriously light-headed, unaccountably irresponsible—looked at it—and froze.

There simply wasn't a single blasted question that one had expected. There were several that had been asked last year, and the others hadn't been asked since 1890, or earlier. He was the victim of a bloody fraud. One looked round for friends—but no, that was the whole point. One had no friends.

A mist began to form relentlessly over his eyes. The moderator was making a routine announcement in a tired voice, but Chote couldn't make it out at all, because the mist was really spreading over his ears, not his eyes. Perhaps he wouldn't be able to write a single word. Apart from everything else, it was so stifling hot. He looked nervously around him. Everybody else seemed to be writing already with speed and composure, except for a girl at the next desk who was sniffling loudly into a handkerchief. 'Oh my God. I can't stand a woman's tears,' Chote muttered to himself and mopped at his own brow, which was to his surprise bone-dry. A chair scraped behind him, and he looked around just in time to see an enormous undergraduate flopping out of it, like a seal tumbling off a rock. The moderator came thundering down the aisle, his enormous gown whirring, and Chote felt a flood of catharsis: 'I'm in better shape than that, anyway.' He picked up his pen as firmly as he could in slithery fingers and wrote his name swiftly on the top of the page. 'Why do you suppose my fingers got so wet when my forehead remained so dry?' he asked himself idly as he twitched down 'Sturdley College'.

Another look at the exam: one hadn't noticed Question 4, which wasn't entirely hopeless; and perhaps something could be squeezed out of Question 7. It could be adapted to something else. He lowered his big, dry head and began to write convulsively. Twenty minutes later, the large undergraduate returned trembling to his desk only to faint again and be carried out for good. Chote smiled briefly like a busy receptionist and continued to write.

Three hours later the moderator cried truce. Chote went on writing until he sensed the black gown looming gigantic over him and the tired, really quite comforting voice: '*Stop* writing please.' In three hours, his brain had shrunk away to nothing. The night before, one had talked blithely with one's friends about celebrating the end of Schools—only eight papers away after all. Now he could see no further than lunch and one had no friends.

Outside on the steps, they were talking in their various ways about the morning's alarums. Some of them were going through it all slowly like coroners, holding up ink-covered question papers in earnest inky fingers to show how one had started to do Question 9, had switched to 10, and back inevitably to 9. There were a few more general comments to be heard, mainly profane, mainly about the deviousness of examiners who ask the same questions two years running, instead of following a more leisurely and traditional rotation. Occasionally somebody would come purring down the steps, radiating silky success. And as many had already been ploughed back into pulp by the tiny paper. But most of them seemed to be like Chote, filled with a functional numbness: their mental faculties stripped down for answering examination questions one by one, with nothing much left for human concourse.

'What sort of morning did you have, John?' asked Hook.

'Damned if I know. It wasn't such a bad paper as it looked. But it could have been better I suppose. What about you?' No use coming to me now, you bastard. Where were you three hours ago?

'I can't really complain. I did two questions fairly well. I may have bluffed them on the others. I don't know.'

'I can't even remember when I *started* doing Schools. Years and years ago,' said Browning.

'I remember,' said Chote. 'I was playing possum in a dimly lighted womb. . . .'

'I say, it doesn't half break your spirit, does it?' said Hook.

At college, everyone made way for the dedicated men. 'How did it go?' they asked timidly, and the Schools men swept curtly past, like celebrities refusing autographs: preferring, to a man, to suppurate in silence.

Judging from the nightmares that became part of his repertoire, the first morning and the last were the ones. The astral Chote would pick up the first paper and find that it was blank, or that it was a history paper instead of a law paper; of course, that was it—he had been studying law by mistake for three years. Or else he would be leaving the Examination Hall for the last time, galloping wildly down the steps, only to feel the heavy hand of the black, bat-winged moderator, coming to land and lay its eggs on his shoulder: 'Excuse me, Mr. Chote . . . one more paper I should like to call to your attention. A paper in Hebraic law, crucially important.' Such a kindly voice.

Schools was just a private episode, a dream within a dream, no connection with the rest of one's life at all. A terrible ache came to visit his arm every afternoon after five hours of writing, forcing him to lower his pen for a few precious minutes. He would rub the cramp this way and that, and flex his fingers with dismay, while hundreds of other men at tiny desks raced inexorably to catch up with him and pass him. The dream where you can't get away. Then came the grateful hour spent soaking in damp grass after each day's work was done. One glass of beer in the college bar to show the chaps that Schools wasn't getting one down (the devil it wasn't) and then home to stare at his notes until midnight, complete exhaustion, sleep and an end to dreaming.

Sunday was a day of rest, and Chote spent it in and out of the limp, chubby arms of Daphne Collins. They looked at the pictures on his wall, which showed him as a square little schoolboy growing up slowly from left to right in hockey shorts and boxing gloves. 'Tell me the story of your life,' said Daphne. 'There it is,' said Chote, 'from shorts to flannels to shorts. A typical English education.'

She couldn't want to hear about his first night at Brinkley College when he cried right through until he had to turn the pillow over? Not very creditable, and yet only ten years ago, still a personal experience, not in the public domain yet, not to be talked about lightly. It was funny to remember so clearly doing something, without any recollection of why. It wasn't from hearing his horrible cockney accent imitated for the first time was it? A ruddy trivial reason, if so, for all that wailing and sobbing. There were other things slightly more recent, and even harder to understand. For instance, one thought of Faunce, the prefect who had tried to corrupt him or something in a roundabout kind of way. He hadn't understood any of it at the time and very little since (perhaps it was all a misunderstanding), but he remembered now a pungent feeling of absolutely unwashable dirt, which shot quickly across his nostrils every six months or so and was gone again. Faunce still cast a prehensible shadow over the endless sunny days of his first summer term, making them useless for reminiscence. He used to have horrifying nightmares about Faunce in which absolutely nothing ever happened. And now there was Chote on the wall, a blank-looking boy in cricket trousers. Nobody would have guessed from the picture that he was going through a large, formative experience at the time. Dull-looking smudge of a boy.

The next term Faunce had gone, and somebody had explained with relish and invention what Faunce had been up to. It was a shock, and only violent applications of rugger and hockey (suitably recorded on film) had been able to revive his calm, and such innocence as was proper to his age. The nightmares took a repetitious form so that he could pretend to be tired of them: they showed him standing on one side of a shadowy line with Faunce on the other, popping his eyes suggestively. 'Ha, there's Faunce,' he would say to himself with all the quavering amusement he could muster. Years later, when he was in the Army, he had actually met Faunce again, a dull man with a big, brown moustache, and it was all he could do not to turn and run like the wind.

And then it was his turn. To his consternation, he found himself in a kind of love with a younger boy called Burns Minor, a little fellow with brown curls and a thin pink face. Chote spent several terms staring stupidly at the boy, chaffing and being chaffed (there was no other word for it) by his lumpy swelling contemporaries. His dour face in the House cricket photo had been too quickly composed after a gorgeous jest about Burns Minor; unfathomable jest, decadence beyond recall: the whisperings and pretended seductions among the faster crowd, the frustrated and confused images (snakes, arm-chairs, Burns Minor, anything) which had kept him thrashing about every night. Say what you liked about the irrational behaviour of American teenagers, was it really so much worse than his own reticent fever at that time? At least the Americans carried on publicly in groups, with stylized mob hysteria. At Brinkley College, the surface of life was smooth as glass, the insanity was hidden and solitary.

His affair with Burns Minor could perhaps be called sub-Platonic, in that it was not only innocent, but that Burns didn't even know it was going on. After a year, Chote became so tired of looking at the boy that he made considerable efforts to avoid him. At fourteen, Burns swelled like a balloon, practically overnight, and in some curious way this snapped the spell for Chote. He joined a select group of older boys who talked about women instead of small boys, and who even claimed to have had 'experiences'. There were no girls within miles of the school so that everybody in the group could make such claims as his knowledge and vocabulary permitted, without fear of dis-covery. Chote, the smug, self-confident captain of cricket in the last photo of all, Chote had a *good* vocabulary along with a wide reading in encyclopædia articles. (All the same, he was always embarrassed when Burns Minor hove into sight.)

There it all was in the pictures—except that to the un-informed eye, the pictures conveyed no expression at all. The school had somehow managed to keep that side of life even out of your face against all anatomical odds. There were so many damned games to play that a fellow hadn't the energy to sprout horns or secondary characteristics. One beat up Godfrey Hook instead. 'A sweet little boy,' said Daphne in unintentional reassurance. The pictures were wonderfully wholesome and insipid. 'A sweet little boy' in fact.

Unwittingly, Chote was beginning a habit of reminiscence

which was to grow alarmingly in the next few weeks; pawing through his life over and over, dribbling onto the pages every now and then. . . . It was the time of year for laughably unscholarly types to try signing up for graduate courses, stopping the flow at this particular point; and in later Junes they would try again, plodding hopefully back to school or university (wherever it was best) as paunchy ghosts, boring and somehow disturbing generation upon generation of young people. The wistful urge to haunt was making its first gentle appeal all over town.

In a few weeks, the habit would have to be recognized as satanic, anti-evolutionary and a bad thing. But at the moment it was a pleasant enough indulgence, languid pleasure for a tense, jumpy brain.

'You'd never guess I used to write poetry, would you?' he asked Daphne.

'Yes I would,' she said loyally. 'Of course I would.'

'Ridiculous isn't it?' His sixteen-year-old self looked extra muddy and determined in his shorts and striped shirt. The sexual beast was down, the midget poet was down and out. The crisp, shadowy woods had once looked wonderfully strange after the dim constraint of London streets, but Mr. Smathers had forbidden him with surprising warmth to go out at night, for fear he might practise smoking, or heaven knows what. And in the autumn afternoons, when a young poet might feel certain benefits, he found himself pressed relentlessly into rugger shorts or hockey shorts and told to keep moving. The sources of inspiration were so narrow, and the spirit so exhausted from endless, meaningless competition. . . . All he had left were a few sonnets written under the vague influence of Burns Minor, the Dark Lady—and a strange religious poem that didn't bear remembering, about the bleeding face of Godfrey Hook. Good God, what brought that up? Crank the handle, you fool!

'Prosaic' was one of his adjectives now, practically part of his definition. And perhaps the school had known best. Young poets at Oxford, long soft hair, humourless vanity, eternal self-importance—wasn't that how it went? At least he and his friends didn't sit around admiring each others' 'things' in the lonely hope of having their own admired in return: behind the dense smog of jesting they could be huskily modest in the best English tradition, and painstakingly unaccomplished.

All he really knew about the 'arty' crowd was what he read in books. He had observed some people who might have been artists, bewhiskered and be-duffelcoated, the sort of chaps who might conceivably have owned teddy bears, and the trappings. He had gate-crashed a few theatrical parties in his first year where he had found it hard to say exactly who was doing what and to whom. A man had hit him on the head with an umbrella, but he couldn't remember the motive—affection, rage, boredom? A bathroom door blocked for hours by a fallen poet with Chote, the practical man of affairs, the Philistine, finally getting him into the bathtub so that traffic could continue. They drank gin instead of beer, and he always wound up feeling unreasonably disgusted. Goat's feet and long crooked tails. Quite unjust, of course—probably they were decent fun-loving people. Some of them, he knew, haunted the Catholic chaplaincy. All the same, they gave off a stink to an old Brinkley man.

The arty crowd responded by rejecting Chote for what he imagined he was, gross and rather too obvious, and after his first year, he did not even bother to crash their parties (a sign of complete contempt at Oxford). 'I don't care what they think.' He smiled bravely. 'I am very happy as I am, honestly.' Was it fair to bring the school into this burlesque? 'Everyone takes it out on the poor old public school,' he said half aloud.

'Do you really think you'll like it in America?' Daphne's flat voice wedged its incongruous way into his thoughts.

'You bet,' said Chote. 'God's country and He ought to know. Besides, they have the right attitude about books—burn the swine. And they know what to do with intellectuals—hound the bastards unmercifully. And actors too—off with their bloody heads. Persecute the lot of them. Who needs them?'

'I expect all that is pretty much exaggerated, don't you suppose?'

'I hope not,' said Chote, hardly bothering to rouse himself

from his drowsy comical imaginings. What, actually, was his batting average when he played cricket for the junior colts? And what about the name of that marvellous chap who supplied the lower school with cigarettes? There was stuff here to occupy him for a lifetime. The comfortable walls of Brinkley closed around him in cool embrace. So much of one's education seemed to be connected with the stink of old stone.

The next day, and he was back at work, wearing out his wrist, brain and sundries, bending and blunting nib, imagination and that super vocabulary. One side of his brain was numb, like that of the man who does nothing all day but put the tops on the bottles; the other lobe was endlessly agile, like a young monkey, crafty and chattering, bluffing and manœuvring his moderate stock of information this way and that to make it read like a full complement. When he could not find a decent question, he adopted a deviously pompous manner which made him sound almost too long-winded and deserving, much too profound for the superficialities of three-hour examinations (a week per question would hardly be enough for such solid scholarship). When he actually knew his stuff, he became magically terse and significant. He imagined the examiners on a hot day going through a vast pile of papers with flies zooming down and taking off again from various pink landing strips, and summer calling softly through the window, 'Hark, hark' etc.—surely in all the distraction they would not notice the unsightly split in the seat of Chote's personality? One prayed that one's paper would never be the fresh one on top of the pile, the one that was marked before the flies had got in their work.

On the last day, the Tuesday, he was tired when he woke up and almost asleep again over breakfast. He had set his mechanism for eight papers, and he couldn't do one blessed question more than that—no, not one.

'I expect you'll be getting drunk tonight,' said Mrs. Worsley severely, waddling in with her groaning tray.

'Well, you know human nature, Mrs. Worsley' (and who knows it better?), said Chote. 'I may have a drop or two.'

'Drop or two,' snorted Mrs. Worsley. 'I'd better leave the large basin in here. I expect you'll be bringing up your heart tonight.'

'Don't be disgusting,' said Chote, between ominous yawns. The *Daily Express* swam downstream for a second. Curious effect, swimming newspaper.

'Disgusting! Who's going to be disgusting when you come home tonight with your head stuck in the gin bottle?' said Mrs. Worsley vehemently, her bosom heaving under the drab chair cover that she preferred to wear before sundown.

'Mrs. Worsley,' he yawned. 'Your obsession with alcohol is downright unhealthy. You wouldn't like me to slip you a drop secretly, so that you can—wuuuh'—it took him a full ten seconds to get his mouth shut. Perhaps it would be a good idea to go back to bed for a minute or two. He slid across his chair and down, and bounced up again at once. The ceiling was beginning to swim toward the open window—if it reached it, he was done. 'Let's get the bloody business over with,' he mumbled. 'Roll on this afternoon.' 'My husband died of drink,' Mrs. Worsley complained.

He wrote in a dream, no longer caring whether he passed or failed, or got the nice jobs in London. He even slipped in a few jokes, on the half-formed theory that the sweaty examiner might appreciate a few laughs during his dry vigil. A week later, when the brainwashing was well behind him, and he was sober again, there was plenty of time to apply the boot for his foolishness, and with justice : it had been a terrible paper, which was to cost him a first-class degree. Chalk up one to the cunning of the inquisitors who knew how to exhaust a man into an indiscretion of some kind. If serious scholarship did not come naturally, the deficiency would crawl out whimpering under the lash of fatigue.

But for the time being none of it mattered. The main thing was physical survival; and for the sake of that, Chote was willing to make sacrifices, even to telling the examiners what they wanted to know about him. God, he was unfit. For the last hour, he stared at the clock like a lover staring forlornly at the moon; and at twelve-thirty precisely, he tottered feebly out of the torture chamber, his confession signed and handed in, himself not quite sure whether he was in any shape to enjoy his freedom.

Outside on the steps, all the demons were assembling for the jamboree. Champagne corks were already popping and raining down on the pale men and women who were coagulating in the entrance. Mortarboards were flung into the air to come whirring back into the crowd. A small jazz band struck up, and men and women in severe black clothes began to caper up and down the steps. Charlestons, cakewalks, old-fashioned waltzes. 'How did you do?' everybody asked everybody else as usual, but there was none of the fastidious analysis of the first day. 'God knows,' was the correct answer; and then something like 'Do you realize, old man, it's all over?' Alan Browning had managed to get hold of a bottle of champagne and three beer mugs, and Chote and Hook were buzzing happily, fatuously around him. Sturdy Englishwomen were embracing each other like so many ruddy foreigners; and strong men shook hands.

Cars and open lorries pulled up, and undergraduates leapt onto the roofs and running-boards, cheering and singing. The corks popped and repopped and champagne fizzed feverishly out over hands and sleeves. 'Don't take it all, you greedy sod.' Chote stretched happily in the sunshine. This was going to be fun after all. Another bottle of champagne appeared miraculously from somewhere, snatched from an unknown benefactor, and as it rushed down his throat, Chote realized that he would never be quite so happy again.

Slowly the cars drove off, with the undergraduates still clinging to the sides and shouting incoherently. The jazz band drove away in a lorry, the musicians in shiny blackface, tooting and jigging their feet. The rest of the undergraduates straggled happily back to their colleges to get out of the sombre clothes into which they had been walled for the past week.

The Schools building returned to its sleepy and austere dignity in the pleasant sunshine, after the briefest lapse into playfulness. And a few tourists, noting the hilarious return of the boys from their daily classes, marvelled at the exuberance and high spirits of the young gentlemen. 'There's life in this country yet,' said an elderly American. 'Mark my words, we haven't heard the last of it.' Months later, back home, he would still be talking about it. 'I saw the young men returning from their studies one morning. And believe me, you have never seen anything like it. There'll always be an England, if those young people have anything to say about it.'

Section

II

Fraud-Baiting

5. Easing Off

THE future lay open. The artificial anxiety of Schools was over.
Now for the real problems, the ones he had been putting off so
long : man's estate, the battle of life, the rewarding struggles
that he had been so carefully prepared for.

The only thing to do was to get potted and stay potted forever and ever. He sat down to a grim tea some six days later,
knowing that amnesia could go no further. By then his mouth
was incurably dry and dusty and his head felt like a badly
packed suitcase. Tea was all and more than he was up to :
even that tasted unpleasantly bitter and punitive.

Hook and Browning had also been forced to seek an intermission in the pursuit of happiness. Huddled over dry biscuits
and tea, the two of them tried to piece out the last few days,
like old men making the most of ancient triumphs. For nearly
a week, they had weaved cunningly up and down, and then
around Oxford like aged tramps, giggling, stumbling and
dribbling—or so it must have seemed to the ever vigilant eye of
the tourists; now they were trying to remember the glory of it,
the wonderful pranks that had delighted their sodden faculties
so much, making them fairly blubber with glee. What did I
do? Chote wanted to know. Wasn't I there at the time? Do
I know these chaps? Can they hear me?

'What I don't remember is going to the Warden's sherry
party,' he interrupted at last.

'Taking one thing with another,' said Hook, 'it's probably
just as well.'

But they told him about it again, how he sang his scabrous
songs and insulted the Warden's wife. 'Frightfully sorry *and*
all that, but the Warden's wife must be made to realize that
the day Chote finishes Schools—on that day NO ONE is safe.

NO-O-O-O ONE. Chote is no respector of persons. Persons, parsons—No respect for any of them.' Chote winced. He must have felt that all this was very telling at the time.

'You're a bloody liar,' he said.

'Damned fine woman the Warden's wife. Don't make them like that any more. Mass production, PAH! But Chote is—norespecterofpersons.' And so on and on. It was almost worse than not being talked about at all.

All he could remember himself was walking about afterwards in the cool of the Warden's garden. Mr. McLavish was holding his arm and talking nervously about the 'jolly good prospects in America' or something like that.

Chote gave a low moan, buried his face in his hands and smiled demurely to himself. Perhaps, on second thoughts, it wasn't such a bad exit as exits went. If one could forget (and one could) the physical misery toward the end, the gloomy threshings about in the darkened toilets, the heavy immovable substance (part fur, part just unusually heavy air) on his tongue. Although one never admitted it to one's playful colleagues, one was slightly scarred by the last amusing stages of collapse when the body, and the periphery of the soul, broke down in a heap.

Later on, he had felt a rush of fatuous amorousness and had zigzagged hopefully over to Daphne's digs for the dreariest of assignations: half an hour in the bathroom while she waited patiently outside; five minutes in her kindly passive arms, and then a mumbled 'Better get home 'fore midnight'—a dyspeptic Cinderella—and finally sick, as prophesied, on Mrs. Worsley's best carpet. End of a lovely evening. It was the backstage side to revelry, and one's friends usually had the decency not to talk about it, unless it was funny as well as messy.

The 'Schools' excuse wore thinner and thinner; with a sigh and a hiccup he abandoned it at last. The shadow of responsibility was stretching out its dry, bony fingers. The evening would be a long one. Henceforth, no more than two weeks holiday a year, spent quietly with the wife, perhaps getting a little tiddly at a seaside resort—hard to take after three years in Arcadia : a cruel joke.

'Frankly, one turns quite pale at the thought of going to work every day,' said Hook. 'One is so superbly educated for leisure.'

'I believe it's hell at first,' said Browning, 'but one grows accustomed to one's chains. I saw Venables the other day, and he told me that the first six months after you go down are the absolute, screaming, bitter end. It isn't only the loathsome, subhuman toil of course; it's the ghastly risings and settings, up at ruddy six, down at bloody ten, every day for the rest of your life.'

'Stop,' muttered Chote. 'I can't stand it.' He could though, that was the funny part: even the well-known twenty quid a year for pleasure. Pleasure indeed: one's wife's clothes, the daily paper and enough alcohol to reduce oneself to occasional, much needed oblivion. Theoretically, one shrank from the prospect—but did one in fact?

Listen to Hook shrinking. 'Nobody expects you to entertain them any more,' Godfrey said fretfully. 'The chances are you haven't a house to invite anybody to anyway, just a grubby one-room flat with your wife's soggy combinations hanging down the middle and the usual vultures on the stove.'

Hook, you miserable man—have you forgotten so soon the thatched cottage, The Manse, only a stone's throw from the vicarage, with plenty of fresh vegetables from the garden, and good Devonshire sunlight to dry your and Mrs. Hook's functional woollies? Chote scratched his ear. Funny about Godfrey. Fate had made him a friend, inertia and mild amusement had kept him one—and, to be honest, the fact that he seemed to admire one. It was a funny kind of friendship, but a real one as far as it went. He didn't want harm to come to Godfrey, and he would miss him—that was about all.

'All very sad,' he said. 'Why don't you blokes emigrate like me? Be a pioneer, show a little spirit. . . .'

'Get a little scholarship you mean,' said Browning. 'I've said it before and I'll say it again: You, Chote, are the jammiest bastard on God's green earth.' There was real grievance there. And yet Browning had never wanted the scholarship himself, and he was the least envious of men. Something else seemed to be eating him. Chote felt, as he hadn't felt since schooldays, that he had done something wrong, unforgivable, but that nobody would tell him what it was.

Bradshaw Soames came wandering into the café by himself. 'May I join you, gentlemen?' he asked in his grave diplomatic way. He looked as if he might be on the prowl for more experience, ready to immerse himself in a new social group and study hell out of it. 'Please be our guest, Bradshaw'—Soames was much more popular than most of his sophisticated compatriots. You could have innocent fun with Brad, pull his leg —the other Yanks seemed considerably more watchful. Not that Soames was a goon, either—far from it. Just a nice, gullible student of human nature.

They talked inconsequentially for a minute or two, but soon the vacuous Future sucked them zipping back, like crumbs off a rug.

'Have you *any* idea what you're going to do when you go down, Alan?' said Hook.

'Hundreds of ideas,' said Browning. 'With my Oxford training, the world is at my feet or thereabouts. I can sell soap, towels, trusses, bog paper—anything you like. I can apply my bottom with equal effectiveness to a hard chair, a soft chair, a cobbler's bench or a lav—'

'Yes, I know,' said Hook, 'but what are you actually going to do?'

'Well to tell you the truth, I'm not absolutely sure. I'm having an interview at Lever Brothers in two days, and one at I.C.I. next week. The usual rounds, in short. I suppose I'll go in with one of our great industrial empires. Help to build a stronger Britain, what?'

'Before I got the scholarship,' said Chote, 'I had all but taken a job selling weighing machines. The pay was disgusting, but it included a rather amusing pension plan. American sort of firm : bags of bustle and ulcers. A weighing machine in every home, men! Faith in the jolly old product! Nobody has ever survived to enjoy the pension fund, so I suppose it continues to expand like the National Debt.'

'I picture something a little more restful,' said Hook. 'On

my thirty-fifth birthday, the manager comes up to my little attic and presses five pounds into my hand. I pause in my stitching to hear how invaluable I have always been to the firm of Gosbaum and Suet, nightshirt makers and button designers. Five years later, he will come up and move me down to the third floor. That's what I want : security, security, security !' Three years ago Godfrey could not have produced half so fluid a speech, and he still felt a tingle of pleasure as the words drizzled thinly out of his mouth.

'That's the advantage of the big industrial empires,' said Browning. 'You crawl slowly up the wall with the other human flies, and by, say, forty-five, you have a bit of money to pleasure yourself with. Perhaps even a naughty week-end or two in Paris, with an elderly secretary.'

'If you're allowed to take any money out of the country at all by then. Perhaps Soames will take pity on us and take us all on a cultural tour,' said Chote.

'What makes you guys think I'm going to have so much money ?' asked Soames, shocked into engagement.

'All Americans have bags of money,' said Chote.

Patriotism didn't come easily to Bradshaw Soames : but there was such a thing as being bored.

'We may have a lot of money,' he said peevishly, 'but at least we don't sit around talking about pension plans while we're still in college. Haven't you guys got any ambition at all ?'

'Certainly we have,' said Browning. 'I for one want to retire with the biggest pension in recorded history.'

'Money is only a sex substitute,' said Chote, 'and a ruddy inadequate one in this country, if you ask me.' He rested his parched seven-and-a-half size head on his hands : the cracks of erosion widened against his fingers. In the last few days he had sighted the bottom of the barrel, and peeped once too often at the idiot face distorted round and round in the empty glass; he had even drowned the taste for sublimating with Daffers; and he had smoked a damn sight too much. 'No climax, no anti-climax, nothing but steady, quarterly increase of ecstasy.' No hangovers, only ulcers.

'Well,' said Soames, 'you call Americans materialistic, but I don't know.'

'And so you are,' said Chote. 'Cars, iceboxes, television, the American way of life—hmm, I can't wait. You never see any of those things over here, do you? No, bugger it, you don't.'

'Look,' said Soames patiently, 'if you don't like it over here, why don't you change the system?'

'Change the system? Are you mad?' They looked at him horrified. 'It's a bloody marvellous system. . . . Besides, it's quite unchangeable by this time.'

'Are you guys, er'—Soames groped for the English phrase—'extracting the mickey by any chance?'

They looked blankly at each other. 'I don't know,' said Chote wearily, 'are we?' The time had come to lower the chipped teacups and begin their exhausting haggle over their inexpensive bill. 'John owes me a tea.' 'No, don't you remember I bought you a beer last night?' 'I thought it was a gift, you stingy blighter.' The entropy of small talk burned them lower and lower.

Soames stared at them between tortoise-shell frames: children? very, very old men? or both? He took out a two-shilling piece and flipped it onto the table. 'That's mighty decent of you, Bradshaw.' 'Coo, isn't he a nice American?' Bradshaw smiled faintly and left them to it.

Chote decided to spend a quiet evening with Daphne, just to restore himself. He walked towards her digs whistling tunelessly, still thinking about the future. After years of hard training to qualify for the intellectual elite, he and his friends were faced with a vexing decision: whether to sell soap or weighing machines. It was funny how they just went over the wages again and again, the wages and the pensions—perhaps that was the natural delicacy of the cultured mind. One couldn't insult a chap by asking him if he really had a future in soap. Had there ever been a period in which educated men had expected so little from life? But then—one had to be scrupulously fair—had there ever been so many educated men? Perhaps *that* was the mistake, a flaw in the system to throw to Soames.

Just for laughs, he had shambled over to the University Appointments Board during his freshman year. First, the inquiries about journalism : hopeless of course. Very few openings, and those to be filled by a pushing mob of gaily spotted young men with dirty fingernails who had been working in newspaper offices from the age of fourteen or so. Chote was already too old to join the scramble; and probably too old also to learn the elegancies of newspaper prose. Anyway, it was an academic question : Chote had been sniffing the air for jobs since he was twelve, and in all that time he hadn't come across anything that paid as poorly as newspapers did. It was a pity that England should have the bulk of its news siphoned through uneducated egomaniacs, but it was hardly worth getting upset about it, after all these years. It was England's problem, not his.

'What about publishing then?' he asked the man at the board, just for more laughs. The dry little man behind the desk looked as if he had been waiting for this question all day. 'Practically everybody who comes in here wants to go into publishing—' so much for his private brainstorm '—practically nobody knows anything about the business. Naturally, you want to go into the editorial side. You are particularly well qualified. You read English or languages I suppose.' 'No sir, law.' 'You are literate and enthusiastic, and money is no object.' 'Well, actually, it is, I'm afraid.' 'And you have always wanted to work with books. I know. So has everybody else up here. Well, I'm sorry to be discouraging, but first of all editing is a tiny part in publishing. The rest is just a business like any other, and a dashed poorly paid one—in this country, at any rate. Secondly, if I may make a personal digression, editing is arduous work, as boring as reading through seed catalogues day after day—and also, damned poorly paid. Thirdly, and who knows? perhaps the most important, all the editorial jobs are taken anyway. You couldn't possibly walk straight into one.' 'I see.' 'However, we'll let you know if anything comes up. In the meantime, what's the matter with the legal profession?' 'I'm too mercenary for that, sir.' 'Well, then, you're *much* too mercenary for publishing.'

So Chote had come blinking out of the oracle's cave, realizing that for him, too, it was either soap or weighing machines from now on. Unlike his friends, he didn't wait until his third year before facing the unpalatable fact. He began right away to make surreptitious trips to London, in his angular grey suit, to be interviewed by captains of industry. They apparently thought he was quite a smart young fellow, too: keen as mustard, and remarkably sensible for an Oxford undergraduate. . . .

'Why, hello John,' said Daphne. She stood at her door in the sad, faded green print dress that had brightened Chote's first spring at Oxford and depressed the very deuce out of his subsequent ones. Daphne had seemed so vibrant in those days: nothing very much in herself, perhaps, but a sensitive seismograph to his own euphoria and bounce. It was a sunny, boozy time, full of vague promise: Oxford seemed to stretch out in front of him indefinitely, a green dream and a girl dressed in green—Good God, did *I* think that? Three eternal springs ago, he had indeed.

By the next spring the dress had begun to fade a little along with Daphne, Oxford and the dream; but Daphne still wore it manfully in all weathers, trudging sturdily about in it wherever Chote chose to lead her. By the third spring, he could hardly bear to look at it. It reminded him of old bedclothes, of ashes in the chair covers, of all the stale tastes. Whenever he offered to take Daphne anywhere, she would respond with that wistful, special-occasion brightness of hers; 'I'll wear my green dress, the one you like.' It was like old Aunt Clara Chote who still gave him rice pudding whenever he visited her: the gesture of a steady, solid mind, almost rigid with loyalty. 'Why don't you wear something else, just for a change?' he had once asked in desperation. 'But I thought you *liked* my green dress,' she answered inevitably. And that was that. He hadn't the spirit or the blood-lust to pursue the point.

'Hello, Daphne.'

'I didn't expect to see you again. I thought you'd left Oxford.' Her face was expressionless as usual, but conscience suggested that she might be sad all the same. He might be sad himself in the circumstances.

'No fear. I've just been frightfully busy. Preparing to leave for America and all that.' His face radiated home-made tenderness and concern : perhaps his silly excuse would somehow make her feel better. In a moment she might begin to look a little disappointed (her only real expression) and one couldn't bear that.

'Yes, I suppose you must be busy. How soon do you leave ?'

'Well, not for three months actually. But there's a lot to do, you know.' He had meant to be kind, but his excuse had turned unexpectedly into a sneer by Dubuffet. Her mouth was sagging a little at the edges. She turned her plump back, with a swish of sad green cotton, and led him up the stairs. He might as easily have kicked her and giggled.

'I'm sorry about the other night,' he said, still trying to be helpful.

'Oh, that was all right. You were quite clean about it.'

'Was I frightfully disgusting ?'

'No, you were very polite and apologetic. I knocked on the bathroom door several times, you know, to see if you were all right. And you said "Very fit" in a sort of muffled voice; and when you came out you kept saying how *awfully* sorry you were. You said it was some bad sherry you'd been drinking, but *I* thought you'd had a little bit too much of something or other.'

Typical middle-class attitude, thought Chote gloomily. He pushed open the door of her sitting-room—wouldn't it be nice to find another man inside ? to make sure that Daphne was in good hands—well, in somebody's hands—before he left her for good. God I'm in fatuous form today, he thought. It was unthinkable that Daphne would do anything like that. She might be dull, but by God, she was dependable.

Daphne was already filling the kettle, her automatic reaction to anybody's arrival. 'I've got some nice chocolate biscuits,' she said over her shoulder. He was still stuffed from afternoon tea, but he felt that he ought to take some, out of that unfailing, wonderful kindness of his. 'Good show,' he said, closing his eyes. He might still surprise himself about Daphne. But he doubted it somehow. A soft thud depressed the sofa; she was sitting next to him now.

Daphne had materialized (there was no other word for that either) in his first spring term. She was going out with Browning at the time, but Alan handed her over good-naturedly when he noticed Chote's rather overdone interest. Now three years older, Chote was wondering if some keen younger man would take over from him some day. Guiltily he flavoured the dowdy pathetic cotton under his fingers, and the too heavy, quasi-middle-aged flesh of her shoulder underneath. Daphne had grown old in his service.

Daphne more or less solved the problem of keeping up licentious appearances. Most of the encyclopædic things he had been pretending to do since his early days at Brinkley could be transferred in bulk to her. When the door to her room closed on them both, it was like a row of asterisks, a leering fadeout. And while they munched away at their chocolate biscuits and sipped their tea, Browning, Hook and the chaps were left outside to conjure up whatever goodies their imaginations were up to.

John went out with them less and less often on their bawdy, predictable rounds—'A bit of basic with Daffers' was the magic formula. And they believed because they wanted to believe. Even this year's joke about his landlady (never meant to be more than a joke) had become a part of the deposit of faith at Sturdley. In return of course one believed in the other chaps' fantasies, and so the folklore grew. Perhaps nobody had ever actually *done* anything at all.

'Did you know,' he said to Daphne, 'that every single bloke up here has a pose of some sort?'

'Have they?' she asked blankly. 'No, I didn't know that.'

'Bless you, yes. It's the whole fun of the place, seeing how long one can keep it up without being debagged, so to speak.'

Daphne was pouring a second cup of tea, and frowning into it. She hasn't the foggiest notion of what I mean, thought Chote. She can't see anything funny in striking a pose and keeping it up strenuously, fanatically, for three years or more. One could hardly blame her, in a way.

'Don't you see the joke?' he asked.

'Well, no, not exactly.' She had, most likely, never struck a pose in her life, wouldn't have known how to begin in fact.

'Well, anyway, all the chaps do it. I admit, it's not always easy to see why'—Oh my, it's beginning to rain again, he thought: Daphne's landlady was bustling about under the clothes-line in the garden trying to capture the flapping sheets and the voluminous 'smalls'. Daphne *was* a big girl, wasn't she? 'One just chooses a part one likes,' he went on. 'You know, a type one admires, and just imitates it like fury. Can you understand that at all?'

'Oh yes,' said Daphne. 'I suppose we *all* do that sometimes.'

'Really?' asked Chote. 'You too?' One never knew with Daphne. He turned from the window to look again at the solid, imperturbable face. What sort of part could she possibly play?

'Especially when I've been to the pictures,' she explained. 'Like a historical one or something.'

'Oh yes, I see what you mean.' Chote shut his eyes, which were still tired from Schools. 'Ann Boleyn and Catherine the Great and all that sort of thing.' Daphne smiled uneasily and began to slice more bread.

Daphne had been slightly more than an excuse, a front for his innocence. His stretch at Brinkley had almost frozen him solid as far as women were concerned, and two years in the Army had nothing like succeeded in thawing him out. The gauzelike, compliant women of his sixth-form daydreams had prepared him poorly for the perky, hot-breathing companions that Browning and his other friends flung at him. Their unexpected opacity, the chunkiness and smell of their flesh, sent the old dreamer scooting for cover: and only that unfailing tongue, working desperately, groping toward an ever greater glibness, kept him from showing his concern. Pound for pound he was utterly unmanned by Browning's warm-all-over, take-it-or-leave-it nymphs; but by heaven, he could, and he would, out-talk the lot of them.

At Oxford, the situation had become in some respects worse, and one began to wonder if one ever would have the confidence to live up to one's by now formidable reputation. (In his Brinkley ignorance, he had made claims bordering on the superhuman.) And Browning still produced earthy, sporting girls, like rabbits out of a hat—girls who knew the rules, and the ropes, and the score. His other flank was harassed by the underграduettes, mostly plain in the best academic tradition, but a few unmistakably pink and pretty—and even more talkative than he was, capable of fast, devastating prattle about 'the most extraordinary little man in tweeds' and 'frightfully funny little men in shorts' and so on, a language which came or didn't come with the mother's milk. The comeliest of them were forever twenty-deep in heaving, determined admirers capable of matching them 'frightfully' for 'frightfully' and 'little' for 'little' in their gaily amusing descriptions of all the people one knew at Oxford. Pimlico and Brinkley simply hadn't trained him for this sort of thing. Perhaps these girls were not all of the leisure class, but they were bred somehow to the patter. (Thank God the merchant class didn't talk like that, he told himself wryly.) It was rather a blow—he didn't yet know how much of a blow—to realize that one's audience would always be limited by the language barrier.

And then he met Daphne, and all that part of it was all right. Here at last was a girl who couldn't possibly frighten anyone—a girl as compliant, though a good deal more solid, than the fantasies that dwelt in the Brinkley dormitories. Eagerly, well nigh- and quasi-passionately, he clutched her to him, and for almost a year she was all womankind to him, all the things he had guessed about (and guessed wrong) at Brinkley, the things he had eagerly, nervously profaned in the Army. Not so much physical things as things of the heart. (Zut alors! Things of the heart from good old Daphne.)

But she taught him too much. By the end of the first summer term, he knew enough about women to know that Daphne wasn't much of one, not the best anyway. Like Godfrey, he hadn't graduated to interesting women. But he began to look around cautiously for more glamorous game—not quite letting go of Daphne, not just yet. Supposing he couldn't get anyone else? There was more to it, of course : one could feel a species of uncritical attachment to the big, solemn girl, with her big comfy body so woefully short in crispness and definition, her fatal tendency to wear her hair in a bun. One couldn't just leave her—not just at the moment. Better to wait for a situation of some kind to arise, or until Daphne perhaps got bored with him, or time did something or other.

Meanwhile, one reminded Daphne over and over again, like a news bulletin, that their relationship was but a thing of today, that she could get out of it any time, that marriage—well, one didn't even mention marriage. . . . Gad, what foolishness, he thought now, as he looked at the mass of sluggish, unwittingly tragic face a few inches from him, staring straight ahead as usual just to be safe. Her attitude toward him hadn't changed a scrap during the three years; she was just as far committed as ever; time had done the wrong things, if it had done anything at all. He had forced the issue with his opening burst of enthusiasm, and now it was his undignified role to crawl out of it somehow, a clown stumbling, hey ho, trouserless down the fire escape.

'What will you do when I'm gone, Daphne?'

'I'll go on working, I suppose. Why?'

'Will you miss me?'

'Yes, I suppose so.'

'Still, you'll get over it soon enough. Won't you?'

'Yes, I suppose so.'

He peeked again at the suet pudding, with its scattering of small features. Slowly, a large round tear crystallized and went sliding down and away. She wiped her cheek, matter-of-factly, and headed for the sink. Life had to go on. The teacups must be washed and dried and put away, or else, where would we all be? He never had seen her cry before—indeed, he had supposed it not to be within her range. He gazed dismally at her industrious back. Him and his amusing exits from Oxford.

93

6. Lounging

ALAN BROWNING believed unwaveringly in the importance of Saturday night. And even though he had declared himself sick and tired of celebrating, he had somehow coaxed Godfrey Hook down to the Harem dance hall to look for women, sleezy search against a sleezy backdrop, pastel tinted and dim lit, and a band that might have been old gramophone records. Browning was liverish tonight, but game.

'There doesn't seem to be anything here,' said Hook hopefully. A group of badly undernourished girls was chatting listlessly on the other side of the floor. Two Americans in leather jackets came in and went out again, after a brief, contemptuous look around.

'They don't look so bad,' said Browning. 'I mean, one has seen worse.'

'Oh come now, Alan. Even the Americans didn't want them. Where's your blasted pride?'

'I suppose they are a bit downtrodden,' said Browning, 'if you're going to be fussy about it. Personally I have never seen any point in being fussy.' The girls were looking over and smiling, yellow and grey smiles, and Browning was beginning unmistakably to smile back. 'That little one in pink looks rather sensuous,' he said out of the side of his smile.

'Yes, if one considers her age,' said Hook. 'Frankly old man, I feel I must draw the line firmly at this kind of thing. Sorry, and so forth.'

'So am I,' said Browning, 'but I suppose it can't be helped. What do you propose doing instead?'

'Well, we could always go back to the faithful old digs.'

'Good grief—at eight o'clock? On Saturday night?' Browning almost stopped smiling. 'You sound like bloody Chote,' he said.

'Chote?' said Hook with quick interest. 'Chote doesn't talk like that, does he?' Browning hadn't said anything either way about Chote since that night on the river, and Godfrey imagined that the churlish mood had passed. He raised his eyebrows to encourage stray confidences.

'He doesn't exactly *talk* like that,' said Browning, whose stomach was beginning to growl peevishly, 'I'll grant you. He *talks* like one of the chaps, all right. Oh Lord, how he talks. When John wants to go home early, he'll say, "Look here, chaps, I have a date with an absolutely smashing blonde. Film star actually. Nymphers of course. Mad about me, natch. Smashing." And off he trots to work and scheme, for all the world like a ruddy toffee-nose. Take tonight—perfect case in point : you heard him saying that Saturday night was a lower-middle-class institution. What flipping class does he suppose he belongs to?' Browning's throat made a tearing, rending sound. 'Excuse me.'

'It's funny,' said Hook eagerly. 'I've always thought of Chote as no end of a chap after dark. Isn't he?'

'Oh, perhaps,' said Browning. 'My own view is that he's a puritan through and through. He may be sitting at home fairly despising us at this very moment—and then again he may not. I really don't know. I say, I am sorry.' Browning's digestion let him down like this occasionally.

'But what about his passionate landlady?' pursued Hook. 'How do you explain her?'

'I'll explain her when I have to,' said Browning absently. 'Look, old man, I *am* going to dance with the one in pink, whatever you say. She looks more voluptuous by the minute.'

Hook watched the smooth familiar approach, marred only by an occasional shoulder-humping burp. The girl smiled sweetly enough and drifted into Browning's well-used arms. The lips were already flapping against her ear; Hook knew the words by heart, even though he couldn't have said them him-self for money. He lit a cigarette and began to blow smoke rings the way Browning had taught him. So Chote might be a fake, eh? The very words took a bit of getting used to. All the sixth-form smoothness and smartness which went with Chote would have to run out slowly, like the colour running out of a pair of socks. 'A puritan through and through.' Why, look at Chote's reputation at Brinkley—one of the few chaps who actually—

But was it really true? Or was it just that nobody could be dirty enough for Browning? He caught a glimpse now of the intimate lending-library smile, the hand tirelessly kneading the cheap pink upholstery. It was really too preposterous that he should find himself on the same side as Browning in the moral struggle, with Chote on the other. If Chote wasn't really playing the game, then he'd better get out, too.

'I say,' he said earnestly to Browning when the music had stopped. 'I'm *much* more of a puritan than Chote is, you know.'

'No, really you're not, old boy,' said Browning wearily. 'Do take my word for it.'

'But with my background,' Hook protested. 'I mean to say, parsons to right and left.'

'That hasn't got anything to do with it,' said Browning. 'Look at *my* background if you like. Hundreds of years of solid citizenship culminating in *me*. It's enough to make one despair.'

The music started, and he was off again in a whirl of off-pink, leaving Godfrey to thoughts which lurched and shunted between the tinny numbers.

'Do you *really* think John is an opportunist?' he said next time.

'Well, I really don't want to malign the bugger, but wouldn't you say there's something fishy about that scholarship, not to mention all those job offers that slip out from time to time? He can't be one tenth as lazy as he pretends to be. Not one twentieth—and one should be at least a twentieth, don't you think?'

'But why does he go to such extraordinary lengths to cover his tracks?'

'Ah, there you have me. Curious habit he picked up in the

Army I suppose. Excuse me a minute, old boy.' He rolled his eyes and began to swerve across the chalky floor.

'I insist I'm every inch as much a puritan as John is,' Godfrey persisted dubiously. Perhaps he was making too much of this. It was an old fault of his. An old school fault.

'Well, have it your own way, old boy. It's really more your affair than mine, isn't it?' Browning answered carelessly.

'I simply can't believe that John has been leading a double life for all these years—a blackened sepulchre, so to speak.'

'Well, if you can't, you can't.' Browning was feeling much better. He had just been annoyed for a moment, because he thought that Hook was going to insist on leaving the Harem early, as Chote had so often done, during the very height of the revels. But it was all better now. 'I may have been quite wrong,' he said generously. 'I say, old chap, are you absolutely positive that you don't want to dance?'

'Quite positive, thank you.'

After the next batch of foxtrots, Browning was happy to report that the girl in pink was coming nicely to the boil. 'Quite a sweet little character, too,' he added. 'I mean, under the skin. I admit that the latter is a bit on the scaly side.'

'I hate to bring it up again,' resumed Hook. 'But to me, Chote has always been virtually the last of the chaps, a swine of the very deepest dye. And remember, I've known him practically since infancy.'

'Oh does it really matter?' said Browning with a gesture of tedium. 'All right, Chote's a bastard, I'm a bastard, you're a bastard. . . .' He was still telepathizing charm across the room, anxious not to lose any hard-earned ground. 'The wretched girl insists on "remaining in circulation", to use her own loathsome phrase, presumably in hopes of snaring a shortsighted American. I'd hate to think that I'd gone to all this trouble warming her up for somebody else.'

'I don't suppose it really *matters*,' admitted Hook. 'It's just a point of curiosity, that's all. What makes you so sure that Chote is a you-know?'

Browning shrugged. The girl in pink was trudging off to the

powder room now, and there was a lull in the action. 'You don't know. It's just something one senses about a bloke. You feel that some chaps are just going through the motions of having a good time, because it's the thing to do. I.e., Chote.'

'And not Godders?' asked Hook, frowning anxiously.

'Good Lord, no. Put your tiny mind at rest, for the love of God. You're a quite unparalleled bastard.'

'You're too kind,' said Hook. 'Heaven knows, I *try*.'

'*Blast* it,' bellowed Browning. 'That ghastly little Yank is sneaking in after all. You can't trust these new nationalities a blessed inch.' A tiny American soldier had intercepted her (the powder room was a bloody ruse) and was already steering her across the floor with brisk, businesslike steps. 'Why is it that you never see a normal-sized American?' muttered Browning. 'They're always either ruddy giants or these blasted pigmies.' The couple swept rapidly past. 'You could at least have the decency to take the chewing gum out of your mouth, you frightful little man.'

Hook smiled. 'We might as well go home, old boy. We're obviously not wanted.' It was amusing to see his friend losing his grip on a girl who had been subjected to 'the method', but for basic economic reasons even Browning was liable to be cut out by an American now and then. It was a situation calling for humility all round.

'Wait a bit,' said Browning. 'There's another girl over there, a lithe creature in blue, who seemed to offer certain possibilities a moment ago.'

'Oh now, come on, dash it,' pointed out Hook in his best Wodehouse.

'I suppose you're right,' admitted Browning, making no move to go.

The little American was whizzing round the floor at a furious pace by now, chewing, it seemed, faster and faster, pumping his left arm expertly and chatteringly winsomely. 'He's a keen little chap,' said Browning. 'One must give him credit for that. You'd almost think he was being paid by the mile.'

'I didn't come here to watch Americans dance,' said Hook impatiently.

'Neither did I,' agreed Browning. 'But one just can't get away from it these days. Everywhere one turns, one sees bloody Yanks dancing.'

Hook went to the wall and sat down on a little tin chair, to wait patiently. Slowly and surely, his hands crept down to his pockets and began to rummage : out came once again the decayed bus tickets and crushed correspondence. 'Why did I buy a fivepenny bus ticket, if it comes to that?' He had never spent so many blank days before in his life. It frightened one a little, like a child's first switchback ride. Ever since Schools, he had been stuffing unaccountable bits of paper into his pockets, to remind him later of the stubbornly unremindable, to locate him somewhere in the great plenum. Among the rubbish were the two letters from Felicity, written from the bishop's residence, crushed now into a hideous carnation. 'Dear Godfrey, your hour of trial is over at last, and the time for rejoicing is at hand. . . .' You said a mouthful, baby, thought Hook, somewhat daringly. . . . 'Dearest Godfrey, my heart goes out to you in this happy season. . . .' As soon as Felicity picked up a pen, something frightful came over her : an older party, in starched cuffs and wimple, squatted down with her, seized the pen and let fly with all this rubbish. Those damned letters hadn't helped much, he thought.

Of course, one knew who the wimple belonged to. 'In this dark hour, while the forces of evil surround us on every side. . . .' He had squirmed and squirmed in his pew, twitchy under the slanting sunshine, while Mr. Hook stumbled through the episcopal letter from Felicity's father. 'We must gird our loins with the armour of faith, and the sword of righteousness.' Little Godfrey (a keen medievalist at the time) could picture the massive bishop being lowered bit by bit into his armour, by a staff of long-suffering servants. 'We must gird our loins—' Mr. Hook had got stuck already, and was beginning to fidget with his glasses. 'I'm sorry. I seem to have read this line twice.' Godfrey felt the embarrassment rising, rising, in wine-dark waves. Thank heavens what with the war and all, there were only four other people present to witness the heroic struggles of Mr. Hook, making his way cautiously through the dense undergrowth of the bishop's prose. Godfrey distracted himself by thinking of old Mrs. Sims in the front pew, girding up her loins—whatever that might mean; the image was a vague but pleasant one—with the armour of faith. She would be the one to try it out on, first. In a few minutes, out we all go and play in the sunshine, and forget about the forces of darkness and what-not for another week. He still remembered that Sunday vividly, because it was during the next week that the bombs began to fall in earnest; and he came to see for the first time what the starchy old bishop had been driving at.

He put Felicity's letters away. They made uncomfortable reading on a Saturday night at the Harem. He hadn't answered them yet, and he really didn't want to. He hadn't the faintest idea of what to say to her, or how, at this point. He had been putting the problem of Felicity off resolutely until Schools : that was last year's deadline. Now he was wondering what else would make a convenient deadline.

Browning's neck seemed to be getting awfully pink in the hot stuffy atmosphere—pinker and pinker, flaring into crimson in fact, as if he were about to have an attack of some kind. Hook suddenly realized that Browning was bringing it on him-self by vigorous talking, although there didn't seem to be any-body near him. Could this be the DTs already ?

'I'm sorry, old boy,' he could just make out what Browning was saying. 'I assure you, I wasn't referring to you.'

He sighted the little American moving grimly forward under Browning's shadow with hands clenched, lips moving belliger-ently. He came to a halt just beneath Browning's chin. 'Out of the question, old boy.' Browning's words drifted over to Hook piecemeal. 'Sent down, you know. Awfully sorry.'

Godfrey hurried over. Browning seemed to be repeating the words 'sent down, sent down' in a foolish singsong. The Ameri-can was leaning against Browning's chest, with his head cocked to one side, uncomprehending. 'Will you step outside, or won't you ?' Hook heard the new American sounds, surprisingly deep and rich for such a tiny man. He must be wired for sound in some way.

'Is anything the matter ?' Godfrey asked helplessly. It was

absurd to feel embarrassed already, but he did all the same. The whole scene seemed so dashed foreign.

'You his friend?' chewed the American. Godfrey nodded anxiously. 'Well maybe you can help me out. I don't seem to be getting through to him too well. I'm asking him to step outside, *you* know, and fight a little. Comprennez?'

'And I'm telling him that I'll be sent down if I'm caught fighting in here,' said Browning reasonably.

'Sent down, sent down,' piped the American. 'Whadya*mean* —sent down?'

'You know,' said Godfrey, 'er, sent down—' An asinine retort, but he couldn't think of any other way of putting it on the spur of the moment. Why the devil couldn't one be masterful, just once in a while?

'Oh, no!' The American gave a bellow of pain. 'Not you too! What's the *matter* with everybody around here?'

'Sent down from the university,' Hook went on nervously. 'Oh, you know.' Browning was smiling aloofly at the straggle of spectators, allowing his friend to carry the ball as best he could.

'But I *don't* know, old boy,' mimicked the American. 'That seems to be the kernel of the problem, wouldn't you say?' The girl in pink had come up by now and was clutching the shiny leather arm proudly. 'Don't hit him, Walter, he didn't mean anything. He's just one of those silly undergraduates.'

Walter turned to pat her down, and Godfrey got a sudden oblique view of the little, lined face. It was shocking. I don't think he's angry at all, he thought. Had the little man actually winked? Anyway he was whirling back on Browning, a raging inferno once more.

'Look, I don't care whether you're going to be sent down, or sent up, or sent sideways. *Nobody* gets away with saying what I just heard you say. Good will or no good will.'

'What did I say?' asked Browning.

'I'm not going to repeat it in front of the lady.'

'Oh, for Godsake,' said Browning.

'Watch your talk,' said the American. And then coaxing: 'Come on, let's go out and fight, huh? I'll find someone for your friend too, if you like.' Godfrey felt a new set of pores opening. Good Lord, how quite insanely embarrassing.

'Come on, Walter. They're not worth your attention, either of them,' said the girl haughtily.

It was an obvious stalemate. Walter was standing patiently, only an inch or so from Browning, chewing contentedly on his cud of gum.

'Look,' said Browning affably. 'I can't fight here, or I'll be sent—you know, expelled, kicked out, canned.'

'Oh, that's all you meant,' said Walter. 'Hell of a funny way to say it, don't you think?'

'We like it,' said Browning. 'Anyway, it isn't worth being sent down just for fighting just before we get our degrees. After that, of course, I'd be delighted to oblige you.'

Browning stepped back, and Walter stepped promptly forward, like the number one boy at dancing school; still crowding in, his head bobbing under Alan's chin. The bad music made a mocking background. 'Don't go away, old boy, while I'm talking to you. Rotten bad manners, don't you think?'

'Look, what do you want?' asked Browning, and they both took another jaunty dance step, back toward the sleezy wall. 'Since fighting is out of the question, let us examine the alternatives,' said Browning, rocking now on his heels like a tired schoolmaster. 'First, we can stand here all night like this until one of us falls aseep. Impractical, but not impossible I daresay, not impossible. Perhaps we can dance a bit to relieve the tedium. Secondly, we can examine the thing in the round. . . .'

Hook realized foggily that it was going to be all right. Both were bluffing well, in their contrasting styles. They were talking men, not fighting men. 'I guess an apology would help,' Walter said at last in an amiable voice.

'Certainly old boy,' said Browning augustly, 'only too happy. Anything to bring our great nations closer, what?'

They shook hands, and a flood of relief drenched Godfrey's system. His admiration for Browning was intense. Perhaps the whole thing had been make-believe—but how superb to have realized this all along, and to have kept one's head. There was a lesson in this. 'Have my card, old boy,' said Browning. 'I hope we shall meet again in happier circumstances.' Graceful, self-possessed, one didn't have to approve of Browning's philosophy to realize that it justified itself beautifully in action. One could go anywhere with him. Tonight's exhibition was nothing special, of course—just another typically smooth performance. 'You talk too much,' said Walter.

The American danced away again, more busily than ever, and Browning wagged his head benignly. 'Extraordinary people,' he said. 'Quite extraordinary!'

'I don't know what you're so happy about,' said Hook. 'You've lost your girl, such as she was, and on top of that you've disgraced English manhood, such as it is.'

'True enough,' said Browning. 'However, blood has been spared. Why, I haven't struck anyone in anger since I was a small child. I doubt if I'd even know where to begin.' He smiled assurance at Hook, who was rubbing his hands together. 'Come along, old chap. There's nothing to be afraid of,' he said. But Godfrey continued to rub.

The pubs were almost closed by now, and besides, they didn't have any money left. They both owed Chote a pound or two as it was, and he had been woefully reluctant to finance them any further: 'I wouldn't have it on my conscience,' he had told them that afternoon. 'You'd only spend the money on something unthinkable.'

They looked in at the Sturdley College lodge, in hopes of finding a free-spending, wistful drunk, thirsty for company. Sometimes, just after Schools, one would come across solitary undergraduates who had run out of chums to celebrate with: dedicated scholars perhaps, who had been hoarding their money for three years or more, and who hadn't made enough friends of the right kind. In such cases, Hook and Browning were always more than willing to oblige. It gave Hook a special kind of pleasure to shepherd his innocent contemporaries from pub to pub: they seemed to look up to him as a man of unlimited experience, a connoisseur of the naughty side of life; and by George he was, too, compared with them.

The lodge was empty, except for Thomson and Soames. They both gave off a fanatical gleam under the bare electric bulb: the serious Englishman and the serious American. They were talking in low tense voices about, what was it? The Treaty of Utrecht?

'Would one of you chaps like to come on a toot?' asked Browning. 'The orange squash at the F.A. is a perfect poem.'

Thomson stared at them like a goldfish through the side of his bowl. There were so many reasons why he couldn't hope to make contact with them. Soames smiled and said, 'Not tonight, boys. I'm in no shape to tangle with orange squash.'

'I was afraid of that,' said Browning. 'In that case, I don't suppose you would consider some more dollar-aid in lieu?'

'I'm afraid not, old boy. I'm practically broke myself, as a matter of fact.'

'It would do wonders toward creating good will between our two great nations,' said Browning, trotting out his phrase again. 'Might make all the difference, in fact.'

'Oh come now, Alan,' Soames smiled. 'You *know* you can't buy friendship. You'd only hate me if I lent you the money.'

'No, honestly, I wouldn't, old chap. I'd think you were absolutely super.'

'Come along,' said Hook. 'Your little tin cup isn't impressing anybody tonight.' He was blinking sleepily in the thin light.

'You're quite sure, old boy? Ten bob would do marvels. Even five would help to bring the roses back to the cheeks.'

'Get up off your knees, old boy,' said Hook. 'You're letting your country down again.' He reached for Browning's padded elbow.

'Nonsense,' said Alan. 'Americans love people to do a spot of grovelling when they ask for money. It's a sign of good faith. Isn't that right Brad?'

'I wouldn't know,' said Soames rather sharply. 'I've never asked an American for money.'

'I daresay you've never needed to,' said Browning. 'Ho-hum. Well, if you won't you won't. No hard feelings, old boy.' He turned to go.

'Listen, Alan,' said Soames a little anxiously. 'I told you I haven't got the money. I'd let you have it if I had it myself, O.K.?'

'Of course,' said Browning. 'I was only joking, old chap. I know you would.'

Thomson was thankful to see them go. He turned back to Soames with a look of 'Where was I?' Soames bent forward to give Thomson an exaggerated amount of attention. Look—he could talk to 'the boys', and he could also talk to people like Thomson.

Browning and Hook strolled slowly back along the High, in the direction of home. The night smelled fresh, after days of rain, and there was that nice sense of stone all around. 'You know, it feels very pleasant to go home sober, once in a while,' said Hook, revelling cautiously in the clarity of night-time sensation, pleasantly aware of the sky for a change and the slight modulations of warm air.

'I don't care for it myself,' said Browning. 'However, each to his taste, and all that.'

'Well, I wouldn't want to make a habit of it,' agreed Hook. 'But once in a while, it seems almost like a new sensation, a kind of vice, one might almost call it.'

'I'd have brought my violin,' said Browning shortly, 'if I'd known we were going to carry on like this.'

They crossed Magdalen Bridge and Hook glanced down at the black, still waters, and the shaggy island that clove them in two: it still looked attractive to him, even though he passed this way at least twice a day. 'I can't believe that you're quite such a hundred per cent red-blooded Philistine as you make out, Alan,' he said.

'Perhaps not. I don't know. One has been rebelling against preciousness for so long that I can't remember precisely where I stand myself any more. I *do* know that all the art in the world would look like nothing if you put it next to a woman's body.'

'I suppose so,' said Hook, a bit dubiously. 'I've never thought about it, really.'

'Well think about it now. Just suppose you had a painting by, well, who? Raphael?'

'I don't care for Raphael.'

'Someone else then. What about Botticelli? Or would you prefer Picasso?'

'I don't care. You choose.'

'All right. Let's say an interior by Sir George Farnsworth, the eminent Scottish abortionist, or even a Matthew Higginbottom nude. That's in one corner. And in the other corner, weighing twelve stone six, we have the fair Felicity. Now, which—'

'You're right, I suppose. Although I'm not entirely sure that there isn't a fallacy somewhere in your argument.'

'Blessed if I can see one. I hope there isn't, anyway. I shall have to cancel my plans for the summer if there is.'

Their digs were in a terrace house, which was looking even more anonymous than usual in the dark. In the downstairs living-room they could hear the two boarders from Christ Church huffing and puffing over their nightly port : from the hallway outside, it sounded like a pair of elderly walruses waffling over a piece of fish. 'Preposterous. . . . Outrageous. . . . Frightful little man. . . . Positive troglodyte.'

Alan and Godfrey shared a sitting-room on the next floor, which was lushly decorated with pilfered signs STOP—GENTLE-MEN—DÉFENSE DE CRACHER and FIVE MILES TO CAMBRIDGE which Browning had tugged and hacked loose from their proper moorings. It was something they'd argued about once or twice : 'It's dashed embarrassing sometimes,' Hook had protested mildly, 'when I'm entertaining clergymen for instance. . . . And on top of that, I'm not entirely convinced that it's funny.' 'Oh, it's funny all right, you can take my word for that,' said Browning. 'Anybody who knows will tell you the same thing.' 'Oh, I don't know,' Chote had chimed in. 'One giggles when one first comes in here, but you can put that down to good breeding and intense nervousness. I must say, it must be a dashed dreary joke to have to live with, day after day, year after year.' 'It stands for a point of view,' said Browning doggedly. And the signs stayed. In fact, only a few days ago Hook had found himself standing in a ditch, hauling away at a ROAD NARROWS sign which Browning wanted to put at the top of the staircase; he vaguely remembered the pelting of the rain and his feet squelching miserably in mud, and Chote lounging on the side of the bank, scoffing drunkenly, 'Come along now, girls. *Aren't* we having a glorious rag, though?' Browning, however, was still quite sure that it was funny.

'Tea or Nescafé?' asked Hook. 'Actually, we're out of both.'

Browning took the poker dice out of his pocket, along with his pipe. 'No tobacco, of course. You haven't got any fags, I suppose?'

'You've smoked my last one, you bloody parasite,' said Hook. 'I was afraid of that. You always were an improvident bastard.'

They played a few rounds of dice, and then they put the dice away. Hook wanted to talk about the future, and in particular, Felicity. But he found it difficult to bring the subject up. Eventually Browning would get back to sex: it was like waiting for a sentry to pass a particular spot on his nightly rounds. And sure enough, at 10.35 precisely, Alan stopped sucking on his empty pipe to inquire after Felicity. 'Rather a delightful creature, I thought,' he added in his chivalrous way. Browning made it a point to say something nice about every woman who was ever mentioned—even when it happened to be someone like Mrs. Fosse, the rugged landlady. It kept him in practice.

'I'm a bit worried about her, to tell you the truth,' said Godfrey, 'a trifle perplexed.'

'You feel she may be cheating?' asked Browning quickly.

'No, of course not, you thoroughly loathsome chap. Felicity doesn't even know how to play the game properly, let alone how to cheat at it.'

Browning made a thin, sucking noise on his pipe. 'I suppose you're the best judge of that. Personally, I never exclude the possibility of cheating, even among bishops' daughters. I've known so many extra*ordin*ary cases—'

'I'm sure you have, old boy. But to get back to Felicity for a minute—before we get completely swallowed up in scabrous reminiscence. What troubles me—and I know you'll laugh when I say this—is that I don't feel worthy of the girl. That seems to be the nicest way of putting it, anyway.' Godfrey frowned apologetically. Browning's eyes bulged, but he didn't actually laugh.

'I don't mean that I've done anything more than averagely unspeakable—well, you know the sort of things I've done, or at least tried to do, not with any outstanding success, I'll admit. It's just that she's so *blasted* pure that it makes me feel permanently uncomfortable. I can hardly bring myself to look her in the eye any more.'

'You don't feel guilty about anything you've done?' asked Browning sharply.

'No. Not exactly. I don't think so. No,' said Hook. 'I mean —well, no.'

It was a difficult matter to phrase : he had, of course, done virtually nothing; but there was no point in going into that again. 'It's only when I'm with Felicity that I feel so hopelessly blackhearted, and, well, unclean—'

'That's absurd,' said Browning. 'You haven't done anything wrong; you've never hurt anybody—'

'No. That's true, I suppose.'

'You've just behaved like a perfectly normal bloke who isn't afraid of life, who isn't afraid of his own body—' Browning was warming up reliably to a favourite theme. 'I tell you, these people make me absolutely bilious, with their timidity and essential dirty-mindedness. Not just Felicity, of course, but all the old spinsters and maiden aunts, of both sexes—'

'Quite,' said Hook. 'I agree with you wholeheartedly, as you know. But before we go on with Sermon Twenty-three, let's just wrap up the subject of Felicity, eh? The question is, do you or do you not consider her a hopeless case?'

Browning was a little annoyed : he hadn't realized that he had made the same speech before. 'Hopeless case? I shouldn't think so for a moment.' Hook received the implication humbly : if Browning could spend a day or two with her, we'd soon see whether she was a hopeless case or not ! 'She struck me as being quite exceptionally responsive,' added Browning.

'But how to tap the hidden resources?' asked Hook. 'You're such a bloody mine of titillating information. So tell me that, if you please.'

Browning stretched pleasurably in his stiff-leather armchair, master listening to protégé, carefully weighing the problem, and packing his little bundle of sagacity. 'There are various approaches,' he said at last. 'But I think that all the experts are agreed on at least one point : that you must stand your ground, whatever happens. In the long run, she will admire you for it—'

Godfrey sat forward in his chair, ready as ever to absorb the anthologized wisdom of the ages. Surely and knowingly, Browning began to fill in his portrait of the man of experience, tenderly awakening his young bride : 'Dear Godfrey, I never thought it could be like this. . . .' Hook blinked, straining to see himself in so unfamiliar a picture. 'She'll actually be glad that you've sown a few oats, learned your way around and so on. Once she's learned that sex is a beautiful thing, not ugly. . . .' Alan's face looked almost radiant, like someone at prayer. Hook could tell that he was already far away, reliving some succulent experience of his own : 'Oh, it's wonderful, wonderful !' Was that supposed to be the girl speaking—at any moment one expected froth to appear at the corners of Browning's mouth : 'Again, just once again, darling.' It was almost a moan. Godfrey felt sick with fear.

Browning sat back with his eyes closed. 'A beautiful performance,' said Godfrey shakily. 'Most moving.'

'Well, that's all there is to it,' said Browning. 'It couldn't be simpler.'

It just might happen like that too, thought Hook, returning to himself. There was an authentic ring to Browning's way of it. At any rate, it was the first time in months that he had seen any hope for himself and Felicity.

'On a point of tactics,' he said, 'do you think I should scrub Doris Flounce and invite Felicity to the Summer Ball ?'

'I shouldn't bother,' yawned the master. 'You have all summer to work on Felicity—and you'll probably need it. For just one night and with two guineas at stake, I should say that Doris is your best bet; one of the best bets in Oxford, in fact. I mean if Felicity is really going to make you feel uncomfortable all evening—'

'Won't Felicity be angry ?'

'I daresay. However, if you play your cards right, a certain judicious coldness might make you seem even more desirable.'

Hook couldn't help blushing just a little at the suggestion that he might make himself desirable : but one saw the strength of the argument. It occurred to him that at last he was making some sort of sense of his problem, and he felt moved to a small word of praise. 'You know, Alan, you're a pretty godforsaken bloke in all sorts of important ways. But when it comes to women, you're incomparable, absolutely incomparable.'

Browning bowed in his chair. 'We aim to please, Mr. Wooster. And now, if you don't mind, it's heigh! for the lonely couch.'

He stood up and moved toward the door, which had a sign on it saying EMPLOYEES WILL PLEASE WASH HANDS, and passed magisterially through it.

7. Leaving

ON Sunday mornings, Oxford's perpetual religious revival swings from the bell rope. The freedom of the air is open to all : thin, harsh chimes, hinting of cantankerous theology, tangle and mingle with the deep booms of orthodoxy. Their consolations may vary widely, but nearly all the churches cling *de fide* to the value of bells on Sunday. Empty churches blast out just as confidently as full ones, all combining in a hearty muscular wooing of the late sleeper. Unfortunately, people who live in Oxford soon become immune to bells, and most of the clanging goes for nothing.

This was the last Sunday of term, the last Sunday of his Oxford career; and John Chote, a little melancholy in the empty, reverberating streets, listened carefully to the lonely smack of his footsteps. None of his friends knew that he went to church on critical Sundays, or even that he believed in that sort of thing. It wasn't something he took all that seriously himself, and there was no point in giving the bloody man Browning unnecessary ammunition. Hook was welcome to the full brunt of Browning's hoary anti-clericalism, his laborious thrusts at 'Dad'.

He sat at the back, a dim figure in a dark church. Some Sundays he believed a little ('in a certain sense') and others, he didn't believe any of it at all; but he always liked sitting in these venerable churches, listening to the stately rigmarole. He had tried nearly all the Oxford churches, and settled at last on this old, very high one, where they sang the good old hymns, and burned incense like the blooming papists, and where they still discussed the Tractarian movement every Sunday with real urgency—if Browning saw him here, he'd never hear the end of it. Not that he cared, of course—no, he really *didn't* care—but why leave oneself open?

Chote had good reason for his conviction that even the most dogmatic ne'er-do-wells had their soft spots—yes, Browning too. In his second year at Brinkley, an ecstasy of excitement had swept through the school when an album of pressed flowers was discovered under the bed of J. D. Stiggins, the peerless captain of rugger and boxing, a fierce jubilation dancing and flashing from dormitory to dormitory like a grass fire : 'Have you heard about old Stiggins's flowers? Pansies I believe.' For days, Stiggins prowled the school with haunted red face, poking the ashes to life wherever he went. 'Chote, what the devilareyoulaughingat?' 'Nothing, Stiggins, honestly.'

It just went to show : the burliest, most apparently flawless men had their little secrets. Perhaps the great Browning chased butterflies during the holidays or cried by himself in the pictures. And then, look at Gosworth—a blubbering coward, weaker than a woman, when it came to an ordinary test of nerve. (Yes, one couldn't restrain a certain pleasure in Gosworth.) If one had a weakness like that, one was quite right to hide it as well as one could, and hope that the chaps wouldn't pry.

And what was wrong with feeling a little sentimental in

church once in a while? Most people would have respected him for it—the only possible criticism being that it clashed a trifle with his other pursuits. Browning would be sure to make the most of that. And somehow the blighter *was* an arbiter of what was acceptable. The perfectly integrated cad—it sounded like an advertisement. He thought again of the innocent rapture which had come about with the unmasking of Stiggins: 'And what were we doing under Stiggins's bed in the first place?' It was a matter for drowsy meditation. He almost chuckled out loud with sensuous reminiscence in the lush velvety atmosphere of the old church.

The organ was beginning to swell now, reassuringly solid and portentous, winding its sure way towards one of the grand old tunes. Chote cleared his throat and prepared to give it his all.

A mile or so away, Gene Fosdick lay on his back smoking a cigarette, not hearing the bells either. From time to time he would pick up a pack of cards and shuffle it, deal himself a hand and grunt.

'What are you doing, Gene?' asked the girl next to him.

'Engaging in a little game of skill, honey. Would you care to join me?'

She was a plain girl in the flat morning light, squinting without her glasses. 'What are you doing that for?' She hadn't much idea why he did anything. 'Give me a cigarette, Gene. Don't smoke them all yourself.' He held up the empty packet. 'Oh,' she said.

What the hell am I doing here? asked Gene. Living a sane sex life, answered Gene. A man of twenty-five has to do something constructive with his time. 'I'm dying for a smoke,' said the girl. Oh my God, thought Gene. This is flat even by my standards. Pair of sevens, Jee*zus*. Who dealt this crap?

'I'm going to get something to eat.' He stood up and stretched. The room looked like all of them, small and stale and untidy. The ash trays were flowing over, and grey English clothes lay sprawled on the floor. 'Get me a cigarette while you're out, will you, Gene?'

He stepped out into the naked street where the bells were ringing. He had an accommodating landlady who didn't care where he spent his nights so here he was a little way down the Cowley Road in the heart of industrial Oxford looking for a place to eat. Flat by anybody's standards, thought Gene.

It was his last Sunday at Oxford also, and as he strolled along the narrow grey pavement, looking for an open teashop, he began trying by force of habit to summarize the whole experience for an imaginary article he might possibly be asked to write when he got home. 'A Sunday in Oxford,' he began typing it out slowly in his mind's eye, 'while the students—or as they prefer to think of themselves, undergraduates—of Oxford worshipped in their historical churches, the young American dealt himself a hand of poker face-up on the snowy bosom of the Sturdley camp-follower, and asked himself if he wasn't somehow missing something that Oxford had to offer.' A racy opening, a little hot for the *Plainsville Sentinel*, perhaps.

He glanced absently at the shop windows to his left : a truss and a pink artificial leg, half-smothered in dust; a bowl of pallid boiled sweets, surrounded by knitting magazines and faded picture postcards of the seaside—a fat lady in pink bloomers diving gaily into the sea, a tiny bald man peeping surreptitiously into the ladies' bathing huts. The grey, authentic face of urban Britain, and only a mile or so from the dreaming spires.

All the shops looked as if they had been shut for years and years. The tobacco shop was especially abandoned, with a pile of empty milk bottles in front of it and an 'Oh, what's the use' window display : yellowing magazines and balls of wool and another helping of boiled sweets; aloof in one corner as if it was pretty damn important stood an artificial pack of cigarettes with a crack down the middle. No trace of American salesmanship or high-pressure vulgarity, anyway—just the depressed middle classes going unobtrusively about their business.

He found an open tea shop at last, and moved in. A gloomy waitress in a faded pink dress came up, slopping tea carefully into a saucer. 'You want a cup of tea?' It looked as if she had been carrying it around all morning, waiting for someone to claim it. Fosdick took it and asked for some buns. 'We're all out of buns.' 'I'll have some cake then.' 'We don't have no cake on Sundays.' She wiped his table absently with a tea-stained rag. There were long thin stripes of tea when she had finished. 'You got some toast?' asked Fosdick. 'I'll see. We don't expect people to come in on Sundays.' 'Why do you bother to open on Sundays?' asked Fosdick. 'Lord knows,' said the waitress with an unexpected smile : she could see the humour of this.

'The townspeople of Oxford', thought Fosdick resuming his informal article, 'are on the whole very miserable, being, to put it mildly, an out-group, and acutely conscious of missing something. But then, who, if anybody, is getting this something that everybody else is missing?'

The café door pinged, and Alan Browning came in at a saunter. 'Have you got any fags, Marjory?' he asked from the doorway. The waitress turned around and shook her long melancholy head. 'We haven't got any cigarettes and I'm not Marjory. She has Sundays off.' 'Oh well,' said Browning, 'anyway.'

He stood there irresolutely, looking at the girl, making his calculations. He hadn't noticed Fosdick a few feet away. 'I'll just have some tea then, Betty,' he said at last, and like magic the girl smiled. 'Why haven't I seen you before, Betty?' he asked quickly. 'Why have they tried to keep you from me?' The girl put the dirty dishcloth in front of her mouth to hide a spasm, then twisted round and hustled into the kitchen with a surprising burst of animation : Browning had somehow managed to galvanize her into brief, misleading life.

Fosdick smiled to himself. It always amused him to watch Browning's old-fashioned techniques, and their no less old-fashioned success. 'Just getting in a little practice, eh kid?' he asked, and Browning jumped. 'Good Lord, man, don't shout like that, whoever you are.' His eyes looked puffy and slow coming into focus. 'Why it's one of our friendly invaders, Senator Fosdick no less. I sure am pleased to meet you, sir.'

He sat down at the table and rested his head on his hands. As usual, after a good night's sleep, he looked dissipated, in a good-humoured way, and triumphantly venal, in a good-humoured way : a small face, especially small at this time of day, noticed Fosdick, cheap-looking but kindly, a carnival barker or a salesman for patent medicine maybe. The sort of fellow a dim sort of girl would trust too far because he obviously meant no real harm.

'Have a bad night?' he asked.

'Yes, rather,' said Browning languidly. 'She didn't half kick and struggle.' Browning made it a point never to admit to a wasted evening, and never to deny a rumour.

'I hope it was worth it,' said Fosdick. He liked Browning and liked to see him doing well with his second-rate girls.

In his second term at Oxford they had taken tutorials together in philosophy, and he had been dazzled and impressed by Browning's easy bored grasp of every new tortuosity. Alan's weekly essays were less than half as long as his own, and much more than twice as pregnant. The fellow might look cheap and rather commonplace, but chance had dealt him a respectable brain, all the same. Away from the tutorials, there was never the slightest hint of it : shake and rattle him as you might, you couldn't get anything of the slightest value out of him. At first, Fosdick used to invite Browning to tea after their tutorials, with a view to picking his brains : 'Look, Alan, I'm on your side about sex, no kidding—I'll sign a statement—I'll contribute to the fund—anything. But tell me don't you *ever* get just a tiny urge to talk about something else, just now and then?' 'Why, I thought Americans liked to talk about sex,' Browning would say in an injured voice. 'You told me so yourself, old boy'—it was a wilful kind of self-mutilation. 'You goddamn buffoon.' Fosdick very seldom lost his temper, but cheezt— 'Wasting a first-class brain on all this goddamn, third-rate dirty-minded drivel. Hell, you'd expect a family of inbred hillbillies to keep up a higher level of intellectual content. . . .' Browning fluttered his eyelashes : 'Why Eugene ! I didn't know you felt that way about my brain'—it was hopeless. The law of averages had given him the brain—it didn't mean anything. He was really very modest about it, and not very interested. His evangelical fervour lay in another direction altogether.

Well, what about politics—surely everybody was interested in politics? 'That was my last area of self-conquest,' admitted Browning. 'I must admit that right up to the end of last term, I underwent spasms of involvement. But thank God, I'm all right now.'

'Can you remember any of the symptoms?'

'Well, I thought, and still think that the Establishment is pretty bloody, and I used to go, off and on, to the Labour Club meetings. But one saw the futility even then. . . .'

'You mean the Labour Party betraying its principles and all that?'

'Oh, bugger its principles. It was seeing the same row of shiny, noncomformist faces—moral uplift, Christian behaviour, the blooming lot—that did the trick. Why, the women were even more respectable than the Conservative bags, if you can imagine. Dawn of a new age, my Aunt Fanny. . . .'

'Yes, but a social revolution—if that's what you want—has to start somewhere.'

'I daresay. However, as the saying goes, what am I going to do tonight? Then I found that Godfrey Hook was working against the revolution over at the Conservative Club, and that we were only cancelling each other out, so to speak. In the circumstances, a pact of some sort seemed to be indicated—and I really haven't given the matter a thought since.'

'But dammit, man, you're reading Politics up here.'

'Yes, silly isn't it? Still, one has to read something I suppose. And of course, no line of study could further underline the futility of one rather sluggish individual's beating his arms for or against the current. Now, with a woman, one can achieve certain tangible results . . . not cosmic, mind you, but by Jove, tangible.'

All the same, Fosdick liked him for what he felt to be certain native qualities. His tastes might be a bit exotic for an Englishman: but his methods of indulging them were typically English —direct, unsqueamish and, of course, unfailingly good-humoured. There was a firm base of middle-class solidity, even respectability to his capers: a warmhearted suggestion of lechery among the tea things, against a cosy background of humorous landladies and patched sofas and dirty songs around the fireside. In Plainsville, a fellow could talk himself blue in the face about the intrinsic wholesomeness of free love, variety, et cetera: but one never felt quite right about it. Neither ribaldry nor earnest philosophizing ever quite washed away the tiny, persistent stain, or anæsthetized the pre-Freudian twinge; a disembodied sense of sin lingered on defiantly, like the smile on the Cheshire Cat. But over here, among comfortable chaps like Browning and Chote, the whole problem seemed to take care of itself quite delightfully. Eros became, with their kindly encouragement, as domestic and conventional as the notorious hot-water bottle: a Saturday night tranquillizer, a blood-cooler, a matter of calmness and pipe-smoke.

In his first term, he asked Browning for some practical advice about English girls, and Browning either was, or pretended to be, surprised: 'Good Heavens, Eugene, not you! I've always thought that you were above that sort of thing.'

'I sure hope I'm not. What made you think a thing like that?'

'I don't know. You scholarly Yanks always seem to be so bloody dignified and antiseptic.'

'When you get to know us a little better you'll find that we have our moments.'

'Yes, I suppose you must. I heard some Rhodes scholars talking bawdy under my window once, and I couldn't have been more surprised if I'd come across a couple of parsons swearing. Big, majestic chaps in glasses—it just didn't seem right, somehow. I only hope they didn't understand what they were saying.'

'Well, this is a nice change. We're usually accused of the exact opposite.'

'Oh, I'm only talking about the scholars. They seem to constitute a special, yes, antiseptic class—high-minded rulers in rubber gloves. Naturally, they encourage the sweaty masses to breed from morning to night.'

After which he gave the information, spotty but copious, and Fosdick had been spasmodically following it up ever since. The two of them shared a casualness of standards, a willingness to subsist indefinitely on a diet of mashed potatoes and gravy, and only a few girls on Browning's list turned out to be completely unsatisfactory. They were on the whole a serviceable and compliant crowd, and Fosdick only wondered why his friend went to such pains to woo these comparatively easy marks.

Browning looked up when the waitress brought his tea. 'Ah Betty. My enchantress.' She stood there expectantly. 'Was there anything else you wanted?' 'Only the warmth of your smile,' purred Browning. Fosdick found it hard to believe that this was going on in the twentieth century. The girl giggled and wiped the table again with her rag. Heaven knows how long it had been since she had had so much fun.

'You never know when she might come in handy,' explained Alan. 'One must lay up one's stores.'

'Well, never mind about that. I wanted to ask you something—'

'Yes, old boy?' Browning was all charming attention.

'I was just wondering. I've been here for two years, but I don't seem to have gotten anything special out of Oxford, if you know what I mean. I know there's something here, because I've read about it. But I seem to have missed it myself. After two years, I'm still a camera-souled tourist.'

'So what's your question, old boy?'

'Well, that's it. You've been here for three years. Have *you* gotten anything out of Oxford?'

'Good Lord, I don't know. I've never thought about it. No, I don't suppose I have. I daresay one would have been equally drunk and fatuous anywhere. As a matter of fact, it's pretty much the same sort of life I lived in the Army, and at school too—only with broader vistas, of course.'

'Well, what about your friends—guys like Chote and Hook? Have they gotten anything out of Oxford?'

'Well, Chote got a scholarship, the jammy bastard, but I don't suppose that's what you had in mind. Godfrey Hook has had a breath of fresh air, after a life in the family parsonage— please God, he'll go on from there. But you can't really give Oxford any credit for that.'

'I hate to mention it, but what I had in mind was the famous Oxford culture, the English Athens and all that crap.'

Browning looked a bit blank. 'Er, yes, I know what you mean. No, I can't say I've come across anything like that. My fault entirely, of course—'

'Don't feel badly about it, old man,' said Fosdick pleasantly. 'All the same, I wish I could get hold of some of this culture to take back home with me. I haven't got too much time left, just one more day. Do you know anybody who could direct me to where they keep the culture around here?'

'Maybe your friend Bradshaw Soames could tell you. He's probably made a note of it somewhere.'

Fosdick waved this aside: he didn't go in for making jokes about Soames. 'I guessed I should never have gone to Sturdley if I wanted culture.'

'That's true, of course. We haven't got any real Oxford men at Sturdley, except perhaps the Warden. When he puts on his straw hat and his shorts and his mackintosh, I can't help feeling that he genuinely belongs here—although, mind you I've heard ugly rumours that he isn't *really* eccentric at all. But most of the chaps are redbrick through and through. Civil servants and Anglican deans, the bloody lot of them. Thank heavens I'm going into trade myself. If they'll have me.'

'Do you think that maybe the whole thing is an elaborate hoax, that there really isn't anything here to get?'

Browning yawned. This was getting entirely too far from the important things. 'I really don't know. I think the chaps who throw bread at each other down at Black's may get something out of Oxford, and the women who smoke cigars, and all the numberless weeds who dive fully clothed into various bodies of water up here—I expect they all get something, though I haven't the faintest idea what. Anyway, they're the ones who write the delirious books about Oxford when they go down.'

This obviously had nothing to do with Athens. It could go on just as well at Lord Squashhead's estate or at Tootle's American Bar, or any damn place where there was bread to throw and water to dive into. Fosdick was no wiser.

For some time, Browning had been watching the kitchen for signs of the girl provisionally named Betty. But she had apparently disappeared for the day, having had all the jollity she could handle at one time. He got up and licked himself all over, in spirit. 'I'd better be getting back to the digs; you never know who's likely to be dropping in. Coming to the J.C.R. tonight?'

'Why not?' said Fosdick. 'I'm in the bloody show aren't I?' After two years, the word was irresistible.

'Of course, of course. Well I'll be seeing you then, old boy. So sorry to see you reduced to places like this. Bad luck on the Stock Market I suppose.' Twitter, twitter, twitter, thought Fosdick. The national noise. 'So long, Alan.' He watched his early influence sauntering past the smoky window. It was true. Browning had long ago made him realize that philosophy was largely a waste of time (all the systems would be exploded next week anyway), thus freeing him for other pursuits. If a guy with his brains can't see anything in it, he had thought at the time, what the hell am I beating *my* brains out for? . . . Let's all give up and go fishing.

He put down sixpence and went out. In a couple of minutes he was back in the girl's room without cigarettes. 'Oh, Gene.' Her face creased with asymmetrical disappointment. He lay on his back and shut his eyes. 'Sorry, honey. How about a game of cards instead?' He fell asleep while she was dressing and he didn't hear her going out to look for cigarettes.

'The college bar was built by Thomas B. Sturdley in 1357. The rest of the college went up two hundred years later.' The tourists from Liverpool looked narrowly at the glib undergraduate. He might just be telling the truth. Oxford was such an extraordinary place. 'The first Warden was a very eccentric man. There are many famous stories about him. For one thing, it seems that he used to take regular leaps from the roof of the chapel, flapping his gown like wings, in an early attempt to fly. Frontiers of knowledge and all that. On one occasion. . . .' The tourists peered dreamily about them. The creeper fluttered gently on the walls, and a wasp buzzed in and out in the warm, musty sunshine. They had picked up this young windbag at the great oak door of Sturdley, and given him sixpence per head to tell them all he knew. It was a tranquil day, and they weren't paying much attention to the chubby dragoman, who was striving so energetically to give them their money's worth. For him it was a felicitous form of valedictory. 'Every year on Chapter Day, thousands of rolls of lavatory paper are dropped through the skylight of the Senior Common Room, a time-honoured custom' . . . 'The statue of Sir Thomas Sturdley is painted bright yellow every Candlemas; the tourists nodded and shuffled their feet. 'Easily the third oldest chapel in England.'

'Don't believe him,' whined a voice. 'We im*plore* you not to believe him.'

'Shut up, Browning. Don't pay any attention to this oaf, ladies and gentlemen.'

'On bended knees,' chimed in Hook, 'we implore you to ignore this man. He is thoroughly and dangerously ignorant.'

'Oh for Godsake, you blokes,' said Chote, momentarily helpless.

'What's the matter, John? Are we interrupting your notable tour of the Stately Homes?' said Browning.

'This chap is famous,' confided Hook. 'For sixpence he'll take you absolutely anywhere—to the bloody moon if you like.'

'Try to be a bit of use, you idle swine, and tell me how old this very, very old chapel is,' tried Chote.

'Don't you remember, John, all those workmen hammering outside your window last year? Filthy noise, but well worth it of course. Most up-to-date chapel in Oxford. Well—er, see you later, John.' And off they scurried with hands in pockets. The tourists were looking blanker than ever. 'Magnificent humorists,' said Chote. 'Genuine Oxford wits, in the real old tradition.' The tourists looked up at the sky and down at the ground. Chote hadn't the heart to go on. 'Well, that about wraps it up. Very ancient bar, statue of Sir Thomas Sturdley. . . .' His voice trailed off, and he stood dismally to one side as his audience, decent middle-aged people with mackintoshes and umbrellas, trooped silently out. They seemed a little reproachful, and one wanted to go up to each in turn and shake hands warmly, tell them not to lose heart. 'Dashed impertinent,' he could almost hear them mutter. Perhaps they had been injured before by cheeky undergraduates: 'Think themselves so dashed superior'; they would none of them come to Oxford again, thanks to those thoughtless clods. The sixpences rattled dismally in his trouser pocket, like so many unearned pieces of silver.

It was the day to make peace with one's gods and god-substitutes. About a third of the undergraduate population was having its last Sunday in Oxford—if ever they came back, it would be quite sadly different—and Sunday was the day when Oxford was most completely itself, being, that is to say, at its vaguest. A number of them looked about searchingly, asking themselves, like Fosdick, what they had missed. Most of them had wasted time there—but perhaps that had been the correct thing to do after all. Some of the few who had really worked hard wondered if they also had missed some of the point; and several of these rushed down to the river, like so many lemmings, and hired punts, to catch up with whatever it was, at the last minute. Up and down the river they heaved themselves, and then sat restlessly under the weeping willows, their hands and eyes baffled without books. Was this it?

Browning and Hook went bravely to the river with a couple of nurses, but they too were restless, trying to get too much out of the occasion. Chote took a long bicycle ride by himself, and lay supine on a hill covered with daisies, his mind a slightly troubled blank, a grey, twitching screen. Bill Gosworth sat in his room and stared at his old lecture notes. The neat black folders full of notes and essays were piled high, ready for a match, and he was going through them slowly and methodically. It was no use, of course. They only let you take Schools twice, then they branded the word failure on your bottom and sent you scampering out into the world. 'Just as well, probably. Wouldn't make any difference if I went back every year'— the stifling room, the men in black, the dazzling white paper, the clock ticking sarcastically—'I'd probably crack up every blooming time.' Might as well burn the bally notes, they're no use now. Four years of damn hard work, and not one bloody thing to show for it, not even a little card saying 'He tried'. One might as well have spent the four years in the Foreign Legion. Well then, forget Oxford, start again. Lots of great men had made up for a start like this. Hard work was more important than strong nerves any day. And sensitivity had its values, hadn't it ? One couldn't remember what they were, off hand— but anyway, for immediate consolation, nothing like Schools would come up again in the course of a long lifetime. . . .

'Ah-ha, what makes you so sure?' The elements of terror were always to hand : tests, clocks, stuffy rooms. One had managed all right at school—but it was just for fun there; and Mr. Thornbery waiting outside to say 'I know you tried, Gosworth.' And he did and one had.

One famous man, now who was it, wrote all his answers in verse, and of course they ploughed him. Another one had an appointment with his publisher, and just couldn't be bothered to turn up for Schools. But those fellows *didn't* care. 'It's no use trying to convince myself that I didn't care. I would have bloody well sold my soul to get a degree.' He continued to leaf through the bland notes. And there on the desk perched Mr. Gosworth himself (he took an angry photograph), founder of Gosworth & Sons Limited, Importers. Blasted cocky old phantom. Nerves of steel—but no sensitivity, so one pitied him really.

A few people, the men with missions, were at the other end of the spectrum. They were already working confidently for the future by way of such things as civil service exams, quite oblivious, as usual, to the thick sweet tangle of creeping nostalgia in the air.

For the permanent residents of Oxford it was just another Sunday. The Warden of Sturdley was racing blithely around the countryside with a butterfly net, while the Chaplain was spending a quiet, unemphatic afternoon at home. Daphne Collins was tidying her room for the second time, and writing to her mother. 'Term is coming to an end,' she wrote thoughtfully, measuring her words like spoonfuls of tea. 'It should be a quiet summer, a bit wetter than usual. Although we have had a few nice days of course. I am enclosing the usual two pounds. . . .'

Evening gathered slowly, bringing even more peace to the nearly torpid city. Undergraduates began to drift from all directions into the college lodge, where they could lounge about together and examine the unchanging notices on the bulletin board. Sunday dinner was the closest thing to a decent meal that the college ever provided, and elderly graduate students, lonely and profound figures only dimly connected with Sturdley, bicycled in from miles around to have a hopeful stab at it. They stood about silently adding tone to the place, talking to each other in whispers, or trying half-heartedly to read over the heads which clustered in front of the bulletin board. Occasional tourists who had strayed courageously from their parties peeped nervously in through the oak doors and scurried off.

The college bar, in contrast, was off and humming. The afternoon's theodicy had given the undergraduates a parching thirst, and they were trampling eagerly over some distinguished Sunday night visitors in dinner jackets who had made the mistake of getting to the bar first.

'Dashed bad manners, this post-war crowd,' said one of them.

'I don't mind bad manners so much,' said a second, 'but these chaps haven't got the *style* that we used to have.'

'That's true enough, by George. Bad manners ought to be an art. If you can't manage them with style, you might as well drop the whole thing. Don't touch it.'

'In my day,' resumed the second, 'we used to break every pane of glass in the quad every single night. Now that had style, if you like. The townspeople used to admire us for it. Even the dons used to admire us for it. I remember sitting with the old Warden one evening listening to the tinkling glass. He said to me, "I miss *your* distinctive note, Mr. Inglenook-MacKenzie." Of course, we could always afford to pay for the damage the next day. *Watch* out you clumsy oaf.' Beer was dripping down his black shoulder.

'Sorry, sir.'

'Sorry, sir!' mumbled Inglenook-MacKenzie angrily to his friends. 'At least he might have had the style to go through with it. We never apologized to anybody for anything in my day.'

His friends were looking a little nervous now, as if wondering whether even they had enough style to suit Inglenook-MacKenzie. 'Scruffy-looking lot,' muttered one of them hopefully.

'Well if you want my quite candid opinion,' said Inglenook-MacKenzie, in a low, confidential voice, 'I'm not all that sure that this present Warden is quite what we mean by the sort of thing, eh? If you follow my meaning?'

'Quite, quite. Just look at the kind of people he's letting into the college these days. Quite frankly, I don't know where he finds them. I've seen some faces down here that shouldn't even be allowed indoors. Fellows coming to dinner in sports jackets and brown boots. Never heard of dressing for dinner, most of them, I daresay. And some of the accents one hears, well bless my soul....'

'Quite,' said Inglenook-MacKenzie. 'The sort of chaps who used to come to Oxford on tourist buses before the war to watch their superiors at play—not that I'm a snob mind you. But there is such a thing as style, if you follow my drift.'

'Quite,' said a friend. 'It isn't even as if these chaps were *getting* anything out of Oxford. They're simply dragging the place down to their own scruffy level. One hardly recognizes the home of one's youth any more.'

'Quite,' said Inglenook-Mackenzie. He leaned intimately towards the barman. 'Tell me, Jack, how are the sales of port these days?—that's the acid test, you chaps. Are they drinking much port these days, Jack?'

'Hardly a drop, sir,' said Jack. 'Nobody can afford port these days. Even the dons.'

'There you are,' said Inglenook-MacKenzie, turning round triumphantly. 'What did I tell you? Hardly a drop of port, Jack says.'

'Chaps without the money to do it properly shouldn't come to Oxford in the first place.'

'I think I'll be pushing on,' said Inglenook-MacKenzie meaningly. 'Are you coming, William?'

'Yes, I think I've had about enough, Ian.'

And the group turned and shouldered its way distastefully through the howling mob of inferiors.

Nearly everybody else was trying to decide whether to go to the J.C.R. that night. The Junior Common Room of Sturdley offered a species of wistful vaudeville woven into a business meeting every Sunday night, to which nobody ever really wanted to go. The business was genuine, but trivial—note-paper, soap, lavatories that didn't work—and so bogged down with pleasantries that most of it had to be settled elsewhere. But on the last Sunday of term, there was always a feeling abroad that the J.C.R. might be a little better than usual that night, and quite a number of undergraduates piled reluctantly into the common room.

They began to feel misgivings right away, and then resentment. The show was late and most of them had to stand in the back, swearing and jostling with other frustrates. 'Why are we waiting, why are we waiting?' they chanted peevishly. The officers flung open the door at last and straggled in behind their beer mugs. The one in front was wearing a chain of corks, culminating in a corkscrew; behind him came a man with a toilet seat draped roguishly around his neck, representing the spirit of Comedy, Sturdley division; and behind these marched the men of distinction, the Secretary, Treasurer and President, in dinner jackets and complex chains of office and loud American ties with hand-painted nudes which a former officer had brought back from America a few years before. The audience wailed dismally as they sat down.

'Order! Order!' said John Chote, the President. 'The time being seven-forty-five precisely, I declare....'

'It's bloody eight-thirty if it's a day,' said a voice from the back.

Everyone began shouting 'Sconce.... Sconce.... For God-sake sconce that man.'

'Order! Order!' said Chote. 'Is it the will of this Society that Honourable Member Chatwind be sconced?'

'Yes . . . yes. . . . For Godsake yes.'

'No,' said Chatwind.

'It is the will of the society that Honourable Member Chatwind be sconced.'

There was a hum of satisfaction. 'No,' said Chatwind again.

A large pot of beer was brought out. Chatwind braced himself. If he could drink the whole of it without removing it from his lips, he wouldn't have to pay for it; such was the code of the sconce pot. He began to swill. Three pints or so later a cheer went up and Chatwind lowered the mug with trembling hands. He rose slowly, stiff and purple, to be cheered all the way to the door and just beyond.

The meeting hadn't even begun yet. Chote felt nervous. The yahoos were in an ugly mood tonight. It was still 7.45 P.M. precisely. Godfrey Hook read the minutes of the last meeting in a high voice. 'As curfew tolled the knell of seven-forty-five P.M. precisely the lowing herd wound slowly into the J.C.R.' Godfrey really cared about his minutes. He had all week to prepare the jokes, which gave them a kind of threadbare polish which was usually quite popular enough. But there was dyspepsia abroad tonight.

'Get on with it, you idle bugger,' roared a voice. 'Your nine months are nearly up.'

'I'm trying to,' said Godfrey grimly. He was no good at answering these chaps quickly. Voices rose, taunts, demands for explanations. He hurried on.

'Is it the will of the Society that I sign these minutes as a true and accurate record of what took place at the last meeting?' said Chote at last.

Only four people had attended the last meeting, so the minutes were allowed to pass with nothing worse than a 'Must have been a jolly exciting meeting' groaned from the back. Godfrey sat down, puzzled, frowning to himself, but glad to be out of it.

Private business proceeded slowly and stormily. The captains of the sports clubs gave their reports, frequently interrupted by unexpected cheers and moans, and demands for inquiries, which were but partially understood by the stolid athletes.

The captain of chess made his annual saucy speech embroidered around such themes as pawnography, chess bawds and stalemates. The captain of chess always received sympathetic attention, because he had been trying for several years to raise a Sturdley College chess team, without success, and he had little to savour in life beyond his annual speech. But tonight he too was sacrificed.

The trouble seemed to be coming from one corner at the back. Bill Gosworth was standing amid a group of apprentice dandies, and he was whipping them to a fine froth. They began to press themselves on Chote now, questioning him about an obscure constitutional point. He stumbled and they were on him, picking eagerly at his chubby flesh. 'Sconce!' 'Sconce the bloody President!' 'Heads must roll!'

Chote strove manfully to contain the riot. 'Order! Order!' he said quickly. 'Is it the will of the house that the President be sconced? As it is *not* the will of the house that the President be sconced, we will proceed with any further business. . . .'

The Gosworthians continued to swarm and the air trembled with endless cries of 'Sconce!' a terrible and primitive sound. 'Order! Order!' said Chote. 'It seems to me that the house would only be bored with further technical discussion between Mr. Gosworth and myself concerning these abstruse points of law'. . . . Cries of 'We're not bored.' 'Go ahead and discuss it, you shifty sod'. . . . 'Therefore I am sending out for copies of the constitution, so that we can all follow the discussion fruitfully and with profit. Now is there any other business to occupy the meanwhile?'

Inglenook-MacKenzie had just sauntered in all unconscious, a dandy of bygone days, and was sitting jauntily in the ex-President's corner. He rose immediately to propose a three-point programme.

'I have recently come across a disgusting and loathsome habit of referring to undergraduates as students, instead of undergraduates. Now that may be all very well at the red-brick universities, and among our colonial friends, but it's not good enough for Oxford. Nothing like good enough. Oxford men are not *stoo*dents.'

Gosworth was already after him in full cry. But MacKenzie pushed on smoothly.

'That is my first point. And I think it's frightfully important.'

'Frightfully important,' echoed Gosworth.

'Now my second point concerns another loathsome habit.' Gosworth applauded: 'Cheers for this smashing man and his loathsome habits.' '. . . habit that I have come across since returning to Oxford for a few days. I have noticed references to "second-year" men and "third-year" men. This is all very well in the provincial universities. . . .'

'And in the bloody colonies, what?' said Gosworth.

'But not good enough for Oxford. Not good enough by half. We are *undergraduates* at Oxford.'

'Blimey, at your age too. You must have ploughed Schoolers more often than I have.'

Inglenook-Mackenzie hurried on. His third point was more in the nature of a forlorn appeal. 'Before the war we used to dress for dinner every night, and I think if the custom were resumed it would add a certain graciousness, a style. . . .' He sat back wearily, out of range of Gosworth's badgering.

After that, somebody wanted to allow women into the college bar. 'Oh, my God,' muttered Inglenook-Mackenzie. And somebody else wanted the college to subscribe to the *Daily Worker*. Inglenook-Mackenzie covered his eyes with his hand.

The copies of the constitution arrived and the rumpus started up again. There was something apocalyptic about Gosworth. He was all ablaze now. Godfrey Hook looked as if he would like to help if he could: but, Chote thought, his aunt had just died or something, was how he looked. Alan Browning, in the lavatory seat, got up and told an interminable dirty story involving an unusual alignment of stuttering foreigners. . . . Chote allowed him to go on for five minutes, over the agonized protests of the Gosworth faction, while he leafed through the constitution himself. Then he opened the floodgates and practically everybody in the house spoke about some small and ancient point he had discovered, and which he alone thought amusing and pertinent. Chote was in minor despair. The meeting was obviously going to last all night, and on top of that he was in serious danger of impeachment. If only he could manage to recite the magic words and blow out the candles, his troubles would be over. Nobody could make him light the candles; business would be buried for the year.

He tried to get another vote on the Gosworth amendment, only to be ensnared by the inspired Gosworth who had found a clause saying that a vote had to be taken at this point deciding whether they should vote. In a bemused ecstasy the house voted against voting, and Gosworth shot up his hand. 'According to Article 17b the house cannot vote again on whether to vote again until at least fifteen minutes have elapsed.' Chote sat back gloomily to see what Gosworth would do to him next. The constitution was buried in impregnable tradition— although, like the Coronation and the C. of E., it was only twenty years old, really.

Somebody got up to make an incongruous complaint about the shortage of lavatory paper in the college. This was real business. Alan Browning fingered his lavatory seat. 'Mr. Gadsby, sir. I'm simply at my wit's end trying to keep you in lavatory paper, that I am. I gave you a whole new roll only this morning. *What* do you *do* with it, Mr. Gadsby? . . .'

Norbert Jones, the only serious undergraduate in the room, spoke next. He had a large intense face, and he came to every meeting of the J.C.R. to raise significant points. His dedication was widely recognized, and every term the J.C.R. devised new minor offices for him to hold : 'assistant book watcher', 'bodyguard to the Chaplain' and so on. There was a show of hands for each appointment, and Norbert was invariably elected. And whenever he could find out what his new duties were, he carried them out with all conscientiousness.

Tonight he was speaking as representative of the International League of Students, a thankless post because the college was always voting to disaffiliate from the league and stop paying dues to it (a mere shilling a head); and it was up to Norbert to woo the college back over and over again.

'Think of the many advantages I.L.S. offers you,' he pleaded. 'Bicycle tours through Europe. Free accommodation at youth hostels, trips behind the Iron Curtain. . . .'

Norbert had put his foot in it again. 'I hear that I.L.S. is just a Communist front, Norbert. Is there any truth to that?'

'None at all.' His large face reddened. 'Absolutely none.'

The others had no idea whether I.L.S. had anything to do with the Communist Party or not. But they knew that the accusation never failed to arouse Norbert.

'We hear you have Communist leanings yourself, Norbert. Would you care to comment on that?'

'Who told you that? It's a wicked slander, utterly groundless.' Norbert was easily distracted and led away from his point.

'Then why are you always associated with such disreputable organizations? Can you explain that, Norbert?'

'There's absolutely nothing disreputable about I.L.S.,' he protested hotly.

'The man in the corner says we mustn't let them call us 'students', either, Norbert. How about "International League of Undergraduates" instead?' Anything was good enough to throw at Norbert.

'You don't have to be called "students" if you don't want to,' answered the solemn Norbert, redder than ever, spectacles shining. Chote intervened and asked for a vote on whether Sturdley should continue to do business with the International League of Students. Out of affection for Norbert several hands went up, and nobody had the heart to vote against him. The house often fluctuated in this way between cruelty and sentiment.

It was time to vote again about whether to vote on the Gosworth amendment. Gosworth announced that he had yet another important speech to make, and he began to filibuster in a travesty of an American accent about the menace of Reds in government. He painted a tiresome picture of the sinister clique that had risen to political power in the J.C.R. 'Chote, Browning, Hook—look at them, helping each other up the ladder of success, and pulling it up behind them. Can any of you remember a time when Chote wasn't holding some office or other? He says he does it for the sake of the community' (Chote had never said any such thing) 'but I say that he has nothing less than a Cæsar complex. Gentlemen, this little man thinks he's God.' People had had enough of Gosworth by now and they began to tell him to shut up; only disembodied phrases of his could be heard through the ensuing din : 'Big brother. . . . The people's party. . . . All power corrupts. . . . Throw the rascals out. . . . Rum Romanism and Rebellion.'

Chote took hasty advantage of the audience's sudden dissatisfaction with Gosworth. 'Order! Order! I see that Mr. Gadsby has something urgent to say. Possibly he wants more lavatory paper. Mr. Gadsby?'

Ralph Gadsby was a tricky man. 'Ah would just like to endorse ever'thin' my friend and colleague Senator Gosworth has said to yo'all this afternoon and in addition. . . .'

Chote ran his hands through his hair. He saw no end to this. Gadsby was already lapsing into a steady, long-winded English English.

'I should like to include the editor of the college magazine in Mr. Gosworth's crushing indictment of our degenerate society. Let's clean house, gentlemen. This decadent filthy rag is puttin' all kinds of *i*deas into the minds of our youth. . . .'

Unfortunately the current editor of the college magazine was Norbert Jones, and he rose heavily to answer. 'There is nothing decadent about the Sturdley *Stump*, nothing at all.'

'In that case, I would like the Honourable Editor to explain —if he can—the obscene drawing on page thirteen. What in the name of tarnation is *that* supposed to represent?'

'It's modern art,' said Norbert. 'It's meant to be an impression.'

'I think it's meant to be an insult to womanhood. And what about this monstrosity on page thirty-nine? Is that another impression?'

'Yes,' said Norbert. 'I think so.'

'A bloody dentist's impression, if you ask me. Of course, I know who's behind all this, the fine hand of Commissar Chote, and his "people's party", softening us up with this bourgeois muck, making us easier to push around, and generally confusing us. The shortage of lavatory paper is only another small symptom of the grand design, the five-year plan, to take over the whole of Oxford.'

Chote leapt to his feet.

'Commissar Chote wishes to announce that there will be no more subversive speeches this evening. The people's party will now hold a vote, and it will announce a suitable result, in accord with the true wishes of the people. After that, group gymnastics on the lawn.'

Chote had not entirely wasted his time climbing up the ladder of power in the J.C.R. He had at least developed an instinct for saving his skin. The house was quite happy to vote by now. Gosworth was carried out squirming by the captain of the rugby team, who was sick to death of all this talking. Gadsby kept prudently quiet, and the Gosworth amendment was rejected without further excitement.

'There being no other private business. . . .'

Gosworth popped his head in at another door, to demand his rights according to Article 43 of the constitution. Chote blew out the candles quickly and made a gesture at his tormentor.

'There will now be a short intermission for watering the college creeper, after which the Sturdley Players will present another edition of their famous follies. A cast of thousands. . . .'

Bradshaw Soames stood at the back, blinking through his thick spectacles, wondering, so everyone imagined, whether he could squeeze all this into his forthcoming novel about Europe : another vast tract of human experience—dons this time and 'students' and college servants, all awash in class and sex conflicts. Unfortunately for Brad's researches, there was only one recognized homosexual at Sturdley, and he never came to the J.C.R. And besides that, he was an American.

And here was that quintessential Oxonian Eugene Fosdick, lumbering in from the wings. The fattest man in college stood up centre stripped to the waist and beating an imaginary gong; Godfrey Hook roared like a lion; Ralph Gadsby posed proudly with his head in a picture frame. Fosdick was smoking a long cigar and waving a briefcase : all but invisible under, behind and inside a stetson, thick glasses, loud tie, camera, a lightweight suite and two-tone shoes, and on his chest a sign saying TYPICAL AMERICAN. ('Say, buddy, can you tell me the way to

Ahxford Cahlege?') Somebody brushed past Soames, a tiny man with the word TITTER pinned on his back, off and running through the audience, followed hotly by two giants in old-fashioned bathing suits: respectively, JOE THE BUGGER and JOE THE BUGGER'S MATE. Around this motley group a fragile entertainment was woven. The captain of rugger ambled about in his shorts with the name ORPHEUS tacked to his backside, while mysterious voices crooned ambiguous advice: 'Silence goes faster backwards, old boy' and 'Birds sing with their finger-tips.' Behind an invisible mirror he found Bill Gosworth crouched low behind appropriate shrubbery reading Groucho Marx jokes; Alan Browning in a padded housecoat playing the eternal feminine, John Chote in his undervest ('Call me a Polak, will you, you lousy stinking slob. Person comes from Poland's a Pole, not a Polak') and Ralph Gadsby once again. For twelve minutes or so they strutted and fretted in their borrowed feathers, and then off they all pranced, kicking rolled trouser legs in chorus, with Gene Fosdick closing the performance with a warning to drive carefully.

The meeting was over, and the clods rushed the piano and began singing their time-honoured bawdy songs. Soames watched for a while, then shook his head almost imperceptibly —nothing more for him here. Chote stayed behind to sing, wistful in his vest because now the excitement was over for good. Gosworth led the mob into a hymn, and out of that into a West Indian calypso. His eyes were blazing sharply, as if he wanted the hysteria to last forever. Browning came in wiping rouge from his cheeks, and he and Chote, Gadsby and Hook went off at last to the Rangoon Restaurant to postmortem the evening and pester the little waiters.

'One dal gosht, four plates, please Win.'

'But, sah, we cahn't do that.'

'Why on earth not? You don't want us to take our custom elsewhere, Win?'

The waiter shrugged unhappily. He wished they would.

'Haven't I always been your friend, Win?'

'Yes, sah.' He hadn't got more than a shilling in tips from the four of them in three years.

Gadsby, who had been stationed in the Far East, said a few words in Burmese. The waiter answered miserably. Gadsby was brisk and friendly. 'Now just give us one dal gosht and four plates, will you, Win? That's a good fellow.'

'Sorry sah. Owner says you don't order four meal, you don't take up four chair. Hungry people waiting downstairs.'

'But we're special friends of Mr. Maung.'

The owner came over finally, a plump, smiling Karen. They insisted on shaking hands with him. He looked at them warily.

'We were just asking Win for one dal gosht and four plates.'

'I'm sorry, gentlemen. Four dal gosht, four plates.' He had to go through this practically every time Sturdley men came to his restaurant. Unfortunately, there was no way of barring them at the door.

'Aren't I a friend of yours, Mr. Maung? An old and valued friend?' said Browning.

'Yes sir. I value our friendship very deeply. But I value my custom even more than our friendship.'

They settled for two dal gosht and four plates, and then as soon as the smiling manager had disappeared, they asked the waiter for one coffee and four cups. This almost made him cry with vexation and they had to tell him they were only joking.

Over at a nearby table Inglenook-MacKenzie was talking to his friends. 'The college has turned into an absolute sewer. I tried to smarten them up a bit tonight, but it's quite hopeless. Absolute guttersnipes, the lot of them. Look at that crowd over there. Don't even know how to behave badly in a restaurant.'

'Quite. Either throw something at the damned waiter, or leave the chap alone I say.'

'Quite.'

The evening was straggling to a close. Gosworth had just finished drinking all the flat beer that was left in the J.C.R. and was weaving over to the Rangoon in his Groucho Marx regalia. He staggered halfway up the stairs and bumped blindly into one of the waiters. '*Watch* where you're going, for Godsake.' At the top, he bounced off the owner. 'Stand aside please. Next queue for tickets.' He plunged into the restaurant bellowing, 'Where are the chaps?'

'My God,' said Inglenook-MacKenzie. 'They don't even know how to get drunk any more.'

Gosworth pulled a chair over to Chote's table and looked around for trouble. 'Isn't that the stuck-up chap, over there? the fourth Duke of Ponsonby. What have we got to throw at him?' The waiter came over. 'Oh just bring me an empty plate, Win. I'm dining lightly this evening.' The waiter went off without a word to look for the management. Gosworth picked up a spoon and flipped it idly in the direction of Inglenook-MacKenzie, who was saying at that particular moment, 'Of course it's the same way throughout the whole confounded country these days—what the devil!'

'It was that thin chap over there,' said one of his friends hopefully. 'The drunk chap.' Inglenook-MacKenzie chewed his moustache in silence.

A moment later, and another spoon was whirring on its deadly way. Gravy splashed onto Inglenook-MacKenzie's sleek dinner jacket. His friends looked at him eagerly. For a second he looked a shade less decisive than usual. Perhaps he actually didn't know what an old-fashioned gentleman should do in these circumstances. His fingers tightened around his spoon and loosened again. No, he was too old to be throwing spoons in a restaurant. 'Confounded cheek,' he muttered instead.

His friends looked openly disappointed. They had trusted to him for a dashing unhesitating response. This was just the kind of situation over which a chap with his views ought to be able to exercise easy mastery. But what the deuce was a chap supposed to do? The line of his conversation this evening had given him certain responsibilities, but he couldn't make out what they were, in the heat of the moment. A fork landed in his lap. He rose quickly.

'My God, this is intolerable. Are you chaps coming?'

One could see that one's friends were still disappointed. Simply leaving the restaurant in a huff wasn't nearly forceful enough for a gentleman of the old school. Gosworth taunted him as he made for the exit. 'What these chaps need is a good horsewhipping,' he shouted. 'We'd have known what to do with them in the regiment, what?'

Inglenook-MacKenzie turned and went over to him, his face red with embarrassment. He wasn't going to disappoint his friends again. 'Would you care to step outside and settle this like a gentleman?' he said in a low voice.

'Can't you see he's drunk?' said Chote. Inglenook-MacKenzie brushed this aside.

'I'm asking him if he would care to step outside like a gentleman.'

'Certainly your lordship,' piped Gosworth. 'Always step outside like a gentleman. Never do it in the house.'

He jumped up before his friends could stop him and bounced merrily down the stairs, taking the last five at a leap, and into the street. He stood there panting under a street lamp, squaring up like an old-fashioned bare-knuckle champion. 'Come on out and fight, your grace. Avenge the family honour, and all that sort of rot.' Inglenook-MacKenzie came down slowly and purposefully. Chote was still trying to persuade him to spare Gosworth.

'You're at least twice as big as he is.'

'He should have thought of that sooner.'

'And twice as sober.' Inglenook-MacKenzie handed his coat to a friend and took a businesslike stance in front of the capering Gosworth. Chote saw that it was too late. 'Of course, you're only half as intelligent,' he said bitterly; but MacKenzie didn't hear him. He was already winding up a long, circuitous punch which was destined ultimately to land plump on Gosworth's breastbone. Gosworth staggered back surprised, and resumed his elegant stance about fifteen feet farther away from his opponent. His feet were beginning to shuffle sideways, and he was thumbing his nose menacingly. MacKenzie rushed at him and hit him ferociously in the face. Gosworth made no attempt to defend himself as blow after blow thwacked against forehead and collarbone, and he began to sink slowly to his knees. 'That's enough, you bloodthirsty blighter,' shouted Browning. Gosworth's nose was dripping and his eyes looked puffy, but he was still smiling, a Groucho Marx leer under pale street lights. MacKenzie stood over him breathing loudly through his thick moustache. Gosworth got up in a moment and MacKenzie clubbed at him again with clumsy ferocity. Gosworth's green velvet waistcoat was beginning to spatter and his cork moustache was drenched through, but he still managed to look remarkably natty. He went down, got up, went down, in a matter of seconds, smiling mechanically all the time. 'I'll-teach-you-to-insult-a-gentleman,' puffed MacKenzie, at pains to explain himself. Even his friends were telling him to stop by now. But before they could get their arms around him, Gosworth was lying face down on the ground moaning incoherently. The harlequinade was over.

'Have you had enough, you blasted sadist?' Gadsby and Browning were kneeling next to Gosworth. Hook was pale as death; Chote glanced at him nervously. Inglenook the Conqueror stood staring and breathing hard. His friends were already beginning to walk away stiffly. He had obviously disappointed them once again. Awkwardly, he made a peaceful move toward Gosworth.

'Get away, you bloody brute. Haven't you done enough damage already?' said Gadsby.

'I just wanted to see if he's all right.'

'He's still breathing, if that's what you mean. Now why don't you just go to hell, and leave him alone.'

Inglenook-MacKenzie walked away, slowly and heavily. Gosworth was moaning and crying. His Groucho Marx face was unrecognizable for slime and blood. The fire that had burned in him all evening had gone out at last. 'One of the best-natured blokes I know,' said Browning. 'I've never heard him say a malicious word about anybody,' said Gadsby. It was so seldom that one had an excuse to praise a friend like this. 'A damned good man,' said Chote. He caught sight again of Godfrey's tiny pupils and said no more.

They had to take Gosworth round to the hospital and leave him there. He was unconscious for two days. After that, he recovered slowly, but, for some curious reason, the fire never got going in him again. The rest of his life was a footnote, the kind of thing he was so bad at. His family found him unexpectedly dull and sad when he got home later that summer. His father didn't get angry with him for failing Schools: on the contrary, he offered to bring him straight into Gosworth & Sons Limited as a partner of weight. But Gosworth remained not especially elated by this and after two years of unrelieved gloom, nobody was too much surprised when he hanged himself in his bedroom. His Oxford notes were open on his desk. Mr. Gosworth, a man of abundant energy, started a lengthy letter to *The Times* even before the body was cold, demanding that the University hire a permanent psychiatrist, and that the 'Schools' system of examination be abolished at once. But the correspondence on this subject had, alas, been temporarily closed.

8. Going Home

HUNDREDS of men lined the platform, waiting for the train to London. Chote couldn't decide whether it was more like the last time he left boarding school, or more like waiting for the 8.32 to take one to work in the morning. Some of them were emphasizing the schoolboy motif, joking and even buying chocolates. Some of them were already embracing the sobrieties of civilian life, talking gravely and reading newspapers. A few were already sporting the bowler hats and tightly rolled umbrellas which would be their uniform for the next forty years or so. The train puffed in sleepily, fashionably late, and there was a brief stampede for the third-class carriages. The men with the bowler hats seemed to get most of the window seats, an omen perhaps. Chote and Browning were left standing in the corridor trying to keep their bags out of the way of the heaving migrants.

The train drifted out again, past the little graveyard which welcomes you to Oxford and sees you out again, out of sight of the dreaming spires and the gasworks. Chote could already feel his Oxford personality rattling away in the other direction. Browning was talking with enthusiasm about his theory of the different levels. There was the highest level of all which, quite candidly, he had never reached (the girls couldn't breathe or something). Several times he had rested within sight of the top. For the next few days in London he would be seeing how low he could go. The train shook rhythmically from side to side: 'How-low-can-you-go, how-low-can-you-go.' Chote rocked back and forth against the window....

'The Poplars', Pimlico, a two-storey house with several fingers of garden. His mother was crouching by the fire, like a domestic pet, down near the floor in a collapsed armchair dripping with antimacassars (one of five such chairs crowded into the tiny living-room) making tea. You could hardly see her at first because of the canary cage and the goldfish bowl on the table next to her. It was a dark room, with the red plush curtains drawn all day, and a fire going, and his mother making indefinite amounts of tea, enough for an army. To the left, there was the upright piano, long out of tune, with brown, sticky notes. It could only be got at by rearranging the furniture, but some evenings, when he was feeling relaxed, his father would fight his way over to it and bang out the old music-hall songs, and sing them too. When he wasn't so relaxed, he fiddled all evening with the enormous radio which had somehow been squeezed into the corner on the right.

The room always reminded one of an old curiosity shop. The brown singed walls were covered with faded pictures: a cottage in the country, a ship in full sail, the siege of Quebec, some flowers in a bowl, nobody knew where they had all come from. He believed that his father must have found most of them in the attic. Visitors always asked whether the beautiful woman with the low dress and the old man with the beard were ancestors; but they weren't. The mantelpiece was covered with little monochrome lithographs, stern, unfamiliar faces, most of which had been found either in the attic or among the remains of dead relatives in the north of England. There were five pipes in a little rack, and a pair of German bayonets crossed on the wall. Altogether, it reminded Chote of the pleasanter kind of Oxford digs. There was no point in deceiving oneself as to why one never brought any of one's Oxford friends home to see it, in spite of Mrs. Chote's open invitation.

His mother would look dog-tired when he came in, but she would hurry to give him his quart of tea and tell him the local news, while he stroked the cat and tried to follow what she was saying. After a while his father would come in and shake hands (his father had been shaking his hand since the first time he came home from boarding-school. It used to make his flesh creep in those days.) Unfortunately, Mr. Chote wasn't comfortable like the rest of the room. He sat on the edge of his chair, never sliding back into the cosy receptacle, and read his paper slowly, as if it were a penance, making his laborious comments as he went along. 'I see the price of tea is rising. I have a pretty good idea who's behind *that*,' or 'It says here the Yanks are giving us more money. Easy enough to see what *they're* getting at.' Chote had never seen his father read anything except the newspaper, but that he read with immense thoroughness, picking his way through motives and stitching together his cynical picture of the world and its ways.

The faded pictures on the piano were, of course, Mr. and Mrs. Chote stepping awkwardly out of the church, squinting in the June 1919 sunshine. His father had come back recently from the first war : in the picture he looked as if he had just got off the boat, a little bewildered but keen as mustard. His mother often went over the bones of the story, ' "Smiling Jack Chote" they used to call him at the works (though don't tell him I told you), always laughing and joking and playing his pranks—harmless you know, but *that* funny. He got ahead famously, and just because everybody liked him. Why, in no time at all, he was one of the assistant managers, just the same as he is today, and all done on personality. As you know, there was no education to speak of.'

His mother never admitted it in so many words, but the Smiling Jack Chote era was long gone. (Look at the square, worn-down face, grey as an old newspaper.) John could barely remember going with his father to the zoo, clutching the big hand which was just about as far above him as a strap in the tube would be now. His father had laughed then all right, hadn't he? All day long, and bought him two Walls ice creams, and sung songs on the way home. He was still a happy man, to all appearances.

But by the time John was ten, he knew for sure that the old man was stiffening up. For one thing, he took to wearing his Sunday-best suit—navy blue with stripes—all the time, including Saturdays. He seldom went out with John or his little sister Sheila any more—it was always time to be getting home for the news broadcast. He never missed the six, seven, nine and ten broadcasts; and John could remember trying to sit still (it was like listening to four sermons on one Sunday) watching back and forth his mother who was knitting patiently by the fire, and his father hunched over the wireless, his face tense and troubled. It began with the war, but carried over into peace. There seemed to be nothing in the world except news any more.

It was only after John had been going to boarding-school for a while that he conceived the crazy notion that it might be something about his own presence that made his father uncomfortable. Absurd, and rather conceited too : but whenever they were alone in the drawing-room there were those terrible long stretches of silence, while Mr. Chote played with his pipe, or went to his newspaper again. John might talk for a bit about what he was doing at school, but his father didn't attend too well; and pretty soon, John fell into the habit of piping 'Let's see if there's anything on the wireless tonight,' before the silence had time to settle on his nerves.

For a while he thought his father must be disappointed with him, and this was distressing indeed, because he had no idea what he could do to correct matters. No use trying to find out from his mother, because she evaded hinting questions nowadays, which only made things worse. She had always been candid before, in an off-hand way : if she had changed, it must be because of him : she must be worrying about him, too. One already felt guilty about certain things that had been happening at school, nothing really bad, just thoughts mostly, but perhaps his parents had found out about those? Adults, one knew, could hold on to secrets of that kind indefinitely, biding their time and driving a chap half crazy. The masters, for instance, certainly had a complete dossier on his case (thoughts and all) that would lead in time to secret, tactful letters to the parents, revealing the pertinent details, but at the same time recommending a common-sense approach to the situation. 'Don't frighten the boy. He's obviously going through a difficult phase.' One saw that a note came with one's report cards, and then one's father reading it thoughtfully, chewing over the nasty little problem with his breakfast.

Holidays became nerve-racking, and John took to staying at school for an extra week or two each term—not a bad dodge from several points of view: some of the softer masters were fatuously delighted with his industry; and then one had more time to loaf when the chaps came back, too. It wasn't until he was sixteen, and he ventured to disagree diffidently with one of the old man's glib cynicisms, that he learned the silly sad truth, or part of it. 'Perhaps the Americans really *do* want to help other countries. People with money sometimes feel guilty about it, you know, "conscience money" and all that,' he said. It might be fun, he thought, to launch a pleasant, academic discussion, as one did in the debating society at school (in fact he had recently used the very same argument there, with moderate success). He was sure that his father was right, of course, and he was prepared to accept whatever reasons Mr. Chote might put forward. Really, all he wanted to do was show that he too was drawing abreast of affairs.

His father had begun to make the restless fidgety movements of anger: 'Absolute rubbish,' he said, cutting into the table-cloth with his knife. John should have left it alone at that point, but he was genuinely curious to hear his father's reasons. It couldn't really be that the old man was having difficulty in meeting that wretched little argument—the one that Mr. Smathers demolished so utterly the day after the debate—no, of course not. 'But Father, people *do* do generous things sometimes, don't they? What about Britain in the first world war?' One knew half consciously that one was probing a nerve when one said this—his father thought of the last war as a real crusade, the only decent gesture of the century—but John was astonished by the roar of pain that followed. 'People who have a little education think they know all about everything!' shouted his father, flinging his knife onto the table with a tinny clatter.

John was shocked: he wanted to cover his face with his hands. So that was the trouble? Mr. Chote was already embarrassed by his son's morsel of education. It seemed incredible. His first instinct was to reassure his father right away, tell him that it didn't make any difference. But Mr. Chote hadn't left any opening for that. John went upstairs full of the painful excitement that goes with obscene discoveries; and he spent the night mapping out this new world of good and evil.

After that his father's fierce cynicism always had a pathetic ring to it, like the chime of a cracked bell, and for a while John made a point of agreeing with it and, so to say, clothing it. 'I see the miners are out on strike again,' his father might say, 'lazy blighters. Don't know the meaning of an honest day's work.' 'That's true,' John would come in quickly. 'I believe they produce about one quarter as much coal as their American counterparts. And of course, their American counterparts are probably lazy blighters too.' Exactly half the time it meant sabotaging his own embryonic convictions; but if one's father really had such a mystical reverence for the powers of education, then the least one could do, as the personification of said education, was to prop up the old man's insights with one's own learning whenever possible—and then of course, one didn't take one's own opinions as seriously as all that. What more could one do with them than give pleasure to others?

This phase didn't last long, because it seemed to make his father more nervous than ever; Mr. Chote would drop his subject in a trice and pick up the paper. He obviously felt unequipped even to agree with his son. With this discovery went all attempts at serious discussion. His father continued to make his grave pronouncements to nobody in particular, while John concentrated on being hearty and unaffected—'Look at me,' ran the legend. 'I'm not really educated at all. It hasn't worked in my case. I'm still one of the boys.' He talked for hours about

144

cars and soccer, which had once been enthusiasms of his father's, until he was exhausted and played out. He spent as little time reading as possible when he was at home and tried to get his father to play the piano more often, though without much success. ('The piano needs tuning,' Mr. Chote used to say.) He even allowed his accent to slip back a little into the pre-Brinkley vowels : thus forming a complex pattern of pretence which one slipped into now almost automatically, as soon as one pushed through the low door of the living-room.

Sometimes his father actually seemed to forget that his son belonged to the sapiential classes, and they fell to laughing and frisking as they had at the zoo. In this mood, they sometimes arranged hasty outings, trips to the seaside, football matches at Highbury, and so on; but then his father would suddenly remember again, and the ease and happiness would leave them both in mid-outing. John would never forget in particular the silent train ride back from Brighton on his twenty-first birthday. His father had suddenly come to his senses as they were having tea on the sands. A chance remark (something about Weltschmerz) had reminded Mr. Chote with a shock of his son's formidable attainments; and he was at a loss right away as to how to deal with this terrifying chap. It came on to rain, and they had to queue endlessly for tickets, while hundreds of babies squalled around them, and mothers whispered traditional words of despair to their improvident little boys. John said something about 'frightful kids' and his father said, 'Why, what's wrong with them?' You're putting on airs, perhaps, affecting to despise the man in the street. But then, it must all be very trying for an educated man. Mr. Chote didn't criticize, mind you . . . John hadn't the spirit to say another word, and they reached home without speaking again. At times like that, he heartily wished that he'd never even heard the word 'education'.

One could only feel wordless compassion. Mr. Chote had worked and saved to a point just short of backbreaking to give his son an expensive education, and to make himself miserable in the process. He must have realized that he could only go so far as Smiling Jack Chote; to go any further, he would need more sheer ability than he could dredge up from his system. Perhaps education would have turned the trick. Mr. Chote simply had no way of knowing.

Of course, his father wasn't even much use as a cynic, but absurdly, almost cloyingly kindly. The sarcasm was a time-honoured device for attaining easy social success, and none too convincing at that. There was really no bite to it at all. Smiling Jack must have found out at some stage that the cynical inter-pretation of events was generally admired; and it certainly didn't take much thinking. Perhaps he thought it would impress his boy too. 'Father may not be educated, but he's got a lot of shrewdness.' At least, nobody in the whole world was putting anything over on old Jack Chote: Roosevelt, Stalin, nobody. He was on to every trick.

Unfortunately, Jack Chote was a sensitive man, if not a specially bright one. He began to recognize at a glance the braying jackasses who would be invariably amused by his mechanical sarcasm, and whose laughter would drive him to further outrageous sayings. He must also have sensed that his son wasn't going to be one of these. Perhaps he began to see the small, self-satisfied eyes wandering as he talked on and on about world affairs: crikey, he's only twelve or so and I'm boring him already.

He must have learned a lot from the boy's face during the next few years. For instance he began to show real hatred for the cheerful title 'Smiling Jack'—it was obviously flashy and cheap. But then, what else was there? He could see his own defects flickering across the little boy's face, but that was all he could see: no remedies were there. John prided himself that his own face was under control now, almost impassive, but how mobile it must have been then. The first, and only day, his father came to visit him at school—the damned little face must have been contorted with embarrassment and fear. It was childish and forgivable: all the boys were ashamed of their parents for one reason or another. But what deep meaning had Smiling Jack Chote read into it? He had never had the chance to be ashamed of his own parents. It was no part of the ordinary course of nature as far as he was concerned: it must be that the boy was already noticing obvious traces of commonness and ignorance in his uneducated father. 'I'd like to meet some of your friends, Johnny.' 'Oh, you wouldn't like them, Father. Silly asses to a man.' The quick answer, lashing like a whip. Jack Chote could hardly be expected to understand that his son was ashamed of his *friends* too, that he was ashamed of everybody, in fact. He couldn't sympathize with the miserable boy, because his own period of nakedness was coming so much later in life. It was soon after that that Mr. Chote decided to cover himself permanently in his smart navy-blue suit. A stab of pain reached Chote across the years. But it was too late to do anything about it now. . . .

'I've enjoyed our little conversation very much,' said Alan Browning. The train was inching its way into Paddington Station. Browning had been talking about women for an hour and ten minutes. Chote rubbed his eyes. 'Did I say anything good?' 'You've had me in stitches all the way from Oxford.' They agreed to meet the night after next and go to pieces together in the old Viennese style. Blast his eyes, thought Chote mildly : he still had to perform tricks for him. Just once more anyway.

John took a bus. He could feel his London self expanding already, trickling through him like rusty sap. 'Thank you very much, ta, ta very much, *thank* you, ta,' hummed the conductor, walking up and down, 'sixpenny, ta, no madam, you should be going in the other direction. Sorry madam. I can't turn the bus round now can I? Next please, ta.' John felt easy and at home. It was a slight strain being an Oxford man, but one only realized it when it began to go away, often enough on board a London bus. 'It's no use coming to me. lady. You'll have to write to the company. Perhaps they can put you on the right bus.' The conductor looked at Chote mournfully, with a sad, shaggy wink. There was always somebody at hand to share the joys and sorrows. Chote smiled back half rude undergraduate, half unspeakable cockney. 'It's a disgrace, madam,' he said, 'more and more buses seem to be running in the wrong direction these days. One is almost tempted to change one's address.' The woman got off with a delicious sniff. 'I wouldn't be her husband,' said the conductor. 'Nor me,' said Chote happily, curling his toes.

He found himself sitting on the edge of his seat now, elbows on knees, ready for action. He used to sit like this with his mates, long before he'd even heard of boarding-school, a trial to the conductor or the passengers according to whim. He might have grown up to become a bus conductor himself, mocking the passenger with faint 'ta's' if his father hadn't worked so hard to make him something better. So instead he had become President of Sturdley J.C.R. and a fellow who played cricket with a ball of paper in one of the libraries at the celebrated University of Oxford. If only he had been able to make his father see how little difference was involved. Any smart bus conductor could have done with distinction the things that Chote had done best at Sturdley : handling the little revolution of Gosworth and Gadsby, for instance, would have been child's play to anyone trained on London buses. He, Chote, might know a little more about law than they did— but then they knew a little more about buses. As for shove-ha'penny and darts, who could say ?

When he got home, he found as usual that the picture was slightly askew. Through the shimmer of the fish bowl, he could see his father, not his mother, sitting by the fire, reading the paper and making the tea. It was rather unnerving : Mrs. Chote belonged in that chair.

'Good afternoon, son'—the formal handshake. 'We were expecting you to roll round sometime this afternoon.' His square face was glowing from the fire, and, seeing it for the first time after a parting, John thought it looked just a little fanatical.

'Where's Mother ?'

'She's not feeling very well. She went to the hospital for a check-up last week, and the blasted doctors promptly talked her into feeling ill. She's upstairs resting at the moment.'

'I hope there's nothing really wrong with her.'

'I'm quite sure there isn't. She's always been a thoroughly healthy woman. But, as I needn't tell you, that's one thing the doctors can never stand for. They take it as a professional insult.' He laughed mirthlessly. John could see now that his father's face might be a little strained from worry. 'Is that you, John?' a reedy voice came quavering down the stairs. 'Yes Mother—she sounds quite weak, doesn't she?'

'I think she's a bit run down. You know how hard your mother always works. And now the good doctors have made a full-dress case out of it.'

'I'm coming right down, John.'

'I'll come up.'

'No, I'll come down.'

She would begin to gather her hair into a bun, and then a wild tussle with the alien lipstick. She wouldn't be down for half an hour at least. He poked at the fire and stroked the cat. Funny how his father still made him nervous. I'm supposed to be the one that makes *him* nervous, he told himself.

'So you're going to Yankeeland, eh, son?'

'That's right,' and forthwith the advice to keep one's wallet nailed to one's drawers. But no, his father seldom advised him about anything any more. He kept his advice for the government, and the world at large, and the stolid brown 'grandfather' radio.

'Have you any idea what you're going to do when you get back?' How one hated this question and dodged it: both above and below one's father's station being out of bounds.

'Well, actually, no—actually. Perhaps I ought to join you in the tool business.' His father might once have wanted to have an educated son who would forge past him when the time came, to a directorship itself, but those dreams had been popped long ago. 'The tool business is no place for an Oxford man,' he said firmly.

'But Father,' once more for the road, 'lots of Oxford blokes would give their back teeth to get into a firm like yours, a steady firm. An Oxford degree doesn't give you any special advantages in business these days.'

'You underrate the advantages of a good education, son.' What's all this 'son, son, son' business, Chote wondered with nervous cruelty. Can he be trying to tell me something tender

149

and true? Mr. Chote made snappy tools, but as a fountain of wisdom he left a lot to be desired. Nervous and cruel.

'If anything, a university education is a liability these days,' John said. 'It means three or four years footled away completely, while the assistant office boys are surging up the ladder ahead of one. We have no special knowledge which can be applied directly to modern business. All we have is a species of seedy charm—and not all of us have that.'

'Rubbish,' muttered his father. He began to pluck at his newspaper. The *Daily Mail* had the answers to the boy's clever nonsense.

'On top of that, employers don't care for us much. They think that we're plotting to take over their businesses right away. They over-estimate our vitality quite sinfully.' I *am* laying down the law, aren't I? We come home from Oxford to educate our fathers.

'Poppycock,' said Mr. Chote. 'Education still tells, in every walk of life. And look at all the Oxford men on every level who will give you a helping hand as you go up and up and up. Why, it would be a sin against nature to waste you on the tool trade.'

Oh, very well, thought John. Just because of an absurd education fetish, he refused to recognize the possibility that he may have sired a clot. After all, even the tool people mightn't have one, if the thing were decided on a basis of talent.

'Treasure your education, my son. It is by all odds your most prized possession. Don't squander it and don't belittle it. Your mother and I have worked hard so that you could have the best—not that we begrudge it to you for a moment.' He had never heard his father talk like this before. Mr. Chote went on, awkwardly emotional, looking into the fire and talking fast. 'In fact we're quite proud of you, son. This Yank scholarship has meant a great deal to both of us. It means that our efforts have not been in vain. You have taken advantage of the gift we have given you.' John didn't know whether to laugh or cry. 'And America should be a grand experience for you too. It will open up new vistas, you will meet important people, make contacts'—the thin shell of cynicism was broken, and the softness inside was running, slopping, over—'There's no limit to your prospects, son. Why, some day I may be proud to be known as "John Chote's father".'

My God, he's cracking up at last, thought Chote unhappily. He's not himself. 'John Chote's father'—what a moth-eaten ambition. It meant the dreariest kind of surrender. The old man was already thinking about the writing on his tombstone. Up to now, John had thought of himself as a kind of unwilling rival, but now, suddenly, his father had collapsed and given up the game. Henceforth, he was going to concentrate on (just think of it) being proud of his son. Was it something the doctors had told his mother? Or was it some new discouragement at the works?

'I wouldn't count too much on that, Father. At least, you're good at *some*thing. I haven't proved myself at anything at all,' and off-hand : 'By the way, how are things at Bingham and Weekly? Business better than ever?'

'All right,' said Mr. Chote. He never discussed business with his son : it was his own private embarrassment.

'How is it that you're not working today?'

'It's Saturday, you young oaf.' It was a fortunate mistake. John kept laughing until he heard Mrs. Chote stumping slowly down the stairs. He trotted into the hallway and she leaned over the banisters to deliver a fragile kiss.

She was small and pretty, a little stooped, and inclined to hold on to things as she walked, although whether she needed to, John didn't know. Her square-looking husband and son piloted her thin body across the drawing-room, through the massed furniture : the armchairs, the canary cage, and round the table with the goldfish bowl. Her slippers flapped and the cord of her faded dressing-gown trailed along behind her.

The tea-drinking began in earnest now. John downed four cups while his mother dilated on the local situation. The people next door had moved, the people who had replaced them had parties every night, and what parties! A fellow in the flower bed, in his pyjamas, eleven o'clock in the morning, fancy. . . .

'But how *are you*, Mother?' asked John for the third time.

'Well truthfully I really don't know. The doctor said he would have to wait and see.'

'Isn't that just like a doctor?' said Mr. Chote. 'String out the case as long as possible, and Lord, how the money rolls in.'

'But Jack, I'm getting this attention on the National Health Service. Surely there isn't any advantage to them in working slowly?'

'I daresay it's just a habit by now,' said the elder Chote quickly. 'But then, on second thoughts, how do we know that they don't get paid more if the case can be made out to seem serious? Or look at it this way—since they get paid by the hour and not by the case, why shouldn't they go slowly?'

John looked at his mother. She seemed to be absorbing everything her husband said, weighing it, accepting it. One could never be sure whether she was really listening at all. She had heard so much of this kind of talk over the years. She poked the fire and poured the tea and answered 'Yes dear', 'That's true, dear.'

These little formulas took on a tragic note when something serious, like sickness, entered the cosy circle. His father preached his own kind of faith healing: ignore the doctors, and you shall be saved. His mother would probably follow his demented directions for the sake of peace. The result would be perfectly suited to the whole pattern of their life together. They would eventually die as they had lived.

Although John felt more at home with his mother, he hardly knew why. She looked intelligent, but most of the time worked at being conscientiously bird-brained, under the watchful tutelage of her pet canary. She couldn't *really* care about the neighbours' children going to the dentist for the first time, or who she found in the flower bed—but she wouldn't admit that she didn't care. She was as insincere as a bus conductor, or as, say, the Warden of Sturdley when he talked about cricket for two hours over tea, as if life itself hung in the balance; it was the Englishman fighting for his interior privacy, even against himself, with every weapon at his resource. Well, he himself knew what it was to play the fool so that people would leave him alone—but his mother, there was no simple accounting for his mother.

Of course, she must have changed too. When he was a child,

she was always very serious with him. She used to take him to church every day for visits, and on the way home she always explained about it. She must have explained it well, because he still went to church, didn't he?—even if it was only to listen to the organ and calibrate the parson's Adam's apple. He couldn't remember much about her explanations, but he hung on anyway, and she never talked about it now that he was grown up. Perhaps religion would come in handy later in life, a comfort, and he would be thankful that he'd stayed in tenuous touch with it. Perhaps his mother had told him that, too, once upon a time (although Mr. Chote knew what the parsons were up to, of course).

It was bewildering at first—this minute interest in the neighbours. He had come home from school during the nervous times, and she was waiting for him with the usual bucket of tea by the fire: and she talked and talked and talked, like someone burning up with fever. At first he was just a little bored and fidgety: '*Who* did you say the Bottomleys were?' but on she went, like someone reciting a lesson, and his discomfort became more precise. 'Why are you telling me about all these people?' he asked her. 'I think one ought to know something about one's neighbours,' she answered primly.

She redoubled her own churchgoing, but of course he was too educated now to share her simple theology. Both his parents knew better than to try teaching a Brinkley boy anything. And meanwhile her garrulousness spread itself like an unhealthy flush on the face of a consumptive. And for all his ability to analyse and patronize his parents, he had no idea why.

His father paused for breath, and his mother ventured a few wistful phrases: 'I'm sure you're right about doctors on the whole, Jack, but this Dr. Walker seems so nice and sensible. And he has such a nice family too. . . .' Her words had a bright tinny rattle. What sort of game *was* she playing? His father stared into the fire, not even pretending to listen.

'Of course,' she summed up her position carefully, 'you know more about doctors than I do.' One thing John knew: she must have made up her mind long ago to take her husband seriously: perhaps young Chote was outside at the time, wading in his gumboots—or perhaps it was even earlier, while he was squealing and snuffling at her breast in rubbery bliss. She was more intelligent than Jack (you could tell just by looking at her) and there must have come that critical instant when she knew it was to be a case of either laughing at him or accepting him. Of course there were bound to be mental reservations at first—she could just keep her own ideas to herself, that was all. But constant agreeing had worn her down and down, and her own ideas had been buried deeper and deeper, so that even she probably didn't know what they were any more.

This, at any rate, was an explanation he could understand himself. And then, no wonder Mrs. Chote had watched him with so much apprehension every time he came home from school with that much more information. He might, without even knowing it, take the path which she had rejected herself, and bring down the whole preposterous edifice of Smiling Jack, the canny observer of human affairs : a thousand shapeless pieces of confidence sent flying by one well-timed giggle. Thus the rapid prattle and gossip which dinned on their ears like rain. She might have been trying to keep fate away all these years by talking it down. No chance of any unpleasant discoveries as long as she kept talking, talking. And now, of course, she was trapped in her own machine.

He watched them from miles away, as if they were at the wrong end of a telescope. His father's mouth was working, his mother was bent over her knitting, apparently listening to something (perhaps him). John had no real idea why they were doing what they were doing. She was ill, perhaps dying, and now he was busy talking the evil spirits away. Perhaps one's education had cut one off from them after all. At any rate, he had no part to play in the tableau. He belonged in a different picture. He stood up.

'I think I'll go over to see Sheila and Bob.'

'Good idea,' said his mother. 'They'll be delighted. Only be careful. They both have colds.'

'Yes, Mother; ta-ta Father.' He shuffled out through the obstacle course of comfortable furniture.

He really liked to see his brother-in-law once in a while. Bob Simmons was a breezy Londoner who had the right ideas about Oxford : he thought it was a bloody waste of time and money, and he didn't mind saying so, loud and often. He patronized John, and told him how to surmount the disadvantages of a superior education. 'We'll make something out of you yet.' It helped to get things back into proportion. Of course John was every inch on Bob's side : he had never expected his expensive education to get him anywhere in life—that was why he had sneaked down to London so often to look for those jobs. He begrudged the three years or more of headstart that his cockney neighbours were getting on him : it was cruel, like being chained to a starting post. And it was with a chafing prickle of irritation that he prowled the smart London offices, asking all and sundry to remember him, to put his name down, to keep in touch— above all, not to let too many of the other boys get past him.

Why ? Well, it was a kind of game, and perhaps a little more, a point of pride. In the last resort, he really ought to get further than his father had; somehow, prove that his father had been right all along; please the old man, and at the same time bury him once and for all. His triumph would certainly break Mr. Chote's heart : but both of them waited restlessly for it all the same. It would mean something solid achieved and an end to struggle.

How delightfully Œdipal, thought Chote, shaking out his umbrella. It wasn't tragic though—just the ordinary thing one did between cups of tea. The rhythm of life. Pretty bloody— but Mr. and Mrs. Chote expected it, and one could hardly let them down.

He pushed the front door open and began to whistle into the wind. Bob Simmons was a million laughs and jokes (the latest ones from the City)—it didn't do to be too solemn around old Bob. He moved off down the road, still whistling. Old Bob didn't belong in the Freudian jungle and neither did he. Whistle, whistle, whistle. It was just a question of making some lolly, settling down somewhere nice with a nice girl, and whistle, whistle, whistle, oh to hell with it.

9. Woolgathering

PICCADILLY CIRCUS at night is considerably more quaint than spectacular. The red buses buzz around the statue of Eros like mechanical toys, and farther out a mild fluster of merry-makers circle and circle. The neon signs are cosy and unpretentious. Their fuzzy, pink glow does not extend very far, making only a minute impression on the greater London darkness.

Chote and Browning turned the corner into Glasshouse Street, and were immediately smothered by shadows of various kinds. Some of the shadows would be real women, drifting women, up one side of the street and down the other, complying with the English law that female shadows must keep moving forever and ever. The elements of seduction were as usual sharply limited by their circumstances: elegant, possibly 'expensive' boredom, the mechanical tick-tock of hips and high heels, the pendulous sway of handbags. And the further penalty, self-inflicted, of dowdy clothes—as if smart ones would not be quite respectable.

Every once in a while Chote liked to come down and watch the girls pacing up and down, up and down, stopping for a moment to let a portly male shadow peer into the hard lines, gathering speed again relentlessly, forever on the walk from the law. From a few feet away, in the thick London air, they looked as desirable as the women in dreams; and then suddenly the dream went wrong and one could make out the cracked skin, and the three-days-dead eyes, the passionless gaze of recognition and appraisal; and then off again, click, clicking past, looking desirable again, dissolving into native shadow.

He used to come down here during the Brinkley vacations

for a delicious brush with temptation—well, it was hardly even a temptation was it? It was something to talk about over the cocoa. You didn't have to *do* anything about it. And now, he still paid the odd visit, safer than ever, gazing around like a ruddy sociologist, noting the existence of the problem. Browning clearly took an opposite view. He had come for action and was eying the hard painted faces with the innocent exuberance of a child looking into a sweetshop.

'My God, man. Where's your pride?' said Chote. It was too late to appeal to Browning's morals: five years earlier had been the time for that. According to the official version, his own were still a shade worse than Browning's. The only objection left was the tawdry old aesthetic one. The thing was ugly, it left a nasty taste, said the vicar. And really how could one live with oneself after trembling in the icy grip of these elderly women with their starchy faces and stringy hair? And besides, hadn't one ever seen a hygiene film?

'I knew it, I knew it,' burst out Browning in exasperated sing-song. 'There speaks the puritan conscience, if ever I heard it. You feel a natural revulsion to things of the flesh. Also, you are stiff with false pride.' Browning was joking, of course, but joking in earnest, with his bit of fun in danger. Chote realized vaguely that he had been waiting for this, for years and years, even before the Browning era.

'I have no objection to the flesh as such, as long as it belongs to someone under fifty,' he said.

'There you go, putting impossible conditions between yourself and pleasure,' Browning said quite affably. 'The puritan can't go it with theology any more, so up goes a cruddy wall of fastidiousness to take its place. It was a bad day when your ancestors lost their faith in God, Chote. They had to find *some* excuse for running away from the flesh, so they invented all this horse manure about self-respect. Thus equipped, they could once again make a strength out of their weakness, and exalt themselves at the expense of thousands of unfortunate women, like these creatures here. And all with a lot of bloody bluster to boot.'

Chote was somewhat unmanned by this outburst: did

Browning really feel like this about him—or was he just irritated beyond endurance by the prospect of going without his crumpet for the evening? Chote went on arguing mechanically —'Don't bring religion into this you blaspheming bugger. Just because you have no taste, and would be delighted to spend the night with an orang-utan. . . .'

'I suppose I am abnormally virile,' said Browning, lapsing reluctantly into more conventional good humour, blowing on his nails and shining them on his lapel in traditional pantomime.

Once more back to the old formula—the one that got Jungle John out of all his worst scrapes. 'I've never had to pay for it in my life,' he said. There it was, unanswerably superior.

Browning had had too many evenings ruined by this hoary sophistry and he was ready for it. 'Does that mean that you can always get it, or that you don't often want it?'

This was a tough one for Jungle John. A mantle of rubber and glue seemed to descend over his head. Browning hadn't tried to corner him like this since their Viennese nights. He reached into his leopard-skin tights for another handy formula.

'In other words, are you boasting about your incredible charm or your incredible stinginess?' Browning persisted, smiling pleasantly.

'Both,' said Chote. 'Frankly, I don't know which is the more incredible.' It wasn't much of an answer, and Browning turned away to look at the women, leaving Chote to patch his defences.

They were standing against a wall a little away from the beaten track. Eventually, one of the girls detoured across to them with raised eyebrows and mincing feet.

'Good evening, madam,' said Browning. Chote tensed—his game might be up for good. 'I'm sorry, madam. I thought you were my mother,' said Browning. She accelerated indignantly, and then whirled round sharply like a sentry. 'Think you're pretty clever, don't you, sonny?' She steamed by them on the way back. Chote was delighted. Alan wasn't going to force the issue after all.

They looked about quickly for more sport, to celebrate their compromise. A little way down the street, a furtive little man was approaching one of the bright-faced ones—a fruity target, set up by the gods.

'Don't do it, old man,' Browning shouted to him. 'It isn't worth it.'

'You'll only regret it tomorrow,' chimed in Chote. 'Stunts the growth and all that.'

The man looked round, a startled rabbit, turned and scurried away in the dark. The woman glared at them and took a few grim steps in their direction, then wheeled back to look angrily for more trade. It didn't do to waste time on petty irritations.

An American soldier came weaving into danger. He looked up uncertainly and hopefully at the first temptress, as if she really might be his mother after all.

'Don't do it, Yank,' shouted Browning. 'Two pounds is too much.'

'We represent your better judgment,' piped Chote. 'The small voice within you. The American way.'

'You never know what you might catch.'

'Think of the girl you left behind,' they volleyed, wildly pleased with themselves.

The American squinted at them through layers of dimness.

'Who're you guys?' He sounded cheerful—any new friend was good news at this time of night. 'Never mind, I'll find out for myself.'

'Thanks pal.' His courtesy was elaborate. 'Would have been very grave mistake, very grave mistake indeed. But,' he frowned at a new thought, 'why do you do it? What's in it for you?'

'It's a public service,' said Chote.

'Nothing too good for our allies,' said Browning.

'Why I think that's *won*derful,' said the American. '*Won*derful. Say, would you fellows like a little gin?' He whipped a full bottle out of his tunic. 'To celebrate narrow escape?'

'We shouldn't drink while we're on duty,' said Browning doubtfully.

'Oh I don't know, Inspector Browning. We might try just a spot behind the hotel, don't you think?'

'You English are *won*derful,' burbled the American. 'Talk like goddam ministers, and all as corrupt as hell.'

They went around the corner and drank the gin.

'And you people are so goddam *sen*sible,' said the American. 'My name is Ed, by the way. So damn sensible. And such bastards.'

'I'm Jack and he's Al.'

'Pleased to meet you, Jack, Al. Man gets a little lonely over here among all you sensible bastards. Good to make a few friends, you know.'

Chote felt the gin tingling into his ears. They had three swigs each and the bottle was empty.

'Got to get back to work,' said Browning.

'Can I join you?' asked Ed. 'Like to see how you fellas operate. Interested in your methods, you know?'

They shambled back to their station and began to bark shrill instructions to the lonely figures ferreting along the street. 'Don't do it, you fool. It isn't worth it.' Through fuzzy eyes, they saw two of the women talking to each other and looking at them. The doorman of the hotel they were leaning against came surreptitiously out after a while and advised them to go easy. 'They're vicious,' he whispered. 'Vicious! Why only the other day they nearly killed a girl who was walking along here, minding her own business. They thought she was trying to muscle in. Decent sort of girl she was.'

'It's all right,' said Ed, who was sitting against the wall with his feet up and his cap tilted over his eyes. 'It's an official service.'

The doorman glanced at him distastefully and redoubled his lamentations.

'They're not women at all, if you ask me. They're monsters. They'd tear your eyes out soon as look at you.' He could do no more : he sidled back to his post, hoping that his words would take root.

'Don't touch them,' shouted Browning to a tubby, sensuous-looking young man who was waddling up. 'They're not nice girls, not nice at all.'

Business had been at a standstill for fifteen minutes now, and the women were beginning to gather in agitated groups.

'Keep moving, girls,' shouted Browning. 'Mustn't loiter,' Chote mumbled. He was finding it hard to concentrate on his work. The girls seemed to be suddenly swimming towards him in a green wave.

'Why don't you leave us alone?' A rasping cockney voice came at him from about ten feet away.

'What's your game?'

'What have we ever done to you?'

Browning was leering at them. 'What's the matter, girls? Business bad tonight?' His voice was unnaturally brassy, like a newspaper seller's. They were moving closer, all the same.

'There's something wrong with you,' said one of the women. 'You're sick.' Chote saw a flash of shiny black and then a handbag came whumping down on his head.

'Leave us alone,' a voice whined and the bag came crashing sideways across his cheek.

'That's enough of that,' he said thickly. The women were round in a tight ring, breathing hard and glaring ferociously. Ed was fast asleep and Browning held a handkerchief to his bleeding nose. The women had tasted blood, and glowed with a new confidence. Faces grinned through the bright chunks of make-up forming a row of comic masks.

'We know how to take care of little boys like you,' said a chalk-white face. A scarlet mouth puckered and spat.

'What we can't do ourselves, we have friends to do for us,' said a gaunt, deep-stained face.

This, then, was the evil thing, and it had got him at last. Chote felt boozily like handing himself over, giving up, swooning into the bony arms. His knees seemed to be dragging him down to the pavement. Browning was looking pensively at his handkerchief, apparently mesmerized by the little red sprinkle.

'That's the silliest threat I've ever heard,' said Chote haughtily. He hadn't even realized that he was planning to speak. 'My friend and I do not believe in striking women, but if we are forced to, I daresay we can make a pretty good job of it. Of course, the law would be on our side. Nor are we afraid of your grubby little friends. The authorities would have no trouble in tracing any violence back to you. It simply wouldn't be worth your while.' Chote listened to his voice in amazement. He didn't believe a word he was saying. His spirit had already capitulated completely, but somehow his tongue continued to wag. He had never realized before how glib he had actually become over the years. The girls were momentarly silenced. They had no idea what to do about this torrent of words. They weren't great talkers, any of them. . . .

Browning took over the attack. 'My friend and I are not without influence, you know. We are in a position to ensure retribution for any untoward actions or breaches of the peace on your part.' And so on.

The solidarity of the women seemed to be melting away.

'We didn't do anything to you.' The delicate balance had shifted again. 'Leave us alone, can't you?' The voices were isolated. The 'Thing' had disappeared leaving a gaggle of disconnected females, unfortunate, pathetic figures: a social problem, really. Perhaps one could help them.

'Do you think we should press charges of assault?' said Browning. Chote was preparing to be generous when he felt a heavy hand on his shoulder.

'What's this, what's this, what's this?' A massive policeman had somehow shimmered along the wall of the hotel, breaking through the ring of outraged females. No wonder Chote and Browning had felt themselves gaining the upper hand. The girls had sensed the arrival of the father of devils. Those on the edges had already begun to drift away as unconcerned as possible.

'It's nothing, officer. A misunderstanding,' said Browning, hastily striving to cover his gushing nose.

'*Something* must have happened,' said the constable in a calm, pleasant voice. Chote felt warm relief as his shoulder squirmed under the vast paw of the law. He might have had his little misunderstandings with the police in the past, but fundamentally he was on their side.

'Were they bothering you or were you bothering them?'

'Neither, officer. Honestly.' His teeth protruded sincerely.

The policeman looked around for witnesses, but there was none to be seen. The doorman had vanished discreetly, leaving no trace.

'Well, I ought to arrest the lot of you for loitering under suspicious circumstances.'

'It was a misunderstanding,' echoed one of the remaining women.

'I wouldn't try to explain it if I was you,' said the policeman. 'The whole ruddy business defies explanation. If you say anything you'll only make it worse.'

'Yes officer.'

'Now, seeing as I didn't see anything, and nobody else saw anything, I suggest we all move along as quickly as possible.'

The girls evaporated, but the powerful hand remained on Chote's shoulder, holding him down like a nail.

'Somebody told me what you was up to,' the policeman confided. 'That's why I'm here. And just so my little excursion shall not have been in vain, I should like to whisper a few words of advice in your dainty ear, before you go on about your business. Prostitution in London is a nasty business, and I wish we could do more about it than we can. But I wouldn't try to fight it single-handed if I was you.'

'All right, officer.' He was trying to work his way loose.

'Here, here, what's your hurry? I haven't finished my priceless advice yet. Now. We like to see young people enjoying themselves. It gladdens our hearts, really it does. But this is no part of the town for your youthful pranks. You're only going to get hurt, either by them or by us. In either case you'll be making our work more difficult. And you wouldn't want to do that, now would you?'

Chote looked up, expecting to see a brutal twist on the policeman's face, some familiar trace of the bully, but all he saw there was bland and expressionless. The heavy sarcasm seemed almost absent-minded and mechanical; the good-humoured bobby going imperturbably about his business.

'May I go now? Is the lecture over?' asked Chote. Browning seemed to be smiling crookedly at his friend's discomfiture, although blood was still dribbling down his chin.

'Not while I have such an attentive audience. You might almost call it a captive audience, eh? What I'm trying to say is that you're both big boys now, and ought to know better. I really have half a mind to give you both a good spanking. However, I'm a busy man. . . .'

'So we see,' said Chote.

'As my dear mother used to say: "Pertness is not clever." Now to repeat, I'm a busy man and my immediate problem is what to do with our transatlantic cousin over there. I wonder if you have any suggestions?'

'Why not give him a good spanking?' muttered Chote.

'I'm afraid that would be exceeding authority. What else do you suggest? If the Yank MPs get hold of him, heaven help him. And we don't want to book him ourselves. Look at him, sleeping so peacefully, like a child. It seems such a shame. . . .'

Browning gave Ed a poke and he opened an eye.

'Where do you live?' asked Browning.

'North London, some place.' He closed his eye again.

'We'll take him home,' said Browning resignedly. 'He's actually a very old friend of ours. Wake up, Ed old man.' He nudged Ed in the ribs with his boot.

'Whadyawant?'

'That's a good chap,' said the weary policeman. 'We'll put him in a taxi and you can take him home. The fact is that we're rather busy in this part of town and we don't want any more work than we can manage.'

Chote felt the blood entering his shoulder again as the hand was lifted at last. Browning went away and came back with a taxi, and in a minute they were rolling out of the street of shadows into the innocent, all-in-fun glow of Piccadilly Circus. Chote was glad to be out of the dark. He had come too close to losing his portfolio as a social worker: he wouldn't always be retrieved by a policeman; and he wouldn't always be able to talk himself out of trouble either. A pleasure was gone from his life forever.

'I don't mind admitting I was a bit windy,' said Chote as he sank back on the hard brown-leather seat of the taxi.

'I felt a twinge or two myself,' admitted Browning. They peered at each other, trying to probe for the genuine emotion as the lights flickered on and off their faces. It was perfectly O.K. to admit fear, even non-existent fear, as long as one didn't go too far. It was difficult, with the sympathetic nerves a-jangling, to hit on the spontaneous note of semi-cowardice that conventional realism demanded.

'It wasn't exactly fear, in the usual sense,' said Chote, circling round the question. 'More a sense of helplessness, of things being out of one's control.'

'Yes, something of that sort,' Browning answered tersely.

'However, Oxford trains one for life. It wasn't so very much worse than a J.C.R. meeting.'

Browning laughed abruptly, almost a hiccup. In a flash of fluorescent light, his face looked unnaturally pale. Chote wondered if he was still shaken; he hoped so. Nobody had any right to be as insensitive as Browning. This might be the chink.

'Just think,' Chote continued, still probing, with dirty fingers. 'You wanted to play footie with those dragons.'

In the next flash of light Browning looked green.

'They weren't any different from other women,' he mumbled. 'They're all savages under the skin.'

'Ah,' said Chote buoyantly. 'So you're one of those blokes who really despise women. That explains a great deal.'

'Nonsense. Lot to be said for savages. Bags of spirit.'

The taxi made a sharp turn, and Browning was flung against the side of the cab like a sack of meal. Ed, who was sleeping in the middle, fell across Browning's lap and had to be hoisted back into place. Browning was looking worse and worse. At last, in a flat, toneless voice, he admitted his problem: 'If I sit absolutely still, without moving a muscle, I may just manage to avoid creating a dirty great scene.' A band of light lingered on him, giving him a look of tragedy and green cheese. 'God save us all from American gin,' he explained.

The taxi was soon winding its pompous way through a succession of neat, moonlit gardens. Ed sat back with his mouth open, while Browning crouched forward as if frozen: his

165

features set rigidly, in a pattern of misery and woozy determination. There was some moral pride in him after all : he wasn't going to make a worse fool of himself than he absolutely had to. With Browning temporarily preoccupied, Chote had nothing to do but look out the window at the clipped hedges, the prim houses. He and his sodden companions were making a brisk, semi-conscious tour of inspection of an altogether foreign world. The people in these houses went to bed early, keeping their faculties fresh and clear for whatever little tasks they had to perform in life. To them, things like prostitutes were always social problems, not personal threats—never for them the faces contorted in rage and hatred, just a few inches away, threatening unspeakable, ungrammatical things. The only violence they ever encountered was in the gentle pages of *The Times*, where it filtered through in their own language, with a marvellous air of remoteness; it had all happened centuries and centuries ago after all, in a different kind of land.

This little realm of gardens, this sceptred bird sanctuary, the music, the madness that nibbled intermittently at his rear (one couldn't describe it more clearly than that on American gin—but all the same he had never described it better) would hardly find him here. With a bowler hat and an umbrella to keep it at bay, it would never again be able to wrestle him to the furry floor of taxis (coo, look at Browning. On all fours). The black coat, the striped trousers were lucky charms against evil spirits with hairy legs, curly-headed whatnots on taxi floors. Was one, Chote wondered, or was one not going to cover oneself in all that paraphernalia, bind oneself hand and foot to the teapot and the umbrella stand, and *The Times*? Thank God, he wouldn't have to worry about it till he got back from America anyway.

The trouble with you, Chote, he thought to himself, the trouble with you, the trouble with you is. . . . He was often suspended in this state of tipsy reflection for hours at a time, while the children of nature were busy passing out or fighting nausea on all fronts. Sometimes, he made his plans. Tonight he philosophized. Those houses and gardens weren't so dashed innocent. People like Inglenook-MacKenzie lived in them :

people in striped trousers, well-known clubmen who always belonged to all the safe clubs . . . wore the lucky charms, said the lucky words, put their tea in before their milk and who never wore brown boots either before Ascot, or after Goodwood, God save the Queen. And yet the sprites had somehow got hold of Inglenook and sent him howling at poor Gosworth like a bat out of hell, with a face and a heart like those of tonight's prostitutes. When a pillar of the Establishment turned up in the colours of the evil thing, where was there left for anyone to hide? After all, Inglenook-MacKenzie wasn't supposed to be a 'social problem' like the poor tarts.

Why was everybody so beastly? He wanted suddenly to wake Browning and ask him—but he knew what Browning would say. His friend knew how to deal with alcoholic remorse. 'You sound just like my grandfather chastising the flock on a Sunday morning,' he would say. 'It's a pity he can't talk to them on Saturday afternoons occasionally.'

It might have been the desiccated streets of Vienna they were driving through again, with Corporal Nevis, the divinity student (who swore in his sleep), remonstrating earnestly with Browning about the pleasure principle. 'Don't you see something grotesque,' Nevis had said strongly, 'in two monuments of belching dyspepsia like yourself and Chote hanging over the car window and carolling the glories of pleasure?'

Chote, hearing the voices in a remote way, like a radio play in the next room, thought that perhaps Nevis had a point; but Browning was adamant. 'An appeal to cowardice (whurf, excuse me) like religion generally. And talking about grotesque, you ought to see my grandfather's congregations, wailing out their fears every Sunday, down on their flaming knees, praying for relief from storms, pestilence and hangovers.' It took character to go on like that in Browning's condition—and there was much, much more, all about how his grandfather salivated when he said the word 'lust' (although he was all in favour of Christian marriage) and about how he, Browning, loved life and human beings and so on. It was all a bit confused now, but Chote remembered the wavering, familiar line of argument well enough. None of that for Charlie, thank you.

That was actually the time when he should have disagreed with Browning, if he was going to. Nevis would have been a staunch ally. He also had a grandfather who loved life and made an ass of himself at regular intervals, so they were well paired. But when Chote at last felt fit to join them, he rounded on Nevis, not Browning. 'You'd have people give up sweating and going to the bathroom,' he remembered saying huskily. 'You're against sin because it doesn't look nice.'

It was a fateful decision, made while of unsound mind. Henceforth he was bound to Browning's point of view more firmly than ever. His Army and Oxford careers were fixed irrevocably.

An accident of history had led them both into one of the foulest-mouthed regiments in the British army. That was the beginning of it. Songs, limericks, novelettes : bloated heroines (freakishly pumped up), verminous villains, corrupted children, prancing in flatulent pageant forever and ever. It was all so bloody unrelieved—no compulsory chapel-going, as there had been at Brinkley, no restorative letter-writing to Uncle and Auntie—and witless. Baby faces (future shopkeepers, bank clerks, respectable husbands) all in a circle; quiet, attentive, moist like babies tugging at the nipple. Before going to Brinkley, to play at being the gentleman, he had known these boys well. Now they unnerved him a little.

But education has its uses, and before he had so much as left the depot, Chote found himself a kind of regimental bard. He remembered the regimental favourites and embellished them better than anyone else, and he had an easily understood BBC accent for recitation. The new recruits began to swarm around him, in deference to his trained memory and verbal resourcefulness, both learned in another cause : and these included one Alan Browning, an amiable, light-comedy soldier from the Midlands, to whom he took a liking on sight.

Chote was delighted to find that Browning was also destined for Sturdley. Compared with Sergeant-Major Worthington and the rest, he seemed like a man of sentiment : he talked about women of course, but not as suppurating and loathsome creatures; quite the reverse. That was the trouble. When they finally got to Austria, Alan began to round up pairs of hefty fräuleins for immediate contact, and Chote found himself in a position of acute embarrassment.

It was all very well to tell stories: they sounded rather less repulsive in one's own words and they established a sort of status too ('Let Chote tell it, that's one of Chote's'); but this was altogether unforeseen. He had unwittingly built himself a reputation; words must now give way to action. And he didn't know what to do.

Almost every night he and Browning would bicycle into town, behind two large bottoms and four chubby churning legs, for long bouts of strenuous Teutonic entertainment: singing and bouncing up and down mostly, with a certain amount of laborious winking, nuzzling and pinching. In no time Chote's knees, lap and morale would be alike, worn down to water, under the bouncing heft of the Austrian maidens, and Browning would be unmistakably primed and mellow. It would then be time for Chote, the well-known coarse clod, who thought of women as playthings, to begin looking nervously at his watch. 'Don't you think we'd better start back, old chap?' In lush, beer-garden colour, there was Browning sitting back placidly, laying his artless plans; Chote trying feverishly to think of ways to ward off the heavy demanding flesh for one more night. The 'let Chote tell it' reputation hung each time by a thread. His manful efforts not to be taken for a public school prig would be in vain if he showed the least uncertainty. . . .

Now—what? Five years later, and with only Browning left —he was still hanging on grimly. Not much longer now, thank God.

They found Ed's house, after a certain amount of trial and error, and piloted him a rambling course up the stairs. He woke up at the top, and suggested that they all go down and start again; but they put this down to American grit and sticktoitiveness, and sure enough, in a few minutes he was asleep again, sounder than ever.

They drove on to the boarding-house where Browning was staying nearby. There didn't seem much to be said, now that they were away from Oxford. It was perhaps the discovery of this that had sent them prowling into Glasshouse Street in the first place. The events of the evening had jarred some of the stuffing out of them too. Browning still looked horribly pale and battered in the stripes of pale light that flashed into the cab at intervals.

This would be their last foray, and Chote felt nothing but relief. The others at Sturdley had shed the Army slowly. For a short time they kept themselves prepared with impromptu drills in the lodge, hockey sticks and cricket bats at the ready, floor : it took time (Nevis writhing and cursing in his regulation sheets) to spew the Army out of your system.

But most of them did come round sooner or later; Browning was almost unique in his failure to convert to civilian life. His monomania, which had been buried in the larger monomania of the ranks, now stood out in splendid isolation. In a twinkling, his lechery became a Sturdley specialty number, like Godfrey's sanctimony—with the difference that it was no joke to Alan. He burned incandescent with a dirty-great flame—and he expected Chote to do likewise.

Thus did John find himself stuck for another three years with his prefabricated Army personality. Alan continued to put him energetically through his paces, rounding up nurses, secretaries, shopgirls in spotty harvest. John, listless, desperate, tried saying that they weren't his type. Like others who start at the top (and Chote's boasting had placed him very near the top) he had never learned the fundamentals. He could hardly learn them now. Browning's leering introductions put that out of the question. The girls expected great things of him.

'And as for not your type,' Browning sealed the last exit, 'you weren't half so fussy in Austria.' 'One doesn't expect so much from foreigners, somehow' was not the most crushing rejoinder.

He might have purged himself then and there; their outings were beginning to get badly on his nerves. Browning persisted in treating Oxford as a foreign town in which he had been temporarily stationed : every night, they had to go out to new pubs and make passes at new women. During the afternoons, they harassed the local shopkeepers (who would never forget: Chote's credit would remain bad with them to the day of his death); at sundown they began to sniffle the watery college beer and map out their dreary assignments. Weak, no doubt, and not what he had planned for himself: but he wasn't quite sure that it was not what he wanted all the same. In the watches of the Brinkley night, he had had dreams not altogether unlike this. If only he could get over his damned squeamishness . . . and meanwhile his reputation at Sturdley jelled, took on a bright wobbly hardness, became the man.

For all that, he must have been near the verge of breaking down and confessing his innocence when Godfrey Hook and Daphne Collins chanced along. He had been at some pains to avoid Godfrey at first. The parson had been such a solemn little pimple at school—and of course, such a victim. One could see him still in humble silhouette, sitting atop his pillow un-ravelling the tightly knotted pyjamas, or hobbling patiently up the dormitory in search of his other shoe. 'The meting out of Godfrey's justice' they called it—the chap had a genius for tapping unexpected reserves of cruelty in the blandest bosoms. John wanted nothing to do with him at Oxford; he brought back painful guilty memories; worse still, he might bring on another spell of sadism, of uncontrollable vileness.

But of course it couldn't be postponed forever. Hook caught up with him at last, at one of the Oxford clubs, socialist or vegetarian or anti-nuclear, or something. He was apologetic about introducing a chap like Hook to a chap like Browning —they would be almost bound to make each other, and him, uncomfortable—but it couldn't be helped. He did it as airily as possible ('Isn't it all too priceless? Fancy going to school with a chap like this—talk about your strange bedfellows', and so on). But to Chote's amazement Browning took a warm liking to Godfrey which was to all appearances reciprocated. The very next day, Alan suggested seeing him again: and in no time at all, he had joined Browning's private army. Chote couldn't begin to understand it. As far as he could see, Hook was the same dull chap as ever, perhaps a little worse with age. It was truly painful to watch him hard at work, trying to think of funny things to say—'Don't bother, Godfrey, for heaven's sake,' one wanted to shout. 'It isn't worth it.' He seemed worse than the worst tortures they'd ever subjected poor Hook to at school—expecting the wretched chap to start making jokes at his time of life!

Nevertheless, Browning never went anywhere without him, and Chote was not entirely sorry about this. Hook was patently a good deal more innocent than he was himself, which tended to distract Browning's attention and absorb his finer energies. It became increasingly easy to slip home early when the old problems arose, and Browning didn't wax half so sarcastic when he spotted his old friend scurrying off. As long as Hook remained (and somehow he always did) Alan's cup was full enough.

With extra time on his hands, Chote fell into the habit of eking out his thin adventures with occasional anecdotes about mythical ones—just for fun, purely for fun. Whenever he went to London, for instance, for one of his interviews with the captains of British industry, he took the opportunity to invent a fruity affair of some kind. It wasn't meant to be sly —at least at first: it was a joke, a game. But Browning and Hook always seemed to believe him, however far-fetched the story—and some of them certainly verged on the fantastic. And now, one didn't like to disappoint the silly buggers.

Tonight's was the last weary challenge. He had done all right, he was still one of the 'chaps'. No point in arousing Browning's scorn this late in the game; perhaps Alan was right, anyway. Nevis had been sure of his ground and Alan had scalded him. Chote wasn't sure of his ground: he was just sleepy.

The driver turned his head slowly and peered at them. 'I think we've arrived, sir.' Browning got up quickly as if he'd been kicked.

'How much do I owe you, old chap?' He fumbled in his pockets. 'I'm afraid I only seem to have seven and six on me.' He sounded genuinely surprised. 'I was sure I had another pound somewhere.' He went through his pockets mechanically. He seldom had as much money as he thought at this time of year—fair enough, because his father had long since cut off his allowance. Nevertheless. . . .

'I'll write you out a cheque,' he said. 'If I can just find my bally chequebook.'

'Don't bother,' said Chote wearily.

'I'm awfully sorry.'

'It's all right,' said Chote.

He had plenty. His father gave him a much larger allowance than he needed, squeezed out of God knew what pre-war savings. When his friends ran out of money, at the end of each term, Chote kept them going with small loans, while protesting his own poverty as convincingly as the circumstances allowed. Without this system, he would invariably have had to drink alone for the last week of term. Browning actually owed him several pounds over the years, and this now hung in the air between them—although heaven knew, Browning wasn't the only one. Chote had some confirmed chapelgoers among his dependents.

'Well, good night old chap,' said Browning. 'Have a good time in America, if your code permits.' He waved and smiled as his old chum was hauled away.

Chote shut his eyes and tried to concentrate; now what exactly was he talking about: 'One of the chaps.' He repeated the phrase several times, trying to make out what each of the words meant, and then, what they meant when you put them together. They sounded portentous and clear, like a dinner gong in the darkened brain, but he still couldn't see them.

He didn't really disagree with Browning. 'Have fun, don't hurt'—why that was his own view precisely. Where did all that other stuff come from? What other stuff if it came to that? Well, too late to think about it now: later would do. One didn't want to change anything too drastically until one had been to America and back: he'd kill himself if he didn't have a good time in America. He smiled at the thought.

But still, pity about Browning, in a way. One had let the chap down, somehow. Mustn't let a legend like that get started in America. Cause a lot of mischief.

He wasn't really drunk any more, but it was a comfortable

173

way to talk. He stopped trying to concentrate, and in a minute voluptuous images were dancing in his brain. But they weren't like Browning's images: they were young, clean, intangible— the old public school dreams, ethereal and unchallenging, bringing nothing but sleep after a hard day on the playing fields. Yes, they were still there, more numerous than ever— and wiser, more fun.

One of them must have switched off the last, soft lamp in his brain: for in a moment he was sound asleep with his mouth wide open and his square chin imbecile-slack on his heaving chest. The stocky torso bounced complacently, rhythmically, over the cobblestones in a weird life of its own.

The taxi driver pulled his scarf tight, keeping out the warm air. It was a long, expensive ride to Chote's part of London— probably just as well that the young gentleman was unconscious, the driver decided, after all this excitement. He only hoped that he wouldn't have to put the young gentleman to bed.

10. Dancing

THE committee in charge of dancing was having its last meeting, over a bottle of warm champagne. The Summer Ball was due to start that evening, and the committee was languidly tidying up last-minute problems.

'Has the man with the coloured lights turned up yet?'

'No, bugger him.'

'Have you heard from Bert LeRoy and His Merrymakers yet?'

'Not a bloody sound.'

Norbert Jones came bustling in, with a sheaf of papers under his arm. 'Sorry I'm late, gentlemen,' he said with bracing significance. 'I have the estimates here from the caterer, and I'm afraid they're rather terrifying. We seem to have made some rather ghastly miscalculations.' His huge face was drawn with anxiety : but one must face the facts. 'I'm afraid we may even be compelled to dip into our own pockets, gentlemen.'

Somebody yawned. It was the same every year. The Summer Ball committee was notoriously inefficient, almost a parody of a committee. The one intense member (Norbert this year) who did the worrying, took notes at the meetings and kept records of last year's blunders, was never quite enough to stem the tide of confusion. If someone like Norbert was treasurer, the money was fairly safe, but then the minutes kept getting lost, and many important decisions had to be made over and over again at each successive meeting; and if such a one was secretary, then of course the finances went gradually haywire.

Norbert himself, with his reserves of unearthly energy, was actually trying to be secretary and treasurer at once this year (the appointed secretary always came to the meetings in shorts, and could never stay for more than a few minutes), but still, things had gone wrong somehow. Norbert saw what was happening as far back as March, and had made one of his strongest speeches at that time—it was all recorded there plainly in his own minutes : if the committee continued its policy of reckless spending, in the face of rising costs . . . and if it did not put its shoulder to the wheel (in short, get cracking) in a sustained effort to sell tickets . . . well he (Norbert) would not be responsible for the consequences. . . . He had been cheered loud and long, but his triumph was illusory. The committee had continued to barrel furiously along the road to ruin, until now, on the day of the ball itself, it found itself unexpectedly face to face with an irreducible deficit of a hundred pounds. Always the good soldier, Norbert was willing to shoulder the blame himself, after all, which was more than anybody else was. Ralph Gadsby, the captain of dancing, and Norbert's chief tormentor, took the occasion to suggest that Norbert himself had absconded with the money and had sent it to Russia, to help support the International League of Students.

'I don't think that's particularly amusing,' said Norbert crossly, 'especially at this particular time.'

As president of the J.C.R., Chote was a member of everything at Sturdley (there wasn't actually much to belong to) and he was happy to suggest a way out of the difficulty. 'I remember, two years ago we had a mess very similar to this—I'm sure Norbert will bear me out—I wasn't on the committee myself at the time, but the method of handling the situation leaked down somehow, and I for one was impressed. Putting it as briefly and simply as possible, the method seemed to be to, er, just leave it all till the following year. By that time most of the committee had gone down and were scattered up and down the country. . . .'

Norbert leapt up and pointed a purple finger at Chote.

'A thoroughly cowardly solution,' he shouted. 'We can't solve anything by running away from our problems.'

'I don't know,' said Gadsby thoughtfully. 'We might take a vote on it. Those in favour of running away from our problems, say aye—'

'If you do, I resign this instant,' said Norbert in a quavering voice. 'I shouldn't be able to live with myself if I had taken any part in such a contemptible proceeding.'

Norbert's resignation was a well-known threat; whenever any of his many committees threatened to compromise its integrity, Norbert would spring to his feet and resign hotly. Gadsby pacified him this time by promising to look into every possible channel before reaching a decision. 'We may be able to raise a loan of some kind,' he said vaguely. Despite his enthusiasm Norbert knew surprisingly little about finance, and seemed to accept this solution, at least for the time being. 'Meanwhile,' Gadsby went on hastily, 'everything seems to be going ahead swimmingly here. Everything in, one might say, ship shape.'

'Good,' said Norbert. 'I suppose Mr. Pringle has started putting up the coloured lights?'

'Well, er, no, actually. He doesn't seem to have arrived yet, drat the man.'

'I'm sure he'll be here in a minute,' said the official in charge of coloured lights, hopefully.

'Good God,' said Norbert. 'You don't call that shipshape do you? Anyway, I take it you've heard from Bert LeRoy and His Magnificent Merrymakers?'

'What about that, Brian?' asked Gadsby, who knew the answer only too well. 'Have you heard from Herbert yet?'

Brian, who was a personal friend of the obscure Bert LeRoy and who had promised to get him cheap for the Sturdley dance, shook his head dubiously. 'He's tremendously reliable though. I'm positive he'll be here.' Norbert had wanted all along to hire a well-known band to be on the safe side, but Brian Johnson had persuaded the capricious committee to take a chance on his friend Bert. Now Brian was beginning to ask himself how much he really knew about Bert LeRoy. He had only heard him play twice, and the second time the club had been raided. The situation wasn't, when you stopped to think about it, so terribly promising.

Norbert buried his face in his hands, and spoke in a muffled voice. 'The dance is due to begin in five hours, and we still don't know whether we are going to have a band, or whether, even if we *are*, anyone will be able to stand its music.'

'Bert's music is smashing,' muttered Brian, who actually was no longer sure even of that. He hadn't been at his critical best either time.

'Also, we don't know whether the dance will have to be held in utter darkness,' went on Norbert with withering irony.

'That might be best, after all,' said somebody. 'I mean, what with one thing and another.'

'And that's what you call shipshape,' said Norbert, still speaking through his hands. 'I really don't know what to do. I really don't.' It was the closest anyone had ever seen Norbert to despair. But the life-force might still be flickering defiantly somewhere.

'We may have to cancel the whole thing after all,' said the brutal Gadsby.

'What?' Norbert looked up, a mask of horror. 'And refund all the tickets? Are you absolutely stark, raving?'

Chote patted the broad, earnest back. 'It'll be all right, Norbert. The college will dance again. I promise.'

Outside in the quad there was a gentle, methodical sound of hammering. The floor was beginning to take shape, and loudspeakers were being lodged in the ivy. Everything was going to be all right. It always was. Undergraduates sauntered about with their partners, carrying bottles of champagne and hired tail coats. They weren't worried about a thing.

Norbert pulled himself together in icy silence. The committeemen looked guiltily at each other. They knew what he was going to do. He was going outside to look at the weather, then he was going to hunt up Mr. Pringle and demand the coloured lights, and after that he was going to ring up Bert LeRoy in London and give him hell. If he had any time left, he might start raising the money to pay the deficit.

'Don't it make you feel guilty though?' said Chote, when Norbert had swept out.

'I don't know,' said Gadsby unrepentantly. 'After all, in thirty years, Norbert will probably be running the bloody country. And then, God help all of us.'

The gaunt features of Sturdley College were lit up in a ghastly smile. Lights twinkled round the quad, brightening the pallid old stones like rouge smudged on an old face. Robust-looking girls in pink evening dresses trudged purposefully through the front quad with their escorts, their bare shoulders looking in aggregate like an extra-large catch of salmon. The air vibrated with a high clatter of sing-song voices, all going as fast as they could : the sound of ice being conscientiously broken around the young ladies. It was only nine-thirty and most of the girls were still looking dour, or apprehensive, labouring their painful way up through the mists of shyness.

They came from Manchester and Birmingham and Weston-super-Mare. When they all began to answer back at once, later in the evening, they would produce a rich and varied sound, compounded of all the accents of England. Their inflections would show (pin the tail on the donkey) where all their partners came from : and some of the smoothest and most sophisticated men would have their masks stripped away at last by sturdy women from farms, factories and Woolworth's—once the ice was broken. Many undergraduates would see each other clearly for the first time, and there would be some gaiety and relief in the air.

In one of the downstairs rooms the committee was already entertaining a shipment of dons and moderately distinguished graduates from the Foreign Office and the middle levels of the Establishment. Chote and Daphne Collins moved dutifully from don to don, talking briefly with each about the clement weather, and passing on. 'I think it's all going very well, don't you?' said the Warden, pulling at his tight collar. 'At any rate, we're lucky to have such an extremely fine night for it this year.'

'Yes, *aren't* we?' said Chote.

The Chaplain, in his annual display of sportsmanship, was looking in for a few minutes. He was standing in a corner with a party smile, holding a glass of champagne at arm's length.

'Ah, Mr. Chote. A fine night.'

The Chaplain shook hands with Daphne, still smiling inflexibly. He mumbled something that might have been 'charming' or possibly 'good evening' and turned his smile expectantly to Chote. Chote felt that it was up to him as an acknowledged man of the world to carry the conversation.

'We're very glad you could come, Mr. Smythe,' he said tentatively.

'I wouldn't have missed it,' retorted the Chaplain, speaking somehow through frozen features.

'We seem to have been blessed with good weather for a change,' added Chote, playing his ace.

'Yes,' said the Chaplain, 'it would have been a catastrophe had it rained.'

They stood there silently smiling at each other. Daphne looked modestly at the ground, as she usually did when two men were talking. She would only make a fool of herself if she tried to say anything. Men were so intelligent.

'Do you remember how it rained last year?' asked Chote. Out of the corner of his eye, he could see Bert LeRoy cutting a genial swath through the crowd. Bert didn't let his clients down. He was a big man with a loud voice, and a sense of responsibility, and his services did not begin and end on the dance floor. He had just finished telling the Warden forcefully about his love for Oxford. 'Believe me, Doctor, this in an unforgettable experience for me, being requested to play in front of your boys.' At present he was unattached, gazing amiably around for somebody to cheer up. Chote beckoned him over: just what he was looking for.

'Mr. LeRoy, I'd like to introduce you to the Reverend Mr. Smythe, our Chaplain.'

Bert thrust out a huge sincere hand.

'Pleased to meet you, Mr. Smythe. I was just telling your Warden about what an honour it is for me to be here at Oxford tonight.'

Chote slipped away, pulling Daphne with him.

'That was a dreadful thing to do,' she said.

'Nonsense,' he answered. 'Bert can talk to anybody. He'll put Mr. Smythe at his ease right away.' Daphne giggled. Across the room they could hear Bert's voice booming. He was telling the Chaplain that he believed in the religion of the heart. 'In here.' He struck his chest by way of illustration. Even playing the trumpet was something of a religious experience, if one approached it in the right spirit. 'Yes, I suppose it is,' said Mr. Smythe weakly.

'Let's go and dance,' said Chote to Daphne.

Outside they could hear the sweet, sickly hum of saxophone music being amplified incongruously through the ancient buildings. The air was heavy with the smell of flowers which was drifting through faceless windows. And the smell and the sound came together in an almost nerve-racking, knife-scraping sweetness. They looked back into the committee room and saw Bert LeRoy pumping the Chaplain's hand. Mr. Smythe's champagne was jiggling and swishing.

The actual dancing was going on in a huge shapeless tent in the rear quad. Bert LeRoy's Merrymakers were playing bouncy Anglo-South-American music, and the couples were heaving energetically up and down on the floor. There were six men in the band, and four of them played the saxophone— a high proportion, even for an English dance band. They were accustomed to getting along without their leader for long periods; in fact LeRoy usually restricted himself to occasional appearances just to lend tone and deliver announcements. Constant exposure would only cheapen him.

Chote put an arm round Daphne, and they began weaving expertly in and out of the little traffic jams that developed constantly among the plodding couples. As usual, Daphne came alive under his hand, moving with a startling grace and intelligence. Most of the other girls were frowning with concentration, but Daphne was smiling to herself, her eyes half shut, a glorious woman, almost first rate. The music stopped, and she woke up and looked at him with empty, lustreless eyes. It was a familiar transformation, but it always surprised him a little.

After that they walked solemnly round the grounds, to see how things were going. Everywhere they went, they bumped into Norbert Jones, who was tearing about in a vast tail coat, trying to remedy a thousand last-minute mistakes. 'It's an absolute shambles, isn't it?' he panted. 'Every conceivable thing has gone wrong.' But away from Norbert all was calm. Couples sat on the lawn, drinking champagne and looking at the moon. The girls were well and truly relaxed by now, and little tinkles of laughter came from every corner of the gardens, including the flower beds.

Chote and Daphne sat down on a pair of deck chairs, to sop up some atmosphere. This would be their last meeting, unless Chote said something to the contrary. Daphne didn't look as if she expected anything—but then she never did. Perhaps she just doesn't give a damn, Chote told himself hopefully. Perhaps, she was really the phlegmatic type of Englishwoman he'd read about so often, or perhaps contrariwise she was seething with inner excitement. He really had no idea.

'What are you going to do with yourself when I'm gone?' he asked her lightly.

She looked startled as if to say 'Who me?' and Chote suddenly realized he hadn't spoken to her for over half an hour. 'Oh, I'll get along all right, I suppose,' she said dully.

'Are you going to stay in Oxford?'

'I don't know. Perhaps.'

181

It was like talking to the ruddy Chaplain, thought Chote. If somebody else didn't speak first, she would probably never open her mouth again as long as she lived.

'I mean, are you satisfied with your job and everything?'

'It's all right, I suppose.'

If one shook her, like a pintable machine, perhaps a light would go on somewhere. He said sharply, 'What do you want out of life anyway? That's what I'm trying to get at.'

She looked away. A man was swaying across the lawn with a glass of champagne on his head. She watched him carefully until the glass fell off, and the elfin laughter tinkled up around him from the dark grass. Chote wondered if the question had been too much for her, with its suggestion of large issues. And then she said: 'You know what I want,' in a surprisingly hard voice, without a hint of tears. Chote nearly fell out of his chair: she really oughtn't to startle him like that. She looked a little bewildered herself, and stood up quickly. 'Let's go inside. It's chilly out here.' She had to say something after that, thought Chote, something about the weather.

They walked slowly through the archway that led back to the main quad, and Norbert came hurtling into them. 'My God, we've run out of chicken.' He was almost crying as he puffed out the terrible news. He stopped and stood in front of them for a moment, crestfallen and indecisive, a tragic figure, utterly broken by fate (but only after a keen struggle). Then he got a grip on himself again, and shot off into the night: he would find some more chicken somewhere, depend upon it. It was a terrifying display of will power, and for an instant Chote felt properly weak and inferior. The night was Norbert's, the dance was Norbert's, life itself was Norbert's. The rest of them were only characters in Norbert's energetic dream. For what was a little intelligence, compared with a will like that?

When they got back to the committee room, most of the dons had left. But the Chaplain was still standing in the corner grinning like a skeleton. All around him hung frowsy bunting: the committee room was beginning to come apart at the seams.

'Ah, Mr. Chote. I'm *very* pleased to see you again. *And* your charming young friend.'

One saw in a glance what had happened. To cope with the animal vitality of Bert LeRoy, Mr. Smythe had overfortified himself with champagne, so that by now he was ready for anything. His shyness had been soaked into submission, and presto! out came the poise. 'I'd like to have a few words with you, Chote, about your future,' he said breezily. 'I must say I'm considerably concerned about it.'

'Yes sir.'

'As we both come from the same part of London, I have always taken a considerable degree of interest in your welfare—'

'Indeed sir?'

'And I must admit to a certain alarm.' The fixed grin gave a fantastic quality to his solemn words. 'I know there is good stuff in you, Chote. In fact, I'm convinced of it. But what have you done with it, eh?'

'I'm afraid I've frittered a good deal of it away, sir.'

'Precisely. Frittered it away. That is the precise phrase for it. Frittered it completely away.'

'I'm afraid so, sir.'

'Well,' and he poked a finger at Chote's stiff shirt front, 'that can't be helped now. The question is, what are we going to do about it, eh? I mean, you can't go on like this all your life, can you? Life isn't a game, you know.'

'No sir. I suppose not.'

'You simply can't go on frittering your life away, can you?'

'I was planning to make a fresh start in America, sir.'

'Good intentions are not uncommon,' said the Chaplain firmly. 'What you must do is stick to, er, it, grimly. You must put aside all this foolish drinking and card-playing and, er, so forth. You must, so to speak, turn over a new leaf.'

'That's what I plan to do in America, sir.'

'I'm sure your intentions are excellent,' said Mr. Smythe tartly. 'But let me repeat : intentions are not enough. Positive, determined action is the thing. Stern application to the task at hand. *That's* the order of the day.'

'Quite, sir.'

There was a pause. The Chaplain was beginning to look a

bit vague. 'Well, er, I think that's about all, Chote. I believe I've said everything I wanted to say.'

Chote began to turn away. 'Just remember what I have been saying, and *act* upon it!'

It was indefinably depressing. One didn't feel like being criticized at the moment, even by a light-headed Chaplain. The accusations lacked precision, to a comical degree: taken on top of Browning's attack of the previous week, they were enough to indicate that he had for three years managed to throw sand in everybody's eyes. Neither the libertines nor the ascetics knew what to make of him, which was really quite a triumph in this home of poses; but one couldn't help wishing that one didn't feel as if one was being kicked simultaneously in the front and in the rear, for one's pains.

This would be a good test for Daphne, see if she understood what he felt. One was always looking for traces of inarticulate wisdom there, which would help one to see her in a different light.

'It's a funny thing about criticism,' he said. 'Even when it completely misses the mark, and has absolutely no relevance to oneself, it still hurts.'

'I think he really likes you, though,' said Daphne. 'He seems to look upon you as a sort of son.'

Oh, all right, thought Chote. One should have known better than to bring the thing up.

The Chaplain was still smiling encouragement under his drape of bunting as if he expected Chote to start mending his life visibly at this very minute. For some obscure reason, Chote felt like tearing off his clothes, and jumping up and down on top of them.

By midnight, things had begun to look better. The Chaplain had peeped at his watch with a pious exclamation, and scuttled away. 'I shall be watching your career with interest from now on,' he whispered to Chote on his way out. 'I expect great things.'

At the stroke of twelve, Ralph Gadsby made a rough-house speech on the dance floor. He began by welcoming all the guests to Cambridge (titters); and followed up by reading out some outrageous telegrams, mixed with random laundry bills and examination papers.

'In conclusion, I should like to thank the man who has made this whole affair possible, by allowing us to hold it in his college. . . .' The Warden began to simper and tug mightily at his collar. '. . . Your own Mr. Norbert Jones.' The Warden was caught in mid-simper. Everybody clapped and Norbert was pushed from hand to hand toward the microphone. He whispered despairingly to Gadsby, 'Don't be a clot. They don't want *me*.' His whisper hissed out through the amplifiers in the ivy outside.

'Step up, Norbert, and say a few words.'

'I haven't prepared anything,' whispered Norbert, redder than ever, struggling like a child in Gadsby's hands, trying at the same time not to create a spectacle.

'Mr. Jones will say a few words.'

Norbert plunged miserably at the microphone. 'Thank you all very much for coming here tonight. Thank you.' Cheering broke out all over the grounds. Gadsby was a bully without a doubt, nobody else would have driven Norbert so far, but this bit of bear-baiting had established a nice mood all the same. Norbert, husky with embarrassment, turned on his torturer : 'That was a swinish thing to do.' His words boomed out for the last time over the loudspeaker system, and everybody laughed again, a great echo coming back to Norbert. The music started again, and a pretty girl came up and asked the secretary-treasurer to dance. He looked a little bewildered, as if it was the last thing he would have thought of doing at a college dance. But he thrust out an arm stiffly and seized her waist with the other, and soon he was forcing his way gamely through the crowd, to everybody's untold delight.

From twelve-thirty to three was visiting hours, and Chote and Daphne wound their way up innumerable staircases in search of friends. Browning had put a jaunty Do Not Disturb sign on his bedroom door. Godfrey Hook sat in the sitting-room outside, holding hands with Doris Flounce, and looking subtly miserable. He had just been home to Devonshire for a few days, and the quiet, ordered ways had, perhaps, brought him back to his senses. He obviously had no idea what to do with the wanton Doris, who was beginning to tap her foot ominously. Perhaps he was wishing forlornly that he had invited Felicity, after all. At least, she would know how to talk : and her eyes wouldn't wander constantly from face to face, like a lost child's.

Chote had also been home too long, and he looked at the bedroom door now with a feeling of revulsion. Why did the blasted man have to make such a display out of it? Why didn't he go off in a corner somewhere?

Browning came bursting out. 'It's all yours, Godfrey,' he said cheerily. 'Sorry to keep you waiting, old boy.'

Even Doris Flounce knew that this was too direct : she looked at the floor for a moment in a token display of modesty. Hook looked at the floor, too. Browning moved smoothly to the champagne. His control of the situation was sure, everybody was playing by his rules. 'Perhaps you would like the use of our facilities, John?' he purred.

Daphne varied the pattern of embarrassment by looking out of the window into the garish night. 'I don't think so, thanks all the same,' said John.

'Suit yourself,' said Browning casually. He turned to give the placid, receptive neck of his partner a brief tickle, like a confident sultan. 'I daresay you know what's best.' Hook still sat hunched over, patently yearning for the bishop's daughter. For a moment, Chote thought of rallying the forces of decency against Browning : two to one, with the girls delicately abstaining. But it was really no affair of his. And he didn't actually have anything very useful to say about it. Browning could make the forces of decency look pretty silly, if he wanted to. And Godfrey probably wouldn't thank him for it.

'I think we'll be tottering along,' he said as soon as he could.

He thought he could make out appeal in Hook's face. The bedroom door hung open, and Browning's personality brooded in the air. There was sly triumph there hanging like vapour. Browning must know, as the bishop's daughter knew, that he was dealing with a lusciously weak character, one of nature's victims. Of course, Felicity would one day straighten him out as easily as Browning had bent him, turn him into a pillar of the community in fact. But tonight, he belonged to Browning.

Outside, Chote said, 'Well, what did you make of that?'

'I don't know,' said Daphne. 'Was there something unusual?'

'I thought Alan was a bit on the crude side.'

'Yes, I suppose he was. But isn't he always?'

When he first met Daphne, he had asked himself in his fever of innocence, whether she was a 'good' girl or a 'bad' girl. After a while the question didn't seem to arise any more. But he was surprised to realize that he still didn't know the answer to it. Probably she didn't know either. It was quite true: the question just didn't seem to arise with her.

Up another winding, rotting, staircase, worn down by centuries of thundering feet, and into the room occupied for the evening by Bradshaw Soames and Eugene Fosdick. They were sitting cross-legged on cushions, talking to two girls with Fulbrights. Chote felt a sudden warm wave of sentiment at seeing them all together, so friendly and serious-looking: a little clearing of civilization in the middle of the jungle.

'Glad to see you, John. Pull up a cushion. Hello Daphne.'

He felt as he supposed one felt in Japan, as if all of life's crudity had been taken away at the door by an invisible servant: these people had really learned the arts of civilization, all right, all right. They lived calmly and wisely, making sure never to get too hot or too excited, never bumping or scraping each other. Of course, that might not be America: it might just be Rhodes scholars and Fulbrights. Or just Soames and Fosdick.

Gene Fosdick seemed to be conducting the discussion like an orchestra leader. A few bars of American politics—

'We were just talking about Senator McCarthy. I expect he'll be after you as soon as you arrive.'

'I have nothing to hide,' said John. 'I've always behaved myself like a gentleman.'

'That'll make you suspect right away,' said Bradshaw Soames, who seemed indefinably more sophisticated tonight, with the two pretty girls around. No matter how cloddish an

American might be, he always seemed to be able to talk to women.

'I guess we'll all be suspect,' said Gene. 'I was reading an article in the Chicago *Tribune* which said that all the Rhodes scholars are being trained over here to take over the American Government in a few years and run it in the interests of the British Commonwealth.'

'That's right, too,' said Bradshaw. 'Every week we have umbrella and briefcase drill in the Old Bodleian library.'

Now a few bars about Oxford—

'It's funny about Oxford,' said Gene. 'The place seems to be so innocent of intention, of any kind, that you can't blame Colonel McCormick for being suspicious.'

'They don't seem to care what you do,' Bradshaw Soames came in on the high piccolo. 'For the first week or so, nobody told me anything at all. I couldn't even make out whether term was supposed to have started or not. The first sign I had that they knew I was here was when the Warden asked me how I was settling in. It turned out that they had forgotten to give me a tutor.'

'It's like that at the Sorbonne, too,' said one of the Fulbrights.

'It certainly isn't at München,' said the other.

Fosdick gently led the talk to Germany, giving his partner a chance for an amusing solo. They took in France on the way back, and then Oxford again. It was dazzling ensemble work, with everyone getting a chance to tell at least one illustrative anecdote, and make one pithy comment. Chote couldn't help comparing this with the usual Oxford dogfight (his Oxford) where two or three brightish men slugged it out with funny remarks, while the girls held the coats and kept quiet.

Fosdick even tried to make an opening for Daphne, but she wasn't ready for it and she fumbled it away. There didn't seem to be anything special she could talk about, anyway. Chote, embarrassed and protective, answered rapidly for her. 'You've lived here for about five years, haven't you, Daphne?' 'Yes, that's right.' She smiled gratefully. Now just supposing he decided to settle in America—no, he couldn't possibly take her. It was a petty thought to be sure, but then one of the Fulbrights asked Daphne another question, and he thought it again.

'You'll have a rude awakening in America, John,' said Bradshaw. 'They'll make you work like buggery, er, pardon my English, reading thousands of books and making endless reports. And you have to be one hundred per cent dull and long-winded, or they won't take you seriously at all.'

'Well, they don't take me seriously here, if it comes to that. That seems to be my fate everywhere.'

He felt that the minuet, or whatever it was, was drawing to a close now. He got up to go, and they gave him their addresses in America (he already had Eugene's, but he took it again anyway). It occurred to him that perhaps he ought to belch or something to convey his pleasure. Their polite faces smiled graciousness in the candlclight, and thc two girls told him with evident sincerity how glad they were to have met Daphne and him. As the visitors closed the door, and began to stumble down the mouldy staircase, they heard the exquisitely modulated voices striking up another number.

'They seemed very nice,' said Daphne.

'You said a mouthful, baby,' said Chote. If American girls were all going to be like that, yummy, yum, yum. His worries would be over. Even an old Brinkleyan could get along with girls like that.

It was like the last chapter of a Dickens novel: everybody was reunited in a series of happy (if somewhat contrived) interiors. In every room there was a surface of welcome and cheer, fizzing champagne and hospitable red faces. The tensions and strains of a largely one-sex community seemed to have snapped and loosened. The big, motherly girls (and the thin shy ones too) had conspired to bring a new mellowness to the cold musty rooms. Clusters of flowers on the cracking window sills, candle-light on the bare walls, festooned waste-baskets—but above all, the girls themselves. Perhaps half a dozen were genuinely pretty, and ten more were 'interesting': the rest were just girls, healthy-looking and durable. Even the most spectacular and apparently complicated men at Sturdley tended, when the chips were down, to be 'sensible' and conservative in their choice of women. For the long haul, the grey years of slow promotion in the civil service or the soap company, you wouldn't want to take a chance on a flighty, demanding girl. A solid, faithful chum was more what you looked for.

Chote assumed that most of his friends were tense. They didn't show it, of course—but they *must* be. They knew too much, and felt too much on one level of consciousness; on another they didn't know anything at all. Unlike the non-University people, they hadn't a chance to glide gradually into the stream of modern life. They were obliged to jump in all at once from a high, remote board, naked as the boys at the old swimming hole. And they had been looking at the water for a long time, getting more and more fidgety. On the whole, the chaps knew more than most people about the facts of life in contemporary England : the chilling climate of frustration and insecurity, and unrewarded anxiety. They even knew the figures on it; but they hadn't really been in yet. Their vantage point was still an eighteenth century Oxford, where one learned to live gracefully and so forth, in a world where grace was still the thing. Granted, Oxford was changing slowly, becoming gradually grimmer and duller. But it still wasn't preparing its sons for the soap company and the one-room flat.

In the circumstances, one didn't want to be fretted beyond endurance by a restless, unpredictable wife. Many of the girls here tonight were fiancées obviously calculated to be a comfort in the years ahead. They were already at home in the bleak waters, and they knew how to pinch and save, how to live from day to day, without expecting too much; and how to stick at dull jobs indefinitely, just for the sake of bed and board. They might, if all went well, be able to train their anxious husbands in the same necessary arts. At any rate, they wouldn't make pests of themselves by demanding the impossible.

And they knew how to generate a modest warmth (like a small electric fire) in the dreariest surroundings. There was a kindly domestic feeling in many of the rooms Chote visited.

The men still strove to be as funny as possible, but with a faint diminution, a slight loss of edge: one could already see them sitting comfortably by their future firesides, far away from Oxford, making their little civilized jokes (no one could take that away from them) while the kettle hissed and the cat purred, as at Chote's place in Pimlico. At the moment, they would all have repudiated this picture *in toto*. But it was in the tea-leaves for most of them.

Perhaps, on the other hand, all these thoughts were only a reflection of one's own panic. As one watched the girls daintily pouring out champagne, for all the world as if it were tea, one felt the trap closing. Thank God he was going abroad in a few days: America would save him yet—but there was a ghastly seductiveness in the scene, a soggy warmth of womb and bosom.

Of course, all the rooms weren't like that. At the opposite extreme was the room occupied by Charles Wagstaff, Sturdley's ambassador to Oxford at large. Wagstaff was a man with a green thumb who knew which buttons to push, and already he had pushed himself into a handsome contract with the BBC, to do something or other big. The world was at his feet, or thereabouts, and he had, by way of proof, brought along a girl with silver nail polish. She had acted in two of Charles's plays at Oxford, and had also been offered a contract by the inevitable BBC to do something fabulous. These were the glamorous people, the talented ones, the friends of the Good Fairy. Everyone in the party seemed to be going places, all at once, even as they sat there.

'Ah, John. I'd love you to meet Gloria.' Charles gave her a kiss on the cheek, light as a feather. 'John is the declining President of our J.C.R., darling, a leader of men.'

'I've heard about you,' she said without interest. She knew right away that he wasn't going anywhere. 'Darling, *do* get me another drink.'

'You already have a drink my dear,' chided Charles. 'You really must pay attention.'

'I'm afraid I'm a most *awf*ul woolgatherer,' she said.

Chote was already beginning to feel itchy in the atmosphere

of success—odd, since he planned on something of the sort for himself.

'John's going to America this summer. Isn't that exciting?'

'Too fascinating. *Do* tell me about it.'

Charles began to talk to Daphne, and Chote was forced to concentrate on Gloria. It was hard work getting the right, inconsequential tone: going to America was *madly* exciting, but all the same, it didn't really amount to anything.

'I shall just float around, I daresay, absorbing the colour.'

It wasn't that he liked talking this way: it was simply the only way to talk. Even so, he felt very clumsy and rustic, as he worked away at her boredom.

'Americans are tremendous fun,' she said at one point. And Chote thought, oh, what's the bloody use. One couldn't think of a remark like that if one tried all night.

'Yes, *aren't* they!' he said, snivelling, so he imagined.

Soon Wagstaff was back, kissing her knowledgeably behind the ear, nuzzling unconcernedly like a world-weary ruminant. He obviously knew his way around the ear. He would do well at the BBC—Home Service and Light. Look at how he had handled Browning that time. Browning had been mincing around the college bar, flapping his hands and screeching 'Darling' to everyone in sight. 'The most divine—too improbable' and 'She was *simply livi*d . . . we threw bread at each other *all* night. *Mar*vellous fun,' and so on. Of course, there had been Wagstaff behind him, all scrubbed and smelly, looking tiny mother-of-pearl daggers.

'Ah, hello there, Charles,' said Alan, not noticeably abashed. Wagstaff tried at first withering him, or at least withering at him. 'I see our village Casanova has been amusing the yokels with a typical performance.' His chubby hands were clenched and a strand of pale hair had fallen across his brow, indicating that he was in the grip of well-nigh uncontrollable emotion. One was reminded of those stories about Oscar Wilde sailing into half a dozen hearty undergraduates and laying them out like ninepins. Perhaps Wagstaff would flare up now in a similar display of virility and drop the coarse, cloddish Browning with a single, scientific punch. There was silence in the bar, and a little heavy, pleasurable breathing among the spectators: whatever happened would be good, whether Wagstaff stayed to do battle or spun haughtily on his heel and marched pompously out of range.

They should have known better, of course : nobody ever fought physically at Oxford except the South Africans. 'If you question my masculinity,' said the ferocious Wagstaff, 'I can assure you that my record compares very favourably with yours. Furthermore, my diet is not restricted, as yours seems to be, to sausage and mash.' It was a slimy-soft way of handling the situation; but to everyone's amazement, Browning took it up, and before long the two of them were comparing exploits, leaving the audience to wander disappointed away.

A funny kind of friendship seemed to grow up then and there between the clod and the dilettante. The delicate Wagstaff had thought up bizarre variations which compelled Browning's admiration; likewise, Browning's complicated bestialities quickly brought forth a series of delicate shudders from Wagstaff. Few of the others at Sturdley had the stomach for this kind of thing (people usually told Browning to wrap up when he became really graphic), and these two were quite affectingly delighted to find themselves brothers under the skin. And although their paths seldom crossed after that first scabrous meeting of minds, they always saluted each other respectfully, from their different sides of the gutter.

Wagstaff was still chewing with deftness and precision at Gloria's well-turned ear while she chatted languidly to a new arrival, a pale fellow with a cummerbund and hair down to his waist—or so it seemed out of the corner of the eye. Chote decided that it was time to tiptoe away again.

Wagstaff disengaged himself. 'Are you leaving, old man?' For a moment, Charles was one of the 'chaps'. 'Have a marvellous time in America, won't you. I'll keep an eye on Daphne for you.' He was shaking hands warmly, intimately. 'I'm sure we'll meet again, old boy—in some compromising situation, of course.' He was smiling, giving it everything. You can't help liking the silly bastard, thought Chote. Funny, a bloke like that still trying to please a brace of peasants like us. Touching.

'Goodbye, Charles,' he said. 'Send me a few bob when you're rich and famous. It'll help to pay for the patch on my trousers.'

'Come now,' said Charles with a *genuine* smile. 'I'm much more likely to wind up broke than you are. After all, I'm an actor.'

The others began to listen now. Charles represented the artistic point of view : this square, commonplace chap clearly stood for security, the steady job, the planned future.

'Anything can happen to an actor or actreth,' lisped the cummerbund hotly. 'Unemployment, thtarvation, public contumely. It'th a continual thtruggle.'

'None of us knows where the next meal is coming from,' said somebody else.

'I thought it was coming from the BBC,' said Chote.

'Nothing ith more undependable than the BBThee,' lisped the cummerbund. 'We might be out on the thtreet tomorrow !'

'It's quite true, actually,' said Charles, brushing back his roguish hair. 'The insecurity is simply intense.'

'Well, I'll help you in any way I can,' said Chote.

'Is that a promise?' asked Wagstaff with a light laugh. 'You don't know what you're letting yourself in for, old boy.'

Outside, the dawn was breaking, turning the college back to a grisly hangover grey. Daphne yawned and shivered. It was only four o'clock. It was her duty to keep going somehow for at least two more hours. The fairy lights in the front quad looked forlorn and inadequate; the music was thin and reedy and repetitious. From here on, it was mostly a matter of will power. Voices were subdued, bow-ties were incurably askew, button-holes were crushed. The hired tail coats looked funereal in the morning light; the evening dresses were sadly rumpled, and the girls inside them looked as if they had been left out all night. Too much laughter in the flower beds.

The committee room was empty, except for Jack the patient barman and an elderly graduate who was reminiscing peevishly. 'We haven't had a batsman worthy of the name in fifty years at least. *Poke* about, that's all they seem to do nowadays.

Poke about!' Jack was polishing the glasses and lining them up on a tray. 'What do *you* think?' asked the old man at last. 'You're probably right, sir,' said Jack. 'Nothing is what it was.'

They went out again and had a couple of lonely dances in the empty tent. 'Let's go and sit down somewhere,' said Daphne. They tried the deck chairs, but it was cold, and the dew was making Daphne's feet wet. It was the season for will power all right.

They finally wandered back to the Browning–Hook room, which was their room too, because they had helped to decorate it that morning and had left some champagne there.

Their feet dragged one by one up the stairs. Chote counted the steps, for something to do: fifty-one. That seemed reasonable.

Browning was sitting back, his eyes closed, humming to himself. His lady was stumping erratically around the room looking for a shoe. 'Have you seen my shoe?' she said to Daphne as she came through the door. 'Alan hid it somewhere.'

'Wakie, wakie,' said Chote, giving Browning a shake.

'Leave me alone, you horrible man,' Browning mumbled sensuously.

'Where's my man Godfrey?' asked Chote, with a sudden twinge of anxiety.

He looked around. The bedroom door was shut again. The Do Not Disturb sign seemed to be swaying obscenely on the handle. The handle must be turning. In a minute Doris Flounce came out, with hair over her face, and then Godfrey. He looked at Chote defiantly. 'What business is it of yours?' he seemed to say. He went over and shook the champagne bottles. 'Bloody man has drunk all the champagne,' he muttered furiously.

Good God, thought Chote. Anyone else, but not him. *He's* not supposed to act like this. It was too bloody grotesque. One thought of Godfrey as an earnest little boy at school, stumbling this way and that in his efforts to do the right thing. Little Hook, the parson's son, trying to do the right thing.

He gazed around in a kind of agony. Daphne was looking, if anything, blanker than usual. Hook was down on the floor foraging angrily for champagne. The two girls were restoring their radiance in front of the mirror, very matter-of-fact and businesslike, making new mouths for the future. Alan Browning just sat there with his eyes shut, smiling and humming to himself. He had had a very pleasant two quid's worth, and now it was time to rest.

11. Waking

In the grey, chalky light, they might have been a middle-aged couple trying to catch some sleep on a train or a bus. Daphne's modest double chin was folded all anyhow, and Chote's lips were puttering in and out in an old man's semi-snore. Flat on their backs on the floor of the punt, they seemed to have spread sideways like sacks dropped from on high, held in place by the hopeless, intractable corpulence of sedentary middle age.

A weeping willow dripped gracefully across the punt, tickling their cheeks from pink to red to purple : Chote's neck bulged ominously against his hard starched collar, which was biting into the soft flesh like two thin white fingers—something would surely have to burst in a moment. Daphne's stays were creating the same effect on her, only lower down : cutting off much needed supplies of blood and driving a savage wedge into the digestive tract. This sleep would do them no good : they needed to be completely rearranged by some kind passer-by. Chote opened his eyes for a moment : the sky was a little grey square just visible through the branches; but he couldn't make out what it was, or whether he was looking up at it or down at it. He closed his eyes again, and dug his chin further into his collar. He didn't know that he'd been awake at all—in fact he would never know.

He had a foul, synoptic dream. He took Schools again, sitting by himself on the lawn at Brinkley. The spray of woods, the morose buildings, and his father's picture on the piano, nothing had changed. The papers were completely blank, which was his fault of course. Mr. Chote would be very upset, but that couldn't be helped. He would have to marry Daphne now—a small wedding, no fuss, no fuss, no fuss, said Daphne, somewhere in the North. It wasn't too bad except for the limp, tedious sunshine.

He opened his eyes again, and saw the sky framed among the branches. A huge frowning face appeared suddenly, ominously between him and the sky. 'Are you all right, John?' asked Daphne.

'God, I feel awful,' he said. 'What time is it?'

'I don't know,' she said, putting a cool hand on his forehead. 'Are you sure you're all right?'

'No, I'm not at all sure.' He touched her hand with his groping heavy fingers. He still couldn't quite make out which way was up, so he lay still. 'I've just had the most awful dream,' he whispered, trying not to exasperate the unaccountable pain in his throat.

'I thought so,' said Daphne. 'You looked absolutely wretched.' Her fingers swam smoothly, lightly across his hot face. 'I'll bet it's that dreadful collar. I suppose you thought someone was trying to strangle you.'

'No, I don't think it was that.' He was getting his whereabouts now—that was the sky up there; the huge face was friendly : it belonged to good old Daphne. And as he became attuned to the world around him, he lost the dream. 'It was very sunny,' he said, clutching. 'Back at school, I think. Or somewhere else. Bloody uncalled for type of dream.'

They walked slowly back in the direction of Sturdley, seedily formal in their crushed evening clothes, mocked all the way by the dull sunlight. Chote's collar hung open like an idiot's mouth; Daphne's dress trailed forlornly in the morning dust. An empty bottle of champagne dangled lifeless between them.

After a silent breakfast of cold sausages (Norbert Jones had made a mistake and ordered too many sausages) they went to the Forester's Arms to join the other mourners.

The coloured bottles twinkled behind the bar like Japanese lanterns: chartreuse, crème de menthe, curaçao, port; bright, exotic, festive colours in a sparkling row, tastefully arranged by Mr. Wilson himself. 'How would you like to take one drink out of each bottle?' whispered a voice in Chote's ear.

'Good grief, no. What a repulsive suggestion. Oh, good morning, Alan. It had to be you, of course.'

Alan Browning was neat and fresh, untroubled by dreams. His shirt front gleamed brighter than ever, and his tie was still straight: 'Come and join our little party, John.' He ushered them across the room like a smooth head waiter, turning this way and that with a smart swish of tails. 'Ah, Mr. Chote. I have just the table for you.' The ruddy man was indestructible: now prancing lightly about, to pull out chairs for them, now tucking them in again with a swift flick of the hand. When Browning's digestion held up, he was incomparable.

Godfrey Hook was a more satisfactory sight, half doubled over, as from a kick in the stomach; his dress shirt had crumpled under him like cheap cardboard. He glanced up briefly and nodded. His face looked stiff, either with pain or annoyance: it was hard to tell which. 'Good morning, Godfrey,' said John as heartily as he could.

'I'm afraid poor Godfrey is feeling a bit under the weather this morning,' explained Alan. 'He hasn't the stamina of the older irresponsibles.'

'I daresay he overdid things a bit last night,' said John. He smiled uncomfortably over at Doris Flounce, who smiled promptly back, radiant in incorrigible innocence.

'Well, you look all right anyway,' said Alan generously.

'Oh, I can't complain. A bit thoughtful, a little tender in the joints perhaps. But you have to expect that at my age.' He put his arm cordially around Daphne. 'Fortunately, I passed a comparatively temperate evening.'

He gazed slyly at each of them in turn, to see how they had taken this little thrust: Alan's girl was studying a small gin and orange, with apparent incomprehension, and Doris Flounce was still smiling at him, as if she'd forgotten to stop. What earthly pleasure did Browning get out of these girls, who were bored—or worse, untouched—by everything one said or did or thought about? Even during love, he imagined that their attention must wander birdlike to all corners of the room: feather dusters glancing lightly off the walls and furniture. In comparison Daphne seemed almost like a German Professor....

Godfrey still didn't look up, but the top of his head looked curiously angry, like the head of a brave bull. No, that must be imagination. How could you tell a chap was angry just by looking at the top of his head? It must be something about the way the brown fuzz was massed over the crown.

'That doesn't sound like the Chote I know,' said Browning blandly.

'Doesn't it?' said Chote vaguely. His head was throbbing and he could still feel the fingers around his neck, as if his collar had not been loosened at all. The pub was hot and airless: one had to suck in an extra quantity of mouldy atmosphere (on the sly) to get just a little oxygen into the lungs. It was no use suggesting that somebody open a window; they were all flung out wide already, and a warm, heavy draught, with very little air in it, was moving slowly and sedately across the pub.

'No,' said Browning. 'The old Chote, what I might call the vintage Chote, wouldn't have dared to come in here today without a hangover—even if he had to fake the symptoms.'

'Perhaps I'm merely faking the symptoms of health, for a change,' said Chote.

'Probably,' said Hook, without looking up: it was like a belch or an unexpected grumble of thunder.

'Godfrey, you startled me. I didn't know you were awake.'

'Blast it, it's beginning to rain again,' said Browning. It was already streaking in, onto the off-white window sills, making the dust swim, turning it to slime.

'Please shut the windows, gentlemen,' said Mr. Wilson in tones of dire emergency and panic—this was just the sort of thing that always unsettled him most.

The windows chunked shut, sealing in the smoke and the stale air once and for all: Chote would have to take gargantuan breaths now, just to stay alive. The problem was to do it unobtrusively. He yawned casually.

199

'Cosy, isn't it girls?' chatted Browning. 'Warm and dark like your favourite womb.' They giggled obediently. 'I can't see my hand in front of my face,' he said, whipping an arm around one of the girls. 'Honestly, were you ever so excited?'

'Chote doesn't like it,' said Hook in a hollow voice. 'He's beginning to wheeze.'

'Why so he is,' said Browning. 'I thought it was the plumbing at first.'

'I must admit, I don't feel quite as clever as I thought I did,' gasped Chote. 'Something dreadful seems to have caught up with me.' It took so much breath to talk; and some pub-land sprite was pinching his Adam's apple at every word, criticizing and carping.

'It's funny, isn't it,' said Hook, 'that the one time Chote acually has a hangover, he has to pretend that he hasn't.'

'Oh, hilarious,' said Browning. 'On second thoughts, Godfrey, what do you know about it? You can't even see him from there.'

'No, but I can hear him, and that's bad enough. God, what a din.'

'Oh, it isn't as bad as all that,' said Chote, labouring uneasily. 'You have to discount some of it as buzzing in the ears.'

These was a moment of silence, so that you could just hear the soft rain outside. Chote tried to hold it, but he couldn't: a deafening, wheezing hiccup tumbled helter-skelter into the gentle atmosphere, like a drunk barging into church. Everyone laughed except Godfrey Hook.

'Did you hear something, Godfrey?' Browning asked. 'A little buzzing in the ears, perhaps?'

'Why doesn't he just go outside?' said Hook, the words coming straight through the top of his angry head. 'Why does he always have to stay and bluff it out?'

'What are you talking about, Godfrey?' asked Browning with exuberant amusement. 'The old brain is beginning to wander perhaps.'

'You know what I mean, and *he* knows what I mean,' said Hook enigmatically. Browning made a suave gesture, apologizing for an outrageous child. Chote looked around at the circle. The girls' faces were glued solid : they were listening now, but they weren't going to help.

'The man talks in riddles,' said Browning lightly. 'Of course he's really in no condition to talk at all.'

'It's just a symbol of his whole attitude,' said Hook.

'There, you see?' said Browning. 'The poor chap is still paralysed with drink. What *does* he mean this time? What's just a symbol, old boy? And whose attitude are you talking about?'

'*Chote's* of course!' said Hook impatiently. Why doesn't he get annoyed with Browning, instead of me? wondered Chote. I'm not the one who's goading him.

'What's the matter with Chote's attitude?' asked Browning, leaning forward, tightening the circle of his acquaintance like a noose.

'You know bloody well what's wrong with Chote's attitude,' said Hook. Why the devil doesn't he look up, thought Chote. What's the matter with him?

'I've always thought that John's attitude was rather charming,' twittered Browning, his merry eyes dancing all over Hook. 'Gross but attractive.'

'Beastly weather we've been having,' said Chote, with another simulated and painful yawn.

'I think Godfrey is trying to tell us something,' said Browning, jerking the circle tighter again, pulling the girls forward with him. 'What's the matter with Chote's attitude, you frightful chap?' Chote suddenly realized that Browning was actually trying to pry something out of Godfrey by main force. 'Come on, Godfrey, don't let it fester.'

'Well, I would have thought it was obvious,' mumbled Hook, wiping his mouth with the back of his hand. Browning smiled expectantly : any moment now, chaps. He held up his hand like a stop signal. 'This is going to be rich—just listen, do please listen,' he seemed to be saying. The girls' faces were half lit with vague, shapeless curiosity—the same curiosity that they felt about film stars and public scandals and ugly rumours relating to the Royal Family. Something, anything, was going to happen. In the circumstances, it was always best to stand in line and wait.

'Well,' said Hook at last, into his hands. 'The chap's a fraud, that's all, an impostor. I thought everybody knew about that.'

'Ho-ho,' said Browning. 'Listen to the man. This is really too much. What on earth makes you think that, Godfrey?'

What are they talking about? wondered Chote. He couldn't make any sense of it at first. He gazed at Mr. Wilson's twinkling bottles, and wondered if he were still dreaming. Emerald green and sapphire, lit cunningly from beneath: the Indies, perhaps, the spice trade. Pirates and sultans. Whoopee.

'The chap's a living lie,' said Hook. 'That's all.'

'Ho-ho!' shrieked Browning. 'Really too priceless.' The girls were trying to see the point—whatever they had been waiting for was happening now. The contagion of Alan's high spirits was doing something to them, but they couldn't put a name to it. They squirmed softly, foolishly in their chairs under Browning's direction. But Daphne stiffened. 'He's drunk,' she said.

'I know he is,' said Browning. 'But isn't he marvellous?'

'He's right, of course,' said Chote quickly. 'I'm thoroughly bogus, in every possible way. But then, aren't we all?'

'No,' said Hook sharply, 'we're not. Nobody else is bogus but you.'

'Oh, come now,' said Browning, still laughing. 'You can't say that. We're all just a little bit bogus, don't you think?' Off to the Indies in a pea-green bottle.

'No!' Hook was adamant. 'He's been getting away with this for much too long. For three bloody years in fact. And I'm just about sick of it.'

Chote was brought to earth on a sudden wave of self-pity. Why did they have to talk like this when he felt so bad? His head was aching dreadfully. 'Open the damned windows and let the rain in,' he felt like shouting.

'He's Mr. Nobody from Nowhere,' Hook rambled on remorselessly. 'He hasn't got any identity at all.'

'You shouldn't encourage him,' Daphne frowned. 'He isn't responsible.'

Why are they talking like this about me? thought Chote. What terrible thing had he done recently?

'You must agree that he's got a certain indefinable charm,' said Browning, smiling at Daphne.

'He just about makes me ill,' said Hook. 'That's all.'

Browning's mouth hung a little bit open, like the mouth of a bad ventriloquist. In fact, Chote had an illusion that Alan's lips had actually been moving a little while Godfrey was speaking. But in a second, he was repudiating his dummy once again. 'How can you talk such twaddle, my dear Godfrey? And about your boyhood chum, too.'

Daphne was fussing with her handbag, opening and shutting it briskly. 'I don't think this is very funny, Alan,' she said.

'No, I don't suppose it is, come to think of it,' said Browning suddenly. 'For Godsake, Godfrey, wrap it up now and go back to sleep.'

'I just thought it needed saying, that's all,' mumbled Hook fuzzily. 'It's high time somebody said it.'

'Well, there's no need to cry about it, old boy,' said Chote a little nastily. 'I hope you'll feel better now that you've got it all out of your tiny system.'

Hook's face shot up out of his hands at last. It was brick-red, amply fulfilling the promise of the angry scalp, and swimming sloppily around the eyes. 'You're a bastard, Chote,' he said in a loud voice. 'A cheap, vulgar, hypocritical bastard.'

'Oh come now, Godfrey,' protested Alan. People in every corner of the pub began to stare in his direction, and sure enough Godfrey started to look embarrassed. The girls were patting their hair distractedly and trying ineffectually to talk to each other. 'Remember the ladies,' said Alan gallantly.

'Didn't mean to cause offence,' said Hook, lowering his head again and shutting his eyes—shutting out the vague, curious stares. 'What did he say?' whispered somebody on the far side of the pub. 'I didn't catch it,' whispered somebody else. 'He said something all right, but I don't know what it was.'

Daphne snapped her handbag shut for the last time. 'Let's leave, John. It's getting awfully stuffy in here.'

Browning bounced up to shower her with attentions. 'I say, I'm frightfully sorry about this. Did you have a coat? . . . I hope you won't get wet.'

Chote raised his flesh, but his blood took just a moment longer, and he suddenly thought he was going to faint. What was he doing in this funny-looking place? He focused hard on the coloured bottles. This looked like the Forester's Arms in Oxford—but what was *he* doing there? He shook his head. Curious feeling.

'Aren't you going to finish your beer, John?'

'I don't think so. Give it to Godfrey.' He glanced at the sandy head, which was now dropping like a dead flower. He had a sudden desire to clutch a tuft of Godfrey's soft hair and yank his red face into the light and punch it senseless—smash it to water. 'He's sleeping like a baby,' he said instead. 'A drunken baby.'

'No, I'm not,' said Godfrey in a low voice.

'Well you ought to be,' said Chote. Godfrey was too embarrassed to make anything out of it. 'That's no way for a parson's son to behave,' added Chote. It was almost as good as punching him. 'What would the reverend daddy say?'

Browning followed them to the door, an anxious head waiter now, hoping that they hadn't been offended by anything, and that they'd call again soon. 'Godfrey's a bit overwrought today,' he explained. 'Too much excitement, you know.'

'He's a bit over-something,' said Daphne. 'And I daresay he's had too much something else.'

'That's rather good,' chuckled Browning, burbling appreciation. 'I'm glad you're being such a sport about it, Daphne. But then, you're always such a sport.'

Chote opened the door and began to push Daphne roughly through it into the rain. Browning made a playful swoop and caught at his frayed black tail. 'By the way, John. There was something I meant to tell you, but all the excitement clean drove it out of my head.'

'Let go of my tail, you frightful chap.'

'Sorry,' said Browning. 'No offence. I just wanted to explain the reason for Godfrey's diabolical excitement, in case you were interested.'

'Well, I'm not much interested, actually. I've seen too much of that sort of thing in my time.' Browning was so damnably frisky, a puppy hanging on to one's trouser leg. Chote stuck his head out of the door, to feel the cleansing rain on his head; he stuck it out farther, but nothing happened. The blasted rain had stopped. He pulled his head in again.

'. . . the most wizard telegram to Felicity,' Browning was saying. 'Putting her fairly and squarely in her place. Godfrey asserted the old manhood like nobody's business.'

'That's nice,' said Chote dully.

'I thought so too. He told her that she would have to wait at least a year, perhaps more. Take it or leave it, he said.'

'It sounds like quite a telegram.'

'Oh, it was, it was. Two overgrown pages, before I got to work with the blue pencil. I shaved away a good page and a half of unnecessary Billingsgate. The remainder was incredibly taut and meaty, "If wish marry other chap, won't stand in way"—that sort of thing.'

'Do you think it was the right thing to do?' asked Daphne doubtfully.

'Oh, indubitably. John will agree with me there. The girl was eating into his virility like a bloody great spider. Wasn't she, John?'

He didn't say anything, so Alan prompted him further. 'You've always said that yourself—in fact I believe I got the pretty simile from your own steaming lips.'

'I thought they were very much in love,' said Daphne solidly, dipping into her bag of phrases.

'Why a year?' asked Chote. 'Why did he tell her to soak her head for a whole year?'

'Ah, that's the point my boy. In the small hours of last night, Godfrey and I came together to a rather desperate decision. We, to put it briefly, have, in a word, decided to stay at Oxford for another year, and acquire a pair of diplomas in education.'

'What a ruddy silly thing to do,' said Chote.

'Oh, I don't know. I'd been thinking about it for some time now. I rather fancy myself as a corrupter of youth—only joking, Daphne—and I think Godfrey would make a satisfactory chalkbag in his own way. But the main thing is to give Godfrey another year to complete his emancipation. It promises to be what the Americans might call "an exciting experiment in living", don't you think?' He smiled innocently at Chote : object if you wish, old boy. Daphne looked at him too, for a lead out of the jungle.

'What are you thinking about, John?' asked Daphne.

'Do you approve of our plan?' asked Alan in his friendly, candid way.

'I don't care what you do with him,' said Chote briefly. 'Come along, Daphne.'

'I must go back and look after my patient,' said Browning. 'By the way, John—we'll take care of Daphne for you next year. She'll be in the best of hands.'

'Thank you, Alan,' said Daphne, with a nice, polite smile. All the nastiness was forgotten—well, it hadn't been anything in the first place : just everyone feeling a bit out of sorts after a nice party. Probably, Daphne decided, the less said about it the better : or to put it another way, the least said, the soonest mended. 'Ta, ta, Mr. Browning,' she said playfully. 'I expect we'll be bumping into you again.'

On an impulse, Chote tried to catch Browning's eye. Had Alan really put Godfrey up to all that crap? Did he really believe he was saving the parson from a fate worse than death? All he got was a blank and distant smile, the old Browning charm, aimed at no one in particular, elicited by nothing special. 'Ta, ta, Miss Collins. We must certainly do this again.' Making fun of her and winning her at the same time.

The workmen had come back to the Sturdley quad, to dismantle the paraphernalia of merriment. The dance floor already lay in disconnected strips all over the place. Strings of coloured lights were heaped in the lodge. Men in overalls doggedly followed in the traces of the dancing people, mutilating, disconnecting and carting away. The only link of continuity was supplied by Norbert Jones, who had already stripped down to tweeds for the day's work. 'Easy on the scaffolding, old boy. We only rented it, you know.' It was hard to tell whether the workmen were paying any attention to him or not, but it was good to see Norbert back on the job.

'Everything in order?' asked Chote.

'Yes, yes,' said Norbert, bustling past to supervise a couple of workmen who were carrying a plank out into the street. 'Watch out, old boy. There's work in progress, you know.'

Standing amid the ruins, Chote suddenly wondered where he was again. There was a persistent hammering going on somewhere, and it set up a tiny replica in his head, with a little toy hammer tapping against the sides of his skull. Of course he knew where he was really—but it all looked so strange. Why were they hammering today? Yesterday was the day for hammering. 'What are they hammering for, Norbert?' It seemed as if they were taking down the whole college, now that he was leaving.

Norbert was trotting past in the other direction, too busy to pay attention. 'I say, are you sure that's not one of ours?' he shouted. A workman was inching forwards with a table on his back and Norbert was accosting him fiercely. 'Yes, it is, it is one of ours. I've begged you chaps to be careful.' The workman inched away again.

'I'm glad everything is in hand,' said John.

'I suppose the rest of the committee's still in bed,' snapped Norbert a touch viciously. 'As usual, I seem to have been left with the whole responsibility.'

'You're an invaluable chap, Norbert. I've always said so.'

'Oh, yes, of course, I know all about that,' said Norbert sarcastically. 'I'm invaluable to you aren't I, Chote? Picking up your mess and so on, and so on.'

As a rule Chote took Norbert's panting indignation with relish. But on top of the Chaplain and Hook, it was really too much. 'What do you mean, clean up my mess, you sweaty bugger? Nobody asked you to clean up anything.' But already Norbert was gone, to convey a word of cheer, and a word of reprimand, to his sluggish charges. '*Must* you have your tea

now? Oh, very well. You've really done very well, actually.'
Chote took Daphne's hand and waddled out of the quad.

Daphne was good to walk with: strong and quiet and
patient. And they walked a long way, past Christ Church,
which seemed to be outlined unnaturally clear and stark, like
a flashy modern skyscraper; in and out of Pembroke (where
was he now? It was getting to be a kind of game, locating
himself, find the donkey); and out over Folly Bridge, into the
nondescript territory beyond.

He still couldn't quite make out the point of Hook's assault.
What had the blighter been driving at? 'Do *you* think I'm
bogus, Daphne?' he asked after a while.

She looked concerned at once. 'He didn't upset you, did he?'
she asked. 'He wasn't himself, you know.'

'Oh, no. He didn't upset me. I'm much too ill to be upset.'
Daphne looked relieved. 'Still,' he continued, 'it raises an
interesting question, don't you think?' They walked another
hundred yards or so in silence. 'I mean, am I or am I not
bogus?'

'Well, not specially,' said Daphne dubiously. 'I mean, no
more than most people, I shouldn't think.'

'That's what I've been saying myself for years, and I'm glad
you've absorbed the lesson so well—but I wonder if we
mightn't both be wrong, after all.'

'Oh no,' said Daphne promptly. 'I don't think so. I didn't
just learn about this from you, you know. I've known a few
other people in my time, you know.' Good God, Daphne
wasn't turning on him too, as part of some universal unmasking? A graduation-day stripping, right down to the glass
slippers. 'I have a brother who's a lot like you,' she said. 'And
he was always showing off when he was your age. It was a
scream.'

'Oh,' said Chote weakly. 'I trust he's grown out of it by now?'

'Yes, he's had to. He works for a respectable firm now, and
only recently, they made him shave off his moustache. It was
one of those dreadful R.A.F. ones, you know, and the manager
thought it might be affecting sales.'

'And do you think I'm always showing off too?'

'Oh no,' said Daphne quickly. 'I didn't mean that—it's quite different with educated people. But it wouldn't be natural if you didn't show off a little at your age. And I'm sure you don't overdo it.'

Her anxiety not to hurt him was transparent—she knew so well what it was to be hurt. She scooped up his hand in hers. 'I wouldn't worry about it, John. I daresay your friends are every bit as bogus as you are. You're all very much alike in those ways.'

They were well out in the country by now. John was vaguely bent on walking himself into the ground, into exhaustion; but so far, only his feet hurt, from the rhythmical pinch and nip of his tight black shoes. 'I say, I didn't ask you if you wanted to change,' he said; a country boy had just wobbled past on his bicycle grinning oafishly at Daphne, and Chote had become aware of their unlikely costuming for the first time. 'I'm frightfully sorry,' he said.

'I didn't want to specially,' said Daphne.

'No, I'm sure you did. You must feel like an absolute fool.'

'No I don't. Or at least, I haven't up to now.'

'All that my enemies say is true,' Chote said remorsefully. I'm nothing but a heartless fraud.'

'You're not, you're not,' chanted Daphne. 'You're really very sweet, and I'm thoroughly annoyed with Godfrey Hook for upsetting you like this.'

Her kindness was humid; there was no air in it.

'Let's go back now and pray for rain,' he said. 'A real, drenching, merciless monsoon to wash everything away.'

'I thought we'd had enough rain to suit anybody,' said Daphne thoughtfully, twisting on a blistered heel and heading back towards Oxford under Chote's morose guidance.

He changed into his stiff grey suit and took his tails back to the hirers. He hadn't the stomach, or the heart, for any more conviviality, and he dodged the next ceremonial opening of the Forester's Arms. Browning would be there, of course, with his nerve-racking vitality, and Hook might be feeling apologetic by now—or perhaps not; he might be looking to get in one more lick at Chote, under cover of drunkenness. In either case, the embarrassment was prohibitive.

Daphne saw him off at the station with a motherly kiss. 'You are *not* a fraud,' she said with a laugh. But otherwise she was gloomy too, and Chote was terrified that she would break out in her great silent tears.

'You will write from America, won't you John?'

'You bet I will, baby.'

She tried to smile, but slipped back into solemn anxiety. 'And you will take care of yourself.'

She stood under the train window looking up at him like a heartbroken minstrel.

'I'll be back before you know it,' he said. But what good was that to her? 'And we'll see what we'll see,' he added. He leaned down to kiss her and her lips smudged across his face as the train jerked him forcibly away. The grey face of the sad girl, spires, gasworks and then the inevitable graveyard; his last view of Oxford, melodramatic, perhaps, a touch overdone, but uncommonly effective. He felt a curious salty taste, and a heaviness about the tongue: and he suddenly realized that it wouldn't be any effort at all to, well, so to speak, cry.

The other faces in the carriage were dim and elfin in the twilight. A choleric country gentleman in brown was rustling his paper indignantly—everything in it was utterly damnable. In the far corner an undergraduate was doing a crossword puzzle in the gloaming, and across from him was a pretty girl Chote remembered vaguely from the Ball. He caught her eye and smiled sentimentally, but she looked haughtily into the corridors, dismissing him once and for all. She obviously didn't realize what a harmless old fraud she was dealing with.

What *did* Hook mean by that? All afternoon long, he had been trying to see a glimmer of sense in Godfrey's accusation. One didn't enjoy being attacked by anybody—even the Reverend Smythe had a tiny sting in his tail, and Norbert Jones could cause an annoying, bumbling sound in the ears—'but surely I could make out a much more damaging case than that myself : meanness and greed and cruelty, real sins, much worse than a little facetious hypocrisy.

'Why don't they turn on the blasted lights?' exploded the country gentleman. 'Blasted inefficiency.' He glared around with bulging eyes at the alien generation, demanding corroboration. 'It is a bit dark,' mumbled the undergraduate with the crossword puzzle. 'Abolutely shocking!' agreed the man in brown, and he got up and strode into the corridor. The young people made faces behind his back : 'Funny old fellow.' The pretty girl allowed herself a small smile out towards the corridor. Elderly people who liked to make scenes were really too priceless.

The trouble with Hook, thought Chote, is that he doesn't really see the joke. 'I am in a framework, you have limitations, he doesn't know what the hell is going on'—an appropriate formula that he and Browning had once made up for people like Hook. Godfrey hadn't seen the joke at school either, and that had really been his undoing : boys had turned on him with absolute frenzy, for not seeing the joke. Chote remembered a bunch of jovial, good-hearted little fellows beating the stuffing out of Godfrey on his very first day at Brinkley. One sensed immediately why they were doing it. It was really the only thing one could do with a chap who missed the joke as badly as Godfrey missed it—but what was the joke? Ah, there.

'Look here, guard, we haven't got any light in here.'

The harassed guard peered into the compartment, as if to make quite sure. 'Inexcusable inefficiency. But it's been like this ever since the war, of course.' The young people smiled cautiously. 'I can't help it sir. They haven't turned any of the lights on yet.'

'What do you mean, you can't help it? You're the guard aren't you?'

It was hopeless, and the country gentleman had to return to his seat. 'We have to sit here in utter darkness, because *he* can't help it.'

'It's been like this ever since the war,' said Chote, who wanted to talk to somebody. 'The ruddy people seem to have lost all pride in their work.'

These indignant old fellows usually accepted one without question as a contemporary, virtually a classmate, in affairs of this sort. But this one was an exception : he peered suspiciously at Chote through the dusk and asked, 'What the devil do you know about pre-war days?'

'Well, only what I read in the history books, actually.'

'Dashed impertinence,' and so on. Chote returned sadly to his thoughts : the old fellow didn't want sympathy after all, but only to be left alone in manly grief and disappointment.

After so much brooding, it was no use pretending any more that he wasn't upset by Godfrey's wild dervish-like assaults— not so much by their substance, perhaps, as by their mood and intent. Godfrey must have been storing up this poison for years. One could hardly blame him, of course. Incidents floated back to mind, incidents forcibly forgotten : the bathroom outrage, for example. 'I won't tell, honestly I won't'—Godfrey staring with shocked fascination at the soggy cigarettes floating like water lilies. 'You know you can trust me.' And they did trust him too : but they plunged his head into the basin all the same, and held it there until it began to blow out sad little bubbles of supplication. Chote remembered the feeling as of lank seaweed under his fingers. 'And you'll get more if you tell. Much, much more.' As he watched Godfrey running down the hall, he knew in his bones that he was going to be punished for this some day. And so he had been at last, today, kismet, in the Forester's Arms.

And then there was the time they had locked Godfrey out all night in the rain, in his pyjamas. Round and round the school Godfrey went sniffling, trying all the doors. But Brinkley, with its precious horde of scruffy boys to be protected, was impregnable by night. 'Hook, what the devil are you doing out here?' 'I thought I heard a noise, sir, a burglar, sir, and the door slammed behind me.' 'Very well, Hook. But remember in future that it isn't up to you to defend the school by yourself. The next time you hear a noise, send for a master.' The authorities were never harsh on Godfrey. They knew from one look that he was a victim—although he never squealed on his tormentors, and they in turn were always careful not to leave any bruises.

The curious thing was that one simultaneously felt the most acute sympathy with little Hook. Although Chote was the one who had pushed the bolt on Godfrey, he didn't sleep at all that night until the victim crept back to bed in the pale light of morning. In his memory now, he could hardly tell whether Godfrey had been out all night or *he* had; or which of them had bullied which.

Only once since, in their first year at Oxford, had either of them ever alluded to the good old carefree school days. As usual Godfrey had shown no resentment. 'I daresay I was a thoroughly ill-favoured little chap, and the rest of you were doing the only possible thing.' 'Well, it wasn't so much that,' John had said. 'I daresay we were all roughly on a par, repulsively speaking. But I always felt that if it wasn't you, it might have been me.' That was true too : he did feel that Godfrey was getting all the pain and punishment that he should have been getting, all that there was in the school, in fact. But Godfrey had dismissed the idea : 'You were the last one they would have picked on, old boy. You were always sickeningly popular.'

At last the lights flickered on, and the young people smiled at the country gentleman, the girl with positive radiance. 'It's about time,' he muttered. 'Too late to do any good, of course.' He was glaring at Chote again, as if he had been responsible for the whole dreadful business. 'Too little and too late—rather typical of our British railways these days.'

The funny feeling of dislocation came back, only much stronger. The naked light bulb shining weakly on the shabby seats; a strange old man in brown snarling at him; a marvellous-looking girl with at least sixty-four shimmering teeth— how had he possibly got into this situation? He suddenly remembered that he hadn't eaten since breakfast. No wonder he felt a little unlocated, a touch displaced.

'Mr. Nobody from Nowhere,' Godfrey Hook had called him. Who was he anyway? It wasn't easy to decide on an empty stomach. He had picked up so many mannerisms along the way—a new accent, a new background and a new style. Didn't everybody? Well, perhaps not. Perhaps Godfrey was right: nobody did but Chote. Perhaps there wasn't any joke at all, and Godfrey was quite right not to see it.

One felt suddenly lonely, under the naked bulb and the old man's glare. Here one was going to a new country, a demanding country, and one wasn't really anybody: nothing but a lot of acquired mannerisms, slapped on like coat after coat of cheap paint. He was, in fact, just like Daphne's brother who had been requested to shave off his moustache—only there was nothing underneath.

What had he been like to start with? One probed back into darkness. But all he could see was Godfrey Hook. He seemed somehow to have merged with the wretched little chap. 'You're all very much alike,' Daphne had said.

A more successful, but also more dishonest version of Godfrey Hook. The same moral standards, the same essential timidity and dependence—but less honesty. The same flatulent desire to be a man among men, one of 'the boys'. . . .

All right, supposing he was that—was there nothing at all one could feel proud of? He rummaged about for a crumb of consolation. Glib; reasonably well co-ordinated; popular? Probably not really. No *real* friends at all. Intelligent, well no, facile, and not very original. He made a grimace at his little list. Fancy trying to identify yourself by such a string of Boy Scout attainments. It was the kind of description you might expect from an employer who didn't know you very well: 'John Chote has always given satisfaction. He is a good worker and gets along famously with other men.'

Then he thought of Alan Browning, and there he saw the one distinction that Godfrey lacked. For all his flabbiness and fraudulence, which now stretched before him in an endless vista, there was one thing he had never done. He had never once done anything that Browning wanted him to do. Alan had never succeeded in breaking him, as he had broken Godfrey. It mightn't be much—but perhaps it had been enough to infuriate both Browning and Hook.

It was a small nub of identity, under the flashy shifting surface: a tiny kind of strength with which to face the future.

By God, he was stronger than Hook, and he always had been. He had whatever it took to survive—and perhaps he could even build on that, although he didn't know exactly how.

He expected that his companions in the carriage had been watching him going through his little adventure: but their faces were blank. He had evidently uttered no groans of dismay or cackles of triumph. Possibly the others had been going through similar contortions behind their own bland skin, deciding to commit suicide or to invest their extra capital. He felt extraordinarily light-headed—he wasn't going to analyse himself again for years and years.

'Ten minutes late,' said the country gentleman. 'A quite disgraceful performance.'

'*The Times* shall hear about it,' said Chote. 'I shall make it my business.' And he danced out into the corridor and onto the Paddington platform, with the last snort of the country gentleman singing like a pastorale in his ears.

Then he spotted the solemn head of Bradshaw Soames ahead of him on the platform, and was brought back to earth immediately. Bradshaw's head, bobbing gracefully above the crowd, reminded him that he was about to go to a mysterious country, a place where, according to all accounts, they valued sincerity highly. The Oxford greasepaint would have to be put away for a while, and he would have to go as he was (whatever that might be). It was a sobering thought, and it reminded him that he was hungry.

So he started to run for the bus that would take him home.

Section

III

*English-Speaking
Union*

12. The New World

'THIS Communist business is pretty much based on perversion, as far as I can make out,' said the little man grimly. 'You can always reduce it to perversion of some kind or other. In my opinion, that's at the root of it, all right.'

Chote shut his eyes and the man's voice blended smoothly with the drone of the motors. 'Have you got any commies in your country, sir?' Chote opened his eyes again. 'What's that?' 'I'm sorry, I didn't see you were resting,' said the man, 'I just wanted to know if there were any commies in your country.' Chote looked at him blankly. 'I suppose so. I don't know. Yes, there must be some, don't you think?' He looked out of the window. A few feet below, a propeller was cutting upward into the clouds, pulling him away from London, and away from the neat green squares of countryside around it, up into the great blank sky, where everything merged into a pale, functional, international blue.

He had already passed through a watershed of forgetfulness: a network of cream-coloured passageways, each of them clean as a hospital and sleek as a cinema foyer. 'BOAC passengers for Shannon, Gander and New York'—disembodied voices echoed and re-echoed off the blank walls, urging him on. And on every side, silent, semi-detached people in twos and threes drifted past like ghosts, answering the voices, doing as they were told. Chote followed them in his own personal trance, clutching his little overnight bag, past a covey of smooth-looking men and women dressed in blue, out onto the apron.

He had never really been in this world before, not body and soul anyway. In the poshest London hospital, say, one would always stumble upon a ragged doctor or better still, an earthy nurse—some reminder that the riper excrescences of life had not been scrubbed away completely. But here, even the people were streamlined: large Americans in oversimplified suits trooped solemnly onto the plane with their well-groomed wives; and an English girl with an American smile stood waiting for them at the top of the steps, with an ethereal greeting for each. 'I hope we'll have a smooth flight,' was the one selected for Chote. 'I expect we will,' he said gloomily. In such company a smooth flight seemed pretty well inevitable.

When he shut his eyes, it was no trick to conjure up the painful contrast. His mother and father had looked woefully out of place even at the terminal in London, which was only the waiting-room to this glossy paradise. Mrs. Chote talked busily about woollies and extra sweaters, as if John were about to leave for the cold moist buildings of Brinkley and Oxford once again. 'Don't be silly dear,' said Mr. Chote gruffly. 'The Yanks heat their buildings something sinfully, everybody knows that.' Their faces were tired and apprehensive as they waved goodbye. Something was wrong, he realized suddenly: perhaps he ought to stay at home and look after them. 'Good luck, son.' His father's lips moved stiffly outside the window of the coach. His mother waved a tiny white handkerchief. A tiny, crumpled, white handkerchief. One good tear would be more than enough to drench it through. But then, as far as he knew, Mrs. Chote never cried.

Chote opened his eyes for the second time. 'I hope I'm not boring you, sir,' said the man next to him.

'No, not at all,' said Chote, smiling at him. He was a little rolypoly with black armbands on his shirt sleeves, and a round skull liberally spattered with earnest, thinker's sweat. 'We feel that if you root out the perversion, the Communist menace will wither on the vine. I really believe that that's what Senator McCarthy is trying to do.' Chote realized for the first time the possibilities of reassurance that could be found in such a patent fanatic as this. There was certainly nothing smooth about him anyway, nothing glamorous—he could have been any one of a thousand Englishmen: he could have been Mr. Chote in fact.

His small eyes were swivelling restlessly on and off Chote. 'What do *you* think we ought to do about it, sir?'

'Well,' said Chote. 'I think we ought to root out the perversion to begin with.'

'Exactly what I've been saying. Root out the perversion.'

'And the rest will follow naturally, don't you think. Wither on the vine, so to speak.'

The man peered a warning at Chote. Was this guy making fun of him? The hostess came mincing down the aisle.

'Please put out that cigar, sir,' she said with such a big smile, as if she were saying something that tasted delicious. 'Cigarettes, but no cigars.'

'Oh, I'm sorry.' The little man fumbled with distress. 'Here, I'll put it out for you,' said the hostess.

The little man was back on the attack in a moment. 'My name is Brinkell. I'm in hardware. You can call me Frank,' he said briskly, getting through the formalities as fast as possible.

'I'm Wiggins,' said Chote mechanically. 'Augustus Wiggins. Private detective.'

The man peered at him again. 'Look, if you don't want to tell me the truth you don't have to.'

Chote took out a cigarette and lit it slowly and expressively. 'You're kidding, aren't you?' said Mr. Brinkell warmly. 'About the Wiggins bit? I mean, if you were an American I'd know for sure you were kidding. But I don't understand you people so good.' Chote blew out a little smoke ring and made a mental note. 'So if you're on the level, I want to apologize here and now,' said Mr. Brinkell.

'That's all right, Frank,' said Chote. 'I know it's rather incredible to meet chap called Wiggins, out of a clear blue sky, as it were. But let's face it, these things happen. Drama in everyday life.'

'I didn't mean to insult you, Augustus,' said Mr. Brinkell warmly. 'Wiggins is a perfectly good name by me.'

'Once you get over the initial shock,' said Chote, 'it's all right, I suppose. I used to be touchy about it at one time, but one can't go on like that, you know. . . .'

Good God! he thought—one certainly can't. He hadn't meant to begin like this with Americans. One had planned on being sincere and direct from the word 'go'. Instead, it looked as if one were about to embark on an unprecedented orgy of deceit and obliquity. Perhaps old Godfrey had put his finger on it, and it wasn't a joke at all but a raging, uncontrollable disease.

Oh well, he thought wearily. We'll just have to see.

It got dark as they left the coast. They came down at Shannon, and Chote moved about among the tax-free souvenirs, finally selecting a bottle of Irish whiskey to give to anyone who might have the stomach for it in America. He didn't have much money, and he began to reproach himself at once for throwing away the ten shillings. He climbed regretfully back onto the plane. The bleakness of a tourist-class night was beginning to close in already. The hostess's smile was wearing thin (she wouldn't need it in the dark) and a hitherto unnoticed baby was tuning up ominously a few seats away. Something had gone wrong with Mr. Brinkell too. His face was sallow and ugly in the light of the seat lamp, and he was glaring venomously at Chote.

'Did you run into any Communists out there?' asked Chote playfully.

Mr. Brinkell shook his head, without shifting his rattlesnake gaze. Oh no, thought Chote. The bloody man's been looking at the passenger list. That was why he would have to be careful in America—perhaps these people really cared! Mr. Brinkell turned his head away distastefully and wedged it into his pillow. Chote had already lost a friend.

It felt like a long night from the very beginning. He smoked some cigarettes and went over the racing results in his evening paper. Mr. Brinkell's back was a wrinkled bundle of disapproval in the next seat. The baby was baying elementally at the moon, deep, unearthly howls and sobs. Chote tried to turn onto his side. He had slept in armchairs before, by George. Outside, the sky was black and empty, an infinity of loneliness. He tried to fill it with some pleasant faces : his mother pouring tea, Daphne smiling uncertainly—and pouring tea. But their faces were unexpectedly huge and cold, monstrous constellar faces. It's really the tea that I miss most, thought Chote, trying to cheer himself up, as cockneys are wont to do under stress, with a little whimsical thought about something commonplace. He had seen enough war pictures to know the sort of thing.

He was distracted by a faint whimpering coming from somewhere behind him. He looked round : Mr. Brinkell was curled up like an unborn baby, with his little fists skewered into his eyes. Oh, no, thought Chote once again. The embryo's face was screwed up like a prune and he seemed to be crying.

It was a long night, all right. Chote dozed off, and had an interminable dream, and woke up five minutes later, gasping for air. Half an hour after that, little Mr. Brinkell woke him up again with a somnolent swipe of the arm. 'Goddammit,' muttered the tiny sleeper. 'Goddamn you.'

The waking intervals wove surely into nightmare texture. He dreamed he was soaring away into space, farther and farther away from all the people he loved and trusted, what people. . . ? No, that wasn't a dream—that was really happening. He could see the blank black sky through fluttering curtains. They were taking him *into that*: right out to the blooming limits. There would be nobody else out there, of course, just John Wilson Chote and a lot of empty space. God? Of course not. One couldn't possibly feel so lonely if God was anywhere about. It was icy cold—God would make it a little warmer if he had to live out here. Chote pulled up his skimpy blanket and jerked his knees onto the seat. Maybe God was there after all : otherwise, one might as well give up altogether. Just—give up. Up give, so to speak.

In the middle of the eternal night, his wake-dream whirred into a new and horrible phase. The plane swooped down into a bare, lighted area, and a metallic voice crackled into his ear. 'We are coming into Gander airport in Newfoundland. We shall remain here for exactly one hour. Passengers are kindly requested to leave the plane. . . .' John tried to stand up, only to find that his seat belt had become mysteriously fastened. The hostess smiled at her little joke : 'May I help you sir?' 'No thank you,' mumbled Chote. 'I have my pride, thanks very much.'

Æneas took his hand gravely. The passengers were led into

an enormous shed and left there to wander about at large under the bright lights until they were ready to be sent for. Some of them clustered pathetically around a coffee and tea counter; the rest maundered slowly up and down the shed, whispering distraught nothings to each other. Mr. Brinkell had placed himself as far away from Chote as possible; in a corner near a souvenir stand—from which vantage point he fired a volley of devastating glances.

Chote groped in his pocket for the envelope, as if it contained smelling salts. It was crumpled, and crammed with grey fluff, but he straightened it out patiently and read it again : 'Dear John'—the writing was small and quite possibly embarrassed—'just a last word of advice and encouragement . . . keep your nose clean, lad . . . remember the flag . . . don't forget the Queen . . . think of what the Duke would have done,' and so on. The signature was small and diffident : 'The Rev. Godfearing Hook' and then the P.S., written no doubt in anguish. 'By the way, sorry about the other day—quite utterly whistled at the time—not the least responsible—must have been two other fellows.' Chote folded the letter and made a face at Mr. Brinkell, who turned away disdainfully and began to examine the souvenirs. Why do all these bloody little twerps pick on me? thought Chote with a burst of light-headed anger. Mr. Smythe, the Rev. Godfearing, this chap : by George, it was insufferable. One of them at least should be brought to book.

He began to stalk purposefully toward Mr. Brinkell—'I'll tell him I'm a Communist, by God'—but the little man scampered softly away, leaving Chote alone among the souvenirs, 'souvenirs of bloody what?'—tired, angry, almost hysterical.

They were all bundled back onto the plane, and before Chote could say a word Mr. Brinkell had folded himself up in his sleeping position and closed his eyes. Chote would have to wait until morning to tell him that he was a Communist. Chote shut his eyes too, resigned to resuming his nightmare proper. He was back in the featureless void right away, hurtling head over heels through the darkness by himself. It was the first dream he had ever had in which there weren't any people at all—in fact, he was hardly there himself : only his brain seemed to be left now, a little scrap of ash-grey, scooting away over the horizon.

During his waking moments he was too tired to dismiss this impression : it might very well be true. He tried instead to picture Daphne against the seat in front of him. But at this altitude, he couldn't get an image; the seat remained blank. They must be plunging him further and further into night. There were no shapes or colours left. Soon, there would be no dreams at all. He would never get out of this one.

Why, of course, this was the black thing itself—and the joke was that it was empty. He opened his eyes as wide as they would go, and looked despairingly out of the window. Just in time, he could make out a faint glow in the distance, a pink light tinting the clouds, and raising the edge of the curtain. Thank God ! It was not really going to last forever, after all.

He turned around to slap Mr. Brinkell on the back, but the little man had disappeared. Chote looked across the aisle and then over the back of his own seat. A pair of bulging eyes stared back at him. Mr. Brinkell had tiptoed away sometime during the night and taken the empty seat behind. 'Morning, Frank,' said Chote breezily. Now at last he would tell Brinkell that he was a Communist. Last night, he would have done it badly, clumsily. Today he would work it in artfully. 'By the way, Frank. . . .' Mr. Brinkell stood up and pattered back to the washroom. Chote didn't see him again until the plane landed.

It was a long morning, almost as long as the night, but better suited for resting. 'No preconceptions, no prejudices,' mumbled Chote reminding himself just once more. 'Take them as you find them.' One was so tired of the superficialities that were brought back to Europe in lush harvesting every year : 'The cars are too long . . . the people are too big . . . the pace is too fast.' One must avoid all that, and dig deeper, much, much deeper. 'New York is not America . . . a house is not a home . . . a good cigar is not a smoke' . . . all the good slogans. He continued to doze and wake and doze again as before, but with

225

a happier cast of thought, nicer pictures and words. He had never realized before how fond he was of daylight. . . .

The grass underneath was pale and lustreless, and scorched away in places. The plane was swinging down over Long Island, pointing its right wing at a row of baseball diamonds, a sprawling golf course, and behind that, a wedge of sparkling blue water; then it dipped the other way to show the offices and factories and shops where the work was done. (That was the good, primary way to look at things.) Now where were the Empire State and the Statue of Liberty? The plane took another swoop into the suburbs. One was actually entering the New World by the back way, a tradesman's entrance of sorts.

They came scudding down onto a thin stripe of runway: whump! the wheels bounced off the hot metal and bounced again.

Outside, the ground was throbbing with heat, sending up a thin haze all around. It was 8 A.M., American time, and the city was warming up slowly but surely—humming with heat, and a variety of exotic new noises. The passengers, silent and dream-like as ever, with only the slightest hold on existence, walked gravely over the shimmering asphalt toward a shed, where a clutch of officials had temporarily nested. They flashed their assorted documents and melted away two by two, leaving Chote and another Englishman sitting alone. Mr. Brinkell had made a fast break, scampering to the head of the line and out, in a cloud of dust and feathers. His last look at Chote was the worst: 'We don't want your kind here,' said the hot little eyes in a final burst. Chote had missed the Statue of Liberty and got Mr. Brinkell instead.

'Welcome to the United States,' said a solemn, kindly man. 'I hope you'll enjoy your visit.' He hammered a greeting into Chote's passport, and handed it back with a small, contained smile.

Outside the customs shed, Eugene Fosdick was waiting for him, next to a radiant girl in shorts. 'Hi, John, old boy,' he said. 'Welcome to God's country, suh.' John was looking at the girl; he had never seen such a long pair of legs in his life. 'I'd like you to meet my sister Mirabelle,' said Gene. 'Hi John.'

Her voice was cool and rich, like a much older woman's. By George, thought Chote. She's mature too. Just like her brother. He felt like a toddler as he held out his hand to have it shaken.

A coloured porter swept up his dilapidated suitcase and flipped it onto a pile which he then rolled negligently away. John was startled, though he was too sleepy to go into reasons. 'I've heard a lot about you,' said Mirabelle warmly. 'You must be hot in that suit,' said Eugene. 'Did you have a nice flight?' chattered Mirabelle. The Fosdicks had arranged to meet him, instead of the University representative, and they were making a workmanlike job of it.

He was wearing his stiff grey suit, and it felt more than ever like fancy dress among the rows of sports shirts. 'I am a bit hot. What have you heard about me, Mirabelle?'

'Oh, all sorts of things. Mostly nice,' she said blandly. 'You're supposed to be a typical English character.'

'Good heavens, me?'

They took a harassed and itchy Chote out into the steamy sunshine. 'Me? A typical Englishman?' he babbled on foolishly. The heat was toasting his bushy scalp and making it damnably hard to concentrate. 'Did you tell her that, Gene?' Fosdick was off along the sidewalk hailing a taxicab, and Mirabelle was smiling, a warm but rather vacant smile. 'What was that John? Did you speak?'

Two long brown legs mounting a set of quite enormous white teeth—could one ever find such a woman really attractive? No doubt Admiral Byrd's men had taken a sort of fancy to the Eskimo women, or whatever, after a while. But this. . . . She sat next to him in the cab, a not unpleasant bony pressure: 'I've always wanted to go to England,' she said vivaciously. 'The Englishmen that I've met over here have been such *fun*.'

'There you are, John,' said Eugene. 'Say something funny.'

The taxi plunged out onto a sparkling highway, a svelte conveyor belt rushing great jumbles of chrome into New York at a furious but steady clip, a superficial phenomenon which any fool could observe—one must dig deeper, much deeper. 'We're not as funny as we look,' he idled. A car swam slithering past the window, a great goggling fish of the roads. 'I made a resolution,' he said, 'not to say anything about the cars over here. But they are rather fantastic, aren't they?'

'Monstrosities,' said Mirabelle lightly. 'Absolute monstrosities. The little English cars are so much nicer. . . .'

'They serve a purpose,' said Eugene instructively. 'Big roads, big people, big country.'

'I suppose so,' said Chote, dismayed at having mentioned the cars like that. 'I knew that there would be a sensible explanation.' One knew too that Fosdick was the man to give it.

The hum of the heat swelled to a sweet, nervous drone inside the city. He had never heard a city humming before. There were sharp sounds too : horns and squealing brakes and jagged cries as of rage and frustration. But behind these there was always the solid hum, drilling at all one's nerves at once, bringing them closer and closer to the surface.

Down the side streets one saw brawny men in undervests, lounging placidly, while mammoth trucks wiggled clumsily in and out of the loading zones, like dancing circus elephants. Private cars squirmed behind them restlessly, with their horns whining and crying for attention. Chote's taxi driver was muttering away ceaselessly to himself, adding his modest bit to the city hum : 'For Chrissake move, you big idiot.' He spoke in stylized cadences to each of the trucks in turn, cajoling, pleading and threatening. 'For Petesake, Mac, give me a break will you? Ah, what's the use of talking.' He hurled himself against his horn and hung there impaled for a full minute, until a big bald man with hairy arms came waddling over. 'Look, fellow,' he said, 'it's kind of warm out today, and whadya say we all just keep our heads, take it easy, and don't make too much noise, you know what I mean?' His big glowing face was already inside the window, looking around familiarly. 'I'm sorry for the delay, ma'am. But we've got work to do and it's going to take a few minutes. You know how it is. Blowin' on the horn won't help.'

'Ah, dry up,' said the cabdriver in a low voice as the bald diplomat sauntered away again. The driver was a thin elderly man, but determined; and in a moment, his hand was over the horn again, squeezing desperately. 'Look, Mac, I made a polite request just now.' The big face seemed to fill the cab this time. 'Do you want me to implement it?' He leaned right across the seat to see how the passengers felt about this. (Public opinion is very important in America. Ho hum. Dig deeper.)

Chote was alarmed. There was an air of brooding, alien violence, cosily mingled with the terrible heat. 'Look here, old chap,' he said—and for the first time in his life, he heard himself sounding like an Englishman: half consciously, one felt it might be wise to emphasize the effect. 'Mac, or whatever your bally name is, didn't you say that you were supposed to be working at the moment? Are you sure that we aren't taking up too much of your time chatting like this? I mean, it's been a treat. . . .'

The craggy face split and cracked and a smile like a great red sunset shone benificently upon Chote. 'You a limey? I was over in England during the war . . . do you know Hertfordshire by any chance?'

For Chote it was a hectic, apprehensive ride, with heat and anger (at least it sounded like anger now) swirling upward in the narrow streets, and the tall buildings falling, falling, falling forward and sideways over them: but all the time, there was a cool place at the centre. Mirabelle Fosdick sat there calm and fragrant, miles above the sweat and tumult, grand as a duchess: none of the vague embarrassment of Daphne Collins, the too evident desire to get out and run . . . she was superbly untouched, unrapt in fact.

He peeped round at her. With her mouth shut, she wasn't quite so implausible: a big chin, but not too big; an amusing nose; bright eyes and glistening brown hair. Above all, a coolness.

'This is your hotel, John,' said Eugene. 'You'd better get a little shut-eye. We'll pick you up around six, and we can go hunting after that.'

'Are you coming too, Mirabelle?' asked Chote.

'Certainly.' Her eyes crinkled like fresh cellophane. 'I've always wanted to go out with a genuine English character.'

The hotel lobby had the same impersonal sheen as the aeroplane and its accessories: but without even the occasional abrasions of noise. The vitality and dirt of the city were sealed out hermetically. The two smart young moderns whisked him over glossy carpets towards a long low desk, where they left him in the hands of a sleek purring manager, many years away from the jungle. 'If you'll just sign here, Mr. Chote.' His bags had already disappeared with sickening, superficially typical efficiency. 'We hope you'll enjoy your stay with us, Mr. Chote.' He thought wistfully of the squinty old couples who ran so many hotels in England, with their comfortable inadequacy: 'The boy who carries the bags seems to have disappeared . . . the gentleman in 107 hasn't moved out yet . . . where is the blasted key? So sorry. . . .'

Upstairs in room 1843 the coloured porter twitched up the window and let the hum come in. 'Mighty warm day, sir, mighty warm.' He flicked on the taps above the basin and gave the toilet a trial flush. 'I believe you'll be comfortable, sir.' Chote was vaguely aware of a massive courtesy, something possibly more human than anything he had left behind. He was grimly determined not to be condescending about coloured people—above all not to think of them as wonderful servants. But the courtesy was irresistibly attractive—and yet not, to one's regret, quite the courtesy of equals.

He reached into his pocket and fished out a nickel and a penny. That didn't look like enough. He probed again and came up with another nickel. 'I don't understand your money,' he said helplessly.

'That's fine, that's perfectly fine.' The porter swept the coins into his pocket and bowed. 'Thank *you*, sir.'

Alone with the hum, Chote tottered about the room aimlessly for a minute or two. 'Room service . . . dry cleaning . . . things to do in New York,' little helpful signs dotted here and there. A Bible and a bosomy novel in a plastic cover sat in tandem on his bed table. There was no little embroidered plaque saying 'Home, Sweet Home' though.

One must at all costs postpone the major judgments, but the minor ones crowded in on every side, oh so familiarly: Bibles and best sellers and long, brown legs. All the clichés had come unmistakably, disconcertingly true. He lay down on the airfoam mattress, and picked up the Bible. The words of the Good Book might take him home, to pastures green and quiet waters and J.C.R. meetings. They might even furnish a profound ageless clue to his new experiences.

The hum insisted; in waves and waves, smothering his thoughts like a hot, dusty pillow. He got up and closed the window, softening the hum, and making a kind of silence. Then he squatted down in an armchair next to the window and went to sleep, to dream of crisp white blouses (that was what it was) and a tangle of incredibly long brown legs.

'I like him,' said Mirabelle. 'He's unusual.'

'Not for an Englishman he isn't,' said Eugene.

'*Don't* tell me about Englishmen, Señor Pomposo, I know about Englishmen.'

'You do?' He smiled paternally.

'Certainly I do. Everybody knows about Englishmen. Only of course *you* have to know more about Englishmen than anybody else who ever lived.' She smiled fondly and he smiled fondly. Nice brother and sister.

'All right, have it your way—he's unusual. And so are the other twelve guys I know who are just like him—they're all unusual, very unusual fellows. But be careful, Mir, about liking him and all. I mean, they play slightly different rules over there. . . . And especially these unusual fellows like Chote.'

She gave him a little shove against the side of the taxi. 'Yes, Mr. Sociologist. Well, it may interest you to know that I also know all about English rules : like not overheating the hot-water bag, and a nice cup of tea in the morning—I'll get along.'

'O.K., O.K., I guess you know what you're doing—'

'Ten times as pompous as you used to be—'

'I'd just hate to have to use the horsewhip.'

'Twenty times—tell me, Gene, how did you ever *get* so pompous?'

'Oh, to hell with it. Do what you like.'

'I think that would be the best way,' she agreed.

The taxi made a sudden swoop at the sidewalk. It had reached the hotel where they were staying for the week: a painfully subdued building on the East Side; not much like a hotel at all, more like somebody's town house. There couldn't be room for more than three or four guests.

'What about Bob, by the way?' said Eugene as they muffled their way through the thick carpet (much thicker than the carpet at Chote's place).

'What about him?' asked Mirabelle, eyes wide. 'What about Bob?'

'Oh, nothing, I guess.' He reached for their keys, and the old clerk handed them across with a grisled, one-of-the-family smile. 'Yes sir, Mr. Fosdick.' 'Nothing at all,' said Eugene. 'Nothing about Bob.'

'That's the boy,' said Mirabelle winking. 'Anyway I only said I liked your friend. What's wrong with that?'

'All right, fine. So I'll see you at six, right?' They smiled very warmly and went off—so Chote would have guessed—to wash themselves all over.

13. New Ways of Relaxing

THEY flopped in and out of the water like seals; or else they lay languid and motionless along the side of the pool. Chote felt unduly pinched and sickly among all the bronzed bodies. His pale flesh had seemed at first to shrink from the sun, then to turn slowly pink from embarrassment, curling up at last in painful little shreds.

'You'd better cover yourself with something,' said Mirabelle. 'You're getting a terrible burn.'

'Why can't I be brown like the other people?' asked Chote. It seemed absurd to cover himself up like a Southern belle while the Fosdicks and their friends were abandoning themselves so carelessly and lazily to the sun. 'I used to sunbathe in England,' he said as Mirabelle slipped a towel gracefully over his shoulders. 'Nothing like this ever happened. Nothing ever happened at all, in fact.'

Behind the pool the sprawling Fosdick acres were kept eternally cool and green by light spray flung out by little spinning devices, of a kind one had never seen before. In the distance stood the Fosdick mansion, a mellow colonial pile, glistening white against the fluffy green of the trees.

'I never realized that Eugene had all this behind him,' said Chote. 'I think he's kept the common touch marvellously, in the circumstances.'

'Oh now,' said Mirabelle. 'Don't tell me that a genuine ivy-covered Englishman like you is impressed by a little shack like this?'

'Oh, but I am,' said Chote. 'You may not realize it, but I'm strictly a log-cabin boy myself. If I went within miles of one of our stately homes I'd probably have to be fumigated by the second butler and deloused by the chambermaid.'

'You're kidding, aren't you?' asked Mirabelle, with a smile. 'I mean completely kidding?'

'Yes, no, not quite completely, I suppose,' said Chote. 'Yes, they'd let me in all right, if it was a Saturday and I had my sixpence with me. But I doubt if I'd be encouraged to lounge around in my shorts like this with the inmates.' He patted her thin brown hand. 'Don't worry about it, Mirabelle. I know my place in life, and I'm quite contented with it, honestly.'

Mirabelle was less amused. 'I think that's a ridiculous way to talk, Johnny, old-fashioned and ridiculous and it isn't even funny.'

'No, I suppose not. By the way, what class do you belong to over here? The best I suppose.'

'I don't belong to any class,' she said. 'We just don't think in those terms in this country.'

'Well, then, perhaps you don't belong to a class yourself—but what class do all these other people here belong to? Any of them from the Lower East Side? How many of them would you say were Negroes or Puerto Ricans?'

'None of them are,' said Mirabelle, 'but I wouldn't mind if they were.'

'Oh, quite. Many of my best friends are Jews, too. Ah, here comes Eugene.' More inscrutable than ever in his sunglasses, Fosdick was making his way slowly up from the house. Funny how the chap seemed to be changing under one's very eyes, taking on a domestic personality. Chote wanted to cut short the discussion before he arrived: one could be reasonably sure that the cautious sage from Sturdley would not be so easy to disconcert as his sister.

'There are ethnic considerations,' said Mirabelle carefully. 'And also environment factors—'

'Quite, quite,' said Chote quickly. 'We find it more convenient to put all those things together and call them "class". Ah, Eugene. . . .'

Discussions of this sort were one of the things he had liked right away about Mirabelle. Where Daphne would have bowed her head modestly and just kept quiet, Mirabelle charged bravely forward, shooting from both slim hips. She had just finished her second year at a place called Jones, and she knew just enough about everything to put up some sort of fight. Since one's mental gifts—if one could call them that—were mainly critical, one's usual technique was to put out a foot as she went charging past: a method which enabled Chote to win nearly all their arguments without having to make any affirmative points whatsoever. 'But what do *you* believe?' she would ask in desperation. 'Oh, a bit of this and a bit of that, you know,' he would tell her cryptically. 'Ever so eclectic, actually.'

During the first week in New York, they had romped through socialized medicine, the Church of England, the Kinsey Report, the Middle East, female emancipation (the list was formidable) in their own peculiar way. By the end of it, Chote hadn't admitted to a single positive opinion. 'Why, I don't even know whether you're a liberal or a conservative,' she said with that *very* nice warm smile of hers. 'Must one be one or the other?' he asked.

'Why of course. Gibert and Sullivan have decreed it,' she said, 'for all people, everywhere.'

'Which are you?' he asked incuriously. 'Then I'll be the other.'

'Mother and Father are conservatives, of course, but I'm a confirmed old liberal.' She knew it sounded funny, and she said it that way, as she so often did.

'Ah, wait till you're a mother,' said Chote. 'Then we'll see.'

The discussion flowed restlessly from night club to night club, twinkling and babbling through a tunnel of blue smoke and off-pink lighting. The Fosdicks took him to Italian places and German places and Irish bars, to give him a feel of the famous melting pot. One could see that the melting had been a great success. All the places were exactly the same. In the Bavarian place, they listened to a group of middle-aged businessmen clad in green shorts, singing a clatch of world-famous German songs, most of which Chote already knew by heart; and at one of the Italian places, a young fellow gave out with 'Santa Lucia', 'Sorrento' and other international favourites. 'No ma'am, I was never actually in Italy, although I've always wanted to go,' he told the Fosdicks afterwards. 'No, I don't speak Italian. But I'd like to.' There were none of the dingy, improvised night clubs of Europe; just these chrome-plated entertainment factories. Whatever the alleged nationality of the place, there was always the same bar in front, lined with the same chubby, anonymous swillers and at least one incandescent blonde; and after that the smart, expensive-looking waiters and the cigarette girls and the grotesquely distended menus, with ham sandwiches selling upward of three dollars apiece. 'Now ve play a good Cherman game. Ve cut off the chentlemen's neckties, and ve pour beer all ofer der ladies'—or something like that : authentic imported horseplay under the steely nationalized eye of the management. Just try paying them in marks or lire one evening, thought Chote.

'It's easy to be superior about this,' said Eugene to Mirabelle, who had been in Europe only the summer before and who was much more upset than Chote by the tinsel and the sham. 'But don't you think that night life is always a bit phony anywhere? I mean the European joints are usually pseudo-American, and vice versa. The big thing is to forget about all that stuff and have a good time. Am I right, John?'

'Oh, indubitably. I'll drink to that any time.'

It was true too. They were outrageous places but he was having a good enough time there. While Fosdick was picking up the tabs, Chote and Mirabelle drank and laughed and talked. 'Don't worry, old boy. You're my guest while you're over here.' Chote protested feebly: 'But I never did a ruddy thing for you while you were in England, old chap. I never even bought you a pint.' But Fosdick's generosity was so casual and somehow inevitable that it wasn't really hard to take, and Chote stopped protesting after a record short while. His scholarship money wouldn't have been enough to pay even the tips at these places. 'Rather degrading being an Englishman these days,' he explained to Mirabelle somewhere about the third night. 'No, it's not,' she said stoutly. 'I think it's a wonderful thing to be. Don't talk like that any more Johnny, even joking.' She smiled gravely and touched his hand for the first time, the best possible time. He never mentioned paying again.

Of course, the Fosdicks did not live in a vacuum. They had their own special crowd, sliced carefully out of the sprawling raw material of the Atlantic seaboard. Chote began to spot the sort of people who might suddenly smile at the Fosdicks and drift toward them through the high-filtrated smoke: big, wholesome men with shaved heads, compound of wind and water, and gaunt vivacious girls, tanned to the bone. 'I'd like you to meet Johnny Chote,' Mirabelle would bubble. 'He's an Englishman and he hasn't got any opinions at all. Isn't that fascinating?' He didn't care for these people much. They always asked him what part of England he came from, and how long he was staying, and then usually left him alone and turned their attention to Mirabelle. The intimacy which had grown up between the two of them was then abruptly switched off and plugged into these new people. Warmth and light flowed from her into them, while Chote sat and shivered in the dark of his own company. He had no special private claim on her, of course, but she had no right to leave him alone like this. Once when she leaned forward and touched the cuff of a huge man from Princeton, he felt himself almost sick with petulance. She was just a kind of emotional tramp, a glorified air hostess, measuring out smiles and lumps of sugar to all the passengers. And then the strangers would drift away again and she would turn back to him with a glorious smile (had he really thought her teeth were too big?) and a cool, kind word, and life would begin once again.

It wasn't so much that he liked her, or even approved of her, but he needed her to talk to. He really didn't know what to say to the other people. They didn't seem to be aware of what he was up to when he tried to be funny, and he couldn't suppose that they wanted him to be serious—anyway, he wasn't at all sure that they actually understood a word he was saying: certainly he didn't understand *them* very well—perhaps they were making jokes too, all unbeknownst. He laughed every now and then, just in case, probably only adding to the tension.

But it was different with Mirabelle. She never missed anything he said, even the things he whispered hopelessly to himself. 'Did you hear what Johnny just said?' she would sometimes say to the others. It might have been embarrassing, but for some reason it wasn't. It always turned out that they hadn't heard what he had said (even when he was most certain they had) and they invariably laughed heartily when Mirabelle repeated it. Perhaps that would be the only way he could make jokes in this country—through someone like Mirabelle.

On their last evening in town but one, Mirabelle got an uncharacteristic attack of giggles during a discussion on American foreign policy; her head bobbed gracefully up and down and her hair brushed against Chote's face. 'You really are the most outrageous man,' she told him. Eugene's date, a handsome but slow-witted thoroughbred from the Main Line (a far cry, Chote couldn't help thinking, from the shopgirls he used to go around with in England), began to look vaguely alarmed. 'Don't worry, Eunice,' said Fosdick, a little sharply. 'They go on like this all the time, particularly in public places.' He was really getting stuffier by the minute. 'Pure nervousness, old boy,' said Chote. Mirabelle continued to giggle. 'John is being outrageous again. That's all,' she gasped delightfully. Honestly, one had never gone down so well.

On the way home, Eugene got out of the car to buy some cigarettes, and John decided that perhaps he ought to kiss Mirabelle. He wasn't familiar with the custom of the country, and he might be making a great mistake; on the other hand Mirabelle might be expecting it by now. One wanted to do the right thing. He half shut his eyes and leaned tentatively toward her, girding himself inwardly for the great social gesture and simultaneously steeling his nerves against the sharp astringent blow that might explode bang in the middle of the experiment. (After all, he told himself, it's only a game.) Her response was, to his surprise, scrupulously polite : there was no trace of affection or encouragement in it, but only a patient willingness to hold still indefinitely until he was quite finished. He withdrew and squinted at her. Her eyes were big and serious, maternally tender. 'Sorry,' he mumbled. 'My mistake.' He hoped she wouldn't say anything too frightfully soothing.

Mirabelle touched his hand with her kind fingers. 'I'm sorry, too, John. I ought to have told you before, I'm kind of engaged to someone.'

'Oh,' said John stupidly. 'Nice chap?'

'Oh, yes. Of course,' she said vaguely. 'He's from Yale.'

'I'm sorry. You weren't wearing a ring. Or were you? I can't say I looked very closely.'

'No. We won't be getting married for a long time. Bob's only a junior.'

It was dark and stuffy in the car, and John began to roll down a window with studious concentration. 'I'd better not see so much of you,' he said over his shoulder. 'As a matter of fact, I have a girl in England. You might say I'm sort of engaged too.'

'No. I like seeing you,' she said. 'I want to see more of you.'

'Oh fine. We'll see what we can arrange,' said John a trifle acidly. This was really too much. Her eyes protested and her mouth opened, but at that moment Eugene pulled the door open and said, 'What's the matter? Mirabelle isn't laughing.

Don't tell me our funny Englishman has stopped being funny.'
His friend from the Main Line had given up and gone home
early, leaving Fosdick unusually ruffled. 'You aren't angry with
us are you, Gene?' asked Mirabelle with concern. 'We didn't
get much chance to talk with your friend, but she seemed very
nice.' Everybody's nice, thought Chote bitterly. Everybody's
so bloody nice. Eugene smiled and said he wasn't mad, just a
little sorry for the girl. Mirabelle said she was sorry too because
the girl seemed so nice. This was obviously the mature way
to look at it.

When he got back to his hotel, he wrote a long, rambling
letter to Daphne, rich with sentimental promise : 'I don't
understand these people, and at the moment I don't like them
very much either.' Alone in the sleazy vault of his hotel room,
with the memory of Mirabelle's tactful, composed mouth still
unnaturally clear and palpable, Daphne's simple-hearted honesty assumed an immense, almost grotesque significance. 'I do
wish you were here, Daphne. Together we could enjoy so many
things that only seem dismal to a chap by himself.' Thrashing
about wildly now in his homesickness, he came close a dozen
times to the ultimate and irrevocable purple passage : but
each time a natural caution steered him away again. Instead
he blunted his frantic emotions in a raging filibuster against his
American hosts, with their commercial good will, their superficial friendliness, and their terrible cold, empty hearts. Whenever he flagged, he would look down at the advertisements and
good-will messages pasted onto his writing desk, and tap new
stores of bile.

It was half-past four by the thudding clock on the insurance
building before his liver was all poured out. He hesitated a
moment at the end, not quite sure what he'd done, and then
he slapped down 'Love, John' and headed grimly for the
elevator with the fat letter bulging in his hand.

Coldly he handed his pulpy diatribe to a sleepy night porter :
'I want you to mail this immediately,' he said in a loud voice.
The drowsy man protested mildly: 'Look, Mac, we have a mail-
box.' 'Mail the bloody letter,' said Chote imperiously. 'Please,'
he added cuttingly. Cold, commercial night porter.

By the time he woke up, Chote had fallen prisoner to a host of tiny qualms. Not because of the things he had said to Daphne —he still wished she was with him, although not quite so passionately as he had last night. But the rest! Where had it all come from? He was fascinated and repelled by the memory of his own hysteria. The throbbing heat and the loneliness of New York had temporarily robbed him of his reason and agitated his British phlegm—well, that brought to mind at least one consolation. Unlike a good many visiting Europeans he had not considered submitting his panicky gibberings to print; fortunately they would be lost forever in the great, impenetrable silence of Daphne Collins. This consolation still left several hundred qualms, and Chote decided to walk them away in the sultry streets.

All day long, his shrill secondhand observations were mocked by reality. Outside the artificial euphoria of his hotel, he was reminded again and again of the unaffected surliness of the city: the liverish bus drivers, worn down by the petty vexations which drip-drip-dripped on them all day long; the exasperated women shoppers, who bumped and wobbled through the crowds on tiny, pinched feet; the mysterious anger of the little man who shuffled past him on Fourteenth Street talking to himself. There was no commercial happiness here: only the tattered nerves of people baked and lonely like himself, only more so. It was embarrassingly clear that any one of them might have been capable at a moment's notice of much the same kind of incoherent outburst as he had let fly last night. The man on Fourteenth Street had obviously given a short lifetime to such outbursts, indefinitely prolonged. But then, he had probably lived in New York a few months longer than Chote.

Several times he had to stop people and ask for directions, and each time he noticed how eerily reluctant they were to speak to him at all. Two men simply pointed, wordless; a third muttered 'That way'; the fourth and last hurried past without stopping. Years spent in the boiling concrete caverns had apparently sapped the desire to communicate, perhaps even the ability. It was the same at the counter where he had his lunch. None of the monotonous chorus of 'Thank you', 'Thank you, sir', 'Ta' that animates English café life, but only the wary silence blown in from the streets. The customers talked a little to their friends, if they had friends : otherwise, they attended to their business. Chote felt garrulous when he said 'Thank you' and fatuously chatty when he said 'Good afternoon' to the stiff-faced man behind the counter. It was easy to imagine the glibness drying up in his mouth like dust, his lips thinning and tightening over the years, as he moved like a ghost in these crowded streets and restaurants; at last, perhaps, he would let it all out in desperation, in a long whining monologue up and down Fourteenth Street, up and down.

But that evening, he had to go back to the breezy world of the Fosdicks and there, even though he didn't understand them very well, the people certainly liked to talk. They were healthy, brown people, too (one saw the virtues now in health and brownness), and reasonably happy people and he was glad to see them again. While he was tramping about in the hazy sun, he felt himself wearing out, like all the worn-out people around him. Something in the air seemed to make terrible demands on one : demands on one's attention and one's responsiveness. There was more to see and more to hear than anywhere he had ever been before; one had to be more excited than ever, too; and one had to wear out faster, use up any spare sensibility, any capacity for being even faintly interested. But now he was with the nice people up from the country : Newport, East-hampton, Princeton (he supposed that that was all in the country), fresh, well-preserved young people whose vitality had hardly been tapped. Chote was curiously comforted by their presence.

Mirabelle was sparkling, more radiant than ever. And she continued to pursue her good-neighbour policy with Chote, focusing attention on him as much as possible, translating his jokes, and telling the others how outrageous he was. He started out trying to ignore her : the siren song was still attractive, but he knew now that it led to nothing, just a gramophone sitting by itself on a rock. She seemed a little disturbed by his frosti-ness, and she whispered, 'What's the matter, John? Why are

241

you such an old bear tonight?' 'Just a touch of the sun,' he told her. She put her cool hand on his forehead. 'You are a bit warm,' she said in a soft voice. Oh, go away, he thought to himself. He noticed once again how big her teeth were. She really wasn't any prize.

He tried talking to the others for a while without her assistance, and all in all, it wasn't too bad, once he got the hang of it. He established definite communication with a couple from Princeton and Bryn Mawr who were mad about Alec Guinness, and the girl that Eugene had brought this evening took to laughing quite frantically every time he spoke, which also represented some sort of communication, he hoped. He was having a pretty good time, and was amused by the attention he was getting from Mirabelle now. She's afraid she's hurt my feelings, he thought light-headedly. Little does she know. She was more or less ignoring the tanned heroes who drifted to and from the table, and concentrating on the glowing, woozily self-satisfied Chote. (He was well into the third person by now.) 'I'm glad you've gotten over your sunstroke,' she said as they got up to go. 'I've always heard that champagne does wonders for sunstroke,' said Chote, his eighteenth century mind cool and amused. 'One only hopes one doesn't have a real stroke in the morning.' When he reached the fresh air, he became vaguely aware that he had made an ass of himself in front of Mirabelle. He didn't care, though : not a fig, not a button.

The Fosdicks drove him back to his hotel, and Mirabelle said, 'I'd better take you upstairs, John. You look a little confused.' She took his arm and steered him firmly into the elevator, although he was convinced that he didn't need steering. Domineering American women that one hears so much about, he explained to himself carefully. That's all it is.

She marched him up to his door and propped him against it. Her eyes were large and motherly again, and he had a terrible premonition. The bloody woman's going to apologize. Oh, please don't apologize, he whimpered soundlessly. Yes, she was moving closer, ominously closer. It could only mean an apology. He shut his eyes and resigned himself; and then, before he knew it, he was pinned to the door like a butterfly and she was kissing him furiously all over the face.

Before he had a chance to respond manfully, or even nervously, she had backed away and was trotting blithely off down the corridor and out of sight, like a girl in a dream : the succuba of Brinkley.

Eugene Fosdick sat down and tucked his bathrobe around his knees. 'You're leaving us tomorrow, John,' he said. 'Just when you were beginning to get a tan.'

Chote nodded his scarlet head. 'Yes, tomorrow the indoctrination begins in earnest.'

'Where are they taking you for it ?'

'The Middle West, of course. The real America, the vital heartland, et cetera. When you next see me, I expect to be one hundred per cent American.'

'Never,' said Mirabelle. 'It would take centuries to turn you into an American. Even ten per cent American like Daddy.'

'That's right,' said Eugene. 'Look at Father.' They all turned around and looked. Mr. Herbert Fosdick was sitting on the terrace in front of his bedroom, sipping a highball and blowing ceaseless ripples in his heavy white moustache. 'Daddy's a throwback,' said Mirabelle. 'By midnight he can't remember where he's supposed to come from. He feels more English than the Pope, or something like that.'

'Anybody who can drink for twelve hours a day deserves the right to name his own country,' said John (who already found it harder and harder to think of himself as 'Chote'). 'Why— do you realize that that adds up to an eighty-four hour week ?'

Mirabelle looked embarrassed. 'He doesn't actually drink as much as that,' she said. John didn't argue with her, of course. But every day for a week he had watched Mr. Fosdick tottering out onto his terrace at twelve o'clock sharp, followed hotly by a tiny Chinese servant with a tray. Half an hour later, Mr. Fosdick would be ready to make an urbane entrance to the living-room, and everybody would get a turn at the bottle. By midnight, the grand old man would be ready for bed; first a round of courteous farewells, and then he would head cautiously for the stairs, with the stiff dignity of an advanced arthritic. 'He only drinks because his rheumatism is so painful,' said Mirabelle. 'And even so, he never takes a drop before noon.'

'Heaven knows, I'm not criticizing him,' said Chote hastily. 'I have the most sincere admiration for his capacity. I think he's a living hero.'

'I don't think that's very funny,' said Mirabelle with unmistakable acerbity. 'You know you don't mean that. There's nothing heroic about alcoholism. The only heroic thing is the fight that Daddy puts up against it.'

Chote felt the same jolting shock that he had experienced several times with Mirabelle. Of course, his remark was indefensible from a certain point of view, but delivered in a flippant frame of reference it seemed harmless enough. 'I'm sorry. I didn't mean that seriously,' he said.

'I know you didn't,' she said. 'But I don't think it's a very nice subject to joke about, do you?'

'No, of course not.' He had never been corrected like this by someone his own age or less, and it was a curious sensation. Most of the time he and Mirabelle would frolic together like children, and then, without warning, her brow would darken and the ruler would come whacking down over his knuckles. She didn't appear to enjoy correcting him: it was more a question of duty. She would say what had to be said as quickly as possible, after which the subject was dismissed gratefully, and Chote became an equal once again.

As a matter of fact, she had a fine knack of dismissing subjects. For instance, she dismissed her 'sort of' fiancé, and she dismissed the implications of Chote too. It would somehow have been bad taste to mention either subject. Every afternoon now they strayed hand in hand into the woods, where they kissed and squeezed each other for hours at a stretch under a shady tree. But she never said a word about what it all meant. He didn't know whether this put him in the same class as the fiancé—or whether perhaps she treated all her friends thus fraternally. At any rate, her tactful conventions made it much easier for him to dismiss Daphne.

And dismissing Daphne took a little more doing. Next to his crumpled letter from Godfrey Hook he had placed three pieces of lavender notepaper. His cry of anguish had touched off little explosions all over Daphne; her response was very nearly passionate in fact. 'Dearest John, how dreadful, dreadful. . . . I *do* wish I could be with you in your awful ordeal. How blissful we could be', and so on. The sunlight threw a golden band across his scrambled eggs and up Mirabelle on the other side of the table, distracting him from Daphne's literary sighs and moans. 'I think about you all the time, John, and count the hours'—the heavy earnest words fell on his conscience like so much dough : gooey, unimaginative sincerity, striking no chord in him on this lovely day. 'Bad news?' Mirabelle asked. 'No—just my nostalgia acting up,' he told her. Mirabelle, one could see at a glance, was all lightness and strength, virtually impossible to hurt; Daphne was such a slow, wobbling target, as outmoded as the battleship. You hit her even when you were aiming at something else. A year from now Mirabelle would still be leading fellows lightheartedly into the woods while Daphne stayed at home methodically drenching her pillow. He read the letter again : perhaps what he was was afraid of Daphne. Too much weakness or strength or something. 'Come along now,' Mirabelle interrupted. 'It's time for our walk.' He got up obediently and followed her out, feeling more and more like a Henry James heroine in reverse: an innocent abroad being used, for good or ill, by the wise, over-civilized natives.

'It looks as if father is planning to join us.' Mr. Fosdick was trudging across the lawn towards the swimming-pool, perceptibly stiffer all down the line than he had been at lunch-time, still pursued by the Chinese with his merry jingling tray.

Chote struggled to get out of his chair, but it was too late. Mr. Fosdick had pulled alongside, obviously full of talk. 'Not much like an English afternoon, eh, Mr. Chote? You can put the tray right over there, Lee. Now what will you have to drink,

Mr. Chote?' he chattered away. John sank back feebly in his deck chair. He had been hoping to avoid a tête-à-tête with Mr. Fosdick on his last day; up to now, he had got on very well with the fuzzy old fellow—but it was a fragile success, built on a gossamer fretwork of misunderstandings.

'My daughter tells me that you are leaving shortly,' said Mr. Fosdick. 'And I thought I'd better take the chance to ask you if you knew my friend Lord Clarwood of Derbyshire.'

There wasn't much to be done with that one. 'I don't think so,' he said, after a moment of apparently pregnant hesitation.

'Pity,' said Mr. Fosdick. 'Perhaps your father knows him though.'

'I daresay,' said Chote. 'Dad knows practically everybody.'

'What about the Montmorency-ffrenches?' pursued Mr. Fosdick. 'You must know them, surely?'

Good God—the whats? thought Chote. But Mr. Fosdick looked so eager, straining forward in his chair and blowing great gusts into his moustache, that one couldn't let him down again. 'Which ones?' he asked.

'The Leicestershire ones,' said Mr. Fosdick.

'No-o-o,' said Chote dubiously. 'I know some people of, er, that name in Staffordshire' (*what* was the bloody name again?) 'but not in Leicestershire.'

'Ah, those must be the first cousins. Would that have been Hubert Montmorency-ffrench?'

'Yes, I think that was it,' agreed Chote.

'Grand family,' said Mr. Fosdick. 'I never met Hubert, but I believe he's the family wit, a quite fabulous character. I hear —and perhaps you can verify this story—that he once set fire to his hair at a banquet for the old Queen.'

'He's quite capable of it,' said Chote dismally. The upper classes at play. 'He does that sort of thing almost every day.' They both chuckled reminiscently. 'Bushy red hair,' said Mr. Fosdick. 'That's the chap,' said Chote.

Eugene had tiptoed away and dived into the pool. Mirabelle still sat next to Chote, silent but alert, ready to cover his tracks if necessary. 'John wouldn't know any of your friends,' she said at last. 'They're all at least ninety.'

'No they're not my dear,' said Mr. Fosdick mildly. 'Hubert Montmorency-ffrench wouldn't be much more than sixty-eight. And Mr. Chote knows him very well. I suppose you stayed at the manor, did you Mr. Chote?'

'Yes, just for a week-end.'

'They've had to close off the west wing since the war, so I hear, and some of the east too. Place is just a shell. Damned socialism. . . .' Mr. Fosdick was safely launched, and it was all right to leave him to his own devices for a while. Chote put on the pair of sunglasses that Eugene had left on Mr. Fosdick's tray so that he could look around for a little without offending his host. The other side of the pool was lined with sleek brown bodies still sprawling motionless in the baking sun. Every now and then one of the brown people would flop over into the shimmering green water; a few lithe strokes and out again, to rest in the warmth once more. The silence and languor harmonized with Mr. Fosdick's slow, deep voice, and made a kind of eternity. Figures on an American urn. Mr. Fosdick would talk on and the brown people would ever sunbathe—'a son at Oxford,' said Mr. Fosdick, in his slow, slightly wistful monotone. 'Maybe you know him, Mr. Chote?'

'You know, Mr. Fosdick, I'm absolutely rotten at names.' Chote could hear the rapid sing-song of his own voice, piercing the thin surface of eternity, cracking the urn. Two of the brown people looked up quickly, as if they had heard a cry for help.

'Young Peter may even have been at your college,' said Mr. Fosdick. 'You did say you were at Eton and Trinity didn't you?'

'No,' said Chote. Of course this moment had been bound to come. He gave himself up to the subtle pleasures of surrender. 'Brinkley College and Sturdley,' he said. 'Oh,' said Mr. Fosdick. 'Yes.' He tugged miserably at his moustache. He didn't have to be told that there were no Clarwoods or Montmorency-ffrenches at Sturdley: only the Gadsbys of Hounslow, and the Norbert Joneses of East Liverpool. Chote wanted to apologize then and there for having led Mr. Fosdick along the garden path, but Mirabelle came swinging in with succour for all:

'Sturdley is very small and picturesque and teddibly, teddibly exclusive. Isn't it, John?'

'Yes, and it's one of the oldest colleges in Oxford.'

Mr. Fosdick surprisingly contributed his bit toward the repair work. 'Everything's upside down since the war. Sir Percy had a deuce of a time getting Peter into Trinity. Before the blasted Socialists got in, the boy would have had gone straight up and no questions asked. As it was he had to wait for two years. . . .' Up, up and away he went. Five minutes later, he was asking Chote what clubs his father still managed to belong to in these tightened days: Chote had licked both his lips twice, and had started to launch a diversion about the criminal rates of taxation when Mirabelle took his hand and said: 'That's enough for now. John is turning into a lobster, and he won't be fit to fly tomorrow.'

Mr. Fosdick saw his chance and took it, still wistfully. 'Can't have lobsters flying can we? Ha, ha. Well, it's been very pleasant chatting with you, Mr. Chote. I hope you'll be coming back this way. Sir Percy may be passing through and I wouldn't want you to miss him.'

In five minutes, he was deep in the woods, a vast green belt that girdled the Fosdick estate, with the house in the position of buckle.

'You're very nice with Father,' said Mirabelle. 'It must be quite a strain pretending to know all those people. But it gives him so much pleasure.'

'It's not such a strain, once you get into the spirit of it,' said John. 'Vagueness is the essence, of course. Your father seems to know England a good deal better than I do—you know, things about the Royal Calendar, regimental ties, the origin of the Boat Race and so on—so the best line would appear to be to sound as muddled as possible about absolutely everything.'

Mirabelle laughed. 'You sound as if you'd done this kind of thing before.'

'Yes, I've been doing it all my life,' said Chote mock-sadly. 'I'm a sort of pathological fraud.'

Mirabelle laughed again, with her deep amusement. 'I'm

sure that's not true. I think you're one of the most genuine people I've ever met.'

'Why thank you,' said Chote, a little embarrassed. Daphne never scolded him as Mirabelle did: but then, on the other hand, it had taken her at least a year to pay him such a compliment as this. 'Your father must have spent a lot of time in England,' he said. 'Years and years and years.'

'Well, no,' said Mirabelle. 'That's the funny thing. He's never been to England at all.'

'What?' said Chote. 'You mean he was just making all those people up? I mean the Chumley-Chumleys and the Honourable Unpronounceables, and so on?'

'Oh no, he's met them all, one way and another. He spends a lot of time at the English-Speaking Union and other likely places, buying them drinks and asking them questions.'

'Why the deuce doesn't he go over to England?' asked Chote. 'He can afford it.'

'Well, he talks about it every year,' said Mirabelle. 'But you know, he has a picture. . . .'

'And he has a picture of me?'

'That's right,' said Mirabelle. 'You're really quite a threat.' She slid her arm under his. It was getting dark all of a sudden, not in the slow, tactful English way, and Chote became aware of a new heaviness as a crowd of insects and evening smells were carried toward him on waves of wet heat. The air here seemed somehow more crowded than the air at home : full and ripe and swarming, almost like a jungle. It was good air for tension to grow in : good for creating painful, painfully silly incidents at parties, say; for setting frantic, damn-fool affairs in motion, for smashing the most durable friendships; it was air, in Chote's opinion, for locking yourself in the cupboard and throwing the key away. In the scalding semi-slums of New York that he had driven through, the younger set must be itching and squirming by now, tumbling out onto the streets and looking for action—any action; out here, the civilized people would drink and chatter as if nothing was going on. But an abnormal number of silly things would be done before morning, all the same.

He could feel Mirabelle rocking gently against him as they walked, crowding him more and more. 'John,' she said at last, in her serious voice. 'John.'

'Yes, Mirabelle?'

'You're going away tomorrow.' She stopped and faced him, as if they had reached the front of an invisible stage; 'I feel I ought to try to explain myself, just a little bit.'

Please don't bother, thought Chote, but one could hardly say that. He stroked his chin in thoughtful silence.

'You must think I'm crazy to be carrying on like this when I'm kind of engaged.'

'No, not at all,' said Chote, lamely. 'Not a bit.'

He thought that putting it like that, so absurdly, might annoy her, put her off stride; but she didn't seem to notice it. She was pursuing her own line of thought. 'I'm not really awful, or crazy, or anything else. I just, well. . . .' She looked demurely at the ground. 'I don't want to say it,' she said. 'But you know what I mean.'

Oh my goodness, thought Chote. He certainly hadn't expected anything like this. He put his arms around her awkwardly and she melted in on him immediately. 'Oh, I think you're wonderful,' she whispered. He ought to have known there was no excuse for being taken by surprise like this.

She pulled him irresistibly to the ground, hissing into his ear and nibbling it simultaneously. With Daphne, every step had always been so slow and premeditated; one weighed all factors carefully, and then decided whether to go a little further. One had ample time to become bored and shortly after that prudent. But here, there was no question of making decisions. Chote had no time to bring his trusty blend of caution and timidity to bear. Mirabelle was like a whirlwind, a dervish, and after a moment, he stopped trying to formulate judgments altogether. He just floated—insofar as his itchy sunburn would permit. Well, that was that. He could look Browning in the eye again. (And wasn't that a peculiar thought to have at a time like this?)

Mirabelle was soon her calm practical self. 'I shall write to my fiancé tomorrow, to break everything off. And didn't you say *you* had a kind of fiancée too, darling?'

'Well, yes, kind of,' said Chote hesitantly.

'I'm terribly sorry for her,' said Mirabelle happily. 'I know just how much she's losing.'

'Oh, I'm not much,' said Chote. 'Red-faced, square, questionable teeth.'

'Nonsense,' burbled Mirabelle. 'You're very distinguished-looking. And what's wrong with your teeth? Lots of Englishmen have protruding teeth.'

'Flat feet, middle-aged spread, dandruff,' chanted Chote.

'You're just very modest and genuine, and I love you,' said Mirabelle. 'There, I've said it first.'

'I'm very fond of you too,' said Chote: it was a dreadful thing to say, but he couldn't think of a better way of putting it.

'Is that all, Uncle John?' Mirabelle asked playfully.

'No,' said John. 'But to tell you the truth, I've never said anything the least bit stronger. It will take a bit of getting used to.'

Mirabelle simply beamed. 'So honest. That was the first thing I loved about you—no, the second. Your wonderful sense of humour was the first, of course.' Chote groaned and she said, 'Yes I know how you hate to be complimented, but you'll have to get used to it. I'm just going to praise you and praise you and praise you until you simply beg for mercy. And,' she added hopefully, 'maybe you can manage someday to stutter something nice about me—if it doesn't violate your principles, that is.'

'I think your simply smashing,' were the only words that came readily to mind. 'I'll try,' he said, 'but it won't be easy.'

She stood up and led him back out of the woods. 'I hope you *will* pay me a compliment someday. Because I know you'll mean it,' she said.

'I'm afraid you're quite wrong about that,' said Chote. 'I really haven't an honest bone in my body, ask anyone. Just because I'm clumsy, and frequently rude, doesn't mean that I'm honest, you know.'

'You wouldn't say that if it was so,' said Mirabelle, and John gave up. 'Now, where can I write to you in Chicago,' she asked, 'and how often are you going to write to me?'

251

Mr. Fosdick was waiting for them on the back porch, beaming like a proud father. 'Just in time for cocktails. What will you have, Mr. Chote?' Mrs. Fosdick, a pale, quiet woman, sat smiling in the shadows. They're all in on it, thought Chote wildly. But nothing happened to confirm this impression.

'I'm going upstairs to change,' said Mirabelle. 'Daddy will entertain you with his reminiscences. Get him to show you Sir Ponsonby Halifax. We've made him into a rug in the billiard-room.' Mr. Fosdick smiled uneasily.

John watched Mirabelle trotting lightly up the stairs. She looked thin and elegant as always in her plaid shorts, moving about lightly in her quality ad, rounding off a restrained romp. So, this was another of those glamorous affairs that one had been dreaming about for so many years: one night of passion, et cetera, and heigh-ho for the open road, with absolutely no regrets. And here he was, practically engaged to the damned girl. Instead of flitting daintily from flower to flower, he was trudging through bloody quicksand.

Well, what were his true feelings about Mirabelle? It was certainly high time he decided. One tried to balance them up with the old self-interest: but all he could find within himself was layer after layer of intense excitement. He felt as he had felt a week before when he wrote that letter to Daphne: as if he might at any moment do something quite exceptionally absurd, and infinitely regrettable. Perhaps he already had: he really must try to clear his head.

The excitement was so heavy and sweet, like the night air. His skull was almost bursting with it. Meanwhile Mr. Fosdick talked about England.

14. Failures in Communication

THE next day Chote went west, to brood about Mirabelle. There were of course plenty of rewarding things to do, and think about. But he found it awfully hard to pay attention. He spoke on a couple of local radio stations, and was mildly impressed by the aimless volatility of the announcers, who read their commercials like Danton or Joan of Arc before lapsing back into a strange native flabbiness. And he attended a drowsy seminar, where he came across ambivalent orientations and characterological motivations for the first time. But he exhausted most of his finest energies in the Golden West thinking about his two admirers, sacred and profane, the fat one and the thin one: Laurel and Hardy, he called them in his short-lived journal, for code purposes.

He got letters from both of them on his second day in Chicago, and the contrast even of notepaper was much more absorbing than the gaudy novelties flashing and blinking on all sides. Daphne came to him, modestly, galumphing on lavender, with a little sprig of flowers at the top of the page: 'Dear John: I hope that you are settling in all right, and getting used to your new surroundings. I always believe that one can learn to put up with anything if one makes up one's mind. . . .'

The beefy stoicism seemed almost a reproach this time. Daphne understood his troubles, of course: but on mature deliberation—and after hearing no more from him—she couldn't help feeling that he had made rather too much fuss. She had borne a good deal of pain herself, let him remember, without making such a song about it, and without fishing for anyone's sympathy. Daphne Collins had nothing to learn about loneliness from him (perhaps none of this was actually in the letter).

253

He turned to Mirabelle's cheery white message, crisp and neat as a starched shirt: 'Hi darling: So dull here without you and your dreadful jokes. . . . Daddy is talking of adopting you, and mounting you in the gun room, right next to Captain Formby of the Ninth Hussars. Wouldn't it be wonderful? . . . Do write lots of funny letters, my dearest, and don't forget that compliment that you were going to pay me some day. . . .'

Already she was more intimate than Daphne would dare to be, but somehow, lightly, impersonally intimate, like a clever child. Daphne, with her massive reserve, got closer to him— sitting on his chest, so to speak, like a heavy cold. Mirabelle was just exciting—nothing more as yet—just exciting.

He stuck some of his own notepaper into a loose-leaf book and wrote on it during his seminar; a brief note to Daphne, assuring her that he was settling in beautifully, and that he was frantically busy—too busy to write much for a while anyway; a long letter to Mirabelle, full of the required jokes. 'I'm still working on the jolly old compliment,' he concluded. 'It ought to be magnificent when it's finished.'

'What do you say to that?' interrupted Professor Agonovski.

'I don't know what to say,' said Chote hastily. 'I would need some time to think about it.' He could tell that the Professor was already disappointed with him: he hadn't contributed anything at all to the seminar. 'Is that all you have to offer, Mr. Chote?' 'I'm afraid so, sir,' said Chote limply. 'At the moment.'

He hoped he wasn't missing anything important, but these damned abstractions were amazingly hard to follow: culture patterns, in-groups, orientations—nothing registered. He imagined that the whole idea was to get him into a good tranquil mood; the substance would follow later. Meanwhile he tried to be as polite as possible. 'If you'd like to write the question down, I could take it home and think about it,' he said. 'No, that won't be necessary,' Profesor Agonovski told him coldly.

In the next letter Mirabelle announced that she was planning to abandon Jones College for Women and spend the coming winter in New York. 'Eugene will be working on Wall

Street trying to keep the Fosdicks in the upper class and I shall probably get a job as somebody's secretary. So we'll all be together again.' By the same post Daphne told him that she was going to take her holiday in Bournemouth. 'It's been quite dull in Oxford since you left, with lots and lots of rain, and I am looking forward very much to the change. By the way, your friends Alan and Godfrey came up to take their degrees (I expect you know that Alan got a third and Godfrey got what he called a very bad fourth) and they took me out to the Forester's Arms and we had a very amusing time. They said that they were livid with you for doing so well in Schools, but I don't think they really meant it.' He didn't bother to answer her. She already knew that he was too busy.

He got back to New York just after Labor Day, slightly regretful at having got so little out of the Middle West. He had bought the small morocco journal while he was there, to record the flat cornfields, and the virile energy, et cetera, of Chicago, and the friendliness of everybody he met : but after a few days he gave it up. 'Too much of everything,' he wrote. 'Too much sound, too much space, too many people. Too many questions about Senator McCarthy.' He closed his journal and threw it in the wastebasket. He hadn't realized before how little he cared about the world at large in comparison with his own private affairs. People offered to show him things indefinitely, but quite suddenly and finally he lost the taste for seeing anything.

The Fosdicks met him at La Guardia Airport and Mirabelle gave him a long, extensive kiss while her brother looked on placidly. Eugene didn't seem particularly surprised. 'Welcome back to the decadent East,' he said when Mirabelle had quite done. Mirabelle took Chote's arm tenderly and led him over to a taxi. 'It's so nice to have you back, Johnny, all brainwashed and everything. Isn't it, Gene?' Fosdick smiled.

'We're all going to a party tonight,' said Mirabelle. 'It's being given by some awfully interesting people.'

'Am I invited?' asked Chote.

'Of course you are. They're positively panting to meet you.'

It didn't seem possible that they could be, but Chote decided to let it pass. Mirabelle always said that people were dying to meet each other, and on her the attitude was strangely attractive, a most beguiling form of make-believe. And quite often she could make people—even shy and melancholy people—act as if they *were* dying to meet each other too : large sulky men would beam with brief pleasure for the sake of Mirabelle's little game; crabbed, dried-out faces would crinkle in smiles; unused voices would croak with delight and fellowship.

The Fosdicks had found a room for him near the University. As they took him uptown, Chote noticed how much less impact the city made on him this time. The buildings were bright and graceful, and not the least bit ominous; the people on the sidewalks were just people after all (Ah there, Fosdick, he thought. I too might become a student of human nature). A cool breeze whipped into the cab, driving away the old humid daydreams and apprehensions. There was nothing to be afraid of.

The new, cosmopolitan Chote—a poem in seersucker, Dacron and straw—stepped jauntily out of the cab and into the dingiest building he had ever seen. The hall was dark and narrow, with peeling green walls and a floor of chipped tiles that felt gritty underfoot, like the floor of a greenhouse. At the far end, there was a potted plant and a self-service elevator, with an OUT OF ORDER sign hanging crooked from it; and next to that a frail-looking staircase, tottering upwards out of sight.

'Are you sure this is the right place?' he couldn't help asking. It looked so empty and abandoned, like the old 'Grand Hotel' in a deserted mining town.

'Uh-huh,' said Gene. 'Mrs. Harrison Griswold. Number fifty-four.' He started up the stairs, followed by John and Mirabelle. 'That sounds like the fifth floor,' said Eugene.

Mrs. Griswold opened the door of apartment fifty-four listlessly, as if she didn't expect much. She stood in the doorway looking at them. They looked at her. Grey and tired. Nobody said anything.

'This is Mr. Chote,' said Mirabelle finally. 'We rang up about him.'

'You prolly talked to my daughter,' said Mrs. Griswold. She

turned and straggled into the apartment. She didn't look so very old, but she did seem awfully tired. 'I guess you'll be in here,' she said, turning into a little room overlooking a courtyard. 'My daughter makes all the arrangements.' She stood by the door.

John didn't know what he was supposed to do next. He went over and felt the bumpy mattress and then he looked out at the hopeless courtyard. 'It seems very nice,' he said politely.

The Fosdicks had retreated discreetly into the hallway, leaving him alone to parry with Mrs. Griswold. He tried to think of a few questions to ask; thoughtful, responsible questions.

'What time is breakfast?' he asked her.

'We don't do breakfasts,' she said.

'Oh, I suppose there's a place near here where I can get something?'

Mrs. Griswold didn't answer. She looked patiently at her fingernails which were incongruously sharp and elegant, wanton with red varnish, the part of her where life went on; and then she looked back at him with almost sightless eyes.

'Where's the bathroom?' asked Chote desperately.

'Huh? What was that?' Her eyes struggled into focus.

'The bathroom, the washroom, the toilet.'

'It's across the hall. You'll be sharing with the Fishmans.'

There was no point in going on. Chote pushed past her unmoving body—'Excuse me,' he said, but she didn't stir—out into the passage. The Fosdicks smiled uncertainly. He expected that they would say a few words of surprise and apology. But they didn't.

'Is it all right?' asked Mirabelle.

'Come in and see,' said Chote. They pushed in, back past Mrs. Griswold who still hadn't moved, into the permanent twilight of his new room. Mirabelle sat on the bed, and Eugene sat on a wooden chair. There wasn't any other furniture.

Suddenly, and when she was all but forgotten, Mrs. Griswold came to life. 'We have some rules,' she said. 'No musical instruments, no radios, no eating in the bedrooms. Leaves crumbs and crumbs attract mice. No girls in the bedrooms, unless the doors are open. No parties. Provide your own towels.'

257

Her voice had become high and clear, a ringing call to stand up and be counted. 'Last one in turns out the lights, kitchen privileges, provide your own food. Those are the rules.' She turned round quite meekly and shuffled out.

Still the Fosdicks didn't apologize, didn't explain. 'It'll be nice, being able to use the kitchen,' said Mirabelle. 'It'll be handy to be so near your classes,' said Eugene. They dredged up his handful of blessings and counted them carefully for him. 'We were lucky to find this place,' Mirabelle concluded. Chote was eager to say something withering about Mrs. Griswold and her mouldy appointments, but he felt that the Fosdicks should attack first. After all, they had found the damned place.

Mrs. Griswold came in once again to ask for rent. 'That will be twelve dollars a week, in advance,' she said. 'Every Monday.'

The Fosdicks got up to go, with their usual delicacy. 'See you tonight, John. Six o'clock at this address.' Eugene handed him a card with a Park Avenue number on it. Phht, they were gone.

John took off his coat and his shirt and lay down on the bed. There wasn't anything else one could do in this room, except sit on the wooden chair. One would get used to it, of course, but it *was* a bit disappointing. After looking forward so long to a year of fleshy luxury, amid the disgusting materialism of the Americans, it was a blow to find himself back in the old squalor, rather worse than anything in England, with a dismal landlady and no daylight and no bloody breakfast. Granted the Yanks made too much fuss about their precious standard of living— still, it was a blasted poor show to be over here and not to get even a whiff of it.

What he couldn't understand at all was the attitude of the Fosdicks. He couldn't picture either of them spending so much as a week-end in a pigsty like this. It couldn't be that they were just being kind again, could it, in some obscure way? No doubt this was all one could expect for twelve dollars a week—no point therefore in rubbing it in. It was delicate on their part, Emily-Post-delicate, to pretend that this was just like the places that they lived in themselves—good, rulebook diplomacy, but

bloody condescending, too. It would have been much less snob-
bish of them if they had admitted candidly that the place was
a dump. One felt vaguely like a poor old down-and-out in the
icy grip of a couple of social workers, old hands at humouring
the poor. 'Look, Mr. Chote. A room all to yourself with a bed
and a chair and everything.' Tears of gratitude welled up in
the old gentleman's eyes. 'Oh, thank you, thank you.'

He caught a glimpse of himself in the cracked mirror at the
foot of the bed. The crack ran down his cheek like a scar,
making his face look twisted and angry, like the face of a pub
fanatic. It made him laugh—he really didn't feel as strongly
about it as all that. He didn't fancy himself as a whining under-
dog, and anyway, the exquisite politeness of the Fosdicks was
one of their great charms, one of the things that made them
Fosdicks. It gave Mirabelle an extra radiance, which would be
nice to think about sometimes in this dark room.

He decided to start thinking about it right away.

At half-past five he put his shirt back on and hitched up his
seersucker trousers, which were beginning to curl around his
legs: he shouldn't have slept in them before going to a nice
party with the Fosdicks. He reached for his Sturdley tie, because
it was such a help in conversation, and headed out into the
hall. He turned the handle of the bathroom door and pushed.
'My wife's in there,' said a hollow voice. Chote looked round:
a little man with blond hair was standing a few feet away in a
patch of darkness, watching him cautiously.

'Oh,' said Chote. 'Then I suppose you'll be going in next.'

The little man held out his hand. 'I'm Joe Fishman.'

'John Chote.'

'Pleased to meet you, Mr. Stote.' Mr. Fishman shook his
hand quite heartily.

'I've just moved in,' Chote explained.

'Oh yes,' said Mr. Fishman. He lapsed into a curiously dead
silence.

'Yes,' said Chote. 'I've just arrived in New York. I'm English
you know.' Mr. Fishman's silence temporarily unnerved him,
like silence in a damp cellar.

'Oh, yes,' said Mr. Fishman. 'So.'

259

'How long have you lived here?' Chote wanted to hear him talk.

'Two years,' said Mr. Fishman.

The bathroom door opened and a pretty woman with a towel round her head came padding out. 'This is my wife,' said Fishman. 'Gloria, I want you to meet Mr. Stote. He's just moved in. He's English.' Gloria Fishman looked him up and down like Alan Browning looking at a girl. Her eyes were bright and candid, and she smiled all over as she looked. 'Yes, Mrs. Griswold told me about you. His name is Chote, dear, not Stote.'

'Sorry Mr. Chote,' mumbled Joe.

'It's nice to meet you, Mr. Chote.' Gloria Fishman was giving him the works, still smiling and looking him right in the eye and squeezing his hand like a flash bulb, all at the same time. Mr. Fishman stood aside, pulling absently at his nose and waiting for his wife to finish her performance. 'It's very exciting to meet an Englishman, isn't it Joe? You people were so wonderful in 1940. I can't tell you.'

Chote watched her undulating her way down the hall, with Joe shambling along beside. He hadn't been waiting to use the bathroom after all, but only to escort his wife back to her room. What a marvellous little chap!

Chote slithered downward into the cool water, and began to cover himself jovially with soap. By George, he thought, by George: this was the sort of thing. He could almost hear the light footsteps outside and the tender rapping on the door as a distant clock chimed two or so: 'Oh, Mr. Chote, Mr. Chote' —well, no, she could hardly call him that. He laughed good-naturedly to himself. Yes, this really was something like the sort of thing. Of course, one had been reading about women like that all one's life and hearing about them from one's more boastful friends (well, Browning anyway) but he had long despaired of ever actually finding one. It was as if the myth of Mrs. Worsley had come to life at last. 'Yes, John,' he told himself happily, 'there really *is* a Mrs. Worsley.'

Unfortunately, he hadn't the faintest idea as to what he should do after letting her in. Would it be best to send her

sobbing straight back to her husband with a few wise words—
or should he perhaps humour her just once or twice out of kindness? Time would doubtless dictate a course. One didn't want
to take this sort of thing too seriously. It was fundamentally
a farce in the classical mode : one must play it accordingly.

He began to sing 'The Man Who Broke the Bank at Monte
Carlo' in a loud inaccurate baritone, soaping himself over and
over again. Those were the orthodox exercises. He didn't have
to put the thought into so many words : but one felt like no
end of a chap, with all these women after one. If only one's
friends could see one in action, *ho-ho!*

Was singing prohibited by one of Mrs. Griswold's statutes?
He couldn't remember. When he stopped it was very quiet, as
if the building had been secretly drained and emptied. But a
moment later he heard, sure enough, the soft, patient, tap-tap-
tap on the bathroom door.

Chote sprang from the tub splashing like Leviathan. 'Just a
minute,' he shouted as he floundered after his towel. 'Just a
jiffy.' This was unbelievable—much sooner than he had expected. Perhaps Mr. Fishman had gone out, leaving his wife
succulently alone for a few minutes. . . .

'Sorry to bother you,' said Mr. Fishman from the doorway.
'My wife thinks she left her hairnet someplace in here.' Chote
stood by, dripping quietly, while Mr. Fishman probed the
washstand. Well it was really very amusing, very amusing
indeed. 'Here it is. Thank you, Mr. . . . uh, yes.'

John crawled back into his seersucker suit, smoothing out
the wrinkles hopefully with his hands. The course of classic
farce never did run smooth, he reflected. There would be more
misunderstandings and disappointments, and nights spent
shivering on the fire-escape too, no doubt, before this thing was
over.

He began to whistle as he tied on his Sturdley tie. The
musty silence of evening was broken now by a woman's voice
shrill and monotonous, coming from a long distance away. No,
he realized that the voice belonged to Mrs. Fishman and it
couldn't be so far away after all. It sounded as if she was using
a megaphone. She was shouting something at Joe, who was

261

defending himself inaudibly if at all. Chote smiled to himself : the tearing shrieks of frustration must be burning into Mr. Fishman's skin, making it hiss and sizzle and shrink. Surely they would both welcome relief from any quarter at all.

Chote stepped smartly out of his new home, a jaunty figure in rumpled seersucker. Fosdick was right, by God. Human nature was the same wherever you found it.

The party was already going strong. He crept in past the little coloured maid and took up his stance in a corner of the vast throbbing living-room. A distinguished old man in a white coat came by with a tray of drinks. 'Good evening,' said Chote and the old fellow looked up sharply. His long face was drawn with what might have been pain. 'Did you speak, sir?' It was an English voice, but of another vintage : preserved with too much care, scrupulously exaggerated by years of service. Nobody spoke like that any more.

'You're English,' said Chote.

'Yes sir.'

'What part?'

'Well, sir, West Ham, actually.'

'You never learned to talk like that in West Ham,' said Chote accusingly.

The old man looked around nervously and then his aristocratic face crinkled into a little round ball of playful pink fun. 'Well, sir, you know how it is. They seem to prefer it. And where, if I may ask, are you from yourself, sir ?'

'*There* you are, Johnny,' said Mirabelle. 'I've been looking all over the place.' She began tugging at his hand in the familiar way, jocular, but firm as steel. 'You *must* meet your host and hostess—they've been dying—'

'So long, Sid,' said Chote. 'See you later.'

'Yes, sir,' said the waiter, with a tiny bow.

The host turned out to be the chubby fellow in Bermuda shorts, standing by the artificial fireplace with a rather dismayed expression, like a baby sleeping badly. 'How do you do, Mr. Chote,' he said with the faintest of worried smiles. 'Glad you could come.'

Mirabelle flitted away, leaving these two exciting people alone together. After all, they had both been dying to meet each other.

'How long have you been over?' asked the host after a minute or two.

'About two months, I think. Yes, that's about it. Two months.' Couldn't say much more about that.

The host nodded thoughtfully. 'I see.' He looked around the room as if for assistance. 'Can I get you a drink? Or a sandwich? Oh, I see.'

Chote held up his drink and a large sandwich. The host (what was *his* bloody name?) jiggled his glass around distractedly and peeped this way and that. Poor chap, thought Chote. Dying to meet me. He wished he could help, but for the life of him he couldn't think of anything to say. 'I've been to Chicago'—one could hardly say that: too much like the little boy who says 'I've been to the bathroom.' What about something like 'It's jolly nice over here.' Good Lord! That *would* be a rollicking one! Or 'What a nice pair of shorts you've got on.'

The host had caught by now the well-covered eye of a thin girl in long-slanted glasses, who was standing by herself a few yards away. He signalled to her enthusiastically.

'Janet,' he said. 'I'd like you to meet—Janet!' She had turned away, but the host was desperate by now; he bounded over and turned her around with a convulsive gesture. 'Janet, I'd like you to meet Mr. em, yes. He just came over from England. Two months ago.'

Janet beamed. John had begun to backtrack, hoping to pick up Mirabelle again. But she seemed to have disappeared behind a row of beefy heroes. He could hear her silvery laugh tinkling away like a bell in a birdcage, somewhere behind a wall of sky-blue dinner jackets: so trim and spruce alongside his own shrivelled seersucker, with its muddy brown cuffs.

'And what do *you* do?' asked Janet in a shrill voice. 'I'll bet it's something interesting.'

'Eh?' Chote said sharply. She had crept up on his flank and startled him.

'Ooh, don't be so ferocious,' said Janet. 'You look like someone in a casting agency.'

'Sorry,' said Chote. 'You frightened me. What did you say?'

'I asked what you did, you know, for a living. Everybody I've met so far this evening does something fascinating. The Pilsons have *such* exciting friends.'

'Well, actually,' said Chote, 'I'm rather embarrassed to tell you what I do.'

'Oh, you mustn't be embarrassed,' said Janet warmly. 'You shouldn't be ashamed of any kind of honest work. I mean, somebody has to do the menial work, even street-cleaning and things like that.'

'It's much worse than that,' said Chote, still looking around for Mirabelle. The sky-blue shoulders were shaking smoothly with flirtatious laughter. Damn it, Mirabelle wasn't as funny as all that.

'I admire a man who does the so-called "degrading" jobs,' pursued Janet. 'A man who doesn't mind getting his hands dirty now and then.'

'Well, if you put it that way, I might as well tell you the truth. I don't do anything. I'm stinking rich and I just can't be bothered,' said Chote absently. 'Too, too boring.'

Janet wasn't the least bit dismayed. 'Oh, you must do something! Everybody does something.'

'Not a blinking thing,' said Chote, 'except sit in the bathtub all day and boast.'

'Why,' said Janet, more delighted than ever. 'I think that's absolutely wonderful. Of course, I don't believe you,' and so on—Chote yawned. He had met this girl before, especially in New York, but once or twice in London as well: she was always excited to the point of hysteria by whatever one said. Whether one claimed to be a taxidermist, a coal miner or a Communist spy (and he had claimed all these and more) it was all wonderful, just wonderful. 'I wonder why you're so defensive about admitting that you don't do anything?' Janet was saying. 'Are you always so defensive about life?'

'You bet,' said Chote. 'Look, do you mind if I leave you

alone for just a moment? I see somebody over there who's leaving and I ought to say "Hello" or "Goodbye" or something.'

He ducked his way through the swirling mob. Mirabelle had shielded herself behind her brawny admirers: one could only peep at her through chinks and knotholes in the sky-blue wall. So he went instead to look for 'Sid' the butler, who was standing stiff as starch by the exit saying a restrained goodbye to some old family friends who were leaving early. He looked a little embarrassed to see Chote again, but he strove to make the best of it.

'Are you having an enjoyable time, sir?'

'Don't come the old retainer on me,' said Chote. 'I'm onto your game, Sid.' Sid's face collapsed into unsightly wrinkles once again. 'Shall we go into the kitchen, sir,' he said.

Sid was dying, it soon turned out, to talk to somebody about the English soccer situation. He followed the scores faithfully in the New York *Times*, but it wasn't the same, sir. Chote perched himself on the sideboard, while Sid (whose name was Alfred Bingham) polished the glasses and pumped him solemnly with sporting questions and drinks. Every now and then Alfred had to go out and raise the tone of the party, and Chote would pour himself yet another drink and wait for his new friend to come back.

'Phew, what a thirsty mob. Now where were we sir, oh yes, we'd reached the last Cup Final. Newcastle United, wasn't it, sir?'

'How do you do it, Sid?' asked Chote, who was sitting in the sink by now.

'Do what sir?'

'You know,' Chote gestured. 'All this stuff—you know the sort of thing you do, don't you?'

'Oh yes, that sort of thing. Well, I don't know. There's an absolute gold mine in it, of course.'

'Yes, I suppose there is. But then don't you get awfully tired of going around with a bayonet plunged up your so-to-speak spine all the time?'

'It's not as hard as you might suppose, sir. You won't believe this, of course, but I attended Harrow once upon a time, and that helped me more than somewhat.'

Chote squinted at him. 'You're a fraud, Perkins. You'd never even heard of Harrow until you came over here. Admit it, now, like a good fellow.'

'I agree it sounds improbable. But I've had an extremely checkered career, and it definitely includes Harrow. A scholarship, of course.'

'In that case whatever reduced you to this? Harrovians usually do a little better than, well, whatever it is that you do here.'

'I honestly doubt that,' said Alfred amiably. 'I don't wish to make a point of it, but my investments over here already total well over one hundred thousand dollars and I expect to do better by and by. Of course it isn't prestige, but it's a living.'

'Well, I'm blowed,' said Chote from his seat in the sink. 'Why haven't I thought of something like that?'

'I warmly recommend it, sir. The better your education, the better you'll do. The gentlemen will give you absolutely invaluable tips, and of course the ladies—' He raised his little grey eyebrows expressively.

'What about the ladies?' Chote asked quickly.

'Well, perhaps the less said the better,' said Alfred. 'But I could tell you some stories about famous ladies who took pity on a simple butler. . . .' His face was rumpled again; it looked somehow greasy with sensuality. ' "Come here a minute, Bingham",' he mimicked in a high squeaky voice. ' "I want to show you something".'

'Now I know you're lying,' said Chote. He felt a twinge like rheumatism of the old disgust. There was the idiot-sly face again, and so much the worse when allied like this with slight decomposition. 'You're just a bloody great dreamer with an over-active imagination,' he said with a thin smile. ' "Come here, Sidney. And tell me what the boys did at Harrow".' No, it wasn't the lechery so much, it was the polish surrounding it, the elegant manners at the altar of the goat. Alfred was a parody of the smoothies in the next room.

Alfred wasn't annoyed. He went on shining his glasses

placidly. 'Perhaps I shouldn't have mentioned it,' he said with his old dignity. 'However, I do most earnestly recommend the career for a young gentleman of discriminating tastes. It has enabled me to purchase a first-class station wagon, you know, and a very presentable hi-fi set. . . .'

The white kitchen door inched open and Mirabelle looked in. 'There you are,' she said. John struggled to get out of the sink. 'I'm going home,' said Mirabelle briefly. 'With you in a tick,' mumbled Chote as the door swung shut.

It turned out that Eugene had already left, along with practically everybody else. It occurred to John that perhaps he ought to make some sort of apology to Mirabelle, who was standing by herself in the hallway, fidgeting with her hat. 'Didn't notice the time,' he said. 'Awfully sorry.'

'That's all right,' she said. 'Are you ready to take me home now?'

'Yes. Better say goodbye to the jolly old host first, hadn't I?'

'That's all right. He's gone to bed,' said Mirabelle. 'I said goodbye for you.'

'Oh,' said Chote. 'Sorry about that.'

She walked very fast to the elevator and then very fast to the front door, and then they both went shooting past the doorman like a pair of roller-skaters. 'Very interesting chap, that butler of theirs,' panted Chote. 'He thinks I ought to become a butler too.' Mirabelle was already out in the street, waving for taxis. 'Not a bad idea, eh?' said Chote. 'Becoming a butler, I mean.' She stopped a cab and yanked the door open viciously.

Inside the cab, he flung his arm around her confidently and told her in a low croon how lonesome he had been in Chicago, but she didn't seem to be responding. 'You aren't angry, are you dear?' he purred, fingering an icy earlobe.

'I'll get over it,' she said.

'It wasn't because I spent the evening with one of the servants, was it?' he asked lightly. 'Instead of with my peer group?' The phrase lingered pleasingly in his mind from some forgotten seminar.

She looked at him contemptuously, and pulled her ear away.

Chote was annoyed. 'What's the matter? Do you want me to apologize again?'

'Not particularly.'

'Well, what is it then?' She didn't answer for so long that he wondered if she had gone to sleep. The cab swung smoothly through Central Park, and then over to Riverside Drive where the air was cooler and there was space to think. 'I'm just a little surprised,' said Mirabelle finally. 'It isn't really anything very important.'

'Oh for Godsake,' said Chote. 'What am I supposed to have done that's so surprising?'

'Don't you know?' asked Mirabelle quietly.

'Blessed if I do. I talked to the butler and I forgot to look at my watch. Anything else?'

'Is that how you usually behave at parties?'

'When I feel like it. Yes.' He was beginning to get terribly angry, though he hardly knew why.

'You don't mind insulting your host and hostess? I might add that you also insulted me—but that doesn't matter. Harry and Marge Pilson are the ones I really feel badly about.'

'Who are they?' asked Chote gruffly.

'They're only your host and hostess, that's all. It was very nice of them to invite you in the first place. . . .'

'I didn't ask them to.'

'And all that you had to do in return was to act reasonably politely, act just the tiniest bit sociable.'

'I *was* sociable. I talked to a bloody silly girl until I could stand no more, and I talked to the host until both of us could stand no more.'

'I think that's a dreadful attitude. What right have you to call that girl silly? How do you know she doesn't think you're just as silly?'

'I don't give a farthing what she thinks,' said Chote sarcastically, 'considering that she apparently has the brain of a retarded flea.' Mirabelle turned haughtily away, but Chote plunged recklessly on. 'I think we ought to get one or two things straight, Mirabelle. I don't mind being told a thing or two about American habits and customs, but I'm damned if I'm going to be ordered around and stood in the corner like a ruddy great child; and I'm double-damned if I'm going to spend my time talking to people who bore the bejeesus, as you say over here, out of me. If you don't like the way I behave at parties, then don't take me to parties.'

Mirabelle's reflection in the cab window actually said, 'Don't you think you're being rather infantile about this? After all, getting along with other people is the most rudimentary step towards maturity. . . .'

'Well I missed it somehow,' said Chote. 'Anyway I've always thought that maturity was rather non-U, haven't you?'

The cab had arrived at Mirabelle's building, which wasn't very far from Chote's new room. John felt sheepish as he handed his money to the hackie who grinned and tipped his cap. He realized that he had been shouting louder and louder, providing some off-beat entertainment for the grateful driver : a petulant Englishman giving it the works.

He took Mirabelle upstairs in a self-service elevator. Conversation seemed pointless, but he thought he would make one more attempt. 'In England we believe that parties are primarily for having fun—not a sort of drill for one's manners.'

'That's nice,' said Mirabelle.

'I've behaved much worse than that at English parties, and the girls I was with never seemed to mind.'

'We have girls like that over here too,' said Mirabelle. 'If you like girls like that.'

They had reached her door. Chote had no plans for kissing her good night, but she darted forward and gave him a peck before disappearing for the night.

He walked home grumbling to himself. He bloody well was not going to be bossed around. He had heard all about these American women who gradually destroyed their men by nagging and sniping, and generally chipping away the old façade. He fulminated like Professor Higgins—he didn't care if she thought he was childish, or what she thought. He made a resolution (which he was to abide by) to avoid American social life as much as possible. It was like ruddy dancing school.

And yet, as with Professor Higgins, there was the after-

thought. He *did* feel childish : Mirabelle had turned the trick
as she always could. The more he blustered, the smaller he felt
—a little boy emerging from the headmaster's study with tears
in his eyes and red welts on his bottom; a smaller boy trying to
kick his mother's shins while she towered above him, absolutely impregnable.

The lobby of his building seemed even more deserted by
night. The potted plant looked gaunter than ever in the thin
red glow of the tiny pointed bulb, and the floor sounded hollow
under his feet.

In his lonely irritation, he half hoped that Mrs. Fishman
would come to his door right away, to wrap him up in her
slatternly arms until daylight came. He made a noise at the
front door so that she would hear him if she slept lightly.
He wasn't sure whether he wanted her or not : but he felt
he ought to make it at least possible. No avenue should be
blocked off.

He shut his door with a modest bang, and then opened it
again and walked into the bathroom, none too softly. It would
do him a power of good just to send her away.

There was a note in the bathtub, a little white note winking
up at him. He made a glad lunge for it. 'To Mr. Chote,' it
said and his heart paused in its tedious work. He turned it
over and squinted at it avidly : what on earth should one do
about it though ?

The words made no sense at first : 'Please do not leave ring
in the tub next time. This is *not* a private bathroom. Mrs.
Fishman.' So that was that.

Chote looked uncomprehendingly at it; and then he leaned
against the washbasin and began to howl. It was a silly habit
he had always had, for moments of surprise and discovery. It
seemed the only thing to do. His harassed reflection shook
helplessly in the mirror. Pagliacci Chote.

And then at last came the footsteps, shuffling demurely down
the corridor, and the long awaited tap on the door. 'Please be
quiet in there'—it was Mr. Fishman's voice, plaintive and
undernourished—'my wife and I are trying to sleep.' The footsteps retreated without waiting for an answer.

15. Angles

DAPHNE COLLINS dusted thoughtfully around the three blue letters on the mantelpiece. She dabbed briskly at the picture frames and threw out the dead flowers, and filled up the pot with fresh marigolds; that done, she encamped behind her small desk and primed her chubby fountain pen for the day's letter-writing.

First a few lines to her mother, to let her know that everything was all right; and then congratulations to her sister in Scotland who had just given birth; and finally something for the scapegrace Chote. 'I'm really very angry with you, John,' she wrote slowly and carefully. 'I know you're awfully busy in America, rushing around and making new friends, but I do think you might steal a moment, just a postcard to say you're all right and everything.'

She looked out the window, to make certain that her comments on the weather would be precise and up-to-the-minute. 'It's a lovely day,' she decided, 'with a bit of haze as if somebody's been burning leaves all over town.' She had a strain of easy lyricism when it came to the weather. 'Oxford's lovely, too, just coming to life for the new term. This morning I saw some young chaps at the station, and honestly, they looked about twelve apiece. Frightfully thin and weedy too. I'm sure *you* never looked like that.' In a corner of the desk, just behind the neat pile of lavender notepaper, she could just see the rumpled, anguished ball of white paper that she had shoved there earlier in the summer. 'I do hope that everything's all right now,' she wrote, remembering. 'I mean, the things that were upsetting you a few months ago, like the insincerity and the commercialism over there, and all the other nastinesses. I suppose you've met some nice people since then (I'm sure there *are* nice people in every country, if you just know where to find them) and everything is all right again. But I do wish you'd write and let me know. . . .' She could hardly put it more strongly than that. She folded the letter and slid it into a lavender envelope and then she took it out again and scribbled on the bottom. 'P.S. Please write so that I won't think you've been in a dreadful accident or something.' Then she put it back and sealed it away as quickly as possible, only hoping that the P.S. wouldn't annoy him too much.

She was making the tea when they arrived. There came a hearty whack at the door and a hoarse shout. 'Anybody home?' She patted down her capacious green dress and pushed at her mousey bun of hair. 'Just a moment please. Who is it?' She could hear them whispering: 'Tell her we're from Whitehall or something.' 'What a bloody dull suggestion.' 'Sorry.' 'You are a dull bastard, I've always said so.'

She opened the door and they swarmed all over her. 'Kiss me Daphne. Here and here and here.' She giggled convulsively: 'I'm not fit to be seen. I wasn't expecting anybody.' 'You look absolutely delightful,' said Alan Browning. 'Ever so unaffected and nice. Doesn't she Reverend? Maiden-surprised-at-the-toilet sort of thing.'

'Oh rather. Yes of course. Damn fine woman,' said Godfrey.

They all sat down together on the sofa, laughing and talking —Daphne very animated after such a quiet, lonely summer. Alan and Godfrey were all tangled up in long college scarves, symbols of autumn and quickening life at Oxford.

During tea they talked about Chote. 'He's a rotten correspondent,' said Daphne. 'But he seems to be having a jolly good time, by and large.'

'Yes I just had a letter from him the other day myself,' said Godfrey. 'All about—well, anyway, he did seem to be having a jolly good time, as you say. Working hard and improving himself and all that sort of thing.'

'What was the letter all about, Godfrey?' asked Browning with a wink at Daphne.

'Well, that, mostly. What he was doing, his little hopes and plans and so on. Frightfully dry stuff, in the main.'

'He says he's very busy,' agreed Daphne.

'Yes,' said Godfrey quickly. 'That was my impression too. Absolutely up to his ears in rewarding activities : speaking at the UN, basket-weaving, the lot.'

'America does that to one, I believe,' said Browning. 'Chaps who have been utterly torpid for years and years suddenly come to life over there and fling themselves into things with the most unexpected abandon. And of course,' he added, 'that's only what it does to the torpid ones. You can imagine the dire effects on a firebrand like Chote.'

'He said something about going into business over there,' said Hook. 'Do you suppose he can ?'

'I'm quite sure he can,' said Browning. 'I can just picture him buttering up old Mr. Woolworth or whoever the big chap is these days. Young Englishman, bursting at the seams with enthusiasm and sincerity, and simply crawling with charm— that'll be the line I suspect.'

'Yes but aren't there all sorts of rules about Englishmen working in America ?'

'Are there ? Yes, I suppose there are.' Browning licked a few crumbs off his fingers. 'But I believe the Americans are frightfully flexible about rules of that sort. I mean, supposing old Mr. Woolworth goes round to the State Department with his cap in his hands and says "Look here you guys, I have this absolutely indispensable chap, simply bulging with key ideas and five-year plans and so on," can you imagine them having the heart to refuse him ?'

'It's all very depressing,' said Daphne with a smile. 'I don't suppose we'll ever see John again at that rate.'

'Well, I daresay he'll be sticking to Wall Street like a leech for the next year or two. But he'll be back eventually with fur lapels on his overcoat and all the various trimmings. In the meantime,' Browning concluded with his gooiest and most chivalrous smile, 'our task is to make the time pass as quickly as possible for you. Isn't that it, Reverend ?'

'Yes, of course. Damn fine woman,' said Godfrey absent-mindedly.

'To which end, we thought a drinkers or two at the Forers to start with, followed perhaps by a spot of dancers at the Harers. . . .'

Daphne took out the tea things, and changed into her other green dress—the one that Chote used to be so fond of—and off they went, clattering and chattering down the stairs. Daphne was laughing uncontrollably by now, deep, painful, unused laughter; the dark stairwell resounded with it, like the tunnel of horrors at a fun-fair. Browning put a friendy arm around her, and they all waddled out into the street together, into the autumn mist, cackling, shrieking, barking with pleasure.

The bulbous figures came apart, like the petals on a sunflower. 'Ah, they've finished huddling have they?' asked Chote breezily. Fosdick nodded. 'Good heavens, what are they up to now?' cried Chote. 'Have they all gone mad?'

Fosdick smiled thinly. 'They gained four yards that time,' he explained. 'Off-tackle smash.'

'Oh, I see. That's what it was.' The air was crisp and cold and the sharp wind was whipping Chote into a fine lather of facetiousness. 'What's happening now? Who are all these new chaps? Reinforcements of some kind, I suppose. The place will be absolutely teeming with chaps in a few minutes. . . .'

'They're substitutes,' said Fosdick.

'The original blokes are simply worn out by now, I suppose. I wouldn't wonder. They must have been going at it hammer and tongs for nearly two minutes by now, huddling away—' He glanced at Mirabelle: she was staring fixedly out at the field, scrupulously abstaining from the conversation. 'They must get very tired running around in that armour-plating,' he went on. 'I suppose they're actually very small men indeed underneath, midgets of sorts. Ah, look, here they go again. . . .'

It was hopeless to suppose that he was amusing anybody but himself. Fosdick's face was set grimly as he made brief notes on a pad. Mirabelle was practically out of sight, buried alive in a fur coat and a cossack hat, but her eyes were cold and infinitely bored. 'Look here, it's only a game,' said Chote nervously. 'Isn't it? I mean I'm not being sacrilegious am I? It's not like making fun of cricket or something like that.'

They both smiled thinly and Mirabelle said, 'No, it's nothing like that.' She leaned over and whispered into his new pair of earmuffs, 'It's just that we've taken quite a few Englishmen to football games in the last few years—and, well, the material's kind of familiar.' She frowned apologetically. 'I'm sure it's the same with Americans and cricket.'

'Yes, of course. I see what you mean.'

The game took on a new dreariness after that. The cold seeped in through his coat and his shoes, folding him in on himself, a frozen bundle of self-pity. The huddles and time-outs seemed to be interminable, the action brief and meaning-less; and all the time the blur of padded figures trotting in and out. Of all the bloody silly amusements!

'Are you beginning to get the hang of it?' asked Fosdick looking up from his studious charts.

'Yes, I think so,' said Chote. 'It's really rather fascinating, isn't it?'

'Well, we think so,' said Eugene expansively. 'I'm crazy about it,' put in Eugene's companion, a languid creation from Vassar. 'Just wild.'

Half-time came at last, and the two girls went off together to discuss the fine points. A band came out onto the gridiron and marched around spelling out various simple words. It was a fine spectacle—red and white formations under an ice-blue sky—and Chote wished the football players would just go away and leave the business of entertaining to the trim major-ettes, who were prancing handsomely up and down the side-lines, along with their brassy followers.

'I like this sort of thing,' he said. 'Noisy and cheerful and nice to look at. In fact, it's one of the nicest things I've come across over here.'

Fosdick was still bringing his charts up to the minute, con-necting arrows and dotted lines. 'What was that?' he asked vaguely.

'I said: What do you actually do on Wall Street?'

'Oh,' said Fosdick. 'This and that. Why?'

'I don't know. I was just wondering how one went about making money in this fabulous country. That's all.'

'I didn't think you were the type that cared.'

'Oh, but I do care. Deeply. Passionately.'

'Really?' said Fosdick. 'Well I must say you had me fooled. I always thought that you were the most insouciant son of a gun I ever met. In fact, I once had an argument about that very thing with one of the guys at Sturdley.'

'Who was that?'

'He didn't say. I couldn't see him too clearly. It was kind of dark in those bushes. . . .'

'All right, all right. What else did Alan say?'

'Well,' Eugene smiled, 'he didn't say much else. He just bet me that you would wind up a hell of a lot richer than any other native-born Englishman in your year. It seemed ridiculous at the time. I mean, Norbert Jones was in your year, wasn't he? Now there's the type of guy that really makes the money. A real, dedicated, undeflected, one hundred per cent jerk.'

'You have to be a jerk to make money?'

'Well, let's just say it helps. A special kind of jerk, that is— a hard-driving, single-minded, unimaginative jerk, like Norbert.'

'I can be all those things,' said Chote stoutly. 'And more.'

'I guess you can,' said Eugene seriously, 'if you put your mind to it. But what a helluva way to waste a lifetime.'

'Are you serious?' asked Chote. 'Are you feeling all right, my boy?'

'Sure I am. I feel fine. How do you feel?'

'A trifle shaken, actually. After all, you're the chap who goes toiling down to Wall Street every day, not I. It does seem a bit much for a chap like me to be subjected to a sermon on avarice from a chap like you.'

'You seem to have a pretty funny idea of Wall Street,' said Eugene. 'I just earn a modest living down there, you know. I don't dig for gold with my bare hands.'

Chote was blessed if he could tell whether the chap was joking. He had always assumed that Fosdick had his share of the conventional self-interest. 'Look Gene,' he said, 'I don't want to be offensive—but you're a bloody rich bloke, by my standards. If I had half as much scratch as you seem to have,

I could afford to take a superior attitude, too. As it is, I have to grub around where the money is; and sometimes my mouth is inclined to slaver a little when I get too close to the scent.' Fosdick was looking at his feet by now, with features drawn tight, as if Chote were singing a dirty song in front of the ladies. 'I'm sorry, old boy,' said John. 'But I haven't been brought up to money as you have, and I don't know how to be very graceful about it. Are you terribly disappointed?'

'If that's how you feel, that's how you feel,' said Fosdick dryly. The girls were mercifully coming back, wiggling their way cautiously over blanketed knees. Eugene jumped up gallantly to help them.

In a few minutes, the bulging heroes were back and the game was on again. Fosdick returned to his charts, recording each tiny manœuvre with the same fussy precision as before. Chote couldn't make out whether his friend had changed since coming back to America, or whether he had just been misreading the English translation of Fosdick. It was hard to imagine the bland philosopher of Sturdley becoming so excited over a mere football game : some boyish streak seemed to have reasserted itself, now that he was back in familiar surroundings.

One felt depressed again, especially with that ruddy game crawling along interminably out there in the frosty air. Clouds had come up, darkening the stadium and cooling it like a new Ice Age. Pennants were drooping from chapped fingers, and some of the sensible set had already begun to make for the exits. And still the game dragged on : '13–13,' said the scoreboard. 'One of the most exciting games I've ever seen,' enthused Mirabelle. 'You've been very lucky, John. This is a game in a million.' The big hand of the clock kept stopping—a special form of torture, which made the ladies squeak with excitement. Apparently the game was getting more thrilling by the minute.

He was just dozing off when the gun went : 'Thirteen-all. How about that?' said Fosdick. Men and women in huge coats began to descend on them, springing from bench to bench, coagulating into a mob. Chote and the Fosdicks were swept away and down in a swirl of fur and wool. Before he knew what was happening, Chote found himself under the tottering goalposts; a tiny man with a grin was looking down at him from the crossbar. The two white spokes writhed back and forth against the slate-grey sky, and Chote tried to focus on them for a second. But the crowd carried him away again and then back, propping him against one of the goalposts. He began pushing at the post frantically—it seemed the only thing to do —and soon he felt a kind of satisfaction as it began to splinter under his hands. The crossbar was twisting crazily overhead and the little man was hanging on grimly. 'Come down, you bugger,' muttered Chote. 'I'll get you down, you silly little sod.' At that point, there was a sharp crackle and the small man hurtled gracefully down into the crowd, knocking people over like ninepins. The little destroyer capered off after that and was lost to view.

Chote was sitting on the grass when Fosdick found him, with his hands up to ward off flying feet. 'You certainly enter into the spirit, don't you?' Eugene smiled. 'You've just finished knocking down your own goalpost, old man.'

'Is that what I've been doing? Good Lord!' Chote scratched his head foolishly.

'Where's your school spirit, man? The old school tie and all that?'

'How was I to know which goalpost was which?' said Chote. 'Why didn't you carry me up to the right end, you swine? They both looked the same to me.'

'You were marvellous, anyway,' said Mirabelle. 'Now let's all go and have a drink!'

'What can this man Chote give you?' purred Alan Browning. 'Money, youth, charm—but what else? Come away weez me and forget thees, thees—man.'

'Oh Alan, honestly. You are absurd.' Daphne giggled.

Godfrey came gliding past holding on to a girl in black tights; he dipped a rigid forearm in salute. 'I'm very proud of Godfrey,' said Alan. 'He's made enormous progress during the summer. Did you by any chance notice the masterful grip? And the long rapacious strides? He's just a new sort of chap altogether.'

'What have you done to him?' asked Daphne.

'Well first of all, I've isolated him from all possible sources of wholesome influence. Absolutely no clergymen allowed in the house. . . .'

'Oh, really Alan. You're dreadful.' Daphne was still laughing convulsively.

'And the rest was just plain hard work: getting him drunk at regular intervals, keeping him up late and so on. Fierce strain on me, of course, but well worth it.'

'I don't want to hear any more,' coughed Daphne. 'You're really the most frightful type I've ever met.'

'Oh I don't know. How about our old friend Chote? I imagine he was pretty rough in spots wasn't he? In a nice way, I mean.'

She didn't answer. The music was heating up, and Daphne was beginning to squirm appropriately. 'And I imagine you've had some pretty pink moments yourself,' said Browning. 'A high-spirited girl like you.'

'That's enough now,' said Daphne. 'Come along and dance, you naughty man.' All around the floor, the pale townspeople were commencing to throw off their cares, kicking and wriggling and snapping their fingers. The girl in black tights was forming lithe convolutions in the centre of the crowd, while Godfrey shook his hips and waved his arms phrenetically. 'Come *on*,' said Daphne, twisting away. 'Oh, very well,' said Alan. 'If we must.' He began to weave a little and then a little more, as the mob hysteria caught at the nerves and set them to tingling. Daphne was already jogging up and down like a mad thing—along with all the other shy ones. A chaos of quiet English people, a sudden tropical storm, building up ominously and leading to nothing, except more quietness, next week's quietness.

They sat on the porch drinking out of paper cups. Now and again a boy's rubber football would come thudding among the wickerwork chairs. Two eleven-year-olds were taking greedy advantage of the last hour of wintery light. Old friends and acquaintances of Eugene's ambled in and out of the colonial house, greeted him casually, said a few words about the game ('Thirteen-all—isn't that something?') and passed on.

The girl from Vassar was talking. 'I wonder what gets into people to make them riot like that? Is it boredom do you suppose? is it frustration? or what is it?'

'It's just the desire for exercise, actually,' said Chote. 'People over here don't get half enough exercise. At least I don't.'

'Do you think that's it?' asked the girl from Vassar. 'Or is it something else?'

'Well, either one or the other, I suppose. Either that or something else, I mean.'

'No,' she went on doggedly. 'I mean the people out there looked so hostile and everything. Didn't you feel that, while you were out there with them? Didn't you feel a tiny bit hostile yourself?'

'Not a bit. I felt bloody peaceful throughout—a regular young dove.'

Mirabelle might have sensed trouble already. 'I know just what you mean, Alison,' she said quickly. 'There seems to be a terrible amount of bottled-up cruelty and hysteria and it just erupts like that.' She snapped her fingers warningly under Chote's chin. 'You see it behind race riots, bullfights, wrestling matches. . . .'

'Chess games, ping-pong tournaments, knitting,' said Chote.

Alison ignored him. 'What do you suppose it is? The will to power, or what? Thwarted ambition, an unresolved rivalry with one's siblings. . . .'

'Yes, something like that,' Chote butted in again. 'Bound to be, don't you think?' Mirabelle smiled apologetically.

'In my own case, it was a mixture,' he said: 'hatred for the gardener, a severe shortage of cheese. . . .'

'Yes, John. We know,' said Mirabelle.

'Well, I was just telling Alison what *I* was thinking about while I was under the goalposts. . . .'

Alison had had enough. She got up and went into the club to look for Eugene. Mirabelle stared out into the twilight where the boys were still groping about after their ball. Chote lit a cigarette and said, 'It's turned out to be a nice evening after all, hasn't it? Nippy but nice. Nice but nippy. Wouldn't you say so? Or would you say something else? Please be frank.'

She frowned in bewilderment. 'I just don't get it,' she said after a pause. 'Don't get it at all.'

'Don't get what, my dear?' He patted her head absently. This was rather a nice club. Elegant, unpretentious.

'How you can be so nice sometimes, and so impossible other times.'

'I d'know. Must ask me astrologer,' he said in his comic Liverpool accent. 'What's the matter anyhow? I was just having a bit of innocent fun. . . .'

'At somebody else's expense. Don't other people's feelings interest you at all?'

'What about my feelings, if it comes to that? I'm chuffed to the ears with these All-American girl psychiatrists. Why should I have to go on suffering week after week?'

'You could always stay home. Anyhow, what she was saying was very interesting, I thought.'

'Except, as you so neatly put it, "the material is kind of familiar".' Mirabelle snorted decorously.

'So why didn't you bring in some fresh material, if you're so well versed in the subject?'

'I tried to, but you wouldn't let me.'

It wasn't a big one like the war in the taxicab, but only one of a hundred tiny engagements, police actions, conscientiously instigated by Mirabelle whenever she thought Chote was going too far. At first, he had wondered why they were necessary at all—he had never wrangled like this with Daphne—but after a while they seemed inevitable, and almost welcome, like cloud-bursts at the end of a humid day. There was a nice freshness in the air afterwards, and a promise of new beginnings. Would that be their rhythm if they lived together? Probably—no peace on this side of the grave, nothing but pain and renewed excite-ment, with love (if that's what it really was) being born and reborn in travail : or just dying stillborn after a game struggle.

After a placid dinner at the club, she started the sniping again, fretfully, like an older sister rubbed raw with too much responsibility. 'Why do you have such an aversion to psychiatry, John? Is it a challenge to you?' she whispered.

'Not that I'm aware of. It's just that back in the old country, we believe that a stiff dose of castor oil generally does the trick just as well.' After a good dinner, and chomping on one of Eugene's Corona-Coronas, he was ready to do irritating battle once again.

'That's snide,' she said. 'And it's superficial. Psychiatry is one of the important ideas of our time . . .'

'Let it be,' he mumbled.

'. . . and it concerns everybody tremendously.'

'Yes I've begun to notice that too. Every dashed person in the room seems to be talking about it.' He waved his cigar around at Eugene's friends, packed tight in annual jamboree. He really had no idea what any of them were talking about.

'Do you regard yourself as a model of mental health?' she asked accusingly.

'Not specially. I have negative thoughts now and then, if that's what you mean.'

'What about your defensiveness? And your aggressiveness? And those funny faces you make all the time? And all those fears you told me about—especially your fear of darkness?'

'I should never have told you about that. It was mostly a joke, anyway.' That was really a dirty trick, bringing that up. 'How dare you read the secrets of the human heart? Haven't you read any Catholic novelists?'

'It's all right. I'm not trying to hold it against you, dear,' she said. 'But can't you see that these are genuine symptoms of inner disturbance? I don't mean that there's anything seriously wrong with you—but I just wish you wouldn't take that hearty "what me?" attitude to the whole thing.'

'That's probably a symptom too. Look, Mirabelle, I know it's a thoroughly sick thing to say, but I'm quite happy, really I am; my friends, such as they are, seem to like me; my mother feels a certain quiet pride; so why in heaven must everyone keep pestering me about witch doctors? I *like* being aggressive. And then I like to run away and hide, and generally go on the defensive. I know it's neurotic, but it suits me, dammit.'

'Are you really as happy as all that? What about those feelings of guilt you were talking about—guilty if you do and guilty if you don't? I know they don't make *me* feel very happy.'

'Oh, bugger my feelings of guilt.' He was sitting in his favourite position, hunched forward on the sofa. A touch would have tipped him over. But he could sit like that for half an hour without moving. Just recently: 'What's the matter dear?' He could still hear her voice trembling up between his chunky shoulder blades. 'Did I make you angry, don't you feel well, what's the matter?' 'Nothing, nothing at all.' She had stood up and then tiptoed out of the room, leaving him sitting there in that silly position, an engineering improbability : his heavy face mottled and creased and anxious in the wall mirror.

He sat back, crunching into the cushions. 'What is it, Mirabelle? Why are we all so solemn tonight?'

'I like to be serious now and then,' she said. 'Don't you?'

'Not if I can help it.'

She looked at his eyes, slowly and steadily. 'Don't you ever get tired of being facetious—morning, noon and night, jokes, jokes, jokes?'

'It *does* take character, doesn't it?'

'I think it's a kind of disease,' she said.

'Oh, God help us all!' moaned Chote burying his face in a cushion. Some of the other guests looked over just then and laughed at the funny uninhibited Englishman.

The dancing was over, and Browning was saying, 'Let's get out of here—there's a depressing smell of bank clerks pervading the place.' The local people were calming down slowly, and letting off a pink gleam. Hook was panting slightly and so was Daphne; but Browning was still the perfect head waiter, eerily calm and stainless. 'I believe you have a pact with the devil,' said Godfrey. 'Why don't you sweat like the rest of us?'

It was raining when they got outside, a misty, abortive drizzle. Godfrey had brought along his customary umbrella, which he flung up triumphantly over himself and Daphne. 'No room for you, old boy,' he said airily. 'Pity.' 'Oh, come on,

Alan,' said Daphne holding out her arms. 'There's lots of room for a little chap like you.' 'He's all right,' said Godfrey. 'I'm blessed if the rain ever really lands on him anyway . . . quite the most uncanny powers, you know.' Browning leered beneficently and said, 'You're both too sweet, but I really mustn't. Apart from anything else, Godfrey would keep getting in the way and spoiling the fun.' He turned away, with his crepe soles grinding like tyres on the wet pavement.

'Where are you going, old man?'

'Oh I have one or two small appointments in the city. Don't bother to wait up.' He wheeled and gave Daphne a chaste peck on the cheek, and a boyish dimpled smile. 'Watch out for this chap—he stops at absolutely nothing,' he said. 'Make sure that he holds the umbrella at all times.' He gave Godfrey's elbow a friendly tweak and was off, dodging the raindrops, back towards Carfax and his invariable appointments.

'Extraordinary bloke,' said Godfrey.

'Yes, isn't he?' said Daphne. 'Most amusing.'

They trudged back over Magdalen Bridge, deflating slowly. 'Are you getting wet?' 'No, it's all right. If you could just hold the umbrella a little bit higher.' 'Sorry, is that better?' 'Yes, that's perfect.'

After all the excitment, they were both glad to be quiet. 'It's nice to be quiet isn't it?' verified Godfrey. 'Yes, it is,' Daphne agreed. Godfrey felt unusually comfortable with Daphne. After all, she was by common consent a good deal duller than he had ever been; no need, therefore, to sparkle. 'I wonder,' he said thoughtfully, 'why a chap like Alan goes around with chaps like us? I mean quiet chaps.' 'I don't know,' said Daphne. 'Perhaps he likes to show off.'

Well, really, one didn't think much of that explanation: still, not worth making a thing about it. But Daphne hadn't finished. 'Most young men like to show off, don't you think? My brother used to—he grew a moustache, you know. And John does, just a little bit, and I'm sure that Alan does.' Good God, yes she is dull, thought Godfrey suddenly. 'I think it's very normal and quite attractive too, for a young man to show off now and then.' Yes, yes, for heavensake ding-dong.

'My father used to wear spats when he was courting. He must have been a scream,' she concluded.

She stopped after that and didn't say any more: perhaps she had said too much already. But it was so nice to have someone to talk to.

'I don't think Alan shows off,' said Godfrey a little stiffly. 'I think his behaviour is absolutely natural and delightfully consistent. He is, in fact, the only person I know who never steps out of character.' Daphne looked modestly at the ground. What on earth did a chap like *Chote* see in such a pudding? wondered Godfrey, suddenly aroused. Whatever one's view of him, one would never have guessed Daphne.

'Alan has the courage of his convictions,' he went on, 'and that sort of courage is a pretty rare thing these days. Don't you think?'

'Yes, of course,' said Daphne.

They had reached her front door, and it was time to say goodnight. Godfrey gave a little bow and shook hands. 'Goodnight, Daphne,' he said.

'Goodnight, Godfrey. I've had a wonderful time. Really I have.' She ran up the stairs, shaking a little under the shabby green dress. Godfrey watched her disappear round the corner upstairs, with mixed feelings. She was really a very nice girl, but oh Lord, how very dull. Not that that mattered as far as he was concerned—but how she must bore Browning! He blushed a little for her sake; he was awfully sorry for anyone who bored anyone. He shut the front door gently and started off for the lodgings that he and Alan were still sharing in Cowley.

The grandfather clock chimed midnight, and then the clock on the mantelpiece took up the cry, and the big church clock down the street. It might have been Oxford in miniature.

'It's twelve o'clock,' said Mrs. Chote, picking up the refrain. 'Twelve o'clock midnight. I had no idea.' She looked at Mr. Chote to see if he were asleep. His shiny black boot was kicking gently against the kettle which hissed by the fireside.

'Look at the time, Jack. Midnight already. Goodness

gracious!' she walked about the room, straightening things up for the night, giving an extra twitch to the curtains. 'Chilly,' she said. She circled behind her husband's chair, examining the back of his head for signs of life. 'You're going to set fire to your nice trousers,' she said. The dark pinstripe was silently withdrawn a few inches. He was still awake, by a thread.

'I had such a nice chat with Dr. Walker this afternoon,' said Mrs. Chote, giving his cushions a pat. 'You really ought to see him. He's awfully nice and kind.'

Mr. Chote snorted. 'Can't be bothered,' he said.

'He's not like other doctors,' said Mrs. Chote wistfully.

'Yes he is,' corrected Mr. Chote. 'He sends us a bill, doesn't he?'

'No, he doesn't,' she said softly. 'He takes care of us on the National Health.'

'Oh yes, that,' said Mr. Chote firmly, disgustedly.

She picked up the kettle and began to pour hot water over the dank tea leaves which lay in dreary chunks at the bottom of the big brown pot. 'Have a cup? It'll warm you up before going to bed. Did I tell you, by the way, I heard from Johnny this morning? Ever such a nice long letter.'

'Yes, you told me about it,' said Mr. Chote.

'I wonder if he's met a nice girl over there? American girls are supposed to be ever so swish.'

Mr. Chote twisted his sallow face around to look at her. 'John has more sense. He's too busy improving himself, studying and meeting important people, as he says in the letter.'

'I know,' said Mrs. Chote hastily. 'I know he is. But a young man needs a little recreation sometimes, doesn't he?'

'Ah, there'll be plenty of time for recreation later on,' said Mr. Chote. 'The important thing at the moment is to get on. John understands that all right. Look at his letter this morning.'

'It was a nice letter,' said Mrs. Chote. She stared at the darting yellow flames. You could see anybody you liked in there: Johnny aged eight, toasting crumpets, Johnny aged eleven reading *Pickwick Papers*, Johnny aged twenty-four meeting important people.

'He's a serious lad,' said Mr. Chote. 'He's never wasted any time with girls. In fact I don't think I've ever heard him mention a girl's name. And I know he's never brought one to the house. He's got too much sense for that kind of nonsense.'

'Oh, yes, he's always been very sensible,' said Mrs. Chote. 'And I'm sure he's going to do well one of these days.'

Mr. Chote lapsed into silence. He took off his glasses and wiped them carefully, put them on again and shut his eyes. The clocks began to tick more loudly, it seemed, in the quiet room. The shadows of the Chotes danced energetically in the firelight like two giant roustabouts, mocking the squat sombre people responsible for them.

Mr. Chote's mouth held for a minute to a thin querulous line: and then it sagged sloppily open. No doubt about him now. There was a pungent smell of scorched cloth wafting from the cuff of his trouser leg. Mrs. Chote pulled him back into his chair, with his heels scraping a mild protest on the ancient carpet. 'Poor dear,' she said. His face was petulant again, disturbed by some indefinable pain. 'Poor old dear.' Mrs. Chote draped a rug across his shoulders, and picked up her knitting again with a gentle sigh. It might be a long time before he woke up, and she didn't want to leave him like this.

The clock ticked very very loud; and the fire dwindled down to a soft fitful glow of grey and red, and Mrs. Chote clacked her needles together patiently, over and over. At two o'clock sharp, Mr. Chote woke up. His eyes were apprehensive for a moment, and his yellow skin was drawn tight over his cheeks. 'I must have been asleep,' he mumbled.

Mrs. Chote helped him to his feet. It was a slow job and he grimaced a couple of times as he creaked erect.

'Are you all right?' asked Mrs. Chote, patting his hand. '*There* we are.' The rug was dripping foolishly from his shoulders, and his glasses hung loose from one ear. 'Off we go now,' said Mrs. Chote gaily. 'Upsadaisy, and up we go.' She took his arm and steered him towards the staircase. He went with her slowly, silently. 'Here we go, one at a time. That's the way,' she prattled. He didn't say anything. His face was gleaming now, yellow and quite ugly with strain. It was doubtful whether he could hear a word his wife was saying to him. But she kept talking all the way to bed. 'Come along, old dear. There we are. That's a good boy.'

The car rolled, with a mellow purr, through the dark, autumn-smelling streets. 'It could be a Saturday night in Oxford, couldn't it, John?' said Fosdick. His headlights had picked up a wavering figure, a student it looked like, standing in the middle of the road with a bottle in each hand. Eugene swerved the car, but the student swerved too. 'Hold everything,' he said. 'Hold everything, hold, hold. . . .' His voice trailed off.

'What do you want, fellow?' asked Eugene. The student trotted round to the open window and squinted in. 'What time is it?' he asked. 'Anybody got the time?'

'It's half-past three. Time to be in bed.' Fosdick started the motor again.

'Hold it, there, hold it. Not so fast,' said the student putting his hand on the steering wheel.

'Now what do you want?' asked Eugene wearily.

'I want to give myself up,' said the student. 'I have some vital information bearing on the Alger Hiss case, and I insist you arrest me.'

'I'm not a policeman,' said Eugene, laughing moderately.

'Never mind about that crap,' said the student. 'I want to give myself up right now, O.K?' Eugene started the car. 'Hey, hold it a second. Very vital information. I have my rights as an American citizen. Deputize marshals. I de*mand* to be arrested. Hold it. . . .'

He stood in the street waving his bottles at them forlornly.

In the back seat, Mirabelle was snuggling up to Chote. 'Are you still mad at me?' he whispered.

'I wasn't mad,' she said. 'But I *do* think psychiatry is important.'

'Of course it is,' said Chote. 'Dreadfully important.'

'Are you two still talking about psychiatry?' asked Fosdick. 'Boy!'

'What was that old boy?' Mirabelle was up to her old trick

288

of kissing his ear with a loud smack, drowning out all other sounds.

He was annoyed at first by her change of mood. An evening like this of biting and scratching left him anything but amorous. Mirabelle's lips still felt venomous against his skin, capable of emptying more poison into his ear. But when they reached his mouth, all was forgiven; a purple hush descended, a rich velvet curtain, cutting him off from the past and most of the present. 'I said : How do you like our fine country?' said Fosdick. 'But let it pass.'

'God she's dull, isn't she?' said Hook.

Browning was pulling off his crepe creepers. 'Oh, do you think so?' he asked languidly.

'She certainly seems so to me.'

'Funny, I think she's rather a sport. Of course you only get out of women as much as you put in. . . .'

'I know, I know. Sermon number sixty-three. You're preaching to the converted, old chap.'

'Oh, am I? Well, anyway, we must take her out again sometime.'

'Must we? Oh, very well. If you insist.' He left the sitting-room scratching his head in drowsy perplexity.

16. Manners

THE winds on Riverside Drive were beginning to howl louder and louder, rattling the windows in Chote's apartment building and pummelling the stuffing out of the cliff dwellers whenever they strayed outside. In the clear blue mornings, the wind seemed to contain some promise: the blood bubbled up to meet the bright vague challenge and one could surge along on the strength of it, purple-faced and billowing, a ship in full sail. But by night the promise was long forgotten; the wind howled dismally and pointlessly, slashing at tired nerves and piercing soft, sleepy skin, which had been prepared for the night by a sequence of cosy radiators.

Chote staggered homeward, propped up foolishly against the blast. His eyes and nose gushed into it; his stubby hands froze hard around the books he was carrying. The wind seemed to be inside him by now, wailing forlornly in and out among dry frosted bones. 'Too bloody much,' he muttered, and the wind blew satirically into his mouth. The Drive was swept bare, a wasteland of gaunt buildings and spidery trees. He twisted sideways into the entranceway, and the wind swung round and gave him a last swift kick against the heavy glass door. Inside, the dead warmth waited with its motherly enervating embrace. He pattered on numb feet across the cobblestones and past the OUT OF ORDER sign on the elevator, and then slowly up the creaking wooden stairs.

The usual note was waiting for him in the bathroom, perched neatly against the taps. 'Dear Mr. Chote. I presume it is too much to ask you to clean the basin out when you have finished shaving. I had to do it this morning and it wasn't very nice. Mrs. J. Fishman.' He rolled the note up into a ball and kicked it under the radiator. 'Bugger it,' he said angrily. 'Bugger all of them.'

He went to his own room and put on his pyjamas. The radiator was hissing and dribbling and shooting a jet of steam up the window. After the cold wind, there was seduction in the bubbling, seething heat and Chote pushed his solitary chair right over the jet, so that some of the steam whistled against the cane bottom. Then he took out his books and lined them up on top of the bed. There was no point in trying to pretend that he didn't work these days : nobody cared whether he did or not.

Those Fishmans were really getting on his nerves, though. He had never realized how many mistakes a bloke could make in a bathroom : and Mrs. Fishman spared him none of them, even one or two that might decently have been left unmentioned. Every day after the Fishmans had gone out, it was his custom to prowl around the community washroom, looking eagerly for peccadillos that *he* could write about. But the Fishmans were scrupulously tidy, leaving nary a hair or a puddle or any other trace.

He took out his pad and began to write: 'Dear Mrs. Fishman. I want to thank you for your many friendly suggestions and household hints.' 'Dear Mrs. Fishman. I found a toad in the bath yesterday after you went out.' 'Dear Mrs. Fishman. Have you been giving any thought to your personal daintiness?' He added some suggestive pictures: and then he tore up the paper and rolled it under the bed. Bloody people.

He began reading his books, lawbooks, reason over emotion and all that: not the unearthly fantasy of reason that you found under the dusty wigs in an English courtroom, but a certain measure of calmness and proportion, all the same. He was taking courses in international law and American constitutional law, culled from the vast catalogue of subjects. In the brisk hurly-burly of registration he had come upon this enormous blue volume: an insanity of freedom lay before him with a thousand choices, all equally bland and equally educational. But the head of his department took him in hand after that, and by prodigies of elimination the possibilities were soon winnowed down to a handful. The freedom in fact was somewhat illusory: one was obliged, it seemed, to build a little pile of something called credits (although he had long ceased to regard them whimsically) which were supposed to mesh in some mysterious way; and then of course, many of the courses were simultaneous. Chote sank back and allowed the department head to weave his skilful way through the maze. It was a far cry from the perennial Oxford don shaking the tobacco out of his sweater, and asking vaguely what one was doing in his room on a Tuesday, when of course it was really a Wednesday. . . . Mr. Snider was every inch in possession of his faculties. 'I think we've planned a well-rounded programme for you, Mr. Chote,' he said. 'Most of your classes will be in the same building, which is no small advantage in a plant this size. Now, don't hesitate to come to me,' and so on. He liked Mr. Snider with his easy command of detail; he was a big blond fellow, amiable and shrewd, and Chote would have enjoyed just trotting around behind him for a few days, observing how he did things. But Mr. Snider was a busy man, with a very full programme, and after a warm handshake Chote found himself propelled once again into the maelstrom, a lonely piece of flotsam expected to bob hopefully this way and that.

'Plant' was a good word for Madison University. Chote filled out some exhaustive forms and stood in line and checked in at a little window; and soon after that, the place was banging away full blast. Determined-looking men in leather jackets and sweaters poured into it every day in relentless shifts; and far into the night, the lights burned bright in every corner of the campus, as education was rapidly manufactured and packaged, and prepared for the June—or February—labels.

'It's a barbaric system,' old Mr. Fosdick warned him. 'You won't like it at all, Mr. Chote. There's no tradition in it, no substance, no sense of the past. And like so many things these days, it paves the way directly to socialism, communism, or whatever you want to call it. You take a boy without any background at all—a cultural leper so to speak—and pump him day and night with the latest sophistries. . . .'

That was one way of looking at it of course. Chote had to have his reservations about this view because he had precious little background himself. In the circumstances he could have no reasonable objection to young men like himself being pumped with sophistries at easy rates—and if sophistries, why not the latest ones?

Actually most of the allegedly 'dangerous' ideas sailed harmlessly over his head. His new professors talked interminably about the role of law, the philosophy of law, the future of law—everything but jolly old law itself. To Chote the law was primarily and preferably the musty old cases : 'Jinks *vs*. Ramsbottom : plaintiff's cow injured by defendant's bicycle, temporarily loaned to one Miss Higgins, on King's highway' . . . the keenest wits in the land straining over the tiniest problems; giants bearing twigs to put up inch by inch a great and durable wall of minute precedent around each citizen, mmm, yes, et cetera. One found it impossible to concentrate for long on airy generalities concerning letter and spirit : law was a question of who paid for the cow and her damaged feelings; and of who paid for the lawyer. Spirit be damned.

In no time at all, he began to cut classes. Nobody seemed to care whether he was there or not anyway; a young humorist named Schwartz used to call out his name in an improbable English accent during roll-calls; and afterwards the same Schwartz gave him the benefit of his own dadaesque notes : 'Law here to stay, famous professor avers. The distinguished jurist, J. Bodley Hammerstein, informed a dangerously over-stimulated class at Madison University, that law was the pillar on which all our freedoms rested. Standing ovation. . . .' Chote spent much of the time in the library reading real cases. This evening, he had brought home a bundle of juicy ones, remote consoling ones, plenty of cows and bicycles. For what with this and that, it had been a pretty taxing day. . . .

The Fosdicks had invited him to lunch, that was the beginning of it. Old Mr. Fosdick was making one of his rare visits to town for the day, and he was bristling with talk—the inevitable consequence of mild excitement piled recklessly on top of towering blood pressure. 'How do you like Madison, Mr. Chote? It's a regular slum isn't it? Waiter, four more doubles and put some whisky in them this time, will you? Right. Yes, an overcrowded slum.'

Chote nodded politely. 'Yes, it is a bit overcrowded.'

Mr. Fosdick raised his eyebrows and looked at Chote with vague cunning. 'What was that? Overcrowded? I'll say it is. Let me tell you. When I was going to school, people who could afford it—people of our class, that is—were guaranteed a little space and leisure in which to grow. We weren't packed in like sardines.'

The waiter came and went, and came again with more doubles; and the Colonel went in turn from red to purple to indescribable; his neck bulged ominously against the stiff celluloid collar, and the veins on his forehead glowed like strips of neon. It was stifling hot at the club, and Chote began to feel a little giddy over the oysters. Mirabelle seemed to be peeping at him anxiously as if round a corner. He wondered if he was doing something wrong. One felt a perfect fool saying 'Yes sir', 'Quite, sir', and 'My own view exactly, sir' over and over again: but what else could one do? One could hardly disagree with the old chap: hypocrisy was the only possible course, even for a stock-company gentleman like himself.

Mr. Fosdick passed through a number of moods in the traditional order: jovial, sentimental, comradely. By the time the coffee arrived, he was good and angry and ready to return, with symphonic gusto, to his original theme. 'I'm sick to death of all this socialism,' he said suddenly. 'Just sick of it. It's taking all the flavour out of life.'

'Yes, sir,' said Chote.

'Well, it's no use saying "Yes, sir",' snapped Mr. Fosdick impatiently. 'You've got to get rid of that damned Socialist Government. That's what you've got to do.'

'Yes, sir,' said Chote softly. 'Right away, sir.'

'Eh, what was that?' The scraggy eyebrows went up into an ocean of red. Chote glanced at Mirabelle, hoping against hope that she had wanted him to say something like that, something a little independent. She obviously hadn't. He looked at Eugene, who was blowing his nose thoughtfully. 'What did you say?' said Mr. Fosdick.

'I was agreeing with you, sir. The question is, how is it to be done?'

Eugene said helpfully. 'They haven't got a Socialist Government at the moment, Father. It's Conservative.'

'Do you think I don't know that?' bellowed Mr. Fosdick. 'They're just as bad as the Socialists, as far as I can see.' Chote turned away with relief; the old man's rage had flowed past him, like a drunken dream, to splash and froth against some new object. He noticed a man at the next table who looked just like Mr. Fosdick: it must be that kind of club. 'Excuse me, sir.' It was Mr. Fosdick's voice close to his ear. 'You said something just now which I didn't quite catch. I'd like you to repeat it.' The eyes were cruel now and surprisingly sly.

'I told you what it was,' said Chote awkwardly.

'No you didn't. It wasn't quite the same, was it? I want you to repeat what you said before, word for word.'

'I can't remember,' said Chote, hoping to confuse him. 'If it wasn't what I said the second time, I can't remember what it was. I'm sorry.' That ought to hold him.

The old man stretched out an agile, unwrinkled hand and gripped Chote's wrist like an iron bangle. 'I want to hear what you said,' he boomed. 'The exact words.'

Chote looked around helplessly. Mirabelle ought to be saying: 'Oh father. Don't be such an old fuff' or something like that. But she didn't say anything. Eugene blew his nose again.

'I'm waiting, young man.' The fingers dug into Chote's wrist.

'I'm sorry, sir. You'll just have to go on waiting.' He could hear the sucking of breath. 'I don't remember what I said. I don't think it can have been very important.' The two men stared at each other with a terrible venom, all the worse for being virtually pointless. 'I'd like you to take your hand away, please,' said Chote evenly.

'Not until you tell me what you said.' It was a child's petulance. 'Or else you can offer me an apology.'

Chote was speechless for a moment. Good God, what a suggestion. 'Take your hand away,' he said finally. 'I'm damned if I'm going to make an apology.'

The drums rolled. The hand fell away like a withered leaf. The Fosdicks stood up in a body. The scene was over. Chote staggered out to the cloakroom, a few paces behind the Fosdicks, who were moving fast.

Mirabelle went straight back to her lodging. There was no need for an argument this time. The case against Chote was transparently clear: 'How could you' and then so on and so on. A poor, sweet ruin, who had treated him with nothing but kindness: a lonely old dear living out his days with a handful of dreams. Chote had had the lot of them: hostilities, father images and all. He headed uptown to find his friend Schwartz.

'I have a class at five-thirty,' said Schwartz who had in fact classes all day long. A man of parts, Schwartz: a genuine scholar who had digested his learning easily with never a belch or a rumble to show for it—also a most dedicated buffoon, forever spraying his own coarse mixture of college humour and horse manure over the world at large; but beyond that, a rich enigma (to Chote anyway) with a curious knack for friendship, and an ease with English dialects. Just the chap for an occasion like this.

'I can see that you're upset,' he said, 'so perhaps you'd prefer me to do the talking, as usual.'

'Yes, please,' said Chote. They were sitting in a booth at the Mayfair Bar and Grill, drinking tiny beers in the half dark.

'Well, to begin at the beginning,' and off went Schwartz in his comforting way, about history and politics and women. 'Mild interest was aroused yesterday in the Senate by a light rain of frogs early in the afternoon. . . . Senator McBean asserted that he knew the names of at least two hundred and thirty-five and one half card-carrying homosexuals on the White House staff alone, not including caddies and assorted hangers-on. Pandemonium broke loose. And the cry of the wild goose was heard on all sides, as members rushed to get at their telephones. . . . Just then a flock of bats, incited by a certain notorious mischief maker, descended slowly from the ceiling of the House, dropping their eggs en route onto some of the most noted domes on Capitol Hill . . . outraged lawmakers labelled the whole affair a "phony peace demonstration which will not fool the American people for long". . . .' In the quiet bar, a hollow place in the mid-afternoon, Schwartz's twittering had a ring of trivial authority to it like radio news.

'You sound just like my father,' said Chote. 'Except that he really cares.'

Schwartz's eyes, just visible through dense bifocals, recognized the words, accepted and acknowledged : but his tongue did not break stride. 'Meanwhile Ex-President Philpot was quoted as saying that the offending bats were nothing but blankety-blank red herrings. . . .'

'What the devil *are* your opinions, anyway?' interrupted Chote.

'So when you get tickets to a farce you have to take sides?'

said Schwartz sharply. 'Who has opinions about *Charley's Aunt*? Listen, Jack, we spend millions keeping this comedy on the boards year after year, but there's no law that says we have to take it seriously.'

'Why don't you just ignore it, as we do?' suggested Chote. 'You never know—it might go away.'

'Yes, but it doesn't, does it?' A curious answer: was the impenetrable Schwartz lapsing at last into the national seriousness? 'It seems to have gotten worse in England, because people like you were just ignoring it. Right?' Yes, Schwartz seemed to be in high earnest. On second thought, maybe he was always in high earnest. Chote felt his foreignness creeping back.

'Yes I know it's all my fault,' said Chote glumly. 'I was told very much the same thing at lunch.'

'Oh, who told you that?'

'Fellow named Fosdick. Father of a chap I know.'

Schwartz gazed around absently. 'Not George P. Fosdick, I suppose?' He smiled secretly at the thought.

'I don't know. Yes, I think his name might be George.'

'No, couldn't be the same fellow. George P. Fosdick has been dead for years.'

'Oh,' said Chote. 'Pity.'

The rings on the plastic top were coupling and melting into each other, and populating the table. 'There goes my five-thirty class,' said Schwartz wistfully.

'Who was George P. Fosdick?' asked Chote.

'Eh? Who?'

'George P. Fosdick. You mentioned him a while ago, remember?'

'No. I can't remember anything like that. It's a pretty name though, isn't it?'

'Well, to get back to what I was saying. . . .' Chote had begun to tell his troubles cautiously and selectively at first, and then one leading to another, so that they all came down at last, pebbles and stones and boulders crashing around Schwartz's ears.

'Yes, old boy?' Schwartz yawned. 'What happened after that?'

'Well I made the absurd mistake of asking the chap—you know B's brother, let's call him C, shall we?'

'Fine, fine.' Schwartz was busy trying to stand a fifty-cent piece on its side, but it kept toppling over. 'C is a fine, manly name.'

'Asking C how one went about making a fortune in this benighted country—an innocent question, you might suppose. After all, we were both grown-ups, and there weren't any ladies around. But no. . . .'

'No,' echoed Schwartz blankly.

'The chap became really upset. Didn't know which way to look; practically crawled under the bench in fact. And ever since then, he has treated me as a kind of Grade B leper, with halitosis and tired blood and all the other native American diseases. I had no idea that Americans were so touchy about money.'

'We're not,' said Schwartz.

'The funny thing is that I was only trying to be friendly. Most chaps *like* to talk about making money. At home, one naturally pretends to be in the grip of galloping avarice whether one actually is or not. It's the done thing.'

'Chote, you don't know what you're talking about,' said Schwartz, looking up sideways through thick lenses.

'What do you mean, old chap? Who doesn't know what?' Chote was honestly confused.

'I mean that you don't know what you're talking about.'

'I didn't mean to be offensive,' said Chote, wondering vaguely if he'd hurt the chap. 'But honestly, I didn't think you *could* offend an American. I thought you people could put up with any amount of abuse. Why everywhere I go, I insult the United States with the gayest abandon, and the people fairly lap it up.'

'You've been mixing with a pretty funny kind of people,' said Schwartz truculently. 'Come round to where I live in Brooklyn sometime and get your head punched.' He threw his fifty-cent piece bouncing onto the table. 'Goddamn thing won't stand up,' he explained. 'Tell you what Jack, these people you've been talking about—A, B, C and infinity—aren't Americans at all—they're lousy international freaks. Let me take you around sometime and introduce you to some real nice girls who never tried to dominate anyone in their lousy lives. . . .'

'I'd like nothing better,' said Chote.

'And fellas who just love to talk about money from morning to night. Real folks.' The tiny eye winked behind the thick glass. Schwartz was being funny after all. 'Of course,' he added cryptically, 'if these kids were really related to George P. Fosdick, that would explain a lot.' He put his head on his hands and pretended to go to sleep on the soggy table.

'Who the devil is George P. Fosdick?' said Chote.

'Eh? Who's that? Hey listen, Jack. I have a class at seven. Let's get out of here.' The twilight outside had joined the permanent twilight of the Mayfair, thickening it, giving it an oppressive richness. 'Let's hit the road, Jack,' said Schwartz.

Chote watched his friend to the door: a contradictory fellow, assembled in committee no doubt—gross head, delicate hands, a good, round capon belly swathed in cashmere; under that, an oaf, a scholar, an all-American boy. George P. Fosdick was his symbol. George might turn out to be a little-known economist or sonneteer of the nineteenth century, or a nephew in Brooklyn, or just a joke. That was Schwartz's world, and those were his people.

But what Chote really enjoyed about Schwartz was his unaffected admiration for Chote. This was a mystical thing. Schwartz didn't admire Chote for any obvious reason; he seemed to be chiefly impressed with the *idea* of Chote, the zeitgeist, the mythos (to quote): the same mind that feasted on minor nineteenth-century economists found all sorts of obscure significance in this visiting Englishman. Chote represented this and that: the nascent self-consciousness of the middle classes, their stoicism under fire, their dreadful dentistry. Without having to say much of anything, Chote found himself one of the seminal people, an English George P. Fosdick in fact. And since one seemed to be a complete cipher to most Americans, it was no end soothing to find oneself a Ph.D. project to at least one of them, especially at times like this.

But it didn't do to take him too seriously—for instance, the things he had said just now about the Fosdicks. Without having to be told, Schwartz seemed to know all about Mirabelle and to despise what he knew. She was rich and spoiled, she was using Chote as a plaything, she was slumming like fury. Perhaps it was a little bit like that: he would never know why Mirabelle had taken him in hand quite the way she had. But it certainly wasn't *all* class struggle. There had been pretty good moments too—moments of candour, and, well, you know.

The slop of beer ran up his elbows and he felt one of his spasms of affection for Mirabelle, the intermittent spasms that kept him going. If suddenly he could run enough of them together he could call them love (whacko! he thought whimsically). She was really a wonderful girl anyway. Face, hair—he reviewed them all rapidly. Wonderful, wonderful.

He floated out of the Mayfair on a high ramping tide of fraternity and sought out a public telephone. The business at lunch had been so trivial. And Mirabelle was such fun. He would apologize, abjectly if necessary. Splendid girl. The biting wind brought tears, which streaked voluptuously down his cheeks, filling out the mood.

He dialled quickly. 'Is that Mirabelle? . . . Oh, it's Daisy. Hello, Daisy. Can I speak to Miss Fosdick, please?'

There was a pause. 'Who'—Daisy believed in taking her time—'do I say is calling?'

'It's Mr. Chote—John Chote. *You* know.'

'And you all want to speak to Miss Fosdick?'

'That's right. Yes.'

'Jus' second. I'll see if she's at home. Jus' hold the line a second.' He could sense the phone being laid down very slowly and carefully so as not to break the shell; and then a great shuffling sound as Daisy moved majestically away. 'Miss Fosdick—Miss Fosdick.'

'Hello there. Is that Mirabelle? This is John here.' The English sounds reverberated around the tiny booth, mocking his efforts, distracting him absurdly. That was what had sapped his strength over here—the knowledge of how he sounded.

'What do you want?' asked Mirabelle in a flat voice.

'I just wanted to say hello,' he said. 'Wait a minute—are you theah?' There was no mistaking the curious sound of the word: 'Theah, theah', indeed. What a bloody asinine noise. He tried again. 'I say, are you theah?' Must stop saying that: sound like a perfect ahss. 'Are you theah, you perfect ahss?' the new words gonged meaninglessly in his head. 'Hello, hello.' The phone only purred back innocently. Mirabelle had apparently gone away.

Good Lord, thought Chote.

He went out again into that cold wind, feeling the sting now as it slapped and slapped at his plump cheeks. 'Take that, you facetious bastard, and that for being superficial, and that for laughing at psychiatry.' The gale smashed at his pride and sent it flying, like a hat or an umbrella; and then it took what was left of Chote and sent him bowling along the street like a ball of newspaper.

Mrs. Fishman's note completed the grim rites. He wasn't even housebroken, it seemed, in the eyes of these Americans: just a noxious, ill-mannered infant. When he cried 'Bugger it,' it came from down near the heart. 'Bugger all of them!' His American triumph.

He read his cases until midnight, taking scrupulous notes, and tearing them up distractedly. The strange habit of studying, picked up so painfully between cold baths and routine bottom-beatings, was a comfort at a time like this. Slowly one mastered the irrelevant information, swallowed, digested, made it one's own: so that forever more one had a little pocket of irrelevance somewhere inside to retreat to.

But there was real loneliness in the room now: and as soon as he put his books away, it came to perch. It was no use thinking of Mirabelle any more. The image was lovelier than ever, but receding now little by little. He would probably never see her again. The old quarrels had been bad enough; but now there would be perpetual embarrassment, discomfort and the chronic threat of silence. And so much faking on his part, as he pretended to feel as strongly as she did about a thousand tiny episodes, like, say, the lunch-time fracas. It was an emotional level on which he could survive only as an interloper and con man. And meanwhile Mrs. Fishman was sitting across the hall, composing her cold touch-me-not messages. . . .

He wrote a letter to his mother, full of tender solicitude. 'Please see a doctor if you aren't feeling any better, and do what he tells you. Father'—is a bit queer about doctors? no, he didn't want to hurt *anybody's* feelings—'may not realize how far medicine has advanced in the last few years. Up until recently, most doctors really were quacks of course. . . .'

It wasn't nearly enough. Brinkley and Oxford weaned one too successfully from one's parents; one could no longer return ad lib to the family bosom. A gentlemanly consideration for the parents' feelings was in itself a measure of one's distance from them. He thought of writing to Hook or Browning: but that meant donning the cap and bells and waving the tambourine, and he just didn't feel up to it.

The calendar on the window sill said October 4. He pulled away the leaves to bring it up to December. That made it, what, five? six months? since his last letter to Daphne. It was contemptible to think of her now; and unforgivable to write as if nothing had changed. And yet, of course, the capacious heart would accept him, absorbing the insult like a great sponge and even thanking him for it. It was almost a kindness, in fact.

No, it was bad stuff. Even Browning—well perhaps especially Browning—would have hesitated . . . it was last-minute selfishness, weakness, brutality really. Oh well, no point in deceiving himself. He took out another sheet of blue air-mail paper and began to write in his small, precise hand :

'So sorry for the long silence . . . very busy, but that's no excuse of course . . . just a low hound, a wart on the body politic, the sort of chap, in short, who always leaves the bathroom in a mess.' Daphne would understand all this and laugh comfortably.

'I'm afraid I haven't got the instincts of a fascinating swine

—although I'll admit I've given it a modest whirl in the last few months. But what with my rheumatism and my other complaints (have you ever heard of tired blood, by the way?) I'm beginning to yearn mightily for those quiet evenings by the fire. Perhaps I'm just getting too old. . . .'

The more he wrote, the more clearly he saw his case. Daphne really suited his quiet unheroic disposition wonderfully well. It was such a strain trying to impress these cold, clever women all the time, trying to live up to their *House and Garden* standards. And besides, Daphne was English—his own culture and his own class and his own manners, too—and there was a lot to be said for that. 'Young men like to show off,' she had told him. What a dashed sensible thing to say when you came to think of it! Well, he was prepared to settle down like her notorious brother, who had shaved off his moustache and become a credit to the firm. Not that life would necessarily be dull on those terms. Daphne was nothing if not the good sport. There would be plenty of pub crawls and songs and the laughter of friends. (All right, sentimentality and be damned!) That was really his speed; and had he ever really wanted anything else?

'I don't think I'll be staying over here after I've finished at Madison. It's a fabulous country and all that but it seems to be a bit much for me, a touch overwhelming if you know what I mean. And England is beginning to seem awfully attractive in my old age.'

He didn't go very much further than that. By force of habit he wanted to leave himself at least one clear path to the exit. But he also wanted to say something kind. 'It'll be awfully nice to see you again and go the well-worn rounds,' he wrote carefully. 'I don't know if I've ever told you how much I enjoy being with you.' He was aware of the tepidity, the thin note of the traditional Englishman-in-love. 'You really are a most wonderful girl,' he added quickly, and then, 'Most affectionately, John.' In the circumstances, he could hardly say more than that. Anyway, Daphne would know well enough what he meant. One never said more than that to Daphne.

He put on his overcoat and tiptoed down the hall, past the

door of the querulous Fishmans and out shivering into the
cold with his tale of passion gripped tight in his hand, relief
settling comfortably in his face. He felt that he had done the
only possible thing; his regret was that he hadn't done it sooner.

17. Permutations

CHOTE had never been a good sleeper. In fact, it was during
the long stretches of the white night that he had developed what
he felt (but only during those very stretches) to be his principle
characteristics: a surly desire to succeed in life; a spirit of
vague, last-ditch defiance, and a hygienic facetiousness. As the
night wore on and his blood thinned out slowly, cooling the
crust of a lifetime, it was time for the hobgoblins to appear in
force: big ones, small ones, fears of all sizes, fears of failure,
pestilence and decay dancing like sugar-plums in his head.
'Good God, Chote. You haven't been to a dentist in three years.
Your teeth must be rotting in your head by now,' or 'A packet
and a half of cigarettes. Have you no self-control at all?' Sometimes, he would crawl woozily out of bed and grope around
for his wallet to see how much money he had left, to make sure
especially that he had reclaimed all his change from the last
bar. If he hadn't, his remorse became something tragic. 'Oh
dear, oh dear, oh dear,' he would moan. 'Bloody undone,' and
he would rock back and forth whispering distraughtly to himself until daylight came to bring sleep at last.

The night he wrote to Daphne again turned out to be a bad
one. The radiator had stopped its companionable clanking,
and in the airless silence Chote began to be convinced that he
was not one, but two people. 'Mustn't wake Chote up,' he
mumbled. 'John Chote, Johnny Jack Chote, good old J.C.
Well played J.C.' He laughed, because he thought he knew

very well that there wasn't anybody else there; well, in fact he was damned certain there wasn't anybody else there. 'But if that's so,' he said suddenly, 'who are you?' and he gave another laugh which startled him. He could see the man in the white pyjamas, stirring uneasily.

'In a few years, Chote will be gone.' He tried that one. 'Rotten, crawling with worms, thoroughly scruffy-looking, in short. Does that frighten him?'

He raised his eyebrows inwardly. 'No, not very much. Chote isn't afraid of that, probably hasn't the sense to be.' Death, extinction, pffft—no, that wasn't bad. It was the merry preliminaries: sitting by the fire, say, with the skin beginning to sag woefully under the chin and the eyes watering. 'Damn the government, damn the Americans, damn the teenagers'—why have they all left me in this terrible state? Growing old on the sly, alone, shivering in one's woollies. 'Damn the weather. What have they been doing to the weather? Nobody cares what happens to me any more. Inconsiderate . . .!' Not funny at all.

Chote could see the old man quite plainly sitting on the crowded bed in his shawls and an old woollen bonnet, grumbling gently. 'It's your own fault, Chote,' he said firmly. 'You should have taken care of yourself when you had the chance. Had a good life, and bugger the rest of the world, when you had the chance.' The old man shook his head uncomprehendingly. Without warning, he began to cry, huge embarrassing tears jerked loose and tumbling down like rocks. 'Oh, my God,' muttered Chote. 'I hope he doesn't say anything. Don't say anything!'

He had passed finally into sleep, but it was bad sleep and he forced himself awake again. It was bad waking too, because the dream lingered, very matter-of-fact and full of cosy detail; the brown lithographs, the ships at sea, the bogus relatives.

He shivered and looked at his watch; five o'clock, nearly time to get up. He didn't want to go to sleep again, anyway. The hobgoblins meant business tonight. It was always a bad sign when the pseudo-Chote turned up like this in the next bed (what next bed? oh dear, oh dear) with his little load of apprehensions and regrets. 'An undigested bit of beef,' muttered Chote. 'An underdone morsel of cabbage. Or possibly too much to drink this afternoon—might make a note to cut down on that.'

He devoutly hoped that it was so : but in the empty unused light of morning refracted off the grey walls and grey windows, it seemed to him that something had gone badly wrong somewhere. Too tired to make it out, too tired and too cold, he pulled the covers over his head and tried to stay awake. He had never had these terrible nights before coming to New York.

To his surprise Daphne did not answer his letter right away. This was not altogether unpleasing : a little spirit, a touch of pride—zut, beguiling! Daphne's flaccid modesty which had hitherto covered her like a tarpaulin might be yielding at last to the flame within—well, not the flame, but at least the humidity. Chote found himself reverting to his old wish that Daphne might become just a tiny bit more exciting, at least at intervals. He didn't want anything as nerve-racking as Mirabelle of course; but there might be such a thing as a surfeit of peace and quiet.

He busied himself with these boyish reflections over the Christmas holidays. They were punctuated by a printed Christmas card from the Fosdicks: 'Christmas Greetings' and a sparse cluster of holly berries. He was amazed at the cleanness with which he had been dropped. 'That just proves they're not real Americans,' said Schwartz, who liked to advise him on points of sociology. 'Members of our tribe always drop each other by a series of exquisitely diminishing phone calls.' It was mainly a relief : he had owed it to himself to have an affair like that with the kind of girl one never got close to at home (cheers for international friendship and the resultant confusion). But he was glad it was over, and no bruises to speak of.

He had Christmas dinner with the Schwartzes in Brooklyn : a dilapidated house of curling white wood where Schwartz was undisputed king. His arrestingly bulky mother spent most of the day immersed in sweet-smelling steam, while his father lay low in the woodshed. 'Visitors make him nervous,' explained Schwartz. 'He doesn't speak de English too good.'

'What does he do out there?' asked Chote. 'He makes pretty good furniture,' said Schwartz.

After lunch Chote offered to help with the greasy dishes, but Schwartz's mother wouldn't hear of it. The young master was already tilted back on the sofa patting his stomach and chomping a cigarillo. 'Have a seat my good man,' he said. 'Work is for women in this country.' Schwartz senior got up from the table and trudged back to the woodshed, through the gathering snow.

The boys listened to German lieder music while the kartoffel and sauerkraut settled; and Mrs. Schwartz came out with some beer; and a couple of nice quiet girls came over from next door and listened to Schwartz talk, and laughed in soft voices. During the next few hours, Schwartz played many parts: a Nazi general rallying the Wehrmacht, Michelangelo prattling about the Sistine roof in Neapolitan English ('plenty bigga da pitch, huh?'), Ed Sullivan. The girls laughed and laughed. Mrs. Schwartz lit a big fire, and began to play the piano, with a nice beer-hall roll, while the Kindeskind stood around and sang. Chote was soon swaying happily from side to side with his arm hugging a warm waist while he bellowed out his dum-de-dums; the Christmas tree next to the piano liberally specked with artificial snow and little cones of warm light, filled him to the brim mit ersatz good will and set him to smiling with infinite tenderness at the striped wallpaper. Mr. Schwartz came in and caught Chote's large mellow eye for a moment. He gave Chote a brief nervous glance and went upstairs.

The music got louder and louder and denser. Mrs. Schwartz's rimless spectacles clouded over with smoke and seasonal emotion as she brought her heavy fists crashing down again and again on the aged keyboard. 'Roll out der barrel'. The old family photos danced ecstatically on the piano, above the throbbing, tinny wires. 'When Irish eyes are smiling', 'Deep in the der heart of Texas', 'Love in bloom'.

In this riot of Weltschmerz, Chote began thinking in spite

of himself that this was really the life for him. He could easily see Daphne green against the green of the Christmas tree, laughing and singing and bouncing gently up and down with these people. 'The good old songs,' by George—they don't write them like that any more. He laughed to himself, but moistly and more than ever tenderly. He noticed that Schwartz was grinning at him slightly now, a wooden, ironic smirk. Supercilious bastard, Chote thought angrily. Ruddy self-conscious prig. He went on haughtily with his singing. The trouble with Americans is that they don't know how to let themselves go.

Through the branches of the tree, he could make out great flurries of snow : and then, incredibly, Mr. Schwartz wading out again in his faded leather jacket, shivering and blue with cold. The little man drifted towards the window and looked in for a moment, wistful and uncomprehending, and then scurried away to his lonely shed. 'Poor bloke,' Chote said almost aloud. The younger Schwartz continued to smile inscrutably.

He stayed all evening and ate cold turkey. Mrs. Schwartz took him aside for a while after supper to talk about her son. 'He's always been very clever—a near-chenius in fact,' she confided, leaning ardently across the kitchen table. 'Mr. Schwartz and I are very, very proud.'

'You have reason to be,' said Chote.

'Of course, Mr. Schwartz sometimes asks himself if all this college is necessary if you know what I mean ? The boy is going to college for nearly ten years it must be.'

'That *is* a long time.' My word, I say, by Jove, thought Chote.

'Yes, it must be nearly ten years,' she said. 'But I say to Mr. Schwartz not to worry, the boy will know when he's ready. After all, he's much smarter than we are, isn't he?'

'Oh, I wouldn't say that,' said Chote vaguely.

'Of course, Mr. Schwartz never went to school too much himself, and he doesn't know why they need all that time to get an education these days. "Ten years, Mamma," he says.

308

"Can you imagine?" He doesn't see how there can *be* so much knowledge in the world.'

'It does seem incredible,' Chote agreed.

'But I tell him, if you want to be a success these days, you just got to go to school, and keep on going until it's time to stop. We know that Gus is going to be a great man one of these days. So why hurry him? You know what I mean, we never ask him his plans or anything like that. . . .'

Nice people, thought Chote. Really nice people. And so familiar. Al Jolson's parents, Eddie Cantor's parents—Nature imitating Art. He went back to the living-room and found Schwartz limp and supine on the sofa, smoking and reading. 'You lazy swine,' Chote said. 'How are you ever going to be a great man that way?'

Schwartz looked up lazily. 'You been talking to mother?' he asked.

'Yes. She tells me that you're going to go far one of these days.'

Schwartz sent a smoke ring twisting languidly toward the scaling ceiling. 'Tragic isn't it?' he said. The smoke ring disintegrated elegantly, and Schwartz resumed his reading.

Mr. Schwartz came stamping in at the front door soon after that. 'Good night, mister,' she said, holding out a frosty hand. 'Gute Nacht, Gussy.'

Chote decided that it was time to go home.

Mrs. Schwartz helped him into his coat. 'Come again mister,' she said. 'Any time you're out this way.'

'His name is Chote, Mother,' said Schwartz a little testily. 'I told you that before.'

'Yes, of course. Good night, Mr. Chote, good night. And Merry Christmas.' Her kindly voice carried to him out across the snow. 'Come again, Mr. . . .? And Merry Christmas.' It was the best time he'd had since coming to America. But was it really worth coming all this distance for?

Two weeks later, he got a letter from Daphne. Ritualistically, he didn't open it until he had gone to the luncheonette and ordered his scrambled eggs and tea; it felt like a nice letter, large and plushy, indicating masses of large soft paper. And there was the little writing desk, and the furrowed kindly brow. Delicious.

He opened it slowly and smoothed it out on the glossy white counter, between the sparkling yellow eggs and the golden toast: it fitted in neatly with the bright promise of breakfast.

'Dearest John,' it began. 'It hasn't been such a bad winter, all things considered. Rainy of course, but not too cold. . . .'

He munched steadily through three pages of weather and general topography, spare and accurate (and yet 'nothing wanting') as an official report. 'A slight depression over Heligoland . . . high winds over Dogger.' This was beginning to look like one of her worst ever. He skipped page four, but there it was again on page five: 'positively soaked through and wouldn't you know, the buses had just that minute stopped running.' It was becoming alarming, hints of something feverish . . . He turned the page over: 'the pipes had frozen solid, as usual' —he tossed it away impatiently.

On page seven there came an earsplitting alteration of tone. 'Oh John,' a sudden wail, in fresh, dark ink, 'why didn't you write? All summer I waited and all autumn I waited and now it's winter. Not one line in all that time, not a single postcard, nothing. Why? . . . You were never so cruel before. At least I don't think so.' The words formed round and grave looking as if borrowed from a child's letter to Santa Claus.

'Anyway, it doesn't matter,' went on page eight, more calmly. 'I assumed that you were tired of me, and naturally I felt free to make other plans. Well, Alan Browning asked me to marry him a few weeks ago, and I said yes. I'm sure we're going to be very happy together. . . .' Good God no!

There followed a brief outline of hopes and conjectures. 'He'll be teaching next year and I suppose I'll go on working for a bit. He's really an awfully nice chap, very kind and thoughtful . . . you must come and see us as soon as you get back.' There was only one reference to that last panting letter of his. 'It was very nice to hear that you have made up your mind definitely to return to England,' she said. 'I know all your friends will be glad to see you.'

That was about all. 'Alan sends his fondest love. Yours, affectionately, Daphne.' The P.S. was a forlorn scrawl : 'I'm sorry. I thought you were tired of me.' The words ran off illegibly at the bottom of the page, off the pink paper and onto the luncheonette counter.

'I can't get over it, old man,' said Godfrey Hook. 'I *simply* can't get over it.' He skipped on and off the narrow pavement like a sparrow.

'Oh come now,' said Alan shortly. 'It isn't as amazing as all that.'

'I think it is,' said Godfrey, twirling himself exuberantly and awkwardly around a bar of scaffolding which was propped against one of the tottering ramparts of Sturdley. 'In fact, I think it's one of the bloody marvels of the twentieth century.'

'Stop jumping about like that,' said Browning. 'You'll only fall over and have to be carried the rest of the way back.' Godfrey was still staggering from his last pirouette. 'People get married all the time,' continued Browning. 'There's absolutely no excuse for hysteria.'

'Yes, but it isn't every day that the great Alan Browning, master of hounds, et cetera, decides.'

'Oh, for Godsake.'

They swung into the lodge. The moon-faces of the freshmen stared at them in the foggy glow of winter twilight : these two were the college characters now, the old vintage, the last of the 'chaps'. If, after three years, one had lived as Browning and Hook had lived—well, one just couldn't these days, that was all. Oxford had become mysteriously and irretrievably stodgy in the last year or so—so ran the talk among the freshmen—with too many chaps doing too much work for one thing, and too much respect for the Almighty Degree and the respectable job. The group in the lodge were in fact busy deploring these very tendencies, while trying wistfully to think up something really original in the way of a prank. They paused as Browning and Hook shouldered past, only to take up their theme more disconsolately than ever. 'Look at those two buggers : carefree, irresponsible, virtually pre-war in fact.'

A thin lad with a wisp of blond beard stroked his chin sadly. 'Let's face it, chaps. We're simply not spontaneous.'

Meanwhile the two demi-gods swaggered on, all unconscious, in the general direction of the college library. They passed Mr. Smythe, the Chaplain, who smiled tentatively. 'Anyway,' said Hook, 'do permit me to congratulate you most warmly, old chap, on finding love's own sweet dream and all that sort of thing.'

'Spare me the middle-class effusions, I implore you,' said Browning. 'You know as well as I do that any damn fool can propagate the species—especially these days.'

'Now don't be an old Scrooge,' squealed Hook. 'Why not just admit that you've fallen prey at last to Cupid's mischievous darts?'

Browning stopped and stared at his friend for a moment. 'What on earth has got into you, Godfrey?' he asked suddenly. 'You're quivering all over like a ruddy jelly.'

'All the world loves a lover,' crooned Godfrey, who did seem unaccountably, deliriously happy at the turn of events. Who would ever have imagined his clever friend, Alan Browning, marrying a dull woman? He could hardly fail to do better than that *himself*. 'You'll build a little love-nest, I suppose,' he burbled, 'and then in a year or two, we may be hearing reports of a tiny stranger . . . ?'

Up in the library the tattered remnants of the old crowd were thumbing over the prehistoric deck and murmuring the antediluvian phrases of disgust and disillusionment. 'Bugger all, as usual', 'Who dealt this crap?' and 'Oh, honestly, chaps'.

Browning and Hook put their books down and went looking wearily for chairs. Alan found one underneath a stout freshman in the next alcove. 'Don't you think you've worked about enough for one day, old chap?' he suggested. 'The brain must be tired.'

'Ah feel very fit, thank you,' said the freshman, a burly fellow from the North. 'Fresh ahs a daisy.'

'There's a bad spirit abroad in the college these days,' Alan reported back to his friends. 'Chap wouldn't give me his chair.'

He squatted down somehow between Godfrey who had been luckier and the perennial Gadsby.

The familiar faces, pasty as death masks by this time of year, squinted through the frosty smoke: 'Look here, I thought this bloody six was a bloody nine.' 'You must ask your landlady for a new pack, William. Really you must.' A chorus of wintery coughs and wheezes ran round and round the table. 'It's the bloody lungs. They won't last another winter like this.' 'Oh, to be in England, ding-dong.'

It was a smaller crowd than last year's: smaller and indefinably more subdued. Once upon a time poker in the college library had been what the freshmen in the lodge were looking for, a spontaneous movement, riding a wide crest of popular enthusiasm: but now it barely survived in the cold hands of a small and dwindling priesthood. Freshmen passed by every night, gaping, as the old gentlemen fussed over their moribund rituals; only one or two of the brassiest asked if they could join, and these lost heart in rapid order. The chatter of the veterans was aggressively inbred, describing ever smaller and smaller circles: old names and forgotten episodes and last year's women, in senile succession.

'Shockingly dull crowd this year,' said Gadsby, as he did practically every night.

'My own thought exactly,' said somebody else. 'We haven't discussed this before by any chance, have we?'

'I expect so. It's so bloody inescapable, isn't it? I mean everywhere one turns, one finds a dull face staring up at one . . . a fishlike pair of eyes, goggling politely. . . . I say Thomas, must you keep dealing me this one bloody, bloody hand? What a dull bastard *you* turned out to be!'

'By the way, I hear you're getting married, Alan?' said Thomas Formby, the beloved dealer. 'Any truth in that?'

'A smattering. Yes, I am, as a matter of fact.'

'To Chote's old girl, I hear—Daphne What'shername.'

'Right again. Yes, Daphne Collins. Nice girl, by and large.'

'I'm glad *you* think so, old chap, I mean if you're going to be living with her and so on. . . .'

'I shouldn't have thought she was quite your type,' said

Gadsby, sucking on his empty pipe. 'Jolly nice girl, of course —but don't you find her a bit on the quiet side? I always think there's something a little sinister about these huge, silent women. . . . My own peculiarity of course.'

Browning took out his pipe and began to suck it in unison with Gadsby.

'I suppose, now that you mention it, Daphne is rather quiet. But she more than makes up for it in other ways.' He and Gadsby gave together a great snorting suck on their empty pipes.

'What a revolting noise,' said Godfrey Hook. 'Haven't you chaps ever heard of tobacco?' Gadsby retorted with another grinding suck.

'She's a good performer, is she?' he said casually. Several faces came suddenly closer in the gloom, shiny and serious like old burlesque patrons.

'First class,' said Browning carelessly. 'Quite superb, in fact. Alpha all the way.'

Hook felt a little embarrassed: after all, Daphne was a decent sort of girl and he didn't like to talk that way about decent girls, not if they were old friends, anyhow. Matter of taste, more than anything. He examined his cards closely, holding them up to the dim light and rearranging them solemnly, 7,7,2,9, Jack. . . . Browning would stop in a moment.

But several celibate veterans were crowding in now, panting for more. 'Really first class, eh? I often wondered what Chote saw in her.'

Godfrey began to twitter : 'Really the bloodiest hand since the memory of man runneth not to the contrary.'

'Bloody mess,' agreed Browning, throwing his cards in negligently. 'Yes it is rather extraordinary—especially as it appears that Chote never laid a glove on her so to speak.'

'What was that?' asked Gadsby.

'Fact. In all those years, Chote apparently remained the perfect little gentleman at all times.'

'I find that awfully hard to believe. Are you sure that you aren't just being taken in by an advanced case of maidenly modesty?'

Browning smiled his most knowledgeable 'really old boy' smile: 'I assure you, my dear Gadsby, that I did not simply take her word for it.'

'Let's get on with the game, chaps,' piped Godfrey nervously.

'It *is* incredible,' said Gadsby. 'You don't suppose that Chote was deceiving us all the time—I mean, when he went on about those mighty feats of strength of his, and so on.'

'I shouldn't be a bit surprised,' said Browning. 'All the weightiest evidence points to it.' Several of the celibates nodded understandingly, heaven only knowing (so they hoped) what secrets of innocence were locked in their own hearts. 'Old Chote, a virgers' . . . 'Who would have dreamed it' . . . 'Well, I'm blowed' . . . 'That is a piece of news.'

Hook swept up the cards immediately. 'Whose deal is it?' He stared around at the glazed unseeing eyes. 'Come *on*. Are we playing or aren't we?'

'I believe it must be mine by now,' said Browning, sucking deeply. 'I put sixpence in last time, didn't I?'

'Yes, I think so,' said Gadsby, sucking back affably. 'So she's really good, is she? I mean one of the best—'

'Oh, for Godsake,' shouted Godfrey. 'Can't you leave the bloody thing alone for five minutes?'

Silence came so suddenly that Thomson, who was studying two alcoves away, came tiptoeing along to see what was happening. He joined a little cluster of freshmen who were peeking around the corner.

Browning was smiling blandly. 'What's the matter, Parson Hook? Have you mislaid a choirboy or what? Speak to us, old chap.'

Godfrey was only a few inches away, and Browning was smiling straight into his face, turning it pink and hot as with the blast of a sun lamp. 'Do tell us the reason for your untimely profanity, Reverend,' purred Browning. 'Too much sin in the parish?' The others were laughing now, little contained laughs, suspended in hope of more, in hopes of something that would really make them explode. God, it was like being back in school,

315

thought Godfrey: faces grinning at him through a dark haze, waiting for him to say something unspeakably funny.

'I just thought we were being rather personal, that was all,' he said quickly.

'Was that it, Reverend?'

'Yes, I suppose we were,' said one of the others in a kind voice. 'You were quite right to scream at us. Browning is such a richly disgusting chap that one quite gets carried away at times. It's like eating too much chocolate fried in batter.' It was generous, too generous.

Thomson whispered away again, and the freshmen went nodding off to their alcoves.

Browning was all good nature, full of solicitations for their dainty stomachs. Hook was still ruffled. Browning tried patting the back of his friend's head: 'There, there, Reverend.' Godfrey shook him off pettishly.

'I think you're every bit as bad as Chote,' he snapped, 'when it comes to bragging and boasting and generally carrying on. I shouldn't be surprised if—underneath the talk—you weren't actually a bit of a ruddy virgers yourself.' Everybody had to laugh at that one, led lustily by Browning.

'My dear Godfrey,' he said, gazing with large liquid eyes. 'Really, Reverend.'

'Is there any truth in this ugly rumour?' sniggered Gadsby.

'None at all, old chap.' Alan wagged his finger at Godfrey. 'Really, Reverend, you shouldn't say things like that, even in jest. You of all people, should know better—a man of God. . . .'

'I'm damned if I know better,' said Godfrey.

'Great heavens,' cried Gadsby, 'our idols are toppling down on every side. First Chote, now Browning. Alan, I implore you —say something—anything.'

From where he was sitting, Godfrey could just see the side of Alan's freckled cheek bulging out in the inevitable grin. 'Gentlemen I don't know what to say . . . this dastardly attack, from such a pious and reputable quarter, has left me temporarily speechless.'

'Speech, speech,' howled the others. 'Defend your ghastly reputation, or be prepared to lose it forever.'

'Well, gentlemen, this is very short notice, very short notice indeed. One needs time to assemble the usual affidavits, testaments, et cetera. The only thing I can actually point to is, well, the fact that I'm getting married next month.'

Hook's mouth flapped open in honest astonishment; but the others were already nodding wisely : 'Just as I supposed', 'It had to be something like that', and 'You can't count on the bloody things, can you?'

'Well, that's how it stands,' said Browning with a good-humoured shrug. 'You didn't suppose I'd be marrying a girl like Daphne Collins if there weren't a good reason, did you?'

Hook was frowning now with real and ugly distress. 'What a bloody thing to say.' The others took it calmly enough. 'You are an incorrigible bastard, Browning,' said one of them in mild reproach : but after all, one took Browning on his own terms. It was futile to be anything but amused at this stage of affairs.

'Do you really mean that?' asked Hook stupidly.

'Of course I do,' said Browning. 'I took it for granted that you knew. After all, we all make mistakes, don't we?' He picked up the deck and began to deal carelessly. 'I'm afraid the Reverend is shocked once more,' he shook his head sadly. 'He suspects me of transgressing the Boy Scout's code, not to mention one or two of his favourite commandments. And then, Godfrey himself was deflowered such a short time ago. . . .'

They looked curiously at Godfrey. 'After all, he's your friend, not ours,' they seemed to be saying. The others might put up with Browning's non-stop depravity for an hour or two every day, and feel all the better for it, too : but they locked their doors against it at night. Not that they disapproved of course : but there *were* other things in life. 'Browning's friend' —even that did not make him quite first rate.

For the first time, Godfrey realized in a flicker of the Inner Light what a curiosity he must be to them : the corrupted parson, shambling around Oxford in the wake of the college sinner, winking and leering and falling over his own feet; a tipsy figure nowadays with his Roman collar permanently askew, and the stink of beer rising like incense from his clericals.

'Once a priest, always a priest,' his father used to say in his solemn way; perhaps he spoke truer than he knew. And even in this role, he depended entirely on Browning's patronage: without that, he was the little minister again, a victim without guile.

'I'm not particularly shocked,' said Hook stiffly. 'But I must confess to being a trifle bored.'

'Typical clerical attitude.' Browning smiled. ' "Personally, I found *Forever Amber* extremely tedious," says the Archbishop of Canterbury. Or "I yawned all the way through *Lady Chatterley*," vouchsafed the Dean of Doncaster.'

'Oh, come now, Alan,' Gadsby interrupted. 'You're not in that class, old chap. We'd be all agog if you were.'

'Godfrey's quite right,' said the kindly voice at the end of the table. 'Browning is, first and last, a crashing bore—dingy without being sensational, dirty without being entertaining. Quite frankly I'm fed to the teeth with this chap and his scabrous little adventures. Do let's get on with the game.'

'Sorry,' said Browning amiably. 'You seemed to be interested at the time. . . . As usual, I was only trying to give pleasure.'

'I'm sure you were.' The deep voice came rumbling doomlike out of the darkness above the alcove. Hook stood up clumsily, banging his knee against the table, and Gadsby stood up too, leaving Browning to slip quietly to the floor between the two chairs. Elsewhere there was a general shuffle of dismay as players stood up briefly and sat down again.

'I'm frightfully sorry, gentlemen,' said the Warden, still only a voice high up in the darkness. 'I'm afraid I shall have to ask you to put away the cards. Tomorrow morning, we can discuss the possible consequences. Would, say, nine o'clock suit everybody?' They waited pathetically for the softening joke, the 'Play the ace, you fool' touch. But the Warden was standing on his authority tonight, as he very occasionally did: and there was no laughter on Olympus.

'Would you care to join us, sir?'

'No thank you, Mr. Gadsby. However, I shall make a note of your request.' And he was gone, never quite having been there.

The group straggled away in ones and twos to face the rigours of the winter night and the prospect of a bleak tomorrow : the more perceptive had realized that something had already gone wrong with the institution. There had been a malaise in the air tonight, a bad feeling in the bones. The Warden had, with his infallible instinct for what was good for the college, picked just the right moment to plant his large heel on the twinkling embers.

Godfrey walked home by himself, while Browning went about his nocturnal business; prowling behind fences, according to college legend, meowing softly, populating the town by stealth.

Godfrey could feel himself walking, almost see himself walking by now, on clerical tiptoe; small dainty strides guaranteed not to distract the flightiest congregations, slippering off down the centre aisle at a deceptive rate of speed. He caught his reflection shooting smoothly past in a shop-window, and he realized to his horror that he was rubbing his soft hands over and over again with the tell-tale unction. In moment of stress, how the old habits came back. He remembered sitting in the parlour on certain Sunday afternoons, watching the Reverend Hook and Felicity's father rubbing their hands to beat the band. He had been so small when he first saw them at it that ever since he had considered hand-rubbing to be an essential symptom of the calling; Mr. Smythe, the Sturdley Chaplain, had kept alive the superstition; and here he was doing it himself. Too many afternoons in the damned parlour.

He almost bumped into the ROAD NARROWS sign at the top of the stairs. He pushed past it through the door marked LADIES and DÉFENSE DE CRACHER (the landlady had somewhat belatedly translated a previous sign of the same sort, and had demanded with reproachful giggles that it be taken down immediately). The living-room looked like a busy intersection with its tangle of notice boards. Browning used to say that he wouldn't be happy until there wasn't a sign or an instruction standing in England—or presumably France, either : but as fast as he picked them, as fast did they sprout, smothering the

319

countryside like wildflowers, crawling, it seemed, even up stair-cases and into sitting-rooms.

This was very much Browning's room. There were several pictures of him in khaki and otherwise on the mantelpiece, behind his rows of invitations and club cards. Nothing fancy about the invitations of course : just 'Tony Jenkins invites you for sherry' and 'Bill Sludge, beer, 8 P.M.' : the last of the 'chaps' scattered and decimated by now, but in their various colleges still doggedly taking in each other's washing. This transcollegiate crowd had never much warmed to Godfrey, although they accepted him as Browning's friend, and nodded to him briefly in the streets. He might be someone of weight in Sturdley, but he wasn't really a 'chap' on the University level.

Next to the mantelpiece, a bookcase was carved into the wall. The books were half Godfrey's and half Browning's—but they were really all Browning's. The humorous books that Godfrey had bought were all by authors that Browning had put him on to; likewise the erotica he had brought home from Paris, and the Japanese prints. What was that new thing that the bloody man Gadsby had called him tonight? 'The first Mrs. Browning?' Not so bloody far wrong, perhaps.

He went into his bedroom to get a glass of water, but the taps weren't running. The cold weather had frozen the out-door pipes as it did every year. Godfrey swore and kicked the wastepipe and went shivering back into the living-room.

What one couldn't get over was the damned humiliation. Four years ago, this 'Parson Hook', 'Reverend Godfrey' stuff was all very well, a necessary part of his tutelage; but now that he was an elder statesman, so to speak, one of the last of the giants, it was more than a little degrading, especially in front of the whole crowd. For whatever earthly reason, Browning had chosen tonight to remind him precisely who was master and who was pupil. And he had been tongue-tied just as in the old days, helpless under Browning's playful thumb.

In all the pictures on the mantelpiece, Browning was grin-ning away, cheery and cheeky, with that indomitable English good nature. But if one looked at them closely enough, Godfrey devoutly hoped, perhaps one could just make out a trace of something that was not quite so good-natured. Godfrey had had some experience of English bullies, and he knew especially well the kind that smiled and smiled, innocent and embarrassingly intimate, while your arm swung back painfully on its hinges. And afterwards, 'We're still friends, aren't we, Godfrey? Here, have some of my chocolate'—chocolate or some other mildly desirable rubbish—the last flick of the thumbscrew, that little touch of kindness that sent one home fairly howling with misery.

Did Browning belong to that sub-species? He peered into the face and saw nothing there that he could put a name to: just the wide empty smile and the small, vaguely humorous eyes, slightly kind, slightly reassuring; but not very. It was the same way with Browning's past of course: it remained blank even after one knew all about it. Over the years, Hook had been taken through a goodly gallery of eccentric uncles and aunts; but they didn't really seem to belong to Browning especially. And here were the pictures. You couldn't see malice in them, even if you wanted to—it was really a very ordinary face.

Chote appeared in two of the pictures, and that was another story entirely. It was still entirely possible to fix all the blame on him. His bloody head was too big, for one thing, like a great balloon with florid features painted on. It seemed to swell as one gazed at it. A face of that size gave itself away every time. All its expressions were magnified grotesquely: a heavy curl of thick lips, as if lips really could curl like hair; teeth, blunt, brown, crooked. . . . And just look at those bloody hands, thick pudgy paws, digging convulsively into the waist of a fräulein, with practically every indication of goatlike affection: but then the great swollen features, frozen in calculation. The limpid eyes never ceased to scheme, no matter what the orgy. That was why one hated Chote, the scheming, the lack of abandonment.

'That's enough, chaps. Somebody's been leaving traces again.' That was one of Chote's at the climax of the last meeting of the 'Friends of Godfrey Hook' society at Brinkley, when all but John had crossed the border from conscious cruelty into the sub-world of inarticulate innocence. One of the officers of

the club had promulgated a rumour shortly before to the effect
that Godfrey had lately been informing on them, and this had
set off an unprecedented feast of blood-letting in the house
bathrooms. One or two of the more sensitive spirits withdrew
after the standard minimum dose of cuffing and kicking, but
the hard core that remained had whipped itself into a fine
frenzy by then. Godfrey opened his eyes every once in a while
and closed them again quickly. He was more or less immune
to physical pain by this time : but their faces were enough to
frighten anybody. Nobody but Chote was really responsible
any more; their eyes were wild, untenanted, his alone responded
reasonably to Godfrey's gaze. But he did nothing.

Godfrey had resigned himself to an all-night session,
crouched against a corner with his head buried between his
elbows; his little contemporaries were much too excited to
stop. It wasn't that they had no feelings of course, but they had
been increasing the dose little by little until Godfrey had
gradually become a sort of exception to the usual rules. And
now, of course, they had justice on their side. 'Bloody little
informer', thump. 'Let's hear you squeal for us.' Godfrey
shrank his spine further into his corner. He knew by instinct
and experience that one cry of pain would have wakened them
and sent them scurrying. But he couldn't bring himself to do
it : he was afraid (he realized now) that they might have dis-
liked him for it. Meanwhile, as long as he kept quiet, they
obviously felt justified in regarding him as somewhat less than
sentient.

It was at the very height of the incoherent revels that Chote
spoke up in a calm voice : 'I say chaps, I think he's beginning
to bruise.' They drew back to look. Bruises on the torso and
thighs didn't count of course—in the wintertime they were
seldom exposed to the authorities; but face and arms and shins
were something else again. 'Some clumsy clot has hit him in
the eye,' wailed a wounded voice : and there were echoes of
outrage as the dream began to vaporize away.

Chote leaned over to whisper, 'You won't tell anybody where
you got that? There's a good chap.' There was no trace of
anger in Chote : nothing but friendliness and concern. You

could swear he meant it. The boys trooped out slowly and soberly and Chote tossed him a facecloth. God, what a thing to do. . . .

It had come home to roost in the college library. All the old crouching vulnerability, the arms flung over the head, the mixture of stoicism and hysteria as before. Nothing had changed. Nothing would ever change. Not even with Browning on his side. . . .

He heard Browning trotting up the stairs at last, whistling and dodging the signs. He got up quickly and made a dive for his bedroom. But Browning had already bounced in.

'Hello, hello, hello. Well I must say that went off extremely well.' As he opened the door of the bedroom Hook noted half consciously that Browning was rubbing his hands too, although quite unlike a clergyman, of course.

'Going to bed, old chap?' The thin door shivered shut behind Godfrey. 'I say, there isn't anything wrong is there?' The voice was full of the old reassuring kindness. 'Godfrey, are you all right? Godfrey?' He was leaning against the door in a posture of solicitude. Godfrey sat up awkwardly at the head of his bed, staring at the door. 'Are you sure everything's all right, old chap?' Godfrey was holding his breath now, as if he didn't want to make a sound. 'Godfrey, old boy. . . .'

Alan shrugged and sauntered away, whistling again to himself and resavouring the night's flavours. Doubtless Godfrey would explain his extraordinary behaviour in the morning. Perhaps—Browning's memory groped back—he was still upset about that bit of nonsense in the college library. But, really. . . .

Chote crumpled up the letter, but it made a gigantic puffball in his pocket, so he straightened it out again and put it in the envelope and threw it in a waste basket near his feet.

He knew at once what it meant. Careless bugger, he thought, mechanically abiding by the convention.

He was curious to know what his own first reaction might be. So, Daphne was a tart after all and I never found out, he prompted himself. Well, well. That didn't make any difference: the discovery did not affect the flaccid image of Daphne one way or the other. Browning was a swine of course—but that wasn't news either. Seducing fiancées was one of his time-honoured japes. He used to come up to Oxford claiming at least one victim every vacation, in fact. And all his friends thought it highly amusing. Chote thought it was amusing, too.

Later, this whole business would begin to stink in his mind : it was all so bloody cheap and rotten and careless. But at the moment it seemed immensely trivial. So he had lost the fair Daphne Collins after all : the foolish girl had spurned his pure overtures in favour of Captain Foulheart's dastardly advances. Pity, he thought, and began to laugh inside himself. By God, they were a long way away and he was well out of it. I wonder how poor Godfrey's going to take this. I suppose he'll be moving in with the young couple.

The man behind the counter noticed Chote beaming and shaking a little with transitory hysteria. 'Did you want something else ?' he asked cautiously.

'Yes, by George,' said Chote. 'Another plate of toast. And damn the ruddy expense.' The thick lips came out wide and the bad teeth glistened with enormous pleasure. Poor Godfrey, he thought. The first Mrs. Browning. What the devil are they going to do with him ? They were all so far away and long ago and the devil take them. He had got out from under two women he didn't love by the simple exercise of inertia. Now he could start again, properly.

The sun slanted a blessing onto the slithery gold of the new toast and Chote addressed himself to it with rare abandon, chomping away and laughing to himself.

Chote had always been particularly partial to hot buttered toast.

18. Nothing but the Smell

EVERY Easter, the Fosdicks reassembled at the Plainsville house. The dogwood was out, and the wisteria arched charmingly over the terrace; and distant nieces and nephews proliferated in the house and grounds like Easter rabbits. For some private, perhaps forgotten reason, Mr. Fosdick chose this most difficult of days to go without his usual nourishment. All afternoon he pattered soberly about the expansive grounds chatting with his tiny relatives and massaging their shoulders with hands trembling fitfully. Only when every last one had gone did he lapse an inch from his strikingly attractive performance.

After the last 'bless you' and sticky handshake, he came tottering back into the house, looking for a glass of milk and a piece of cake, something to keep him busy part of the time until midnight. Out in the kitchen, the airy sweetness of the day gradually thinned out. A slice of chocolate cake capsized in the middle, smudging its icing against his shaky fingers, and then falling onto the floor in a spray of crumbs. 'Goddamnit,' he said.

'Here, I'll pick it up, Father,' said Mirabelle.

'No you won't,' he said, going down on his knees. 'I'll get it.' He crawled wheezing under the kitchen table, and out again. Mirabelle looked at the clock—ten past eight. It was going to be a long evening.

Mr. Fosdick straightened up slowly, clutching two handfuls of dirty crumbs. The knees of his good suit were dusty. 'Goddamnit,' he said helplessly. 'My pants are dirty.' Mirabelle led him over to the sink and helped him to get rid of the crumbs. He gave a testy slap at his knees, shifting some of the chocolate icing onto them. 'My best pants,' he muttered. The two maids who had withdrawn to the far end of the kitchen began to giggle. 'Come along, Daddy,' said Mirabelle hastily. 'Let's go sit in the living-room. I'll get you some more cake.'

'No, I want to stay out here,' he said stubbornly. 'I'll get the cake myself.'

Mr. Fosdick started hacking into the brown goo once again, and then he changed his mind and said, 'Whatever became of that English fellow that used to come here?'

Mirabelle smiled patiently. 'I don't know. Why?'

'I was just thinking about him recently. I didn't like him, you know.'

'Yes, I knew that.' Mirabelle took the cake and put it away in the icebox.

'I could tell right away that he wasn't a gentleman, not even the beginnings of a gentleman. But of course, I made it my business to treat him as if he were one. It never does any harm, you know.'

Mirabelle nodded. The maids had stopped giggling to listen.

'You never can tell—some of it may rub off. But then, he pushed me too far, eh?'

'Yes, that's right,' said Mirabelle, glaring at the maids.

'I had to be blunt with him. He didn't like that, of course. Those fellows never do.' Eight-twenty. He was obviously going to try filibustering through to Monday. 'It's my experience that these rootless fellows haven't got much in the way of normal feelings,' he said. 'The state, religion, the family, they don't give much of a damn. But you can get at them with a few home truths now and then. They're touchy beggars you know. . . .'

Mirabelle wandered out of the kitchen, with the querulous voice piping her on her way. 'Oh, yes, they're touchy all right. . . .'

Eugene was sitting on the sofa in the living-room, listening to some modern jazz records with eyes shut and dreamy. He looked very composed in a plaid sweater.

'Move over, Señor Pomposo,' she said, and plumped down next to him on the sleek brown surface. 'Father's giving John Chote hell out in the kitchen. Again. . . .'

'Oh yes?' Eugene asked with a yawn.

'Have you seen anything of John lately, by the way?'

Eugene shook his head. 'No. But I had a letter from a friend of his the other day. Fellow at Sturdley.'

'Oh, yes?' It was Mirabelle's turn to yawn. These Easter Sundays were a terrible drag.

'Fellow named Alan Browning.'

'Oh.' She paused and read the record cover for a while. 'And what did Alan Browning have to say?'

'Nothing much. He said that he was marrying John's old girl friend.'

'Ah, these English are so civilized. "Have one of mine, old boy". "No, I insist that you try one of mine, for a change".'

'I doubt if it was quite like that,' said Eugene. 'I don't know how Chote reacted, of course. But there was a third guy who reacted pretty violently.'

'Oh, who was that?'

'Another old buddy of Chote's, name of Godfrey Hook. Strange sort of a fellow.'

'And what did he do?'

'Apparently he just quit Oxford then and there—at least, according to Browning, that's what he did. "Overcome with my vileness" (or words to that effect) "the Reverend Godfrey has returned, with head lowered, to the bosom of the church : girl named Felicity." He then puts in a limerick about a bishop which I needn't bore you with. . . .'

'Oh please.'

'And then he sent his best to John, and that was about it. Nothing very interesting.' Mirabelle frowned.

'Is he really so vile? I mean Alan Browning?'

'Uh-huh. He was just about the friskiest thing I ever met outside of uniform.'

'How about John? Was he vile too?'

'I guess he must have been. Heck, we were all vile. You know college guys.' He rubbed his eyes sleepily.

'English ones, too?'

'Of course English ones.' He laughed reminiscently. 'Only I'm not sure that vile is the right word. I believe that this fellow Browning, for instance, had the healthiest, most natural attitude to sex I ever came across. I wish we had more people like that over here, sometimes.'

'Really? Stealing his friend's girl is natural?'

'Naturally it's natural. Why not?'

'I don't know. *Something* about it must have smelled sort of sour to make his little friend what'shisname go running off like that.'

'Well, as I was saying, Godfrey Hook has always been kind of peculiar. I wouldn't attempt to account for his movements one way or the other.' He closed his eyes firmly, and Mirabelle went back to reading the record cover: solemn programme notes on the emetic ecstasy.

'It's a pity,' she said, after a while, 'that John turned out to be so hopeless.'

'Hmm?' said Eugene. He squinted peevishly at the interruption.

'Did you ever guess at Oxford that he would turn out to be like that?'

'Like what? You mean, hopeless?'

She nodded.

'It's a funny thing,' he said, 'but I don't remember too well. It seems like an awfully long time ago. I guess he seemed pretty much like everybody else. Now, go ahead, ask me what everybody else was like.'

'It's a pity,' she said again. 'I liked him so much at first.' Eugene slapped the eyelids shut once and for all. He wasn't so very sure why Chote was supposed to be hopeless in the first place. It was Mirabelle's idea, not exactly his. All the same, he wasn't sorry that they had stopped seeing the guy; about half-way through the summer he had realized that he didn't much care for his English guest after all. Amid the artificialities of Sturdley, he had always assumed that Chote was the same sort of fellow, as say, Browning. But he wasn't the same at all. Not at all. Instead of Alan's rude health, there was something indefinably unpleasant, foul-tasting, disagreeable.

Of course, Eugene had punctiliously forged ahead with his duties as host and possible brother-in-law; he would never have dreamed of telling his younger sister how to run her affairs. But he was distinctly relieved when Mirabelle suddenly announced that John had become impossible. He was tired of paying for Chote's amusements. Chote was certainly a prince among freeloaders, and he was tired of lugging him around to the points of interest : but most of all, he was tired of the endless dribble of facetiousness—not humour, nobody could call it that—just silliness for its own sweet sake, hour after hour, day after day. Once or twice (God, that terrible day at the football game) Chote had become briefly too much for him, and he had picked the makings of a quarrel over nothing at all; but then generations of politeness had reasserted themselves, and he had relapsed into low-pressure hospitality. (Hell, Chote was expensive though : and never *once* offering to pay for anything.)

So all in all, when Mirabelle stated her proposition that John had passed beyond the feasible limits, he was highly disinclined to question her. She must have her good reasons : he didn't want to hear about them. Whenever she brought the subject up, he shut his eyes, or the equivalent. It would be a pity if she talked herself out of such a nifty idea—as she was, he well knew, quite capable of doing.

He had been lulling himself toward sleep with these thoughts, and the aid of a brace of atonal saxophones, and he didn't realize at first that Mirabelle was talking to him again. 'You and your healthy Anglo-Saxon attitudes,' she was saying. 'Well, I suppose that's all right. I don't know. We must be healthy, mustn't we? But I know one thing for sure. You never learned anything like that from John Chote.' And she got up and trotted out to the kitchen, to pick up the thread of her father's grievances and, if necessary, help the quivering old man on his way to bed.

A few weeks after that, Mirabelle had to go up to John's neighbourhood on a secretarial errand. The winter gales had turned by now into coaxing breezes and on the way back she found herself being puffed gently along past the Chote Memorial building. She stopped her mild progress and stood for a moment gazing up at the deceptive Edwardian curlicues. This was as good a time as any to do what had to be done. She pushed through the heavy glass door and started up the rackety stairs.

'Is Mr. Chote at home?'

Mrs. Fishman pulled her kimono tight under the chin, as if it were advisable to be extra-decent in front of a female visitor. 'No,' she said. 'Mr. Chote isn't here.'

'Oh, well. Do you know when he'll be back?' Mirabelle looked past her along the empty hall.

'Mr. Chote doesn't live here any more. He moved,' said Mrs. Fishman.

'He did? When was that?'

'Oh, a week ago, maybe two. I really don't know.' Mrs. Fishman rested her gaudy hip patiently against the frame of the door and examined her nails. 'I'm afraid I'm a mess to be answering the door,' she said.

'Do you know where he moved to?' asked Mirabelle.

'I really can't say. He just left. Maybe he went back to England.' She shrugged and nestled the silken hip further into the woodwork.

'Maybe he left a message of some kind,' suggested Mirabelle. 'With the landlady.'

'He left a message of some kind with me,' said Mrs. Fishman with unexpected heat. 'You can have that if you like.'

'What kind of message?'

'I'll go get it for you.' Mrs. Fishman snapped back into alignment and went tick-tocking elegantly down the hall. Her bedroom slippers flip-flopped in antiquated ragtime on the dusty floorboards, leaving a shapeless smudge. She went into her room and shut the door carefully.

When she came back, her hair was tidier and her lipstick considerably clarified. 'I'm sorry I'm such a mess. I wasn't expecting anybody.'

'You look fine,' said Mirabelle, reaching for the note. Mrs. Fishman took a step backwards, pressing the note to her bosom.

'Here it is, from Mr. John Chote,' she said, biting the words out slowly. She thrust it out distastefully to arm's length to

330

read it: a piece of Mrs. Griswold's iron-bound toilet paper. The neat handwriting was splattered all over the mildly absorbent surface: 'To Mrs. Fishman, in memory of those many happy exchanges in the bathroom. Keep up the good work, Mrs. Fishman. Suggest that any further suggestions concerning my personal habits be sent to my representative, Mr. Schwartz, c/o the Mayfair Bar, 9–5 weekdays, all day Saturdays. He will know exactly what to do with them.'

Mrs. Fishman was staring balefully at her. 'Well!' said Mirabelle, at a loss for the moment.

'Well is right,' said Mrs. Fishman. 'Did you ever see anything like it?'

'No, I don't think so.'

'We didn't find it until after he'd gone. Otherwise Mr. Fishman would have called him out. Mr. Fishman may be small but he's wiry, as they say, nuggety, and he doesn't allow people to insult his wife.'

'No, of course not,' said Mirabelle.

Mrs. Fishman took the note and read it again, shaking her head woefully from side to side. 'My God, the nerve of him. "Happy exchanges in the bathroom". Just look at that will you? And "My representative, Mr. Schwartz". Did you ever in your life see anything like it?'

Mirabelle stood there uneasily. She could see Mrs. Fishman's kimono working itself loose in the general agitation: and she knew very well that when it came apart, Mrs. Fishman would come apart too. 'I already met his friend Mr. Schwartz,' she was saying. 'There's another fine gentleman for you. I would be lying in bed sometimes listening to Mr. Schwartz staggering up and down the hallway half the night, singing and swearing and carrying on. Mr. Fishman went out one time and found them wrestling out there. Wrestling, by God! The hall lamp was down, of course, and the telephone. . . .'

'Well, thank you anyway, Mrs., er'—one more outburst, and the kimono would be past praying for—'I'm so sorry to have bothered you.'

'That's all right. I wasn't doing anything.' Mrs. Fishman recollected herself, the kimono was attended to.

'Well, anyway.'

Mrs. Fishman stood there adjusting herself primly and patting down her hair. 'I'm sorry I couldn't help,' she said quite sweetly. 'Gloria Fishman is the name, by the way.'

'Thank you, Mrs. Fishman.'

'What's your name, honey?' Mrs. Fishman smiled ingratiatingly.

'Mirabelle Fosdick. And thanks anyway.'

'Won't you come in, Mirabelle? I'll make you some tea or something. Mr. Fishman won't be home for a while, and it gets a bit lonely around the middle of the afternoon you know? It's awfully dark in here.'

'No, really. It's very sweet of you. . . .' Mirabelle took a step backwards and began to pull on her long white gloves. 'I really must be running now.'

'Those are nice gloves,' said Mrs. Fishman, reaching out a hand, 'very nice gloves.'

'Do you think so? Well, goodbye, Mrs. Fishman. And thanks again.' She was halfway to the stairs already. She turned slightly and gave a little wave, and Mrs. Fishman waved back enthusiastically. 'Poor thing,' Mirabelle said to herself as she started down the stairs. 'I wonder what really happened between her and John.'

She asked somebody down on the street the way to the Mayfair Bar, where the last traces of Chote were apparently to be found.

Although the spring sun was warming the sidewalks and the buds were popping down on the Drive, dozens of collegemen were packed in like moles in the everlasting dark of the Mayfair. At first, Mirabelle couldn't make out anything but the little white glistening screen at the end of the bar. She seemed to be staring along a narrow black funnel filled with disembodied, reverberating voices. Gradually the darkness lifted an inch or two, revealing a stripped-down dispensary, with a large, solemn man in white measuring out teaspoons of medicine to a chattering row of patients.

After soaking up the gold of the afternoon, there was something sinister about this jabber-jabber in the half-dark. But she advanced bravely and asked the man in white if he knew anybody by the name of Schwartz. 'Eh? What was that?' Not only did he not understand a word she had said—he never would understand: his features contorted with a kind of despair. 'What was that, lady?'

'Did you say Schwartz?' asked the man Mirabelle was leaning over. 'Hey, Schwartz, there's a lady here wants to see you,' said somebody else. There was a shuffling sound at the other end of the bar, and in a moment a swart fellow with a large head like Chote's and very thick glasses was standing by her side. 'Can I help you, madam?'

'I don't know. Are you John Chote's personal representative?'

'I guess so,' said Schwartz. 'Why, are you Mrs. Fishman?'

'No, I'm Mirabelle Fosdick.'

'Ah-ha!' said Schwartz. 'So that's it.' The thick glasses raked her up and down slowly and thoughtfully. 'Mirabelle Fosdick, eh? Well, well, well.'

'Is that all right?' she asked frostily.

'Oh sure. That's fine.' He put his hand to his chin and tilted his head to one side. Mirabelle began to wonder if anything were the matter. A quick peep down at her shoes, stockings, spring coat demurely buttoned—everything seemed to be in order. Her hat was on tight. Her hair was too short to get into serious trouble. Schwartz's glasses were so thick that it was hard to tell exactly what he was looking at anyway: the convex bowls sent his sight splaying off in all directions at once.

She began to pick up the dismal waves of noise again, rising and crashing and churning all around her, as pointless and brutal as the sea itself. And she began to notice the smells too, dingy and motionless. God, why did people come into these airless, stinking holes when they could be out in the clean sunshine? Schwartz was still goggling at her patiently: Well, well, well, Mirabelle Fosdick. What do you know?

'Can you tell me where John went?' she asked impatiently.

'Sure. He went back to jolly old England, and all that sort of thing.'

'Oh,' said Mirabelle. 'I see.'

'Rather a blow, what?'

'You do imitations, I gather.'

'As John's personal representative, we attempt to capture some of the authentic flavour, madam.'

Mirabelle started to edge her way out. This place didn't want her: Schwartz only spoke for the whole crowd. People stood aside, sarcastically it seemed to her now, to let her get by. When she reached the steaming glass door, she found that Schwartz was still with her.

'Where do you want to go?' he said. 'I'll tell the chauffeur.'

'What chauffeur? What are you talking about?'

'Oh, John told me all about the chauffeur, and also about the upstairs maid and the downstairs maid and all the maids in between, and the ladies in- and out-of-waiting and the third-string butlers warming up on the sidelines. . . .'

'Oh, for heavensake,' said Mirabelle disgustedly. 'Did he really tell you all that?' there was something dolefully familiar about the recitation. She seemed to remember Chote saying something silly about chambermaids.

'Uh-huh, that and more. Although, mind you, he wasn't complaining about it—no sir, that boy never once complained.'

Mirabelle thought for a second to defend herself: to give him the names and particulars of the three servants (two of whom were only kept on out of kindness) and to let him know about how her mother bought all her clothes at the Thrift Shop, and so on, but she decided that it was all much too childish. She pushed against the glass door and plunged out into the soft day.

'Maybe John was exaggerating, huh?' said Schwartz, following amiably.

'Oh honestly, who cares?'

'I do, for one. Didn't I tell you, I'm really an unreconstructed Wobbly at heart? I resent every last damn butler of yours. And when I think of those nonunionized chambermaids —cheezt!'

Mirabelle was walking vaguely down the street, hoping to shake him off somehow. He sauntered along beside her, with his hands in his pockets, chatting away undismayed. 'How does it feel to be an outpost of feudalism, eh? A little chilly sometimes, I'll bet, when the cold winds howl through the old castle. Now, I know just what you're going to say: "We've always treated our slaves jolly decently—never had any serious complaints, don't you know?" Of course, Louis XIV made very much the same point in his day, and so did Czar Nicholas. . . .'

'Look,' said Mirabelle. 'I don't want to have to ask you to go away. . . .'

'All right, all right. I'll change the subject. I was only warning you for your own good.' He paused and chewed his thick lower lip for a moment, before resuming in a low, tense voice: 'Of course I'm on your side really, you know. All these damn snivelling university socialists—pah! Never seen an honest day's work in their lives, most of them. Bleeding hearts, squash-heads, parasites. . . .'

They had reached the Drive again, and Mirabelle stopped and wheeled on her narrow spikes. 'Mr. Schwartz, I'm sure you're a very amusing fellow, but honestly I'm not in the mood this afternoon.' He was trying to say something to her, she supposed, but it took so long and she had a headache.

'O.K., O.K. I guess this is pretty exotic stuff when you come right down to it—you have to be keyed up for it.'

'That's right. I'm not up to it.' She started up again along the high bank overlooking the river. That ought to take care of Schwartz.

'Let's see, what shall we talk about?' he said. 'Politics is out, economics ech!—say, how about religion?' The silent treatment. 'Do you dig the Christian mumbo-jumbo? In your position, you probably have to, I guess.'

She had lost her sense of transportation. The convenient thing now would be to get on a bus and sail away. But these buses looked unfamiliar. And she didn't want to encourage Schwartz by asking him. It looked as if she would just have to walk all the way home.

'Hey, let's sit down a minute. I'm getting winded,' said Schwartz. 'All right, let's not. Where are we going anyway? O.K., let's make it a surprise.' He was indomitably affable. 'I know what let's do. Let's can the small talk and get down to the larger issues. What happened between you and John?'

She turned her palm upwards and kept walking.

'You want to talk about John?'

'Not particularly.'

'It was funny about how he left. Just one day he came around to the Mayfair and said he was leaving. So what's so funny about that? I know, I know. But it seemed funny all the same. I asked him what had come up and he said nothing special, that he wasn't getting much use out of Madison and that I could pretend I was him, he, ah to hell with it, until the end of the year if I felt like it. I probably could too. Am I boring you, by the way? No, I didn't think so. A couple of days later, he told me casually that his father had died. He didn't seem too broken up about it, but you never can tell with these unemotional Englishmen, can you? John was very frank about a lot of things, but just when you'd expect him to tell you something, he just wouldn't. He was really back to front by our point of view—open about his secrets, and secretive about his openings, or something. Didn't you find that?'

Mirabelle didn't look at him. 'What did he say about his father?' she asked, very off-hand.

'Well, like I say, nothing much. Shouldn't say "like", should I? Naughty, naughty. No, he just said he was surprised. He knew his mother was sick, but he thought his father was in the pink. Apparently the old boy had been ailing for some time, though. Cancer, it turned out, I think.'

'He told me his father didn't believe in doctors,' said Mirabelle.

'That so? Well, anyway, that was that. I guess John wanted to go home for the funeral. I asked him if he was coming back afterwards, and he said "Why should I?" So I didn't know. Why should he?'

'Let's sit down for a minute,' said Mirabelle. 'I'm getting winded too.'

They went over to a bench and sat down together almost like friends. 'Do you know why he should?' said Schwartz. 'No,' said Mirabelle.

The sun was inching down, preparing for its nightly plunge. The air was cooling off slightly after the cordial warmth of the day, allowing new possibilities for loneliness and reflection among those so inclined. Mirabelle was still a little bit peeved at Schwartz, but she wanted to hear more about the vanishing Englishman.

'I don't know why he should want to come back,' she repeated slowly, shaking her head. 'No, I don't.'

'He got kind of a screwy impression of America from you people didn't he? I mean, you're pretty unusual people.'

Mirabelle smiled involuntarily. . . . . After all, you could get a pretty screwy impression from Schwartz too.

'All the same,' he went on, 'he seemed to like it pretty well. All those chambermaids tickled his fancy, I bet you.'

'Oh, please. Spare me the chambermaids.'

'Anyway, whatever it was, he had a pretty good time. He used to like to sing around the piano, you know, so I used to have him out to my place a lot, and he met a lot of ordinary people, the "little people", as you might say, and he liked it pretty well. That was really his style, you know.'

'Ah,' said Mirabelle.

'You don't agree? You think he preferred jazzing it up at the Palace with your crowd?'

'I don't know. He was a funny kind of fellow, wasn't he? After all, he went back to England, even after he'd had such a wonderful time at your place, didn't he?'

Schwartz smiled one of his rare smiles. 'You've got a point there, kid. Maybe the "little people" treatment wasn't such a success either.'

They stared out silently across the river. This thing would be much easier to discuss if they liked each other even a little bit. By now the discussion of an absent friend should have done its work, generating at the least a kind of working intimacy, if any possibility of one had existed. But it was just hopeless. Schwartz disapproved of her, doubtless for his own good reasons : and in the circumstances, real politeness on his part would have been a serious breach of honour. She didn't know exactly why this should be so—in her world, one was

337

polite to practically everybody; but Chote had made her all too familiar with this virtue—you might call it 'ill-natured integrity'—and she knew better than to try wearing it down with kindness or copybook gentility.

'I'd better be going home,' she said. 'There doesn't seem to be anything to talk about.'

'I thought we were doing famously,' said Schwartz. 'You just scored a good point, remember? After all, you're right, he can get singing around the piano anywhere—Oxford, London, anywhere. But what you people have to offer, oo la la.'

'Do you know what buses go over to the East Side?' asked Mirabelle politely.

'I thought you used to live around here. What happened? Back to Butterfield?'

She stood up and dusted herself mechanically. 'Sorry about the pigeons,' he chatted. 'They're shocking at this time of year. They come all the way over from England, I believe, and make a mess, and go all the way back. How do you like that? So we retaliate with G.I.s, but it isn't the same—Hey, we're going the wrong way. The bus is back that way.'

'I don't care,' she mumbled petulantly, and at the same time hunching her shoulders and accelerating.

'All right. It's a lovely evening for walking. And it's only about sixty blocks from here. I can always take the bus back. So I meant to ask you, what happened between you and John?'

What was he trying to do? He seemed like a moderately perceptive man, in his brutish way; and he was a friendly man too, according to John—yes, she remembered a little about Schwartz: John's 'mucker' who had dropped his Christian name 'out of protest'. It came back haltingly now: a thin shower of comic attitudes, poses and opinions. Funny hats, card tricks, impersonations. A scream at parties.

'I will say this about John,' said Schwartz, 'he had terrible manners. And I don't just mean things like chewing with his mouth open, although he certainly did that, or not carrying a handkerchief. He did much worse things than that. Things like saying just what he had on his mind, talking back to older people. . . .'

Mirabelle noticed with interest that Schwartz hardly opened his mouth when he talked : apart from a slight trembling of the jowls now and then, his face was all but motionless. Very different from Chote, whose features worked fast and furiously, sometimes winding up in the most unexpected configurations.

'That was certainly one of his worst ones. Dignity, respect for age, meant absolutely nothing to him. And tactless. . . .'

It must have taken years to develop that great stone face. Sedulous practice in front of the mirror. The eyes were safe behind the opaque glass, but to freeze the rest of the features like that took some doing, years of dedication—well, not years perhaps. Taken one by one, they were young features. Stripped of the gravity of repose they might have been very young features.

That was a line of thought to while away the time, while Schwartz was talking. A boy who got ahead of himself in the school system could become an adept at this kind of facial composition : always a little younger than he should be, always striving to make the most of his skimpy years. She was sure that that was the point of Eugene's unusual solemnity too : the secret of youth had been well kept in his case, but at a cost. He was really quite a stuffed shirt.

And this was really very young talk, too. Brash, not necessarily honest but fearless undoubtedly; poorly judged but manfully delivered. Giving the rich girl a good talking to. Tuning in again : 'I don't know what we're coming to—talking back to the rich indeed !' The big-stick sarcasm, a man's weapon in the hands of a child. The prehistoric college radical, with bobbing Adam's apple, telling the footloose debutante a thing or two. If he only knew. . . .

'I'm glad to see you smiling,' he said suddenly. 'To what do we owe the unusual privilege?'

'How old are you, Schwartz?' she asked quite gaily. 'I was just wondering.

'I'm thirty-one. Why?'

Good Lord. 'Nothing,' she said. Thirty-one.

'I expect you find me very immature,' said Schwartz. 'Girls

like you are always finding that men are immature—and so they are, from a certain special point of view. John, for instance. . . .'

Didn't they have any taxis at all on Riverside Drive? She thought she could see a tiny light glittering in the distance, but it seemed to be going the wrong way. Her feet were pinched and aching prodigiously in her smart spring shoes.

'Of course, I'm young in heart,' rambled Schwartz. 'That's why I still go to school, you know, and suck my thumb and all.'

Oh, for heavensake shut up and find me a taxi. The tiny glittering light seemed to be edging towards them after all, but slowly and reluctantly. Somebody was sure to intercept it and carry it off.

She darted over to the edge of the wide sidewalk to flag it: Schwartz came trotting behind, still talking, incredibly, relentlessly.

'Ooh look, it's coming,' she said breathlessly. 'Goodbye, Mr. Schwartz.'

The cab had to make a U turn (or, as Chote might have said, a non-U turn. How a habit could stick) around one of the slim traffic islands, and Mirabelle stood on her toes waving urgently. 'I'm sorry you have to go,' said Schwartz. 'We have so much to say to each other.'

'Oh by the way,' said Mirabelle. 'How can I get in touch with John?'

'Want to write him a "Dear John" letter? O.K., only kidding.' Mirabelle was not annoyed, but Schwartz pretended she was. 'No, seriously,' he said, 'I guess Sturdley College, Oxford, is your best bet.'

She was afraid for a moment that he was going to bounce into the taxi alongside her with a view to more talking, but he only stood by the door bowing courteously. She backed in awkwardly and he flicked the door shut.

It was dark already, and she could make even less than before out of the passive features. But there was a glint on the heavy glass eyes that suggested a notable self-satisfaction, as from a difficult job well and faithfully done. He had defended his friend, in his own, peculiar way. The taxi tugged her away.

So much for John Chote: one friend and one enemy. Apart from that, he had left very little trace. A mess no larger than a pigeon's.

All the irrelevancies had come back in force: the noisy eating, the fabulous rudeness, the crazy-quilt of concealment and candour; the rubbery face going this way and that over its food—the images were obtrusive and distracting. She wanted to know more about the bad dreams, the fidgets and the assorted hobgoblins—all the things that might have saved the day—and here she was with the old stereotypes, the faded prints of 'John Bull abroad', gruff but endearing . . . the truth was hidden as before behind the flashy art work. All the dreary mistakes she had made about Chote had apparently been repeated in spades by Schwartz. Aged thirty-one. No fool like an old fool. The very same formulas, too: Freud, Karl Marx and Emily Post, offered to the adult patient through a sterilized rubber nipple. The description was Chote's, of course: one of his last as far as she personally was concerned. Over the bleak Thanksgiving week-end of the annus Britannicus.

She had been chastising him for his manners, just a little bit this time, toning them up, really, and now she was coating the pill with a little love. For the first minute or two, she concentrated on her own performance, so it took her that long to realize he wasn't responding at all satisfactorily. She nibbled his ear and asked him what was the matter.

'Nothing,' he said. 'It's just that this always comes as rather a shock after the well-known sermon on etiquette.'

'That wasn't a sermon,' she said lazily. 'Just a word of advice about the local totems and taboos.'

'No doubt, no doubt'—she could still hear the astringent voice. 'But sometimes it seems, how shall I put it, perverse? to worry so much about manners, and then so little about, er, other things.'

She sat up sharply. 'What do you mean, other things?' Once or twice before she had sensed the same spectre of frowning dissatisfaction, but he had never put it in even as many words as these.

'Well, *you* know,' he was honestly embarrassed, 'other things.'

'There isn't anything wrong with what we're doing, is there?' she said tartly. 'You might have told me sooner if you had any objections.'

He looked at his hands. 'I'm sorry. No, there aren't really any objections. Just a few atavistic twinges. Must be the weather.'

She was pretty annoyed at first, and he was full of his own kind of apologies. 'I know it's perfectly all right and one hundred per cent healthy,' he said. 'And I'm really awfully grateful—if that doesn't sound too fatuous.'

Well, it did, in the first spasm of her indignation. 'If you'd only try being honest with me for a change. I really thought you wanted to. . . .'

I thought so too. I'm really very sorry. I know it's the normal thing for Viennese doctors, American teenagers, and probably for most Englishmen too. But to someone with an old non-conformist conscience, and occasional delusions of Anglicanism, it all seems rather, well, tasteless, now and again, if you know what I mean.' It came stumbling out, a shocking disruption of the usual smooth stream.

'No, I don't know what you mean. Those categories of yours seem pretty parochial and accidental compared with the universal, human tendencies, drives and needs'—she'd said all this before, and she knew very well that he couldn't make any sense of it. He sat listening attentively, apologetically, all awash in abstractions. The least he could do, of course, was let the poor girl say her piece.

They argued for a little while, out of habit. But she felt that too much indignation in the circumstances would look cheap; and anyway, she hadn't the heart for it.

They were in his room, sitting side by side on the shabby cloth counterpane. There was nothing to look at, to concentrate on, except the cracked mirror with its handful of scarred reflections and the sound of the blurting, forlorn radiator. She began to think about crying. It was such a wretched room.

'I feel like a terrible fool,' she said. 'It *does* all seem cheap, if *you* think it's cheap. But why didn't you let me know?'

His answer was thin and useless enough for her to start sobbing in earnest. 'It's my fault entirely,' he said. 'I'm the fool if anyone is. I don't know what it is—my mind isn't at all clear.' She shivered with her sobs, making the springs creak woefully in the inadequate $12-a-week bed. 'Really not very experienced, not very satisfactory. Perhaps not even very normal,' he was saying, but there was no weakness in his voice: something much more like patience and even perhaps a faint whisper of boredom, now that his own crisis was temporarily resolved.

'I feel so exposed,' she said softly and truthfully.

'Entirely my fault,' he said, putting his arm generously around her. 'I can't apologize enough.' His arm was very cold, but infinitely patient. She looked mistily up at him: his eyes and mouth were respectfully shut, in the presence of an exposed female. And she had a sudden uncanny notion that he must be counting to himself: to a hundred, to a thousand, to whatever was necessary.

That was just a guess, of course, but it was part of a new way of looking at him. She knew from that moment that she couldn't really get at him, with tears or sermons or anything else. On the surface, he might be pleased or irritated. But underneath, he was counting away to himself, marking out his own private time, waiting patiently for the end of it. All her various attempts to bring his attention into focus had failed dismally: he remained triumphantly unapproachable, behind a spiky wall of mannerisms, jagged eccentricities, broken bottles. . . . He might worry about his own conscience a little —but precious little about anyone else's feelings.

That being the case, there didn't seem to be much point in telling him—well, no point in telling anything. She got her things together soundlessly, except for the irregular creaking of the mournful bedsprings, and left.

It was a mark of what she now assumed to be his quite formidable indifference to other people that Chote didn't seem to notice that anything had happened. He took her out several times after that and chatted away like a magpie, chuckling effervescently at his own inventiveness—exactly what he had been doing all along, except for the uneasy intervals when she got mad or sulky or otherwise obtrusive. He really seemed so much happier when she sat quietly and left him alone. He bloomed, he blossomed, he became delightfully himself. It seemed almost a crime to distract him with her little displays of temperament. Far better to tiptoe away and leave him smiling to himself, playing with his toes.

At the end of each of these last dates, he raised his eyebrows inquiringly, and she shook her head vigorously 'No'. All the same, he found reason to say, 'These last two weeks or so have been awfully pleasant—don't know what it is. We just seem to get along better and better.' He seemed to be growing rosy and prosperous with each refusal. 'Remember how we used to make each other feel so rotten with our quarrelling? Thank God that's over.' She smiled while he talked now, and hardly said anything at all. 'I've never felt closer to you,' he said, squeezing her hand and raising his eyebrows for the third time.

'Not tonight,' she said politely.

'I say'—a cloud seemed to gather, no bigger than a man's hand. 'It wasn't anything I said the other day was it? I was feeling out of sorts, you know. . . .'

She shook her head and the cloud fell apart. In fact, he seemed almost ecstatic with relief. 'I'd hate to think it was anything like that, especially now that we've given up wrangling and jousting on a more or less permanent basis. You know—I can say it now, I suppose—you used to get so ugly when you were angry, really quite repulsive sometimes, and I did feel a bit squeamish about, you know—hope you don't mind my saying so?'

Yes, impossible was the word for it. Some minimum of insight, or reasonably intelligent kindness was necessary: and here was only the cold thoughtlessness of a child. At that, she had to admit that Chote was unique: his boisterous lack of normal, human responsiveness added up to a kind of genius. His refusal to admit to any convictions was only one symptom of the same thing: it wasn't scrupulosity, or humour, but a vast and deadly indifference to anybody outside Chote. She had

344

never come across anything like it before. She hated to get really angry, but she couldn't help it by this time. Otherwise, she would have avoided that clumsiness in handling the final formalities. A cool explanation was called for—but then how could one explain anything to someone who was counting to himself all the time? He would leave, all right, but dumb, uncomprehending to the last, he would feel himself most unfairly put upon : and hurt, of course, they always felt hurt. One couldn't let that happen. Not to a big baby like John Chote anyway, with his child's heart.

All she could say was that it had seemed like a good solution at the time. Stuffed and uncomfortable that day from the greasy pleasures of the table, indefinably restless in the old gentlemen's calidarium, she had recognized the outlines of one of those rare opportunities. In the heavy after-dinner fuzz, it had seemed like a small triumph of cunning just to find an excuse to leave the room like that. Within an hour or so, she knew that it hadn't been a good way of handling things at all. It was, in fact, fundamentally sloppy and not a little undignified. And there was something especially shabby about accepting poor old semi-conscious Mr. Fosdick as deus ex machina. Nothing could be done about it right away, but eventually she must try again, explain things a little bit more honestly. Poor old Mr. Fosdick, everybody laughed at him. She laughed at him herself sometimes. John must have known that : she really would have to give some sort of accounting of that part of it. He must think Americans very queer to get upset about a thing like Mr. Fosdick and the socialists. It was the kind of chance thing that led people to get funny ideas about countries.

By springtime, John should have made some nice new friends. She would talk to him then, and trip out all the dear, good clichés (stored conscientiously during the winter): how it never would have worked, how it was better for both of them, how wonderful it had once been, for all that. No regrets, no indeed—a tender smile, a light kiss, et cetera, and home again, mission accomplished. Nothing very distinguished perhaps, but a big improvement on the dining-room fiasco.

Instead of which, of course, she had met Mrs. Fishman and Schwartz, and the clichés had dried in her mouth. All they had given her was a comic picture of how her old flame had been spending the winter : annoying a silly, lonely woman mostly (over weighty matters of bathroom protocol), and building up fabulous theories with his friend Schwartz about what made the various Fosdicks tick. Imagination groaned over these two childish men putting their outsized heads together day after day, trying to decipher the secrets of her, in particular, heart. Heaven only knew the full extent of the jumbled mosaic : Schwartz's devastating innuendoes had only deepened the mystery. What *did* Chote think about the Fosdicks ? What sort of story-book villains had he and Schwartz turned them into ? And what sort of story-book clown had she made of Chote ?

She shook her head sharply. There was something wrong with her own picture : the man in the corner was wearing a moose's head; and the girl was standing upside down. Mirabelle frowned, focusing on the cabdriver's wall-to-wall neck.

She had really wanted to see Chote again—that must be admitted, if the picture were to be put right. To explain things, of course, but also, well, to see Chote again. Perhaps something would have happened : she might have remembered some key thing. It had been such a dull winter, all the old faces back, better scrubbed and more considerate than ever : helping her into her chair, laughing at her jokes, remembering to buy flowers. They had the kind of manners you didn't have to correct. The boys in dancing school had grown up, spreading this way and that, but they still wore their patent-leather shoes and their little three corners of handkerchief : and then (one must remember, they were grown men now) they tried to make love with obscene politeness. Bob Wilkins, her former fiancé, was back too, depressingly dependable, inexhaustibly faithful, unfathomably dull.

Compared with that crowd, Chote had seemed like a wild boar galumphing out of the Black Forest, snuffling his food, interrupting everybody, laughing brutishly at his own jokes, pouting—no this wasn't quite right either. She had been making her own pictures this winter : his manners weren't as bad as all that. There was that big face that always looked a bit slovenly; and not very much respect for women as such. And—oh what was the use of going through all that again? Anyway, at first it had seemed rather refreshing and later it hadn't seemed so refreshing, and now it seemed altogether unimportant. She had made much too much out of it. It wasn't that, it was something else.

It had been such a disappointing day, starting out with a high heart—some nice surprise might so easily have happened —and winding up with Schwartz. Everything would have been all right if there really were nothing more to Chote than there was to Schwartz: but one couldn't be sure of that. Schwartz was a local boy, and she knew all about him. Chote was a foreigner, and she might have missed something there. The day's nonsense shimmered fitfully in a glaze of fatigue : silly, wrong pictures of everybody. An older, truer memory came back outlined for convenience against the cabdriver's steamy, indented neck. Chote's harassed, good-humoured face the day he arrived, with its broad acres of new possibilities . . . after that, the sturdy comedian's figure walking away apologetically, by himself. Of course, by himself. Very independent fellow. 'My fault entirely . . . take the entire responsibility.' Jolly decent of him, to use Schwartz's patter, but it didn't do much to help. It would still be a pretty dreary summer. With an awful lot of Eugene, the distinguished Oxford man. Damn Chote for being so hopeless. Damn him for being so selfish— if he was selfish.

'Over on that side,' she said tartly. 'How much is that?' She handed over a five-dollar bill in the dark, and got out quickly, slamming the door. The taxi driver smiled complacently at her mysterious, rewarding anger. She made resolutions across the sidewalk and into the elevator, and kept at least one of them when she got upstairs. She couldn't let things go quite like that : she must find out just a tiny bit more.

Section

IV

Soap Futurities

JAMES *and Oswald, he of the ominous nephew, sat in the saloon bar of the Forester's Arms. They had come to Oxford once again, James to jeer and Oswald to savour the complexities. They were customers very much to Mr. Wilson's taste: quiet, unobtrusive, mindful of the civilized arts. They responded appropriately to Mr. Wilson's courtly ways, with grave nods and sixpenny tips: it was always much better in the vacations.*

'We're right next to Sturdley,' said James. 'Why don't we pop in a minute and see that nephew you were telling me about?' (Oswald had told all during the winter months.)

He gave his friend the elbow, expecting a wince of embarrassment; but Oswald was all smiles. 'Oh, he's gone down by now. He isn't here any more.'

'Can't say I've noticed any improvement,' said James. 'He's taken his curse elsewhere, has he?'

'Yes, he has. As a matter of fact, I've just come from his wedding. Nice girl—very sensible she seemed. Nice family, too, come down from the North.'

James laughed. 'The ra-akes's progress like. What's happened to lad? Has he gone soft?'

'He's learned to behave himself, if that's what you mean. His father wouldn't believe it, at first. He's strong on the predestination, you know, and he says boy's damned. But damned or no he chartered a bus at last minute and us of Lancashire branch chartered bus and we had a proper do. Lad's uncle officiated and all. . . .'

'You mean,' *snorted James,* 'they got married in a church?'

Oswald nodded serenely.

'Lad belongs to club,' *James said shortly.* 'Just a vertical

351

congregationalist or whatever, like his father and his grand-father. . . .'

'It was like a devil going out of someone,' said Oswald dreamily.

'And leaving him as dull as everyone else,' chimed in James.

Oswald shook his head sadly—it was all much more complicated than that. There were after all such things as conventional devils—and suppose you were possessed by one of those? But just try explaining something like that to James.

He sighed and Mr. Wilson smiled sympathetically. The undergraduates wouldn't be back for weeks and weeks, and Mr. Wilson could afford to be benign. Perhaps, who could tell, the Sturdleyites would find another pub to fester in next term? Or learn miraculously to behave themselves? No cause was ever lost, even up here. Mr. Wilson would restore his tissues during the Easter vacation, and the fight for Decency would go on.

19. Back to Sleep

THE insistent drizzle made everything seem much worse. Altogether, Mr. Smythe couldn't remember a worse winter-spring than this one.

Of course, Godfrey Hook had been one of his failures for some time, but not a shameful one. Four years ago, one had promised the Reverend Hook (also Bishop Wagstaff) that one would keep an eye on the boy : but after all, there were limits. If Godfrey chose wilfully to fall in with bad company, it was really more a reflection upon the Reverend Hook (and upon Bishop Wagstaff) than upon himself. There was no excuse for not realizing—especially in these days, with all the new knowledge—that the early years came first, so to speak.

He had warned Godfrey quite explicitly about people like Chote—people who just seemed to go hopelessly wrong from the start; pathetic, really, but none the less insidious. 'Pity them by all means,' he had told Godfrey, who was staring blankly into his cocoa, 'but do not, I implore you, harbour the delusion that you can help them.' Help, if it came at all, came from above the battle.

Henceforth Godfrey was on his own, although Mr. Smythe continued to keep an anxious eye out, and send home baleful bulletins. One didn't want to upset the Reverend Hook, of course (such an unworldly man!) but facts must be faced. Godfrey was fishing in turbulent waters. If the Reverend Hook were too preoccupied, or worse still, too timid to take his own son in hand, well, there one was.

Thus the matter stood for three faintly regrettable years. Godfrey didn't seem to get so very much worse. He managed somehow to squeak through Schools—a feat that occasionally proves Mr. Smythe knew) beyond people like Godfrey, who combined laziness and nervousness with considerable ignorance and lack of facility. A failure, yes—Mr. Smythe accepted his share of the blame, perhaps overscrupulously : but surely not a disaster, not a disgrace.

And then, this *thing* had happened and here were the hurt letters from the Reverend Hook and His Grace : 'Nothing that you had told me had prepared me for anything like this.' Well, no : Mr. Smythe hadn't honestly been prepared himself. One had hoped that, with Chote gone at last, the lad might get on with his late maturing. But instead, Godfrey seemed to have become rather worse than before; when he wasn't playing cards in the Senior Library with his questionable cronies, he was out caterwauling underneath Mr. Smythe's window, or tottering bleerily in and out of the lodge, in and out.

And really, Alan Browning was almost as bad. He didn't get drunk, as far as Mr. Smythe could tell, and his manners were always very good; but in his quiet way, he still seemed to waste an awful lot of time. One couldn't be sure whether Chote's influence lingered—or whether, perhaps, one had oversimplified in laying *all* the mischief at Chote's door. Whatever it was, they had turned out to be rather an unfortunate trio, and he wouldn't be at all sorry to see the last of them.

It was while he was renewing his mild, urbane melancholy for Michaelmas that Godfrey suddenly decided to leave Sturdley. Oxford life being what it is, nobody was aware of his absence for several days. Alan Browning seemed to think he had gone home to Devon : 'I shouldn't be surprised if we hear wedding bells any day, sir.' But there was deep silence from Devon, too, and for the first time Mr. Smythe found himself good and rattled. Hook was overdue for a stint of practice teaching, and apologies would have to be made, but that wasn't the worst of it. One's modest failure had mushroomed into a professional disaster. This was no sudden aberration on Godfrey's part : the signs had been there all along—slack, silly eyes staring at one in the lodge night after night, brainless chatter under one's window, the gradual erosion of character. . . .

It wasn't really his fault, or his responsibility. But dash it all, he was supposed to be a pastor to these chaps, even if they didn't pay much attention to him, even if (and one had to face the thought sometimes) they thought he was a tiny bit ridiculous. One suddenly realized that one had been making excuses for rather too long about people like Godfrey, saying over and over that one had done one's bit. Well, he clearly hadn't done enough, and he certainly could have done more. One had to judge sometimes by results rather than by one's private (and sometimes very moderate) notions of duty. If all his little flock ran haywire, it didn't matter a damn (that's right, a damn) whether he had done his duty or not. Thus Mr. Smythe set to scourging himself that February.

And day after day it drizzled, deepening the slush of his misery. Nobody else seemed to care: the Warden remained imperturbable, and the other dons went absently on about their business. Well, he must do the caring for all of them. If the college was dead at heart, he was as much to blame for it as anybody.

And then, as if that wasn't enough, it came unmistakably to his attention that something had gone wrong with Alan Browning, too. A few days after Godfrey's disappearance—well perhaps before that (what did Mr. Smythe really know about these chaps?) Browning began to go on an unholy jag. For the first time since Mr. Smythe had known him, he appeared in the quad well and truly squiffed, swinging a hockey stick, as it happened, at the downstairs windows: a routine fine and damages followed, and then the very next night Alan wrenched a fire extinguisher down from one of the walls and began spraying it into the street that ran in front of the college.

There didn't seem to be anything funny in it: just witless violence. Mr. Smythe wrung his hands over and over, feeling more responsible than ever, and correspondingly more helpless. He went to see the Warden about it, but the Warden could offer no comfort. Yes, he knew what was going on. Yes, he had talked to Alan. There was nothing more to be done but wait: either Alan would come to his senses, or he would go too far. Reports were coming in from other parts of Oxford—

acts of stupid vandalism, piling up. It wouldn't be long now.

'But isn't there something we can do about the boy himself?' wailed Mr. Smythe.

'What would you suggest?' said the Warden, quite sharply. 'He isn't really a boy any more you know. It's a bit late in the day to try little homilies on him, don't you think?'

It was all so cold and thoughtless. Surely something more could be done? Alan wasn't really a bad chap. He had just gone wrong somewhere. Losing his friend like that had probably unhinged him temporarily: and hadn't Mr. Smythe heard that he was planning to get married? Perhaps he was having second thoughts about that, too. One had to understand the psychology of these young men. It was ridiculous to talk of giving up on somebody at the age of twenty-five or so. One should at least try reasoning with them—and not in little homilies either. He trusted he could rise above that!

Obviously, it was up to him to waylay Alan and try talking some sense to him. For several days, he hung about the lodge in and out of the spring drizzle, on one pretext and another. Again and again Alan came swaggering through, drunk and sober, but Mr. Smythe found to his dismay that he could never quite drum up the nerve to go over and speak to him. This was a terrible discovery indeed for a pastor to make and he made up his mind grimly not to give in to such unprofessional weakness. All the same, his presence in the lodge was beginning to look increasingly peculiar: and he found himself feeling steadily more vulnerable rather than less so.

One evening toward the end of term, he managed to catch Alan's eye: but the eye he caught was so cold and empty that he was quite unmanned by it. Not that it was hostile exactly—it was too far away for that; but one hesitated somehow to bring it any closer. There was some quality there, too, that he didn't understand. Alan had turned away with what might easily have been contempt, only that contempt seemed so unreasonable in the circumstances, and Mr. Smythe slunk off, defeated once more.

It was shortly after that that the tremulously desired opportunity came. He was floating drizzle-washed in his cloud of private gloom past the Junior Common Room late one evening when he heard an ungodly rumpus going on inside. He went over to the window and stood on tiptoe : two men were rolling on the floor in a wild tangle of furniture—just like a Western bar-room, thought Mr. Smythe mechanically, not pausing to check his reference. They were fighting clumsily with their coats on, hacking and chopping and wheezing.

Very regrettable, thought Mr. Smythe, but quite outside one's jurisdiction of course. The J.C.R. belonged incontestably to the undergraduates. He flinched a couple of times with wistful compassion, and was about to turn away, when one of the two men jumped abruptly to his feet and picked up a chair, which he began to wave with tipsy menace. Mr. Smythe could tell right away that it was Alan Browning, if only from the attractive smile. The other chap (could it be the lout Gadsby?) was on his feet, too, edging sideways into a pile of furniture, talking as he went. Browning stood there smiling seductively and wiggling his chair foolishly.

Mr. Smythe was transfixed by the unseasonal violence. He watched Gadsby go tipping over against the furniture, and up again with a frantic jerk. Browning stamped his foot threateningly and began to laugh. Oh dear, oh dear, said Mr. Smythe to himself. He hadn't seen a fight for years, not since refereeing the fourth form championships at Womley—how many years ago was that? And anyway those were quite different, quite different. Why these two could cripple each other if they went on, concussions, fractures. . . .

That was it, then. Of course, one had to act : there was no gentlemanly alternative. He abandoned his perch at the window and went scampering round to the door. Were dons ever allowed to go in? Of course, of course. Special circumstances. He shut his eyes and turned the handle bravely.

'Good evening, gentlemen,' he said in a low, slightly quavering voice. What on earth did one say next? The two combatants stood gaping at him for a second or two, and then Gadsby uncoiled and took a leisurely step forward.

'Watch out!' shouted Browning, and the other two jumped

obediently. 'Ha, ha. Sorry, Mr. Smythe. Didn't mean to frighten you.'

'Have you gone quite mad?' Mr. Smythe's voice went shivering uncontrollably up the scale. 'Put down that chair immediately!' he bleated. 'Immediately.'

Browning lowered it gently. 'I was just trying to frighten this frightful chap,' he explained. 'Put the fear of God into him, you might say.'

'Alan,' said Mr. Smythe more firmly. 'You've been drinking this evening.'

'I have? Good Lord!'

'In fact, you've been drinking rather a lot lately, haven't you? Rather more than is good for you, I would say, a great deal more. Now I—what are you smiling about?'

'Nothing sir. Just good nature.'

Mr. Smythe frowned : he didn't want to be sidetracked into a wrangle about impertinence. That was always a hopeless start to a pastoral chat. He was also becoming uncomfortably aware of the lout Gadsby, who was standing by, lumpishly attentive. He wished the fellow wouldn't 'hang about' like that : but then on the other hand one didn't really want him to go away either.

'Look here, what I'm trying to say is simply this : that while one fully understands and indeed sympathizes with a measure of high spirits at your age—a need to let off steam, so to speak —there does come a point when these very high spirits that one welcomes so much can turn on their owner and fairly rend him. Now I realize that moderation and temperance can seem like the dullest of virtues to a lively young man—but surely there is something to be said for conserving one's steam : the mens sana and, er, so on.' Little homilies, oh dear, oh dear. 'There is nothing unmanly about temperance—quite the contrary, in fact. It takes the greatest—' He noticed out of the corner of his eye that Gadsby was looking at him sympathetically, cheering him on. Oh, this was dreadful! 'Well, that's about all I have to say. But remember if anything is worrying you, please don't hesitate to, er, come to me. That's what I'm here for, you know.'

'Thank you very much, sir,' said Alan. The words went in like needles.

Mr. Smythe hesitated to give up completely. 'I know that I may seem like rather an unlikely person to come to for advice on contemporary problems. Well, I don't set myself up as an expert, of course. But it sometimes helps to get a second opinion, you know, an older person . . . and, after all, I have had some experience.' Oh God, what was he saying. These people didn't want his help. It was an absurd presumption for an Oxford chaplain to make, butting in where he wasn't wanted, pestering undergraduates with old-fashioned advice—advice they could have taken at school, if they'd wanted it : heaven knows they'd heard enough of it there. He had nothing to add.

'Well, goodnight all.' They were waiting silently for him to go. 'I implore you to lay aside the tools of violence.' He smiled thinly and wagged his finger. 'Those who take the sword must perish by the sword, you know.'

Mr. Smythe turned and walked away, almost tripping over the furniture. He hadn't quite fumbled the door shut when he heard the obscenity. It was Browning's voice, quite loud and clear, using that dreadful, ugly word. . . . Mr. Smythe's face went white and his hands began to tremble in earnest. But that was a detail.

'Oh dear, oh dear, oh dear,' he groaned.

Half an hour or so later he saw Browning and Gadsby going out together through the lodge, laughing and joking like old friends. Mr. Smythe tugged at his little curtain and went to bed sorrowing in the dark.

Mr. Smythe never told the Warden or anyone else about that shameful encounter. But a week or so later, Alan Browning was sent down all the same. He had uprooted one signpost too many. One of Oxford's finest found him straggling back toward Sturdley with a mammoth No PARKING plaque under his arm. 'Officer, I want to report a lost signpost,' he said bravely (drawing on his wide reading), but the game was up, of course. The Warden did what had to be done quietly and without fuss.

Mr. Smythe hadn't the heart to discuss the affair any further. The spring vacation was only a few days away, and he kept his own counsel till then. As soon as he reasonably could, he set off for Wales, where he hoped to find comfort among the lonely hills. He had often taken groups of boys over those very tracks, and come home altogether toned up. It would be a spiritual retreat sorely needed.

He booked into a country hotel, homely and charming, and day after day he set his pale face against the wet and trudged doggedly up into the hills. At night he came back to his hotel, drenched to the skin and weary to the bone. But comfort did not await to reward his exertions. The stark surroundings, together with the rain pounding incessantly on his little felt hat, reminded him powerfully of his personal insignificance: but he found this less consoling than usual. 'One likes to get things into proportion,' he used to explain to the boys as they gazed around the impersonal wilderness and the blank grey sky, 'see the ego for what it is.' But this time, he seemed altogether too insignificant. Several times, when he was by himself, he spoke out loud: but it was a squeaky voice against the wind, and the force that makes for righteousness seemed a long way away. Meanwhile, the God of the Hebrews lurked just above the clouds, and pelted him angrily for his sins.

He caught cold, and had to lie in bed and listen to the soggy patter of the rain, and watch the whip and splash against his windows. He sat shivering on his pillow to sniff at his nose drops and make resolutions about improving his ministry—but how, if the chaps were only going to laugh at him? He crept back under the covers. It wasn't really a ministry at all: just a set of private exercises.

He had brought a book with him, a hearty one by a colleague in the East End of London: mix with the lads at the pub was his advice, talk their language, open new vistas for them—Mr. Smythe winced to a halt. What good would it do if he tried these tactics at Sturdley? He would only open new vistas of embarrassment. He could just imagine the chaps leaving the dartboard and crowding round with their troubles! The picture of the author munching his pipe serenely on the back flap told the story. 'Mr. Forbes—or "Alex", as he is known at the Boar's Head and other places—used to be a distinguished rugby forward, before he received his calling. . . .' Usually one smirked a little at that kind of thing. But Mr. Smythe, peeping gloomily at the dry white skin between his pyjama buttons couldn't help wondering which was really the pathetic one : 'Alex' Forbes, rolling up his sleeves to do the Lord's work, or himself (good old 'Monty' Smythe no doubt) with his fussy tutorials in early English literature, and his reserve of public school homilies for those in need. . . . Anyway, Forbes was the coming thing. They would soon have one at Sturdley—standing shoulder to shoulder with the Warden, facing the future.

With mucous rolling up like thunder clouds, Mr. Smythe lay in grim inquisition, searching his soul frantically for clues. He couldn't do it the Forbes way, and, truth to tell, he didn't want to do it the Forbes way. And what was the use of grovelling in his own insignificance, if he was too proud to change his ways? He buried his head in his inhaler and sucked up the fumes : his meditations were endless and fruitless.

After a week he was on his feet again more or less, but in no mood to renew his search for peace in the wilderness. All those hours spent communing with a stuffed head had soured the taste for solitude, and in his still-shrunken condition, the Welsh wastes looked positively alarming—what could be seen of them through the smoky windows of the hotel lobby. 'Happy to see you restored to health, Reverend,' said the manager.

He packed his little suitcase with a view to creeping back to Oxford, to his books especially, and his little group of friends. He dreaded the opening of the new term. The undergraduates would seem bigger than ever this time : bigger and coarser and louder. He wouldn't be able to do anything with them, of course : no, obviously not. If they wanted a distinguished rugger player, they should have thought of it sooner. On the other hand, if they wanted a sound scholar, who really knew his Beowulf. . . . He sneezed miserably into his suitcase. Four weeks or less and they'd be back, big, noisy, sarcastic, crude : his parishioners. His little flock of souls.

The very first day he got back to Sturdley he ran distractedly into the Warden who said, 'You're looking very fit, Mr. Smythe. Come and have a cup of tea and tell me all about Wales.' The Warden stayed at Sturdley all through the vacations, following out his own eccentric rhythms. Now he was bounding up the stairs of his annexe ahead of Mr. Smythe, hearty as any big undergraduate.

'I've just been talking to an old friend of yours,' he said as he helped to settle Mr. Smythe into the big leather armchair by the fireplace. 'John Chote back from America and looking remarkably fit, I thought.'

'What?' said Mr. Smythe sharply. 'You don't mean it?'

'Yes, he's chucked his scholarship.'

'Good heavens.' Mr. Smythe's chin sagged against his stiff collar. 'Oh dear, oh dear.'

'Yes, a blow, I grant you. Although I daresay Sturdley will survive it.'

'Sturdley?' said Mr. Smythe. 'I wasn't thinking about Sturdley. It's, I don't know, all these young men. . . .' He gestured feebly.

'Well, I'm sure John Chote will survive too, if that's what you mean. Uncanny survival value that chap, I would say.'

'Browning, Hook, Chote,' chanted Mr. Smythe in a tremulous dirge. 'Who will be next?'

'I think that'll be about all,' said the Warden sunnily. 'They were quite a company, weren't they? I take the blame for Chote of course. I can't remember how the other two got in.'

Mr. Smythe looked at his boots for very shame. Four years ago or was it more, yes more, six, he had played a decisive part in helping the college to pick Browning and Hook out of an amorphous sea of aspiring adolescents: Hook on background, Browning on character. The Warden had, as he said, insisted on Chote. 'Yes, my fault entirely,' he repeated. 'I thought it would be nice to have a good cricketer just to balance things. And then, of course, the wretched chap had to go and abandon his cricket entirely. You have every right to say "I told you so".'

Mr. Smythe shook his head mutely. He couldn't possibly say such a thing.

'On the other hand,' the Warden went on brightly, 'apart from the stark tragedy of the cricket, I always felt that Chote was rather good value.' That intolerable holiday-camp phrase of his.

Smythe leaned forward and began to crush his anxious hands between his knees. 'Oh dear, oh dear,' he said. 'One feels so helpless.'

The Warden raised an eyebrow: this seemed to be, in some respects, a new Mr. Smythe. 'I wouldn't take it too much to heart if I were you,' he said kindly. 'Chote really behaved quite reasonably in the circumstances. His father died a few weeks ago, as you probably know, and Chote had to come home anyway. He expressed every willingness to go back and carry on with "the harlequinade" as he described it; but there really didn't seem to be much point.'

'But weren't the Americans frightfully upset?'

'Well, I made a few inquiries, and to tell you the truth, there seemed to be some vagueness among them as to who Chote actually was—and quite impenetrable darkness concerning what he was supposed to be doing. However, with the sportingness one associates with the top nations, they very generously offered to fly him back and do what they could with him.'

'And Chote refused.'

'No, not exactly. Although, yes, I suppose he did, really. We had quite a long chat about things, and he told me what he had been doing over there, and I must say, it did seem rather futile to go on with it. His attitude was that it verged on the dastardly to go on taking money from the nice Americans— rather a novel point of view, I thought. Though not, perhaps, one that ought to be encouraged among our young men.' The Warden splashed some more tea into his guest's cup.

Mr. Smythe smiled weakly at the pleasantry. 'I suppose it could have been a good deal worse.'

'Yes, Chote was quite tidy about the whole thing, told them that he had to stay here and settle his father's estate, but that he would never forget, and so on. Still, I can't help feeling a twinge of self-reproach,' he said, puffing complacently at his

363

pipe. 'Just the merest twinge. I had always assumed that Chote was quite infinitely adaptable, and yet, according to his account of it, he was out of his depth from the word "go". He didn't understand them, they didn't understand him, nobody understood anything.'

Mr. Smythe realized dimly that the Warden was being more than generous in offering himself as a sacrificial victim; but he wasn't up to taking advantage of it. He continued squeezing his hands disconsolately between his bony knees, hoping that things would get better.

'I don't know whether chaps like Chote simply aren't meant for export,' said the Warden—'although, good Lord, look at Wiggs, practically running for the presidency by now, so I believe. Or whether Chote isn't quite as adaptable as we had all supposed. I had assumed that Chote was the absolute wave of the future—and here he goes reacting like an eminent Victorian on his first trip to the colonies.'

Mr. Smythe was far away. His concentration had been quite dreadful lately, and the Warden was the most soporific of orators. . . . 'May have to give up the scholarships altogether' . . . one must try to catch some of it . . . 'Perhaps Norbert Jones would have been a safer choice, eh?' The Warden stopped talking and looked curiously at Mr. Smythe.

The Chaplain strove to collect his thoughts. 'The one that I really feel sorry about is Alan Browning,' he said somewhat inconsecutively.

'Oh, why?' asked the Warden with interest. 'Undistinguished sort of scoundrel I thought, thoroughly routine.'

'I suppose so,' said Mr. Smythe humbly. 'I was rather dense about all that.' 'There, there,' said the Warden's eyebrows. 'All the same,' continued Mr. Smythe, 'he became so excessively vile in the last week or so, didn't he?'

'I can't say that I noticed any particular change. As far as I could see, he had decided to leave Oxford anyway, for his own very good reasons, and he thought that it might be a good idea to have a bit of fun before he left. He was very pleasant about it, I thought, paying his fines and so on with quite remarkable gusto. I found myself almost liking the fellow towards the end.'

'That wasn't my experience at all,' said Mr. Smythe sharply. 'I found him quite vile.'

The Warden looked genuinely concerned. 'What? Did something happen?'

'No, er, no, I don't imagine so. No.' It was too embarrassing. 'I just found him rather more unsavoury than before.'

The Warden nodded thoughtfully, which made Mr. Smythe fidget—he must have said too much.

'Of course it's necessary for us to put a premium on formal good behaviour,' said the Warden, relapsing into geniality. ' "Je suis royaliste, c'est mon métier" and all that. All the same, I thought there was something rather splendid about Browning's last fortnight at Oxford. How many of our undergraduates have the vitality, or even the character, to stage a one-man performance like that? Why at one point I was tempted to rush out and offer him the American scholarship on the spot. I exaggerate, of course,' he added, trying to suit his words a little better to Mr. Smythe's unearthly pallor, 'but when I see some of these mealy little fellows who seem to find their way to Sturdley so unerringly. . . .'

The old distaste ventured a brief comeback. The Warden was to blame for the whole thing. A man like that should never have been put in charge of an Oxford college in the first place. All sorts of peculiar appointments had been made during the post-war confusion, but really, this one was inexcusable. Why, the man didn't even know about boys and their vileness . . . his distaste crumpled. What did he, Mr. Smythe, know about such things?

'However, I wouldn't quite compare Browning with Chote,' said the Warden, unaware of Mr. Smythe's hectic reversals. 'I daresay Browning would have had a better time in America— well, imagination reels, doesn't it?—but I'm afraid he was never quite as, let us say, trustworthy as Chote. Not that either of them is exactly a Christian gentleman, as we used to under- stand—and officially exploit—the term : but at least Chote made some quite conscientious efforts to clean up after him. Clumsy but not altogether contemptible efforts. As for Brown- ing. . . .' He shrugged good-naturedly. 'By the way, you'd

365

never guess what Chote suggested to me this afternoon. He said he'd like nothing better than to come back to Sturdley next year and read for a diploma in education.' He shook his head happily. 'Chote can really be a most amusing chap, when he sets his mind to it.'

'You're not going to let him?' A strangled sob.

'Oh, good Lord no. But I thought it was a decidedly droll proposal.'

It was time for Mr. Smythe to beat a retreat. He never could make head or tail of the Warden: what on earth did he find so amusing about Chote's demented proposal? After the Hook-Browning fiascos, Mr. Smythe could see precious little humour in that sort of jest: therefore he was all the more horrified to realize that he was smiling conspiratorially at the Warden.

Yes, definitely time to go. He stood up and began to back-track distractedly. 'More tea, Mr. Smythe, are you quite sure?' Mr. Smythe shook his head, and then, to the Warden's surprise, turned briskly and marched out.

The Chaplain stood at the door of the Warden's house. It had begun to rain again, and he thought nervously of his bare head and his late sniffles. His own rooms must be at least fifty yards away. Perhaps he should borrow one of the Warden's umbrellas. No, better not—only fifty yards, after all. He girded himself to make a run for it.

Down the path he sped, at a very respectable trot, into Park-minister's triangle and out again, whizzing through the main quad like a bat out of hell—home and dry. Quite invigorating, a run in the rain. A massive figure seemed to be sheltering itself just inside the entrance to the staircase. Mr. Smythe braked sharply and approached with caution, allowing the drizzle to catch up with him and do its dreary work. Yes, the undergraduates were getting bigger, or at any rate, broader.

'Good afternoon, sir.' Mr. Smythe squinted suspiciously. His glasses were still high and dry in his breast pocket, but it sounded very much like the abominable Chote.

He was about to push through with his gruff 'Afternoon, Chote.' It was all and more than the chap deserved after his dreadful behaviour in the last few months. And yet—one had to start somewhere. He paused in the rain, and gave a diffident smile : it was the least a pastor could do. 'Good afternoon, Mr. Chote. Back from America, I see.'

'Yes, sir. I was just up in your room looking for you.'

'Well—come up, come up.' Mr. Smythe bustled nervously ahead. 'I was out,' he explained. 'And as you observe, I got a thorough wetting.'

He fussed about the room drying himself and looking for the sherry decanter, and wondering what to say to this impossible chap. It was hard enough conversing with the sheep in one's flock without tackling the goats as well. Look at what happened with Alan Browning—no, he wouldn't be able to say a word if he thought of that. 'Did you have a good time in America?' he said from deep in the cupboard, where he had taken sanctuary and was slowly changing his coat.

'Yes and no,' said Chote. 'I found it a trifle overwhelming, I'm afraid.'

'Ah yes. I suppose so.' Mr. Smythe came reluctantly out of the cupboard. He had an unpleasant feeling that Chote was waiting for him to settle down.

He poured two small glasses of sherry and sat down opposite Chote in his number two armchair. 'Well,' he said, as if with deep contentment. 'Here we are.' Chote was supposed to be no end of a humorist : perhaps he would go on from there.

'To tell you the truth,' said Chote unexpectedly, 'I made rather a hash of things in America.'

'Ah, well,' said Mr. Smythe deprecatingly.

'I wasted a lot of time—well, there's nothing very new about that, I suppose. Still, *you* know,' Chote said vaguely.

'Oh, yes?' said Mr. Smythe.

'Hard to explain, really. Do you mind if I waffle a bit?'

'Not at all, not at all,' said Mr. Smythe warmly. This was something like the stuff. He almost said, 'That's what we're here for, you know,' but restrained himself. Still, it *was* a capital start for the new Mr. Smythe.

'I hope this isn't too embarrassing,'' said Chote. 'Stop me if it is. The truth is that after my father died, I wanted to talk to somebody, you know, in a general sort of way. And I'm afraid you're the one.'

'I'm delighted,' said Mr. Smythe rather inanely. 'But isn't your mother still living?'

'Yes,' said Chote shortly. 'She is. Anyhow, as I was saying, I felt worse than usual about wasting time when I was in America. Nothing specific, mind you, just a feeling of rattling about in a vacuum. I suppose that sounds a bit silly?'

'Not at all,' said Mr. Smythe, who was beginning to grope a little wildly. Was this what the young men were talking about these days?

'Previously, up here for instance, when I wasted time, I felt I was wasting it shrewdly and to some purpose. But in America, I don't know, it was different, if you see what I mean.'

'Of course. Yes. I *do* see what you mean.' The young people were so incoherent these days—at least when they spoke to him.

'Well, I know only too well that I wasn't brought up to waste time, quite the contrary in fact—I say, this does sound rather too soft to be true.' Mr. Smythe shook his head unconvincingly. 'The point I'm trying to make is that my father worked very hard all his life and expected me to do the same and I—you know,' he said very quickly.

'Ah, yes.' This was something Mr. Smythe could understand: in fact, he had operated on much the same principle himself. The elder Mr. Smythe had also had his expectations. And one trusted, or rather one hoped, that one. . . .

'So when I found that I wasn't getting anywhere in America, I decided to come home and go to work.'

'Quite,' Mr. Smythe heard himself saying.

'I would have enjoyed myself much more over there if I hadn't been so infernally queasy. But there it is: one is what one is. When I heard of my father's death, it was like a bell sounding. Godfrey Hook will probably discover the same sort of thing eventually. We were really very much alike, you know.'

'Do you really think so? You surprise me more than I can say.'

'Yes, of course. Consciences made in eighteen-ninety. I

seldom envy anybody, but I honestly envy Alan Browning *his* conscience. It was a superb instrument.'

'I don't know,' said Mr. Smythe. 'He didn't seem at all happy just before he left.'

Chote waved his empty sherry glass. 'A temporary indisposition, no doubt. Something had gone wrong with his plans—could happen to anybody. But on the whole, Alan was an extraordinarily happy man, quite the happiest I have ever met, I think. How the wicked do insist on prospering, don't they?'

'I never understood him at all,' said Mr. Smythe sadly.

'Who did?' said Chote. 'When you get a bloke as simple as that, all of a piece, so to say—'

'I thought he was rather two-faced,' interrupted Mr. Smythe, with just the hint of prime indignation that the word deserved.

'No, Alan really was an awfully nice chap in his way. I mean, he was nice to everybody—nice to you, of course, and nice to poor Godfrey, nice to, er, all sorts of people. Why, if unfailing kindness and simplicity mean anything at all, he was one of the best characters at Sturdley. Certainly, much better than Godfrey and me.' Mr. Smythe looked dismayed. Not only was he alarmed at the sentiment, but he had never felt entirely happy about the disjunctive pronoun in English.

There was a pause, and Mr. Smythe felt that he'd better ask his question now. 'Tell me, John,' he said casually, flicking at his clean grey lapel, 'would you say that Alan was, say, typical? I mean, are there many young men like him? One tries so hard to get the, er, wavelength.'

Chote didn't respond right away. Is he going to try to please me? Mr. Smythe wondered anxiously. Tell me something soothing? My word, what a lot of dishonesty a parson had to listen to. 'I honestly don't know,' said Chote at last. 'It's a puzzle, isn't it?'

'Yes, I suppose it is,' said Mr. Smythe with a sigh.

'But to get back to my own case,' said Chote, gesturing with his empty sherry glass '—why that's very kind of you sir. I'd love a little more—as I was saying, I felt guilty about wasting, er, time, and so on. And so many people seemed to think I was a fraud of some kind, and to tell you the truth, I was even having nightmares about it—dreaming that I didn't know what I was, or where I was; or sometimes even worse, dreaming that I *did* know.' He looked at Mr. Smythe, who was nodding his head rhythmically, 'Yes, yes, yes, I understand.' 'Well, never mind about that,' said Chote quickly. 'The long and short of it is that I have decided to take your advice.'

'Ah, yes,' said Mr. Smythe vaguely. What advice? He remembered saying something to Chote at the last Summer Ball, but couldn't think what it was—for some days after, he remembered hoping that it hadn't been anything too ridiculous. Well, he was very glad that whatever it was had proved helpful after all.

'That's about it,' said Chote shortly. 'Thank you very much for listening to my nonsense, sir.' He finished his sherry and stood up.

'I'm afraid I wasn't much use,' apologized Mr. Smythe, rising slowly. He really hadn't been, either, he was glumly convinced of it. He had missed a sterling opportunity. If only he'd begun to understand what the fellow was talking about!

'Oh, yes, you were,' said Chote. 'Most useful. You know, I've always felt that one could come and talk to you, and that you would understand perfectly.'

Mr. Smythe gave a little start. 'That's most gratifying,' he said. 'Of course I've always felt that one should "know the men", but it's so difficult to know some of them these days.' He shook Chote's hand gratefully.

'I think you've done remarkably well,' said Chote, 'if you don't mind my saying so, sir. I don't suppose any chaplain in the University is more liked and respected.'

'That's really most encouraging,' said Mr. Smythe. 'One does so much of one's work in the dark, you know . . . it's a real pleasure to hear a word of assurance now and then.'

He followed Chote to the head of the stairs. 'Good luck, John. And do let me know how you get on.' He tweaked the lad's shoulder in a rare gesture.

The sun had broken through miraculously. He looked out of his window at the clouds scudding away, and he could almost have cried for joy. The winter was over and gone, at long last. The rains were gone too (for the time being at least); and Mr. Smythe was no longer being pelted for his sins.

He cleared away the sherry glasses carefully and rearranged the chairs. And then he went down on his knees and said his, somewhat self-conscious, thanks.

20. Shaving Off the Moustache

AFTER buttering up the Chaplain—no, that was putting it rather too cruelly—and coming to terms with the Warden, there was nothing more to be done at Oxford. The authorities of childhood were squared away—education and organized religion too (although poor Smythe could hardly be called organized, perhaps).

If, by any chance, one had hoped for a little bit more—well, clearly there was nothing to be gained by embarrassing Mr. Smythe. Floundering as he was in the dead-air space between the old theology and the new, the Chaplain was in no shape to deliver messages to anybody : and as for consolation, it took only a few nervous minutes in the Chaplain's company to know who was most in need of *that*.

Still, the old boy had made a jolly praiseworthy stab at being helpful; and it was nice to have made one's peace with him. Those fellows in black have great power, as Schwartz used to say; and once they put a finger on one, phhht ! Once again, that hardly applied to Mr. Smythe, underplaying everything in his non-sectarian grey suit—one couldn't imagine him calling down the elements, not so much as a sun shower. But he was a *good* man, and an innocent one, and therefore somehow the most depressing enemy yet. And one was getting more than a little tired of making enemies (one didn't know exactly how, but there they were, all right). Years ago, one hadn't minded having enemies, but now. . . .

He got as far as the lodge and turned around for a last look. The ugly little quad was making a frankly sentimental appeal : pointing archly, by way of its tufts and blotches of creeper, up to the unfortunate neo-Gothic accessories and down again to the grass that had never come in right. Small, undistinguished sort of place, fit only for the humble work of polishing up its quota of rural deans and minor officials : the kind of place where a second-rate man of God like Mr. Smythe could tilt with a second-rate bounder like Alan Browning—virtue and vice having it out on a terribly small scale. Browning would probably send his son here one day. His accidental son. Well, perhaps not : but little Brownings would appear from somewhere and little Hooks and Chotes—it was a matter of architecture more than anything else. 'The Sturdley type', sprouting like fungus in the old stone, year after year.

If he took so much as one step out of the lodge, he was as good as lost. Industrial England lapped right up against the walls these days : a false move, and he was up to his knees in soap, weighing machines, insurance, and what the Americans called the 'intangibles'. Looking back under the arch, one captured in a small frame the moth-eaten enchantment of Sturdley : within its asymmetrical girdle, it kept out the rising waters. That was enough to make it a paradise of sorts.

And here came the fairy godmother himself, striding across the quad in artful disguise : khaki shorts this time and his best straw hat. The Warden had spotted the sky clearing and was off at once to take his exercise : 'Good afternoon, Mr. Chote. Having a last look round at the home of one's youth ?'

'That sort of thing, yes sir.'

'Have a good look while you can,' said the Warden jovially. 'Quite a lot of it should be coming down this summer. We're putting up a new building in the Tapwater quad, and new rooms there, there, and there.' He pointed around. The floppy hat was no disguise. This was a very sound businessman talking. The world of money had made its way into the little stone girdle, and was nibbling fast.

'Pity, in a way,' said Chote.

'Yes, in a way.' The Warden scratched himself apologetically.

There wasn't much to be said for the present buildings, of course. They were drab and impractical, and not even very old. And they had proved dismally inadequate to the post-war boom. It went without saying that people like Chote, Browning and Hook had to be housed somehow. All the same. . . .

'Have you any particular plans, Mr. Chote?' asked the Warden. 'Or have we talked about that already?'

'No sir, we haven't really. I was rather counting on the diploma in education as a matter of fact. Or, I know, what about a B.C.L? That would keep me out of mischief for another year at least.' One knew how to amuse the old Warden all right with his unfailing weakness for the outrageous.

The Warden shook his head. 'I doubt it,' he said. 'I'm afraid you've gone about as far as you're going to go academically, Mr. Chote. The time has come to take the plunge at last.' This with a kind of sepulchral relish.

'Yes, I suppose so. Don't feel a bit like it, though.' One had only to think of all the soap outside. 'I mean, it's all rather soul-destroying, isn't it?'

'It can be,' said the Warden. 'On the other hand, so can Oxford, can't it?' Ah-ha there, Mr. Chote.

One could never forget for long that the Warden was a tycoon: yes, of course, the joys of competition, the fun of making the wheels go round, the satisfaction of engaging one-self. The Warden would now proceed to run through the lot; touching upon the personal awards, the thrill of building a beefier Britain, the assorted enrichments, basic and fringe. This was the chap they should have sent to America—perhaps they already had.

'Do you feel that you got any benefit at all from our little American experiment?' the Warden asked suddenly. 'It's the sort of thing that can be immensely useful if handled with intelligence. I'm not referring to your scholastic performance, of course.'

'Well, no, I'm afraid, sir, nothing to speak of. I never really got to grips with anything over there. I mean, I still don't know very much about *America*. . . .'

'Did you meet anybody interesting?'

'Well, I saw rather a lot of Eugene Fosdick.' The Warden nodded whimsically. 'But then I could have done that over here, couldn't I? Then, after that, I met a priceless fellow named Schwartz—it doesn't sound like much, does it?'

Mr. McLavish smiled. 'Perhaps you'd have had better luck with Bradshaw Soames. Tell me, did you form any general impressions?'

'Only the usual ones—nothing you couldn't have picked up from Evelyn Waugh, Simone de Beauvoir, Geoffrey Gorer, and the rest of the crowd. The men work like dogs, the women are cold, despotic and svelte. . . .'

'Well you must have learned *something* for yourself.'

'Er, no, not really. I got my information about the women from a series of smashing articles, in the *Reader's Digest*, I think it was, about five years ago. I should never have noticed it on my own.'

Mr. Smythe was coming through the quad now, smiling shyly above a pair of long grey shorts; a heartening harbinger when Smythe got out his shorts. 'Thought I'd take a few pictures,' he said. 'Take advantage of the sun.' He padded softly past on his tennis shoes, beaming seraphically at both of them. With his right hand he was massaging the silver-lettered news about Godfrey and Felicity which someone had just slid —*R.S.V.P.*—under his door. Of course, of course.

'The thing actually is,' said Chote, watching Mr. Smythe disappear quietly through the oak door, 'about business I mean, is that I'm quite keen on being a success, and, yes, I'm quite willing to work for it, too. But it all seems sort of ruddy point-less at the same time, if you know what I mean. After all, who really wants to be a big man in soap? All the time, I was dreaming of something rather fruitier.'

'Yes, I *do* see the problem. But of course, if you really want to be a success, you will have to conquer a certain amount of squeamishness. Soap, for instance, is not altogether contemptible. . . .' His voice trailed off absently. He had nothing to add at present about the joys of competition, the cog in the wheel. . . .

'But it's the whole business,' said Chote, 'making contacts, watching beady-eyed for openings, clambering up the jolly old ladder. Those are the things I should have been doing in America, of course—but when it came to the point, I just couldn't bring myself to do it. Four years ago, I would have like a shot, but not now. So I mucked about with useless people like this chap Schwartz I was telling you about. . . .'

'Do you suppose Sturdley is responsible for this apathetic state of mind? I thought we gave our men bags of incentive.'

'I can only speak for myself,' said Chote, 'but for the past six months or so—and especially now that I've met a few rich people in the actual flesh, I have lost virtually all desire to get ahead, as such. I didn't much care for the company at the top, and I'm afraid it didn't much care for me. I would like to do some one good thing in life, really well—well, you know what I mean.' He was back in England now, and he must go easy on these solemn declarations of intention: it simply didn't sound right, amid the brisk, high patter of English conversation. One said what one had to say as quickly and prosaically as possible, keeping the poetry where it belonged. Forget that simple rule, and one could bore one's friends dreadfully within a matter of seconds.

'An admirable sentiment,' said the Warden smiling. 'Although I'm sure the government will give the fullest consideration to any scruples you may have about becoming rich. And of course, you never know,' he went on, looking around at his little kingdom, 'how things are going to turn out. After all, one might start out in soap and wind up in something, er, altogether different.' He looked Chote in the eye, and gave him a little nod. 'Well, I must be on my way while the weather holds.' He began to lumber towards the mouth of the lodge and Chote noticed for the first time that he had an enormous knapsack bulging against his back. Heaven only knew what the Warden did with himself when he got out into the country.

'Hail, Thane of Cawdor . . . hail, Warden of Sturdley.' The

old charlatan was dead right as usual. There must be considerably more to business than met the eye. It might lead one indefinitely onward and upward and outward (even in Britain); it might be the golden master key, in the right hands. And yet somehow, at the moment, one hadn't quite the stomach for it.

He hadn't been entirely honest with the Warden (perhaps one couldn't be : it wasn't what the Warden seemed to call for). Out of a fuzzy delicacy, he had failed altogether to mention the late Mr. Chote as an influence. And that was rather to leave out the whole point.

The news of his father's death had given a violent twist to the kaleidoscope. Chote felt that his head, which after all (he now realized) was just a shell-like dome with stars and moon painted on the ceiling, was being splintered open with a heavy spoon. Darkness came flooding in on all sides, obliterating the dear old ambitions, the 'success' which his father had believed in so fervently, because he hadn't known any better. Mr. Chote had never seen the outside of the egg. But now, with his ghost liberated from its small cares and rattling about in infinity, the difference in education was squared : they both *knew*.

Eventually the little artificial roof would have to be repaired and life resumed inside the egg (even the death of one's procreator—the great life-giver himself—might eventually be hammered down to ovoid scale). But John was relieved forever of his obligation to improve himself in a wordly way. He would become, what? an Anglican monk? a gatherer of leeches? Something tranquil and gnostic seemed most appetizing at the moment—now that he knew about all else being vanity, and so on.

The original plan had been to go home to England and wait for things to mend : a certain amount of tranquility, a few hours with his mother and a few more on his knees perhaps, would restore the classic proportions. The wound in the sky would heal over. And then, the pursuit of wisdom could begin in earnest.

When he had got home, his mother was already fussing about the funeral. 'Ah John,' she greeted him, ever so businesslike. 'I'm so glad you came home in time to practise with us. Now *you* will have to walk on the right. . . .' He tried to catch her eye right away, to reopen the primal understanding, but all he caught was a vague flurry, the wild, scattering gaze of the nervous hostess. Well, at least she hadn't broken down or anything.

'How was it, Mother?' he managed to interrupt at last.

She looked confused by the question. 'Oh, he went off just like that,' she said finally, 'the poor dear. It was really as nice as it could be.'

'Is it true that he had a cancer?' Surely that couldn't have been too nice?

'Well, yes, dear—but it wasn't a very painful one. I mean, it was all over so quickly. . .' and she was off again in a moment about the funeral arrangements, birdlike and almost jubilant, as if she was looking forward to a great occasion. John thought of putting an arm around her, but she seemed to be moving about too fast.

The funeral was quite a small affair after all. A couple of old friends from the office, and a sprinkling of neighbours. John's sister Sheila had gone to New Zealand with her husband a few months before. Mrs. Pringle from next door took care of the sobbing, and made such a business of it that the others, including Chote, rather lost the taste for it. But they all were properly grim and withdrawn—it seemed to John at several points as if they might be faking, but this must be unjust. Mrs. Chote was still on the move, making sure that everything was running smoothly. The vicar gave a little talk about the merits of the departed—it would have applied equally well (and badly) to any male member of the parish—and then they set off at a trot for the cemetery, where thousands of grey head-stones stood waiting patiently for Mr. Chote to be filed away. The rain squibbed against the dull wood of the coffin, and the vicar and his helpers tried to do the job as quickly (without actually hurrying) as possible before everybody got drenched. 'It was lovely,' bellowed Mrs. Pringle afterwards. 'I thought it went very well, didn't you?' said Mrs. Chote.

John went back to the church for a while after that and

sat in front of the bare altar. It was a low low-church designed to help the faithful to be alone with their God : and Chote felt very much alone there. It was almost a case of 'bring your own God', and Chote knew only too well how little he had to bring. One sat waiting for something to happen. The time was ripe for religion to start playing a significant part in his life.

He tried an act of love, which didn't ring true at all, at all (what, or who was he pretending to love, anyway?) and then the conversational approach, 'Look, whoever you are, I know I'm not much of a chap'—it lapsed fatally into parody. One couldn't do this sort of thing once every six months or so and hope to get into the swing of it. He went through the words of one of his old favourite hymns, slowly and trying to make some sense of them; but they only echoed around and around, brassily mocking. 'Piety Chote'. Browning had hit the button : it was contemptible to go to church only when one was in trouble, or sorry for oneself. Contemptible and useless. One only lost one's scrap of faith.

He stumbled out again into the richer air outside. (God was everywhere, except in that church.) He would try again sometime when things were going better—though he still wouldn't know what to say.

He had one more whack at his mother that night. She was sitting in her favourite sunken armchair by the fire, looking a bit calmer, and it seemed like a good moment to ask her about her plans.

'I suppose I shall stay on in this house,' she said quite brightly. 'We have so many friends here now.'

'How about, er, money and so on?'

'Oh, don't worry about that, Johnny. Your father left me all I need.' He glanced up hopefully : but there was no sign of recognition. 'He even left enough to help you with your career.'

'Yes, about that career.' He took a deep breath. 'I've had some second thoughts about that, you know. As long as Father was alive, it seemed like something pretty important. I mean, he'd spent so much getting me ready—so much of himself and everything—that the least I could do was play along. . . .' That was what it was, playing, the gorgeous game of getting ahead. One did it to amuse one's parents. There had never been any other reason, as far as one could see now.

Mrs. Chote showed no flicker of interest. 'Oh, I think you ought to think about your career, don't you? It would be such a pity, now that you've made a good start.' John stared at her, horrified. 'Mother, for the love of God'—he almost shouted. She looked up and saw that he was disturbed. 'Don't worry, dear. I know that you're *going* to do well, whatever you decide to take up. . . .' She smiled tender encouragement. 'I'm quite sure of it.'

He had set out for Oxford the next day, hoping to find something there. But all he found was poor Mr. Smythe, in his own obscure distress. Perhaps Chote's mission in life was really to help other people. He smiled wryly. Or he could always try his old landlady, Mrs. Worsley. She would have some folk wisdom for him : his own attempts to widen his understanding had bogged down pretty badly.

'Good Lord, it's Chote!' The perennial Gadsby had crept up stealthily behind him. 'Gaping around like a ruddy tourist. That's the Fosberry Room up there, in case you'd forgotten.'

'That'll do now,' said Chote. 'And what are *you* doing here, you frightful chap? I thought you went down years ago.'

'You know, chemists, world of our own,' said Gadsby yawning. 'I'm afraid your muckers have fled, though—in a blaze of glory, fertilizer and bright yellow daisies, but nonetheless fled.'

'Yes I heard about that,' said Chote. 'I don't suppose you happen to know what's become of them, by any chance?'

'Oddly enough, I do—Browning that is. Nobody knows what happened to the Parson : I doubt if we'll ever hear from him again. I ran into Alan down at Brighton of all places, just a week or so ago. It was one of those glum encounters— the wretched chap couldn't even afford to come drinking. . . .'

'Did he say what he was doing now?'

'Yes, and that was the gloomiest part of all. The bloody man has apparently been reduced to selling chocolate biscuits for a living. Yes, in Brighton. God, it's depressing, isn't it?'

'I suppose so. Oh, by the way, do you know if he ever got round to marrying Daffers?' Chote asked casually.

'Oh, indeed he did, oh yes, rather.' One had forgotten how Gadsby enjoyed his bit of talking. 'Extraordinary business, wasn't it? I mean, preggers or no, I'm quite sure he could have wriggled out of it if he'd wanted to—a man of his resources—'

'Did you ever ask him why he didn't?'

'Oh, frequently. But he was too far gone during most of his engagement to make the remotest kind of sense. He rambled on, you know, at length about what a splendid performer she was—any truth in that, by the way?'

'No,' said Chote mechanically, 'none at all.'

'Well, then, I give it all up,' said Gadsby. 'I thought of bringing the subject up again when I saw him in Brighton, but it didn't seem quite the thing to do.' Gadsby looked at Chote questioningly: Ralph wasn't too sure about these points of etiquette. 'I don't know, perhaps you'll think I was being too scrupulous. But the whole thing seemed *so* dismal—and it was too late to do anything about it, anyway.'

They started on another turn round the quad. 'Most amazing,' said Gadsby, 'that last little bit of Browning. I suppose you heard about it. Rather put one in mind of the glorious hundred days, or whatever it was. But it was quite different when I saw him again in Brighton. He seemed very subdued—well, one hates to say it—almost respectable, if you know what I mean. Of course, I'm sure it's only a front: as soon as the chap makes a little lolly, he'll be himself again. But still, one finds it depressing, the way the very worst sods *will* insist on letting one down.'

'It must be dreadful for you,' said Chote.

Gadsby glanced at him craftily. 'Why,' he said, 'if it comes to that, Browning even told me that *you*—'

'Don't you believe it,' said Chote quickly. 'Alan was only jealous. I was an even more consistent sod than he was. Stronger constitution, and all that.'

'Well, I *am* glad to hear that,' said Gadsby, all sunny again. 'You're a dwindling band, you know. . . .' He was irresistibly willing to believe. What was surprising to Chote was how the words began to form now in his own mouth. One had surely outgrown all the old pretences, the childish need to impress : but here, under the slavering promptings of the perennial Gadsby (whom nobody had ever taken seriously), up came all the old foolishness. If one stayed at Sturdley for a hundred years one would still be lured into the droll fertilizer.

'Did you get up to any worthwhile mischief in America?' coaxed Gadsby. 'I hear the Yank women are incredibly cold and calculating.'

'Don't you believe it,' said Chote. 'Why, I could tell you stories—regular schoolboy classics,' and out came the first dribbles, seeping through from what muddy underground streams. Good God, what's the matter with me? thought Chote. Just so happy to be one of the 'chaps' once again. A few months before, he had tried talking like this, the old way, to Schwartz, and Schwartz had been pretty bored. Gadsby wasn't so demanding : he was happy just to hear the dear old words and situations, again and again, in simple arrangements. He seemed to get particular pleasure out of Chote's variations on Mrs. Fishman. . . .

'That'll do for today,' said Chote sharply.

Gadsby let out his breath. 'My word, you *must* have had a good time in America! Why'd you come back, old man?' His round face was aglow now with shared excitement; a symbolic chap with a muddy streak of chocolate running down from a corner of his mouth. A curious, rosebud mouth. Nobody ever looked very closely at Gadsby, he was just there. But Chote took a look at him now. He wasn't quite what one expected. He looked younger than one had remembered. How old was he? Twenty-five or so, and still swaddled in puppy-fat : eyes all a-twinkle in their pouches, from other people's experiences; mouth half open with perpetual self-induced astonishment. This was one of the 'chaps', heir to the Sturdley spirit. One of the people one had been trying to impress since the Army days. No, even longer than that. You could put the chap in a school blazer, and he might have been one of the 'Friends of Godfrey Hook' urging one on to the hackneyed public school brutalities.

Any kind of excitement was good enough for the Gadsbys of this world.

'No, I didn't as a matter of fact,' said Chote shortly. 'I've been making the whole blessed thing up, for your porcine amusement.'

'Ah, well,' said Gadsby philosophically. 'I was very much afraid of that. Nevertheless, it filled a few pleasant moments.'

They had reached the lodge again and stood outside it awkwardly with their hands in their pockets, looking down at the cobblestones. Gadsby was at it again.

'I suppose you've guessed *my* little secret,' he said in a matter-of-fact voice. 'Not that it's much of a secret. Anyway, I'll be very glad to get away from Oxford.'

It wasn't like Gadsby to be cryptic and Chote had guessed no secrets (perhaps he had missed part of the conversation). But he nodded wisely all the same. It might be amusing to try, in the years to come, to guess the clod-Gadsby's little secret. Or then again, perhaps it might not. One was losing interest in Gadsby at a fearful rate, which was somehow heartening.

'Oh, by the way,' said Gadsby. 'There's a letter in your box. It's been there for days and days.' For once Chote hadn't bothered to look: after all, he didn't belong here any more. 'Sam isn't very good at forwarding mail,' Gadsby rambled. 'He never remembers who's gone down and who hasn't. So I help him by snooping in the boxes.' He ran ahead and brought back the letter. 'It looks rather American, and it smells simply delightful. So everything you said just now is true, true.' He clasped his hands ecstatically. 'It's all *true.*'

It did smell nice, at that. The handwriting was pleasantly familiar—Mirabelle Fosdick, well, fancy that. So—another letter to bugger his life about with. He knew, just by looking at it, that it would do all of that. He stuffed it into his pocket, and said goodbye quickly to Gadsby. 'Look me up, I'm in the book.' 'I wouldn't dream of it, old boy.' He oscillated the pudgy hand. 'Your secret is safe with me.' Gadsby smiled mysteriously. Who cared about the bloody man's secret? 'Can't get over Browning, though,' said Gadsby ruefully.

Chote turned once more back toward the quad, for a last

poignant glimpse, but Gadsby was already standing in the doorway, blocking out the view.

So that was what turned out to be his last view of Sturdley: Ralph Gadsby's red velvet waistcoat, and his pink perennial face, standing guard over the lost innocence. Chote headed for the station, for positively the last time.

It seemed as if all the same people were sitting in the compartment to London as last year—the same kind of people, anyway. Someone was frowning into a crossword puzzle: a pipe smoker, a baby smothered in grime, a chap doing his National Service—all the usual railway people.

Even the baby looked to him incredibly English, and John was not too surprised when it eventually said 'Mummy' in a clear Oxford voice. On second thoughts, it was rather a large baby—but that was neither here nor there.

It was amusing to sit and watch these people, looking so damned English. Even though the compartment was cold and uncomfortable after a soft winter, and the baby smelled depressing and so on—one felt pleasantly detached and vastly diverted.

Now what about that letter from Mirabelle? There was something extraordinarily nice to the touch about an unopened envelope. He ran his finger over the seal, without taking it out of his pocket. He would look at it in a moment. He was in no mood for trouble.

The chap doing the crossword had on a navy blue suit very much like Mr. Chote's old one. Now there was food for thought if you liked. John had half expected to find the suit gone when he got back, given to the poor or something, but it was still hanging in the cupboard, stiff as a corpse—and, of course, there were two. In all these years, he had never guessed that—although it stood to reason. He gave them a flick with his finger and they swung together creaking on their hangers. They shouldn't be left up there, he thought at the time: they ought to be cut down: something obscene about two suits hanging empty. He ran his hands over the harsh, unwieldy cloth. They were good suits technically, expensive suits. He had no idea why his father had spent so much money on them, though. They were unstylish, even in death.

One was half tempted at first to get a pair of suits like that and go into the tool trade. It was just as good as soap, better in fact—and it would be a nice gesture to his father's memory. 'See, after all, I really did admire you, and your life, and I never wanted more than that for myself.' Since it was only a game anyway, what did it matter? A philosopher, one who *knew*, could adjust himself to anything.

A nice gesture, but a little artificial. Like the Bourbons dressing up as shepherds and romping in the meadows. One couldn't sacrifice quite as much as that for a gesture. 'Daddy wouldn't have wished it.' The inevitable burlesque brought up an ugly fact : one was returning to normal, by inches. The period of mourning was almost over—hadn't he really begun to realize it even while he was talking to the Warden?—and it would soon be time to make his plans. 'Daddy would have wished it.' Did that really have anything to do with it? Perhaps, perhaps not. Whatever it was, one would wind up playing the damned game after all, after the mourning was over. And the silliest part of the game was that one had to take it seriously. What about all those contacts he'd made in his freshman year—well, one couldn't just drop them, could one? If one had the ability, it was hardly right to waste it. . . . And, of course, one had to do something. Couldn't just do nothing, I mean. . . .

All the same, there would be differences now. No more cheap go-getting, no sycophancy, no truckling to people like old Fosdick. The only point of the thing was the plain, hard work of it. 'The joys of competition, the struggle at its keenest, a stronger Britain?' Well, all right, if you wanted to put it like that. But it wasn't precisely so, all the same. One was born and bred to work hard, with no particular object in view; one felt uncomfortable if one didn't, that was all; and one took the work that came to hand. Incidentally, and apropos of that, it might be a good idea to get in touch with that chap at the weighing-machine place, as soon as possible. . . .

Thus the waves rose around him, slapping up against his chin, and beyond. The delicious sensation of drowning . . . the sea around Sturdley—and, yes, the waters were seeping into Sturdley too; the Warden was already handing out the water wings. It was depressing beyond words. But what could one do? One had no special talent, no gift to give to the universe, nothing but a modest talent for getting ahead along the most commonplace lines. What indeed could one do? One certainly couldn't play at being the philosopher much longer. One really hadn't the patience for it or the training or the imagination or something. The pursuit of wisdom had begun unmistakably to bore him.

Well, there was one thing he wasn't going to do, anyway. It was hard to say why he suddenly felt so strongly about it—one didn't know most of the other rules, but this at least seemed to be a recognizable test of one's house-brokenness. Perhaps even Alan Browning would bow to that. (Indeed, he had already bowed, all the way to the floor—and what a relief that was! What a liberation!) Now that one was embarked on the game it was more than ever necessary to behave honourably. Otherwise, it didn't make any sense at all, even as a game.

He pushed back the glass door and stepped quickly out into the corridor. The window was wide open, sucking in a foggy gale. He took the letter out of his pocket and tore it carefully into narrow strips, envelope and all. He stuck his fist out of the window and down to beat the draught and spread his fingers and let the paper go scudding off down the track and out of sight. Better not to play around with it. Mustn't use people one doesn't like. Rule No. 1.

After all, that daughter of Mrs. Pringle's (what was her bloody name? Lavender? Heather? Primrose? Primrose Pringle) looked rather promising; and if not, there were bound to be other possibilities. That wasn't exactly what he thought— but it was a *way* of thinking, the way one should have been thinking years ago. One wasn't afraid of that any more—well, not as afraid as before, anyway. So perhaps one's trip to America hadn't been a complete frost. One had sown a wild oat, the necessary minimum. And now, more glamorous romantic doings? Good Lord, no—something steady, a little brighter than Daphne, the very top of the Second Division.

He went back into the carriage and plumped down into his corner seat, from which the English could be observed at their endless pastime of being English. Now for the melancholy pleasures of surrender and second-best decision.

In the clack of the wheels he could hear the martial music that ought properly to attend a hearty stoic as he rides out to do meaningless battle. One was engaging oneself without hope, tarantara, tarantara. Roll on the bloody weighing machines, bring on the damned soap. The six months he had spent reading what'shisname, the one about the small-town American lawyer, had not been wasted: he knew how a man of sorrows faced the bad news about life.

The people in the compartment were staring, of course—one was making faces again. Funny, one had never realized about that until old 'Finishing school Fosdick' had pointed it out.

Well, it really was pretty funny—Chote the proud pagan, resigning himself to life; taking the pain of it in the gaunt stride, living honourably in a valueless world. What a chap! What a marvellous chap.

This was great stuff, best enjoyed alone. A grunt of well-bred annoyance went spiralling up as he stepped out once again over tweeded ankles, into the corridor.

They were past the cemetery now, but the countryside was grey in the twilight; and there was smoke hanging over it, from a spring bonfire—no, from the engine of the train, of course. It was small countryside, cut up precisely into small fields and gardens, and it brought one down to earth, down to one's allotment of earth. An acre and half a cow.

John Chote Jr. was not the man for the bloody great gestures, the windy heroics. Even if he did something big—and he might, at least in his dreams—it would be small by the time he got through with it. Heroism was large and unconscious—and where would he have learned anything like that, on his way? His brief attempt to see things in the eye of eternity had ended in dismal failure: he was, let's face it, a small-bored chap. Whether he went into tools or weighing machines, it wouldn't be the big symbol, the gesture that everyone had been waiting for for so long; it would just be a chap going into tools or

386

weighing machines. And it was just a chap throwing a letter away. From a girl whose memory he had come to loathe with all his mind and soul. That was all it was.

Thus, and not all together, but in a series of small puffs, another dream was carried sputtering back to Oxford, past the cemetery, to dissipate itself, puff by puff, in the sleepy air.

And Chote stood out in the corridor and laughed and laughed.

It seemed the only thing to do.